The Sacrificia
By Peter Mer

Thanks Chris!

Peter Meredith

Fictional works by Peter Meredith:

A Perfect America
The Sacrificial Daughter
The Horror of the Shade Trilogy of the Void 1
An Illusion of Hell Trilogy of the Void 2
Hell Blade Trilogy of the Void 3
The Punished
Sprite
The Feylands: A Hidden Lands Novel
The Sun King: A Hidden Lands Novel
The Sun Queen: A Hidden Lands Novel
The Apocalypse: The Undead World Novel 1
The Apocalypse Survivors: The Undead World Novel 2
The Apocalypse Outcasts: The Undead World Novel 3
The Apocalypse Fugitives: The Undead World Novel 4
Pen(Novella)
A Sliver of Perfection (Novella)
The Haunting At Red Feathers(Short Story)
The Haunting On Colonel's Row(Short Story)
The Drawer(Short Story)
The Eyes in the Storm(Short Story)

"...it would gather all the power to the supreme party and the party leaders, rising like stately pinnacles above their vast bureaucracies of Civil servants, who are no longer servants and no longer civil."
Winston Churchill

CHAPTER 1

There was something behind her.

In the forest.

A sound came out of the black shadows of the pines. A small sound, a human sound. It was the sound of a branch running along nylon. It was an accidental sound and it stopped quickly. Whoever had made it hadn't meant to. They wanted to be quiet instead. They wanted to be sly and slick.

It brought her up short. Jesse spun around, peering into the dark, holding her breath, trying to listen with every part of her. Even her skin seemed sensitive to the least vibration of the still air. Nothing stirred.

Early winter in a night forest can be a silent place. Yet this was too much so. This length of the woods seemed eerily hushed as if nature itself was afraid to make noise; afraid to call attention to itself; afraid of what would happen.

She had been walking along, quiet in her own right, the pine needles barely crunching beneath her white Nikes when...zzzwip. That sound stopped her feet, cold.

Had her mother been right? The warning about going out alone had been shrugged off easily enough in the light of the Clarke's living room. After all, as a senior in high school, Jesse was practically an adult and hadn't been prone to childish fears for some time. Yet now peering into the underbrush, the warning certainly seemed to have some validity. There was a shadow that didn't fit with the tall slim pines surrounding it. Its outline, though black against black, stood out. It was different. It didn't belong.

Involuntarily Jesse took a step back. It was one thing to hear a quick noise, which in truth could have been anything—a plastic bag caught in a tree or two branches swaying against each other—it was quite another to see that shadow. It couldn't be explained away as anything but what it was, the outline of a man.

A freaking huge man.

He lurked in the scrub just off the trail perhaps thirty yards away.

With her heart in her throat, Jesse turned, wanting to put some distance between her and this stranger, only her feet felt weighted down and they were slow to respond. She almost tripped. It was a very near thing. Her sneakers clicked together and she lurched into the rough edged bark of a pine tree. It was tacky with new resin, something that she absolutely hated but now barely noticed. That minor thing, the little trip, suddenly made her feel weak and frail. She felt girlish, which was rare for her. It ramped up her fear, revving it up until she felt possessed by a strange rabbit-like panic. It made her want to up and run, wild-eyed and dead-brained toward the distant lights of the town.

But that wouldn't do.

Partially giving in to the rabbity feeling, Jesse took off in a very fast walk. She was both afraid to run and afraid not to. The civilized part of her was barely holding on and she feared that if she began to run she would end up shrieking her head off and dashing off into the forest. A forest which, as far as she knew, went on for miles and miles.

At the same time, not to run could mean...what? She didn't know that either except that it would entail something very bad.

A part of Jesse was astonished at her behavior. Thirty seconds earlier she had been tromping along, feeling somewhat eager to see the town at night for the first time but now her breath seemed to be stuck in her throat. It was nearly perfectly lodged there and she began to think that if she had to scream, she wouldn't be able to.

Logically, there was no reason for this.

It was prudent to be wary of strangers in the forest at night, but prudence had never entered the picture. She was straight-up freaking out. From the second she had heard that noise she had begun a freak-out that was incomparable to anything she had ever experienced in her seventeen years.

Jesse fast-walked, with her head cranked around, watching with a growing pain in her chest, as the shadow, muted and monstrous, swept along keeping pace. The unthinking rabbity part of her mind grew and began to eclipse all reason. Her feet felt light and full of energy; they wanted to run, and unknowingly she picked up speed. She raced along, keeping to the trail only with the use of her periphery vision and a whole lot of luck.

However, the trail was rugged and her luck only held for so long.

Her right foot snagged on an exposed root and she went down aware of a distant pain in both her knees and her palms where rocks had bitten into them. She was full out, splayed on the frozen dirt of the path, exposed and vulnerable. Her fright became a bomb, exploding out from her chest, blotting out rational thought and suddenly the rabbit in her took command of her mind completely.

She had a vague realization that, although she didn't want to, she was going to run. This was an odd and frightening sensation. No longer was she in control of her body. It was as if she was only along for the ride. She pictured herself running blindly off the path, getting lost in the woods, hearing the Shadowman's heavy breath as he drew closer and closer.

This image was too much for the rabbit, and that crazed part of her scrambled and clawed Jesse back to her feet and, as she had imagined, her panicked body fled. Unthinking it tore directly away from the shadow, sending her feet racing down a small slope. At first she stayed to the path, but quickly it curved to the right and Jesse left it behind, heading straight down the hill. She didn't care where she was going just as long as it was away from danger. The concept of "lost" was too great for her at that point. The only concept she understood was "death".

By a small miracle, she ran over two hundred yards without breaking a leg or running a tree branch through her eye. And by a larger miracle, she stumbled again upon the path, which had meandered back to the left. Seeing the path going off in two directions forced her mind to reassert itself. A choice had to be made. Only she was clueless as to which way would lead to town and which way would send her back towards...it.

Feeling like a rudderless boat at the mercy of tide and wind, the girl swung her head back and forth at the two options, her blonde hair flying. With her panic and the dark, Jesse had no idea which way was right. She was completely turned around, so that both directions looked the same to her. Painfully, it felt as though her life hinged upon the flip of a coin. Left or right?

She had to choose before the Shadowman came and took even that from her. While she debated, a sudden rushing noise swept down on her and she cringed with her hands coming up protectively to her face.

It was only a charging gust of new wind. It dashed merrily about the forest and as it did the trees swayed in gentle appreciation. As if to music, they gently danced together and between their boughs Jesse saw the golden warmth of the town's lights. An explosion of stupid relief burst within her; she knew where she was. She was closer to safety than she had realized. From where she stood she was practically at the ponds and the town was only a few hundred yards beyond them.

She could make it. As long as the Shadowman wasn't too close, she could be at the ponds in a minute. With a last look back before she took off, Jesse stumbled to a halt.

"What the hell?" This came tumbling from her numb lips as she slowly spun in place staring all about. Her eyes searched the dark forest. The evil shadow was nowhere to be seen. The woods were empty. Her eyes darted to each bush, each little outcropping of rocks, carefully examining everything. She peered all the way up the hill that she had just run down—it was empty.

Just then the stupid relief that she had felt at seeing the lights doubled, and a giddy smile cracked her lips.

Had she just imagined the shadow? Had there actually been anything lurking in the woods at all, or had it been just some guy taking a shortcut on his way home; one of her new neighbors perhaps? Had she just made a great big fool of herself? That was certainly a possibility but, Jesse reasoned, if were so then it had been her mother's fault.

Just before Jesse had left the light and warmth of her new house, Cynthia Clarke had dropped this little bomb on her daughter: "Don't go on the trail, dear. I heard a rumor that a boy was murdered down by the ponds. It's not safe at night."

That was practically a challenge to Jesse's imagination and was also a guarantee that she would take the trail. Rebellion was Jesse's hallmark. Something her church-going mom knew perfectly well. It would have been smarter for her to have warned Jesse about the dangers of the well-lit streets if she had wanted her to go in that direction.

With a shrug and a snort of derisive laughter at her own foolishness, Jesse once again began walking down the trail toward town. Though she was almost certain that the shadow had just been her imagination gone wild, she kept her eyes out, scanning the forest all the same. Shadow or no shadow the woods were very spooky.

The opposite of how they looked earlier that morning when she had made her first trip into town. The sun had been shining, and the birds chirping. It was just gorgeous. Now it was cold and bleak. The snow clashed with the shadows; harsh white against the black.

Even though her fright was fading, Jesse noticed her hands were shaking. She stuffed them deep in the pockets of her black coat, only to pull them out again quickly. Her right hand had come up against the frozen weight of the chain she carried. She gave the night another little laugh, again feeling foolish. What was the use of carrying a weapon and then not pulling it out when danger arose? It was stupid.

A weapon was a necessity for a girl like Jesse. Despite the fact that she had been living in sleepy little burgs for most of her life, she always carried a weapon of some sort. Actually, it was *especially* since she had been living in sleepy little burgs that she carried one. Had she been raised in a big town or even a city, she could have blended in, disappeared. But there would be no disappearing in Ashton, population six thousand and twenty three. For Jesse, Ashton would be just like Copper Ridge, which had been just like Crisfield, which had been just like Denton.

In each of those towns Jesse Clarke had been hated with a venom usually reserved for child-molesters.

A sigh escaped her as she ran her hands along the outline of the thick links. The chain, which had been pulled in self-defense only twice before, was like a security blanket to her. She considered tugging it out right there, but it had felt like ice and her hands were already almost numb from the cold. Besides, she thought, what was the point? What good would the chain do against a Shadowman?

Shivering, Jesse suddenly realized that the Shadow-man could, even now, be darting through the trees. She could imagine him looping around on the other side of the hill, looking to cut her off where the trail split the ponds, and she could imagine herself taking the chain out only to swing it ineffectually through the black nothingness of the creature. And she could imagine the cold of the thing as it swept over her.

The very notion that the thing could be moving to cut her off raised an army of goose bumps on her flesh.

Ahead of her lay two long fingerlike ponds. They were separated by a low berm over which the trail ran. If the man could get between her and the ponds she would be in huge trouble; the path back to her house was a half-mile or more. A long way to run, and worse it was too far for her screams to be heard by anyone.

"Damn!" The word was a hissed whisper and like a starting gun it spurred her into a sprint. Although she was slim and athletic, the dash was terribly difficult for the already tired girl. The trail went up small steep hills and down into gullies filled with frosted-over mud. A low hung branch slashed a thin cut across her cheek and then a jutting rock sent her sprawling and, finally, a slip on a patch of snow turned her ankle.

Nevertheless, she made it to the berm unmolested. It stretched long and thin, the length of a football field or more. With the last of her strength, she turned and walked backwards on it, sucking wind, gasping. The Shadow-man was nowhere to be seen...at first. When she was half-way across, she saw him moving along the edge of the pond to her left. This was not her imagination run wild. There was definitely a man there scrambling along the lee side of the hill toward the berm and it was clear that had she not sprinted he would have surely cut her off.

Once again the rabbit-like panic took her in its mindless clutches. After sprinting for nearly five hundred yards in the last few minutes there was no more racing, or dashing left to Jesse. All that she was capable of was a lurching, stumbling half jog and she only managed to keep this up until she had crossed the berm. After that, her stride became a drunk's stagger, as she moved from the support of one tree to the next, using her relatively fresh arms to push her onwards.

Her entire focus was on reaching the lights of the town. They were her salvation. Those low-hung golden stars were everything to her and nothing else mattered, not even the shadow that loomed up from the other side of the trail. She barely saw it in time.

It was a man coming at her. His eyes were sinister black and filled with explosive rage. Jesse screeched and dodged around the trunk of a large fat pine, putting it between them, while her hand dug at the cold lump of chain in her pocket.

"Hey, it's ok," the man said, and just like that he transformed from an evil, hate-filled person to something else entirely. He exuded nice like a friendly neighbor or a favorite uncle. "It's ok, I won't hurt you." His hands were up and empty.

Jesse felt tears of relief coming before she knew it. "Th-th-th...huh-huh." Her oxygen-starved lungs weren't close to being able to form words just yet. It was all she could do to just breathe. The man came closer and despite the fact that he was obviously someone to be trusted, Jesse stepped behind another tree.

"Look, I'm not going to hurt you... It's me, Jerry Mendel, Kyle's father?"

There was something in the way he said this that struck an odd chord in Jesse. It sounded to her like a rehearsed line, one that he had used many times before, and it was spoken in such a way that it was clear that Mr. Mendel was expecting a rote response.

Whatever that response was supposed to be, was beyond Jesse. First, she had literally just moved into town the previous day and knew absolutely no one, and second, at the moment, she didn't really care who Kyle or Jerry Mendel were. She only cared about getting away from the Shadow-man and getting into town.

"Suh-suh..." Her breath was still coming so raggedly that all she could do was point down at the berm, fifty yards away.

The man's demeanor changed, turning cautious. He squinted down toward the berm, which was almost completely hidden by the intervening trees.

"Someone!" Jesse was finally able to gasp out. "Down..."

A charge seemed to go through Jerry. "Someone's down there? Who is it, do you know?"

Jesse didn't have a clue and thought the explanation of an evil shadow was too childish to bother with, so she only shook her head. Jerry eyed her for a few moments and then looked back to the berm for two more before he reached out and grabbed her arm. Jesse flinched back and tried to pull away, but he held her with an iron grip.

"It's not safe here," he said in the tiniest of whispers. "Come on." He gave her a firm tug and had it been in any other direction but toward the town she would have screamed and fought him. Thankfully, however, he propelled them up the trail in the direction of the lights and she was so spent that soon she began leaning on him for support.

Jerry kept quiet until they had cleared the last of the trees and then he too seemed to sag from their little mini-adventure. "Have you seen Kyle, anywhere?" he asked, eyeing Jesse closely.

At first she resented the look, until she remembered she was too new to be hated just yet. That probably wouldn't occur until the next day.

"I don't know who Kyle is. I just moved to town."

"Oh...well Kyle is..." The man seemed suddenly at a loss, as if it was unheard of for someone not to know his son. "He's..."

"Your son," Jesse tried.

Jerry nodded, but acted like there was more to it than just that, yet he didn't elaborate. He only glanced back the way they had come, before turning again to her. "Miss..."

"My name is Jesse." Purposefully she left off her last name.

"Jesse, it's nice to meet you. I'm Jerry Mendel." His hand was a block of ice, even colder than hers was. "Sorry," he said rubbing his hands together. "I've been out all night looking for Kyle."

"I haven't seen anyone but you and..." Perhaps this Kyle was the person who had chased her. "Is your son really big?"

"Not especially. Wait, was the person you saw in the woods a really big guy?" Jerry put his arms out tall and wide. She nodded and he continued. "That's not Kyle, that's a man that you want to steer clear of. Look, I gotta go. Do you need a ride?"

Jesse figured she would call her mom from the library. Cynthia was home and didn't have the luxury of an excuse not to come get her. "No, thank you. I have a ride. But, can you tell me about the..."

Suddenly agitated, Mr. Mendel cut across her, shaking his head, "I don't have time, sorry." He started walking away, but he turned and spoke over his shoulder, "Don't go out alone at night anymore. At least not until the next body shows up."

Chapter 2

The next body? Jesse opened her mouth to ask about it, but Mr. Mendel had continued to walk away from her and, in moments, she was all alone and freaking out, once again.

The next body? The question kept running through her mind, at least until she made it to the library, whereupon a new confusion kicked out any thought of bodies.

For a late Sunday evening the library was strangely jam-packed. Kids talked and tittered everywhere; they overflowed the private study rooms, and lounged down every aisle. There were a dozen make-out sessions going on in every corner and a hacky sack circle had formed in the large open foyer. There were kids of all types there: Jocks and cheerleaders, punks and emos; there even appeared to be a gang in long black trench coats sitting against the emergency door in the very back of the building. This they had propped open with a brick, while they sat about smoking cigarettes and trying to look tough.

None of this made sense to Jesse who walked about with what must have been a shocked expression on her face. In every other town she had lived in, the library had been the preserve of nerds and outcasts like her. It wasn't for regular kids.

Her purpose for coming out as she had that night was in the vain hope of finding a friend...or at least an acquaintance. Someone she could sit next to at lunch the next day or at least smile at in the hallways. Her one chance at this was to find a person who looked lonely and strike up a conversation. Sadly, if she didn't get a friend that night she would never get one. It was just the way it was for her.

Though she looked everywhere, strangely no one was sitting alone. Even stranger, dweebs sat with preps, and nerds sat with hot chicks. Jesse found herself in Bizarro world.

She made a full circuit of the building without finding what she had come for. Only then did she head to the front desk where an elderly woman in a grey cardigan sat.

"Hi, can I get a library card, please?" Jesse asked as she eased around some milling middle-schoolers were loitering near the front desk.

"Sure thing, dear." Despite appearing frazzled by the commotion going on about her, the librarian, who was sitting on a tall stool, and looking more like a lifeguard than anything else, had a pleasant air about her. But also a curious air; a new person in a tiny town like Ashton was a rare thing indeed and sure to be a seven-day wonder. She stayed very close as Jesse filled out the form and the girl could feel the older lady's eyes hot all over the little paper.

When Jesse had entered all the information that she could she slid the card over to the lady and it was then she felt the first chill.

The librarian glared down at the card, then slid it back and said icily, "We don't accept incomplete applications."

"I don't know the zip code here. I forgot it. Could you just tell it to me?"

"I'm sorry, but I'm not an almanac. Go look it up." The tone was as snotty as an adult could go without sounding like a teenager. Not only did this cause a stir among the middle-schoolers, it made Jesse's cheeks go red and her ears feel hot.

There was no use arguing with her, the librarian could rule supreme as a tyrant in her little kingdom. Jesse was just about to turn away and look for someone, other than one of the middle-schoolers, to ask when she saw that the librarian had a little stack of business cards sitting right in front of her. The library's address sat only inches away. Jesse snatched one up and jotted the zip code onto her form.

The librarian took the application, glanced at it and said in a loud voice, "That'll be twenty dollars,"

"Twenty dollars! That's ridiculous," Jesse exclaimed. She had never paid for a library card in her life.

"Yes, it is terribly ridiculous," the lady replied in a nasty manner. "It's the new town manager's fault. He thinks the library should be self-supporting; as if a price could ever be placed on access to this much knowledge." She waved her arm to the hundreds of shelves laden with books.

This was a new low for Jesse's father. He had done some unconscionable things before, but never something as stupid as this. Scowling, Jesse dug out what was supposed to be her lunch money for the coming week and slid the twenty dollar bill across to the grey-haired biddy behind the desk.

"If you don't like it Miss Clarke, why don't you bring it up with the new manager? I can give you his address." The librarian held up the application and pointed at the address that Jesse had just filled in.

"Maybe, I will," Jesse replied, coolly. She then looked at the librarian, who only smiled at her in a nasty way. This went on for a few seconds until Jesse blurted out, "My library card? Could you get it, please?"

"Sure thing. It'll be ten-to-fourteen business days." Saying this seemed to make the librarian very happy. Jesse could only shake her head in bewilderment, so the older lady explained in an over-loud voice, "Sorry, *Miss Clarke*, but the new town manager, *James Clarke,* slashed our budget and we had to let three of our part-time employees go. And right before Christmas, too! What a shame." Here she put on a sad face and clicked her tongue.

The younger children behind her commenced a low whispering behind Jesse's back. This was just the beginning, Jesse thought. She knew from past, painful experience that over the next few days the whispers would grow like a storm. Everywhere she'd go the soft murmuring would tag along in her wake, but that would seem like a treat compared to what will invariably follow.

The whispering would turn into catcalls and insults; and then would come cruel mocking laughter. After that she would have to endure threats...and then violence.

Jesse felt the heat of shame at being the daughter of a bastard who could fire people right before Christmas. She wanted to denounce him right there in front of everyone as being a son of a bitch, a jerk and every other name she could think of only, again, she knew it wouldn't save her. She had tried it before.

Like no other, she felt she had been born to be hated.

Not even her father, the bastard himself, was so despised. Certainly there were some that hated him, but mostly he was feared and his butt was kissed by everyone. He was referred to as decisive, while she was called a slut. He was described as a leader in difficult times, she was labeled a bitch. He stood defiant against political opponents, she ate her lunch alone.

And there was no one she could turn to.

Her father worked sixty-hour weeks, but that was nothing compared to Jesse's mother. Cynthia Clarke worked from sunup to long past sundown and she had the much harder job of the two. Her sole occupation was to try to convince everyone, including herself, that despite her husband she was truly a good person. To that end she volunteered her time to a dozen charities at once. She was always baking cookies that Jesse couldn't eat. She was always donating clothes that Jesse still wore. She was always out mentoring "at risk" children while Jesse was left to fend for herself.

And the worst of all, the very worst, was that once James Clarke's stringent budget-cutting and Scrooge-like streamlining began to take effect, people who had once hated him would clap him on the back and thank him for his hard work. Whenever they would move on to the next bankrupt town, Jesse's mother would be gifted with going away presents and told with all honesty how much she would be missed.

But Jesse would remain hated.

No child, or adult for that matter, had ever come up to her and apologized for their mistreatment of her. Not once, and she no longer bothered to hope that it would ever happen. In fact, she really didn't care. If someone was going to be mean to her because of what her father did, then screw 'em. Even if they did apologize, she would simply spit in their face.

She was an angry girl. A desperately lonely, angry girl and just then, with the librarian sneering the way she was, Jesse had never felt angrier.

"Was it really a shame that they were fired?" Jesse asked the librarian. Despite being pissed off she tried to keep her tone calm to show that she was a cool customer, but her voice rose nonetheless. "If they were as lazy as you are then I say good riddance."

"How dare you call me lazy!" The librarian came off her lifeguard chair and, as she did so, Jesse stepped forward aggressively. This was something the old lady wasn't expecting and she flinched back.

"You are lazy. You've done nothing since I walked in here but sit in that chair like you're a queen. And now you tell me that typing a library card will take you two weeks? It's a wonder that you weren't fired as well."

Now the lady's face went as grey as her hair. "Get out. Right now! I never want to see you in here again."

Jesse smirked at this. There wasn't a ghost of humor in it—instead it was an angry, hard smirk. She loved the library. It was her refuge from the world. It was her refuge from the hate and the insults and the cruel laughter that came after the stupid, stupid jokes at her expense. However this library was clearly infested with the very roaches she looked to avoid. Just then an image of herself holding a flaming torch popped into her head. Her lips were twisted in a smirk as she turned the torch on the building and it went up in flames. The fire ate up the books and the children with equal delight and the smirk grew into a wicked smile.

She was a desperately lonely girl who had been hated for so long that the hate had baked down deep into her soul where it roiled and burned. For some time, the hate had begun to radiate back up, coming out in little ways: the hard uncaring looks, the cutting insults, but mostly the hate came out in her imagination.

"I said get out!" The librarian rose to the challenge behind Jesse's eyes.

"This is a *public* library, ma'am, and as a member of the public I have every right to be here. But..." Jesse let that hang in the air for affect. "...I think I will take you up on your offer to speak to the City Manager. He and I have a surprisingly close relationship. He buys me ice cream and he frequently listens to my recommendations. Maybe I'll suggest he hires back one those part-time workers you mentioned and get rid of some of the dead weight around here instead."

"I have a contract with the town. It's..." the librarian's words were hollow and Jesse spoke over her with ease.

"So *did* a lot of people. In every contract, there are always loopholes. A lawyer's whole job is either to discover loop-holes or to create them." Jesse had overheard her father say those exact same words only that morning at breakfast. As was usual, when he was at home, he had been on the phone with someone from work.

The librarian went greyer still, but rallied for one last effort. "My contract is ironclad. It was written..."

Again, Jesse spoke over her, "Nothing is ironclad in this economy." It was another little gem of her father's and, because he had said it with such self-assurance, Jesse believed him unreservedly. She employed the same tone and it shut the librarian down completely.

The librarian looked as though she had been punched in the head and Jesse began to feel a touch of remorse. The hate within her, what she thought of as "rebound hate" wasn't all-encompassing; there was still plenty of room for guilt. But she didn't apologize to the librarian or try in any way to calm the fears that she had stoked. Her anger over how the old lady had treated her was too fresh, instead she raised an eyebrow by way of saying good-bye and walked to the exit. As she did the whispering behind her back increased, just as she had known it would.

Chapter 3

Stepping from the light and warmth of the library to the lonely streets of Ashton, made Jesse feel like a switch had been thrown within her.

Her blood had been boiling with anger only seconds before, but the cold night, which had turned bitter in the half an hour that she had spent in the library, doused the feeling quick. The air was sharp and it ran up her sleeves and down the neck of her coat. It searched out the spots where she had begun to sweat and froze the damp uncomfortably against her skin.

Remember the body, a voice inside her spoke up.

"How can I forget it," Jesse replied. She pulled her coat tighter and strained to see into the shadows.

The dark and the quiet of the night, like the cold, had also changed; they had grown. The air of the town was thick with silence, the buildings deep in gloom. Nothing stirred on the streets, no people, no cars, not even a forgotten stray making its rounds.

Most of the towns that she had lived in rolled up their sidewalks at six, and shut down for the evening, but this was much more than that. This was weird and quite a bit scary. Apart from the library, the town looked altogether dead. Not a light could be seen in any of the nearby buildings and they appeared abandoned. It was as if she had wandered into a ghost town.

That thought made her realize just how alone she was. Normally that wasn't an issue, she was used to it. For the last ten years she was the most hated and lonely girl wherever she went, but again, this was more than that. This wasn't just being apart from people as they went merrily about their lives. This was being so alone that her screams would go wasted on the empty buildings. So alone that her body would decay right there, untouched and un-mourned until the...

Stop it! the voice commanded.

Jesse's was surprised at how quickly her imagination had turned sinister. It ran wild with images of her running in a panic from empty building to empty building, each of which was chained with her own lock. This flashed through her mind, but then that same mind recalled her earlier fear: the brain-dead panic she had felt at seeing the Shadow-man down the length of the berm. That's what this sudden fear was really all about. The Shadow-man.

It had been real.

There was no denying it, though desperately she wanted to. Jerry Mendel's reaction had cemented that fact within her. His look of shock over her announcement that someone else was in the forest with them hadn't been faked. He believed her, and he had been...what? Afraid? Probably or at the very least unnerved.

And now she was very much alone and the thought of the Shadow-man kept her feet from venturing off the steps of the library. Beneath her heavy coat her skin rippled with goose bumps and she began shivering. He could be out there snugged down in the dark watching her, either that or waiting in the forest that ran right up to the edge of the town. Waiting for her to come back.

Like that was going to happen. No way she was going down that path again, at least not in the dark. She would call her mom first...

"Damn it!" She remembered that she hadn't yet memorized her new home phone number, and she couldn't call her mom's cell. The cell coverage out here in No-wheres-ville, USA was spotty in town and non-existent ten feet outside of it.

It would have to be a ride home with dear old dad then.

The thought of her father went a long way to calming her fears. He was such a rational man that the irrational idea of the Shadow-man's frightfulness wilted in comparison. But still she hesitated on the steps, wishing for another option.

The Shadow-man, in her mind, represented a swift horrible painful death, while her father represented a long horrible pain-filled life.

It was a testament to how much she loathed him that she actually cast a look at the forest rising up behind a darkened laundromat across the street. The trees were nightmare dark.

A sigh marking defeat escaped her. She hated to turn to her father for anything; even the least favor had strings attached. Yet her harsh feelings stemmed from more than just that. Being in his presence was another chance to be ignored by him, or worse, lectured to. He certainly would never take the opportunity to mention that he was proud of her, or God forbid, for him to ever tell her that he loved her.

No, the only emotion that he ever seemed to demonstrate was disappointment.

Jesse took a peek at her watch, 7:46 p.m. This early on a Sunday night meant that he would still be at work and it also meant a long wait for her ride home. He probably wouldn't be finished until close on a half past nine.

Heartily she wished that she had a third option. Being kidnapped by a Jehovah's Witness with a latex fetish might have been preferable.

With a final piercing glance into the nearby shadows, Jesse hurried down the steps of the library. This time if there was going to be trouble she'd be ready. Her right hand found the chain in her pocket and she curled its cooling links around her knuckles. Had she been in the forest the chain would've been out and ready to plow a deep notch in someone's forehead, but on the town's streets it was wiser to be more circumspect.

With the parking lot full of cars and possible ambush sites, Jesse sped along over the building's snow covered lawn and then out onto what passed, in that dinky little burg, for a main street. Though compared to say Lansing, or even Flint, it wasn't much more that a wide spot in the road.

At breakfast that morning, upon seeing the glum look on Jesse's face— she hated moving nearly as much as *not* moving—her father had tried to cheer her up by expounding on the wonders of Ashton. This was nothing new. He was always the head cheerleader for whatever town was crazy enough to imbue him with dictatorial powers. Another thing that wasn't new was that he would always over-sell.

The people of Ashton were the friendliest he had ever met—he had said the same thing about Chrisfield. The school is the one of the highest ranked in the state—he had said the same thing about Copper Ridge. On and on until his breakfast was plunked down in front of him. The town had formed a hundred and thirty years earlier at the junction of two of Michigan's most unimportant highways...though in Jesse's eyes the definition of the word highway had been dreadfully abused to make that statement.

With big eyes that darted up and down the street, Jesse crossed one of these "highways", jaywalking in a diagonal, going at her fastest pace that was still technically walking.

Her father's office was in the town hall that was a block past the next intersection and though she was loath to see him, she was even more loath to be out there like she was. It bothered her the way she was so exposed. If there were eyes in the dark watching her they had a perfect view of her slim form. The thought was unsettling.

When she got to the other side of the street, straight away she hopped up onto the sidewalk, like she had done a thousand times before, but this time the tall heel of her right boot hit an odd crack. Her ankle buckled beneath her and she went down clutching her lower leg.

"Ow! Crap!" The pain was sharp, but not debilitating. Out of a cold fear she was up again in a second, cursing her bad luck. "What a damned night," she hissed between sharp intakes of breath. After testing her weight on her gimpy leg and finding that it would support her, she began to hobble on again. She went for half a block hoping that she would be able to walk off the pain, but it only started to stiffen up all the more.

"Damn," she groaned again in dismay.

The sprain was worse than she had thought. She reasoned that it was probably only so bad since it was the second time in an hour that she had turned that particular ankle. The first time, running in the woods, she had barely felt even a twinge.

Just thinking of that first time made her want to look back the way she had come. The trail and the pond were back in that direction, and so was the berm and of course what had been on the berm. It was a strangely powerful and terribly fearful desire to look. It was as if she knew, perhaps psychically that if she turned she would see the Shadow-man bearing down on her.

She fought the need to look, at least that is until she heard a soft noise coming from behind. With her heart blocking her throat, she wheeled and her eyes ran up and down the sidewalk and then the street. There was no Shadow-man.

It was perplexing; she could have sworn she heard something behind her. Jesse stared for a second and was just about to turn away when she saw the cause of the sound.

A car as black as the night and nearly as quiet was creeping along behind her with its lights off. When she had looked back for the Shadow-man it had been moving so slowly that she had thought it to be only parked and empty. But it wasn't and now that she had noticed it, the car came on faster.

Jesse turned to run, but it was no use. The building she stood in front of was boarded up and ran the length of the block, which was too far. There was no way she could out run the car even if her ankle had been fine. Instead of running she dug for her chain with its attached lock, however it snagged on something in her pocket and before she could get it all the way out the car was upon her.

Chapter 4

The night had been one of the oddest in Jesse's life. Everything was topsy-turvy. A Shadow-man haunted the forest behind her house, the library was filled with normal kids chatting it up with geeks, and now she was practically paralyzed with fright. This last was something that she couldn't believe would ever have happened. Even in the woods she had at least ran, though admittedly it was in blind panic, she had at least ran.

But this was different.

She felt like a mouse on the receiving end of a serpent's stare. Jesse could do nothing except feel the pull of her eyelids as they went further and further back. The car crept right up to her, still dark, still terrifying, and as it did her breath sucked quietly into her chest, deeper and deeper until she thought she would explode. She was ready to scream only she was too terrified to. The scream was there, but it felt stuck, corked in her throat.

Then the car paused along side of her. The window slid downward an inch or two and now she was watched by a pair of dark, shadowed eyes. They stared at her and as they did the paralysis holding her became complete. Her heart seemed to stop, her eyes were as wide as they could go, and her lungs were full but air refused to leave them. Her entire body was numb; the ache in her ankle disappeared, the cold of the chain in her hand was forgotten.

For a span of seconds she stood unable to budge even the smallest muscle, until at last the car's window edged up silently and it drove away.

The air hissed out of her in combination of relief and anger, "Ooooooh man."

What was that all about? This was the foremost question in her mind, followed immediately by: *What's wrong with this town?*

She had never heard of anything so bizarre as what she had experienced so far that night and she felt a fear of the unknown like she hadn't ever before. Jesse began hobbling again, but this time she freed her chain from her pocket. It hung down and swung gently as she made her up the block. She didn't care who saw.

When she got to the corner of the intersection she was just about to turn, but stopped briefly in surprise. Down the next block she saw actual light. It streamed out of what appeared to be a crowded little poolroom. Had her night not been so crazy, the lights would have been a temptation to the naughtier element within her, but as it was they were easy to resist. So far she'd found the town so bizarre that it wouldn't have shocked her to find the place filled with Amish people sword fighting.

She took the right, away from poolroom, and scurried as fast as she could toward the town hall. She knew where it was situated because her mother had given her the fifteen-minute grand tour of the entire town only that morning. Ashton was so small that the tour had been overdone by about fourteen minutes.

The town hall itself was an ugly two-story block of cement that looked to have been lifted straight out of a prison yard. Jesse was sure that its complete lack of beauty and refinement was a plus in her father's eyes. His motto was: *Beauty is to be found in the eye of the beholder, not in the wallet of the taxpayers*. Her motto was: *My dad is an ass*.

But as the front doors to the building opened easily under hand she was glad that he was at least a predictable ass. James Clarke had a literal open door policy. Any time of day that he was in his office he would accept visitors whether they had an appointment or not. That night was a painful demonstration of that.

"I understand your point of view. I really do, but there is nothing I can do at this point."

In the empty building, Jesse could hear her father's booming voice and was not so secretly relieved by it. Without knocking she slipped into the office and was surprised to see he had a visitor; she had thought him to be on the phone. A tall lady with a long horse face stood over his desk. It was no shock to Jesse to see that she was unhappy.

"Is it that…" she started to say, but upon seeing Jesse the lady stopped and glared at her.

"Excuse me, I don't mean to interrupt," Jesse turned to go, but her father wouldn't allow it. He saw moments such as these as teaching moments.

"No stay, please. You might learn something," James said so fluidly that the condescending word "might" was barely accented. "Miss Weldon, this is my daughter, Jesse. She will be starting at Ashton High tomorrow.

"It's *Ms* Weldon." The way she said Ms, it sounded as though the word had two Zs at the end of it. "Pleased to meet you," the lady lied to Jesse with a tight fake smile.

Jesse returned the fake smile with one of her own, but said nothing. She didn't want to be there. Her ankle was throbbing and her muscles were shaking up and down her body with the unspent adrenaline of her fright. In addition to that she felt oddly thirsty; her mouth was like cotton. Gingerly she lowered herself onto a leather couch that ran along side of the room and tried to put a look on her face that could possibly simulate interest.

"We were just discussing next year's school budget," her father explained. "And Miss Wel…"

Ms Weldon interrupted, "No, we were talking about you slashing the budget. Thirteen percent is unheard of and it's ridiculous for you to even consider."

"Perhaps it would be, *if* I was considering that number. The actual budget cut is closer to four and a half percent."

Jesse realized that there was almost no chance that she could feign interest in a subject as dull as budgets. Feeling a headache coming on, she rubber her temples and thought about closing her eyes, only she didn't bother. Ms Weldon's shrill voice would ruin any chance at a nap.

"I have the budget in my hands," Ms Weldon said with ice in her words. "You won't be able to gimmick your way out of this."

James Clarke smiled at the paper. "That is the projected budget that was proposed before I came here. It's not the actual budget. Remember what the council and the School Board discussed when I accepted the position as Town manager? I operate strictly on zero-based budgeting. What you have is a version of base-line budgeting, which is something else entirely."

"All that is economic mumbo-jumbo. Maybe you can explain the difference between zero-based or base-line budgets to the kids who will be affected by your cuts."

"That would be no problem," James said easily. "But my daughter knows the differences well enough." Jesse's head came up at this and her father caught her eye. "Go ahead, Honey. Explain the difference to Miss Weldon."

Just then the term, *Honey* sent a hot coal of anger burning her belly. "I'm really not in the mood..." she started to say, however she paused at the nasty way Ms Weldon was looking at her. The lady was clearly visiting upon Jesse the sins of her father. Though it was far from unexpected it still angered and Jesse decided to answer after all.

"Ok...base-line budgeting is founded more upon assumptions than upon reality," Jesse recited. Her father had expounded upon this topic too many times for her not to have remembered the basics. "It uses existing spending levels as a basis for future spending, generally without regard to the health of the existing tax base or the actuality of need. Zero based budgeting demands that every line of the budget is justified before approval."

Ms Weldon looked as if she had swallowed something particularly nasty. "Like I said, *mumbo-jumbo*," the words came out of her mouth with exact slowness. "You can fancy it up all you want, but the school district still has seven-hundred and twenty six, K through twelve students to accommodate. Seventeen percent of whom are on assisted or free lunch, the very program you wish to cut out entirely."

"Where the cuts come from is up to you and the board. You asked my advice and I gave it," James replied. "I ate peanut butter and jelly everyday for twelve years. I didn't like it mind you, but it was cheap and back then people lived on a budget."

"And what about the cafeteria personnel?" Ms Weldon fired back. She looked frazzled. "Six more people collecting unemployment? This is going to be great for your so called tax base?"

Here he was eight o'clock on a Sunday night and James Clarke looked as fresh as if it were a Monday morning. He loved this sort of thing. "Ok, if not the cafeteria personnel then talk the state into allowing the schools to drop a non-core class...art for instance."

Ms Weldon seemed ready to explode at this. "Drop art? Is that supposed to be a joke?" She fairly screamed this at James.

He remained cool despite the lady's tone. "I am serious. Compared to say-English, math, and science, how many of us ever use art in our daily lives? Outside of school, I've never known anyone to make anything out of paper mache. And a kiln maybe the most useless device still in existence. Water-colors, charcoal drawings are great, but they are hobbies and should be treated as such."

She seemed beside herself at what he was saying and she screamed at him again, "I can't talk to you…I can't talk to you! You are impossible!" Throwing a nasty glare at the two of them, the lady stormed out of the room. She could be heard fast marching down the hall and a few seconds later a door slammed shut.

"Nobody likes it when their ox is the one getting gored," James said and then bent to peer at some paperwork in front of him.

"What do you mean?" Jesse asked.

"Oh, she's just the art teacher at the high school."

"What?" Jesse was on her feet in a second. She couldn't believe what she had just heard. "That was a teacher at my school? And you let me… you made me go on about budgeting? Oh my God!"

Jesse began to pace, but only made one turn of the room before her ankle forced her back onto the couch. Her father hadn't responded, he was still reading, still ignoring her. Her anger grew frothy. "Well? I asked you a question."

"There's no reason to get upset. You were correct on your points, though you should have elaborated on the basic pros and cons of each…"

"I don't care about budgeting, ok? That's your deal not mine. I care about the fact that I just pissed off of one my teachers. In case you didn't know, in order to graduate I still need to take an art class. Didn't you see how she looked at me?"

Her father hadn't glanced up from his paperwork and Jesse left off shaking her head. Was he being obtuse? Or was it that he truly didn't care about her?

"I'm sure it will work itself out. Just give it your all." James was quite the multitasker. He could throw out a useless cliché, scan a contract for errors, and alienate his daughter all at the same time.

Give it my all? Like that would matter in a subjective class like art. If an art teacher hated a student, he or she could be the next Rembrandt and could still fail. It had happened to her before. In her junior year, her English class was little more than a creative writing seminar that she passed with a D minus-minus. She had to jump through hoops and turn in extra credit work on a weekly basis even to get that pathetic grade.

The worst part was that she was actually a good writer. Jesse had been writing stories and poems for as long as she could remember and still she had barely passed.

She wasn't a good artist, however. Even drawing a stick figure gave her trouble. This was literal. For some reason they all turned out to be boy stick figures as she would frequently draw the legs a little too high on the downward line, leaving a little something extra between the inverted V of the legs.

Her headache grew worse as she thought about how Ms Weldon had glared. There was no getting around the fact that the lady would likely take out her anger at James on Jesse. She sighed tiredly.

Her father must have heard. "Jesse, I'm rather busy. Is there something you need?"

The question focused her mind from the dread of the future to the dread of the very recent past. "I need a ride home."

"Really? You're a big girl. It's only a fifteen-minute walk. I think you can handle it."

She thought about telling him about the strange frightfulness of her night, but the prospect of James Clarke trying to rationalize away her very real fears only soured her mood further. She could picture the...*why are you wasting my time on such silliness*...look that he would wear and she knew that if she saw it, it would make her want to punch him in the face.

She decided to go with hard unassailable facts instead. "I sprained my ankle…in the forest."

"In the forest, oh ok. Well if you want a ride anytime soon, I'm going to need some help. I'm so far behind it'll be hours…" James went on with the stipulations necessary for a ride home and Jesse only half listened to the details of the clerical work that would ensure a safe trip in the car.

Chapter 5

"I like your skirt, and your hair," her mother commented in a chipper voice when Jesse came down for breakfast. "You look beautiful."

The navy blue skirt was the second finest that she owned, she didn't want to go overboard after all, and above it she had slipped on her long-sleeve white satin blouse. Her hair, recently dyed back to its original gold-blonde, had been painstakingly curled and even with the slight crook in her nose where it had been broken the year before, she did indeed feel pretty.

Jesse was about to give her a warm thank you when her mother added, "Why don't you try harder like this all of the time? You usually look like such a slob."

With the stress of her first day of school, it was a struggle for Jesse not to flip out on her. "Just be happy that I'm trying today," she replied between her clenched teeth.

Normally her attire matched her mood, which meant black with barely a touch of color. She thought the vampire/goth look that many kids wore was silly, but all the same the style of clothes that she preferred to wear was close to it.

But that day, her first at Ashton High, she didn't dress according to her mood, which was an anxious, jittery nervousness.

That day she dressed to impress.

If that was still even possible. Despite the fact that she had been in town just shy of two complete days, her father had been there three months already. There was no telling how many people he'd had fired in that time and in a small town like Ashton everybody seemed to be related to everyone else. With all the first, second, and third cousins, as well as aunts and uncles running around, one firing could mean a dozen or more angry students.

And then there was Ms Weldon who would probably turn most of the school staff against her, if they weren't already.

Jesse was definitely behind the eight ball and she knew it. Therefore she put on her nicest school outfit and her most pleasing smile. She was determined to face her new school head-on in the friendliest manner possible. Who knew what the day would hold? Perhaps today she wouldn't be hated; perhaps she could even find a friend. This time, this school could be different.

It wasn't.

If anything, it might have been the worst first day in the history of first days. From the receptionist in the front office, who eyed her with a cold sneer, to her counselor, who couldn't stop saying things like: *I look forward to seeing you graduate from Ashton High... that is if I even have job in May*, everyone was downright nasty.

Everyone that is, but one boy and the best he could do was ignore her completely, even going so far as refusing to say his name when she asked directly. He was rude and frustrating, but was an angel compared to the rest of the students.

Registration took close to two hours, which meant that not only did she miss her first two classes: English and calculus, she was late to her third. The receptionist, Mrs. Daly, had done this on purpose. With five minutes left until the bell rang for the end of second period, all Jesse needed was a printout of her schedule. With the schedule sitting on her computer screen, Mrs. Daly could have had it printed out with two clicks of her mouse, but instead she answered a call from a friend.

They chatted and Jesse fretted. Walking in late to class on your first day of school was a singularly painful event. Everyone knew this. When the bell rang, Jesse tried to get Mrs. Daly's attention, but the woman simply turned her chair away and went right on talking. She seemed to be in absolutely no hurry.

Next Jesse tried to lean over the tall desk to get a better look at her schedule, thinking that she would write it down if she had to.

"Do you mind?" Mrs. Daly crabbed before switching off her screen. She then went back to her banal conversation with her friend. "It's nothing. You know that new town-manager…it's her daughter. Already she thinks she's queen of the school."

Jesse's eyes rolled in her head at the words. She put both of her hands in her hair and gripped her blonde locks hard and before she remembered how she was going to try to be positive, a growl of frustration escaped her throat.

"You have something to say to Mrs. Daly?" Asked a man, Principal Peterson, she assumed from the plaque sitting on the wall next to the doorway he stood in. He was a tall, angry, rat faced man with an over-flowing paunch. Not a person Jesse wanted mad at her.

"No, sir. It's just that I…"

"Then get away from her desk," he ordered. "It's not polite to listen in on someone else's conversation. Didn't your parents ever teach you that?"

"Yes, sir." Jesse dropped her eyes and went to sit down at a nearby bench. A minute later the late bell rang for third period and her stomach knotted unpleasantly. Ten minutes after that Mrs. Daly scolded her for loitering when she should have been at class.

"But…"

"Your schedule has been sitting right here for ages. Do you even plan on attending classes today?"

Jesse had learned long ago that as a child and a student there was no use arguing with a person such as Mrs. Daly. "Yes ma'am," Jesse said glumly and the pain in her abdomen grew slightly.

A look down at her schedule made the pain grow. 3rd period: Art at the Speed of Life. Ms Weldon rm. 213

"Mother-puss-bucket." The words came out as a groan. Ms Weldon was the last person she wanted to see at the moment. Jesse checked her watch and saw that there was still thirty-eight minutes left to the period. She decided that ditching was the best course of action. It was either that or she would get an ulcer at the age of seventeen.

Jesse figured that she would find an empty classroom or a bathroom to hide out in, but just as she turned toward the stairs she saw Mrs. Daly eyeing her. It was a shrewd, been-around-the-block kind of look and it sent warning bells off in Jesse's mind.

She decided that it was best not to ditch.

Instead, she moped her way up to the second floor. The school, like the town, was small; it had only four-hundred and ten students and Jesse was at room 213 in little over a minute. She stood outside it for another minute trying to gather her courage. It never got gathered. The only thing that occurred was that her stomach began to ache all the more. It felt like she had swallowed a razor.

Finally she stepped in. The art room looked exactly like a high-school art room. This was Jesse's third high school and every one of them had a room that looked just as this one did. Except that is, for one large horse-faced difference.

Ms. Weldon accosted her the second she walked in. It was as if she had been expecting...and hoping for this very thing to occur. "You are late. Do you have a proper excuse?"

Jesse felt ambushed. She barely had time to take in the twenty or so students staring at her. "No. Registering took longer..."

The art teacher cut her off, striding to stand over her, "Do you think you can walk in here anytime you please?" The tone sounded sweet, but the words were poisonous ice.

"No of course not. I only..."

"Then perhaps you'll be kind enough to follow the rules of this school and go get a note from Mrs. Daly," Ms. Weldon said in her sickly-sweet manner.

Jesse was so astounded that she couldn't find even the simplest words to respond with. "I...uh...I," was all that came out.

"Go," the teacher ordered. "And don't come back without a note. We have rules for a reason and don't think that just because of who your father is that I'll bend them for you."

Red-faced and with ears that felt as though a match had been taken to them, Jesse left. Tittering of the art students could be heard as she walked down the hall in utter disbelief.

"Mother-puss-bucket!" This time it wasn't a groan. This time she was angry.

"Excuse me, Mrs. Daly?" Jesse paused for a response, yet nothing came from the receptionist but a cold stare. After an awkward moment Jesse went on, "Ms. Weldon says that I need a note excusing me for being late to her class. Could you write one for me please?"

"No."

Another awkward moment passed between them. Jesse scratched her head, thinking. "You won't write me a note because you believe you gave me my schedule with plenty of time to get to class is that correct?"

Mrs. Daly stood up and placed her pudgy little fists on her desk. "I don't *believe* I did. I *know* I did. You asked for your schedule and instead of taking it and going to class you sat around day-dreaming."

Unbelievable. Un-freaking-believable, Jesse's voice of reason said in her mind. It had good reason to be mad.

A fury began to mount in her, but she bit it back, relying oddly enough on the part of her that was her father. Mrs. Daly and Ms Weldon were nothing but cogs in the high school machine and should be treated as such. The idea tempered her anger and allowed her to think.

"Well I guess I'm in a bit of a pickle then," Jesse acknowledged. "Is Principal Peterson available? I will probably need to talk to him."

Mrs. Daly began to laugh at this. She laughed so hard that she had to sit down. "What do you need to see him for? Do you think he'll believe anything you might try to make up? If so you are sooo mistaken. He has seen your transcripts from your previous schools. They read like a felon's rap sheet. Fighting, stealing, cheating...the works. So whatever you have to say, you might as well save it."

"Actually I was going to turn myself in for cutting class."

Mrs. Daly looked dumbfounded. "What?"

A millisecond later Principal Peterson's office door came open and the rat-faced man stepped out. "Did I just hear you say you are cutting class?"

Jesse glanced up at the clock and jerked her thumb toward it. "Yes, technically I think so. Third period. Ms Weldon won't let me in without a note excusing me for being late and Mrs. Daly won't write one, so...here I am."

The two bureaucrats looked at each other in surprise with eyebrows raised. Neither could find anything to say to this. Jesse was sure that no student had ever turned themselves in for cutting class before and she went on speaking as only a cog in a machine would really appreciate.

"I hate to be taking so much of your valuable time for something as simple as this. It would be terrible if people got the idea that the faculty around here had nothing better to do than to give the new kid in school the run around. Especially when so many budget cuts are being enacted. It would seem like such a waste of time and resources."

Now the surprised look on their faces faded through the full spectrum of apprehension. They went from unease to the first trace of fear...but this didn't last, a glower of anger settled on both their faces. Secretly this struck Jesse as humorous. They would have laughed at her had they known how little James Clarke valued the opinion of his daughter.

Principal Peterson barked out, "Just write the note."

Chapter 6

Jesse couldn't decide if the note represented a minor victory, or just a mitigation of an obvious defeat.

There were many votes in the mitigation category. After all she was still heading to Ms Weldon class halfway through the period and she would still have to suffer whatever unnecessary barbs the art teacher had to throw in her face. In addition to that she had, by invoking the ghost of her father, probably forever linked the two of them together in the minds of the teaching staff. This of course meant that since he was hated then she was hated, but at the same time, clearly this had already begun anyway.

In the victory category, she held in her hands a note Ms Weldon would be very surprised to read. Because her day had started so poorly Jesse decided to claim victory, though hollow it turned out to be.

When she walked back into the class, the art teacher was obviously ready with some snide remark about crawling back empty handed. Before the girl got halfway through the door Ms Weldon rounded on her.

"I thought I told you not come back without a…"

With a neutral look upon her face, Jesse flashed out the paper and presented it to the teacher.

"What is…" Ms Weldon read it over once and then eyed the signature closely. Callously she crumpled the paper into a ball. "You are still responsible for everything that you missed. Take your seat."

Jesse groaned under her breath. The only chair available was at an empty three-person table in the very front of the class. Feeling every eye in the room boring into her back, she hurried to the chair and sat down.

Just as she did, Ms Weldon spoke up, "Jesse please stand up and face the class."

"Mother-pus-bucket," she said so that no one could hear. Slowly she climbed to her feet, fearing the next bit of torture that Ms Weldon had in store for her and wondering if her cheeks were as red as they felt. "Yes, ma'am?"

"Class this is Jesse Clarke..." Here Ms Weldon paused, perhaps expecting the name to be known, but in this she was disappointed. No one so much as batted an eye. She continued, "This is her first day here at Ashton and I want you all to stop your work and give her your undivided attention as she tells us a little bit about herself."

What? This was ridiculous! "I...I haven't had to do this since the second grade," Jesse began with a shy smile. This earned her a few grins, which rallied her. "I'm only seventeen so there's not much to tell just yet. I...uh, just moved into town with my family. We were living in Copperfield. So that's about it..."

She was just starting to sit when Ms Weldon asked, "Your entire family just moved here?"

So this was the deal. The horse-faced bitch just wanted to make sure every kid in school knew exactly who she was and more importantly who her father was. Jesse had a strong temptation to simply lie straight out, but she held back and instead went with a modified version of the truth.

"Only my mother and I just moved. We got to town on Saturday." She almost made it back into her chair which would have been nice since her sprained ankle was beginning to get twingy.

"And your father?" The voice of the art teacher was dead cold.

Jesse wanted to blurt out: *I'm an orphan. My father was killed in Iraq. Thanks for bringing up that painful memory!* Instead she said quietly, "My father works for the town."

"In what capacity?"

The exact truth was that James Clarke was sort of a janitor. His whole job was to clean up the messes the idiots who ran the town before him were too gutless to handle. Of course that couldn't be mentioned since some of the children of the cowards were possibly in the room.

"My father is the town manager," Jesse announced.

Now came the whisperings that Ms Weldon had been hoping for and along with the sound, which reminded Jesse of a basket full of snakes, came quite a few hard stares. The teacher let the students murmur to each other for a long minute until the classroom was all astir and only then she took control again.

"Quiet down. Jesse you can take a seat, unless you have anything else you wish to say?"

Jesse had plenty to say, all of it enough to get her expelled. Instead she sat. Her face a stony mask.

She tried to tell herself that everything was going to be fine and that either way the truth was going to have to come out sooner or later. At least this way her secret was revealed all at once, like ripping off a band-aid…it was always better done quick.

"Let's get your graphs out," Ms Weldon said to the class. There was a general confusion as large rolls of paper were laid out upon all of the desks. All save Jesse's. "Remember these have to be done by Thursday and I will not tolerate excuses."

Jesse stared about her as the other teenagers went about marking up long rectangles of paper that were drawn over with pictures and bubbled wording. From where she was sitting she couldn't read any of it and had no clue what was going on.

She raised her hand. Eight minutes and twenty seconds later Ms Weldon strolled up.

"You have a question?"

The question was dreadfully obvious to both of them and Jesse felt strength slip from her at the silly need to ask it. "What is the class working on?"

"It's a coordinated studies program. The artistic portion is using *I Madonnari* to protest." She said this as if it were the simplest thing in the world.

Jesse waited the appropriate amount of time for her teacher to explain what *I Madonnari* meant and then sighed, "Alright, I give up, what's eye moderny?"

Ms Weldon handed her a hefty textbook. "I'm busy. Look it up."

By Jesse's count she had one hundred and six days until she graduated. The way things were going she feared that each day would feel like a year all by itself. "You want me to look it up? Isn't it your job to teach?"

Jesse's tone had been over the line rude, but she didn't care and neither did Ms Weldon, who replied calmly, "My job is also to teach you how to think for yourself; something clearly lacking in your upbringing. I repeat Look. It. Up."

"Could you at least tell me what language it is?"

The art teacher surprised Jesse by answering, "It's Italian."

For the remainder of the shortened class, Jesse tried and failed to find anything in the book that sounded like *eye moderny*. Eventually, she just took to reading about Cubism, which was mildly interesting. When the bell rang her shoulders drooped in relief at the sound.

"Miss Clarke?" Ms Weldon called to her as the rest of the class escaped to the halls.

"Oh crap," Jesse whispered to herself. Louder she said, "Yes ma'am?"

"Do you have the definition of the word yet?" Jesse shook her head and Ms Weldon smiled grimly. "Then you get a zero in class participation for the day. And to catch you up with the rest of the class, I want a five page essay on *I Madonnari* finished by tomorrow."

Anger and outrage coupled with a sudden despair that nothing would go right had her emotions taking over her mind. Jesse had to blink back tears. "That seems rather excessive."

"I just want the tax payers to get their money's worth," Ms Weldon said with feigned innocence. "Isn't that what you want as well?"

"Yeah...sure." Jesse turned to leave and saw on one of the side chalkboards the word: *I Madonnari*. Finally a flippin break! Hurriedly she jotted it down. She had been looking up an altogether different spelling of the word. With that done she darted from the classroom and pulled out her class schedule.

"Lunch!" she cried with more enthusiasm than she had meant to. People stared.

She left the area around the art room and limped down to the cafeteria on her gimpy ankle. The three-inch heels that she was wearing, though they looked great, were really starting to put a strain on her. She had to stop and slip them off. This was an immediate relief, but it also made her last in line for lunch.

She came up behind a boy who was slim and of average height. From behind he was nothing special, but when he turned around he was something else entirely.

"Excuse me?" She tapped him on the shoulder. The boy hadn't been in her art class and probably didn't know who she was yet. Jesse was hoping that a little small talk would lead to an invitation to sit with him. She would even flirt if that's what it took. Though she had everyday of her high school life, she dreaded the idea of sitting alone.

The boy didn't turn, nor did he make any sign that he knew someone was behind him. She tapped again harder.

"Hi. I was wondering if you knew..."

She stopped in mid-sentence because the boy had turned in the oddest manner. Instead of just turning halfway about and looking back, he turned fully toward her, as if presenting his front to her. He paused for half a second and then turned back again without ever once looking her in the eye.

She had looked however. The boy had striking hazel eyes and thick dark eyebrows. His skin was smooth and unblemished with the youthful color of apple in his cheeks, but despite that he had the air of a man. Not a goofy teenager like those all around them, but a man.

It made her heart do a little tap-dance within her chest. She coughed, afraid that her voice would crack and said, "Uhh... excuse me?" The boy made no indication that he heard. It was very strange.

Perhaps he was a retard, Jesse mused. Or maybe he was gay. If so...what a waste! But she didn't think he was gay and the idea that there wasn't something right in the ole attic stuck with her. If this was the case he wouldn't last long at the school. Her father absolutely hated retards in school. He was fine with them learning and growing to the best of their ability, he just thought it was detrimental to all the other kids around them.

In an otherwise perfect society he might have a valid point. Yet Jesse had seen so many "normal" kids being far more of a disruption in class: selling drugs, talking on phones, mouthing off to teachers, that in her mind a retard wasn't going to change things much. If there had been...

"Miss Clarke!"

The stern voice calling across the cafeteria disrupted her thinking and made her jump. She looked up to see Principal Peterson standing with the cooks behind the tins of food, glaring at her. "This is a cafeteria, not the playground; get your shoes on, now!"

Laughing and whispering followed on the heels of the booming voice. Jesse hurried to comply, but her ankle was swollen and it took a minute to get the shoes on. By the time they were on the cooks were removing the trays. Hurriedly Jesse grabbed a plate and held it out.

"Excuse me, can I have a little of..." She couldn't tell if what she was pointing at was lasagna or stuffed shells. "A little of that, please."

If she thought that the angry stare of the librarian from the night before or the wicked malice of Mrs. Daly was bad, it was nothing compared to the looks the cooks were giving her. Just then she remembered her father's conversation with Ms Weldon about closing the school cafeterias. Oh crap!

The cook did not spoon out a small portion; she dug out a great big heap of the marinara filled dish. It was much more than Jesse could eat in a day, let alone at one sitting at lunch. Yet it was the single act of kindness that she had received in a long time.

"Thank you very..."

The cook smacked the great gob onto Jesse's plate and it couldn't have been anything but purposeful. The food hit the back end of the plate and a large portion of it shot in an oily red mess onto Jesse's white satin shirt.

"Sorry," the cook muttered with a shrug.

Chapter 7

Laughter, cruel and mocking, followed after Jesse as she left the cafeteria. Her shirt was ruined; it ran with red sauce and oil. She fled to the nearest bathroom where she attempted to clean it in the sink. This seemed only to spread the stain and when she was done, it was so wet that *everything* beneath showed through. She looked like a dying hooker from a horror movie.

"Damn it!" Jesse screamed and then the tears came, they were hot on her face. Ashamed of them—they made her feel so weak—she went to a stall and hid there...and cried some more.

Girls came and went. The bell for fifth period rang, then six minutes later the late bell rang as well and still Jesse cried. She was furious at everyone in the school. They hated her and she hated them right back. It was a passionate hate on her part and they could all rot in hell for all she cared. After a while, being half-naked, she grew cold. Sneaking out of the stall she took her shirt to the hand dryer and ran it repeatedly until the shirt had dried well enough to put back on.

Jesse then went to mirror and looked at the person who was hated to such an awful degree. She couldn't understand it. How people could be this way was simply beyond her. Heavy tears began again to fall from her cheeks and just then the bell for the sixth period rang. Like a coward she ran back to the bathroom stall and locked the door. There she sat... alone.

Girls came and went. They giggled and laughed and talked up a storm. The subject of boys came up and everyone agreed that Allen was by far the dreamiest. This brought about the topic of the coming Christmas ball and a parade of hopes floated along the white tiles of the bathroom. The talk turned to dresses and shoes and who would look most like a princess. Then the words Jesse had feared the most popped out of someone's mouth. The words were—Jesse Clarke.

Whatever nasty things they were going to say Jesse refused to hear. She clamped her hands to her ears and began rocking back and forth. A muffled bell rang. It was the late bell for sixth period. Slow and tentatively, Jesse pulled her hands back. The bathroom was mercifully quiet again and there she sat... alone.

Eventually her legs grew numb from sitting in one place for so long and she got up and went to the mirror again. The girl there was pathetic looking. Her makeup had run down her face, her eyes were red and puffy and her stupid marinara stained shirt looked idiotic. The shirt, the skirt, the shoes, the blonde hair had all been a bad idea. The girl who had dressed so thoughtfully that morning was a putz. She was a weakling and a coward; a person afraid of eating alone.

Who could like someone like that?

Jesse dunked her hands under hot running water and began washing away the makeup. Beneath it she saw the hard girl that had walked the halls of Copper Ridge High. That girl had been hated, but unafraid. That girl had once stabbed a boy with a wickedly sharp pencil. At Copper Ridge all of her pencils were wickedly sharp.

When her face was scrubbed clean, she rolled the sleeves of her shirt far up and then untucked the bottom of her shirt. She undid half the buttons and then tied the loose ends of her shirt just below her breasts. It made her look a touch slutty, but not for a second did she care since at least the stain was halfway hid. Next she pulled off her shoes and then groaned in relief.

Not a minute later the bell for seventh period rang.

For her, AP History, room 235 was her next class. It was all the way down the length of the school. In actuality this wasn't very far, but as she opened the bathroom door it seemed like the hall was a mile long and was filled with thousands of laughing, jeering teenagers.

Was it her imagination, or were they all staring at her? Were they all pointing? Did the name Jesse Clarke roll down the hall in a whispered undertone beneath the hated laughter?

Jesse gave her head a brief shake and then gritted her teeth in determination. *Remember, you are tough and you are strong,* with this mantra going through her mind, she strode down the center of the hall as if she owned the place.

As the most hated person in every school that she had ever attended, Jesse had learned a few things about walking down crowded halls. The first thing she had discovered was that there were going to be jerks who would want to smash into her as she passed by. This was an inevitability.

The trick to combating it was a simple little maneuver. She would act like she *wanted* the shoulder-to-shoulder confrontation and as her assailant would brace in preparation to send her sprawling, Jesse would make ready in the opposite manner. At the last second she would dip her shoulder back and step deftly to the side.

This worked almost every time, though it depended upon a state of awareness that was uncommon in teenagers. The hated one hadn't initially been blessed with this hyper-awareness, but over time, and with many a bruised shoulder, her mind and body had adapted. Her eyes would flick about with startling speed, going from person to person, judging *their* mental state by how they walked, who they were with, and where they were positioned amongst their friends. Were they slouched, bored with school and just wanting to get to class? Were they with a girl in a nice dress and wished to look gentlemanly? Or were they alone?

Rarely did people alone ever bother Jesse. Sure they might sneer or drop the word "Bitch" as she passed, but a physical confrontation was an uncommon thing with a lone person. It was when they traveled in packs that she had to take the most care. Then the least little dweeb might want to try something to impress his or her friends.

On that stroll through the halls of Ashton High, she was likely just too new yet to actually have to worry about any of this. This was the part in her little Greek tragedy in which she would be sized up. This was the stage where her physical and mental presence would be judged and it was important to come across as someone not to be messed with.

Therefore she held her head high and looked the other teenagers in the eye as she passed... at first. Then something caught her attention that was so out of the norm in her school experiences that she was shocked into staring.

In front of her a ghost moved down the hall.

There was a second tactic to moving in crowded corridors, one that worked better even than the first. It was simple. All Jesse had to do to move from class to class safely was to get behind a group of football players...linemen she believed they were called. The very largest and strongest kids played on the line and when they sauntered down the halls, they were like battleships plowing down a narrow river. People scurried out of their way and Jesse found that if she stayed in their wake, she could drift along behind virtually unnoticed by all.

Amazingly, this ghost, though slightly built had that same ability.

He wasn't a ghost of course, he was the boy who had stood in front of her at the back of the lunch-line, and he was quite solid. However, for all intents and purposes he was the ghost of Ashton High. The other kids seemed to look right through him. They noticed his presence among them but pretended they didn't. He drifted soundlessly down the hall and although he was only average in size, Jesse was amazed to see the crowd part for him like he was the biggest leviathan on the football team.

It was so strange to Jesse that she followed along after him and she passed her own classroom without even a glance into the room. The ghost went to the next and last room in the hall where two girls stood in the doorway. He walked right between them without even the courtesy to say excuse me and only one seemed to even twitch at his passing.

She was a big haired girl with pasty skin that seemed to crawl as he went by and when he was safely in the room, she gave the slightest barely perceptible shudder, just as if a ghost out of a book or movie had gotten too close. Jesse walked between the same two girls.

"Excuse me," she said by reflex only, her mind was too absorbed in the ghost for actual thought out politeness. She watched him go to the back of the class to a desk that was purposely set apart from the rest. As he passed, the ten or so students in the classroom all found convenient things other than the ghost to look at. Heads were turned slightly away, eyes were averted, and awkward conversations picked up in volume. The ghost sat down and taking a book from his bag, began to read, ignoring those who ignored him.

Jesse turned to the girl on her right. "Can you tell me who that boy is?"

The girl, a blonde who had apparently applied her make-up with the hopes of being mistaken for a transvestite said, "Yeah, his name is John McScrewyourself."

Jesse blinked in surprise, having momentarily forgotten that she was hated, but she rallied quickly. "Oh, so you two are related then?"

The larger girl with the 80's teased hair, whose skin had crawled with the passing of the ghost, looked stunned at first at what had just been said. She then realized who it was that stood in front of her. "You're that bitch, whose dad fired my mom, aren't you?"

Jesse could have made an attempt to side with the two girls and denounce her father as the straight up bastard that he was, only she knew it wouldn't work. Instead she stepped up in the girl's face.

"And you're the bitch who will be missing her front teeth if she thinks she's ever going to call me that again." Jesse stared hard into the girl's eyes, knowing what was coming next. The big haired girl thought she knew as well, but in truth she hadn't really thought past her next word.

"Bitch," she said slow and obvious.

The word seemed to set a spark in Jesse's eye. It was a lusty spark that denoted danger and she hoped the big haired girl read it properly. The key to not fighting is to actually want to fight, or at least to seem like you wanted to. For Jesse, she was in a semi-bluff position. As a street fighter she was very good for a girl. In fact against other girls she was thirteen wins against only one defeat and two draws. On the other hand, the big hair of her opponent sat atop a very big girl. And she wasn't fat either, more like a volleyball player. She had Jesse by at least thirty pounds in weight and four inches in height.

The girl saw the spark in Jesse's eyes, paused for a moment and then her own eyes sparked as well. She was game for a fight, or so she thought.

In a semi-bluff position it paid to keep betting, it put the pressure on one's opponent and Jesse was sure that her opponent thought the fight would be a modified hair pulling event in the hallway that would go on to the cheers of the other students until a teacher broke it up. But Jesse had other plans. A fight such as the one the girl was envisioning would only cause many more fights down the road. Instead, Jesse wanted to take it out back and go at it girl against girl.

The fight she envisioned would have her pummeling the girl into a half-conscious state and then coming back into the school alone. And when she did, it would be with a smile of pleasure on her face at having ripped the big hair off the girl's head. That sort of fight would discourage other fights. It wouldn't stop them all together, but at least there would be far fewer.

"Let's go," Jesse said simply and began to walk away. She turned to see the girl looking slightly perplexed. "Come on. We'll do this out back, behind the cafeteria. Just you and me...it'll be fun." There was no hesitation in her words and her voice was like cold steel.

The girl hesitated, the spark in her eyes dimmed. Jesse had put a lot on the table and her demeanor suggested very strongly that she could back it up with her fists.

"I'm not going out there...I have class."

"So you're all talk?" Jesse made sure the distain was clear in her voice for all to hear. "You call people rude names and then you hide behind excuses. Fine, you don't have time now, how bout down at the berm after school?"

There had been a growing crowd around the two girls and with it came an increased murmuring, but at the mention of the berm, the hall grew silent. Big haired girl's eyes looked about with a touch of wildness to them. The idea of the berm frightened her and that very obvious fact brought back the memory of the Shadow-man in Jesse's mind.

Maybe fighting down at the berm wasn't such a good idea. Still there was no backing down from this sort of dare once it was out there, not in a situation such as this.

"Well?" Jesse asked as the pause lengthened.

"What's going on," a man's voice spoke up sharply. "What's going on?" A dapper man in a three-piece suit pushed through the crowd. He stood staring for a moment at Jesse and the girl, he then asked in a somewhat fussy manner, "Have you two been fighting?"

"No Mr. Irving. We were only arguing," the girl said, speaking for Jesse as well.

"That's good, Amanda. I don't want to have to suspend anyone so close to the holidays, but I will if I have to," Mr. Irving threatened. "Now get to class, all of you before the late bell rings."

With a last glare at the girl, Amanda, Jesse turned to leave, but Mr. Irving called her back. "Miss Clarke? You were absent from my sixth period economics class. Have you anything to say for yourself?"

"I...I was sick." It was the truth in a way, but sounded extremely lame nonetheless.

It sounded lame to Mr. Irving as well and he cocked an eye at the excuse. "Then you will need to go to the nurse's office for a note excusing you."

After the near fight, Jesse was deflating rapidly. "Sure. Could you tell me where..."

"Where the nurse's office is?" The teacher interrupted. "It's the front desk. Mrs. Daly is both the receptionist and the nurse." Jesse's mouth came open at this, which made the economics teacher smile sourly. "Budget cuts, you know."

She knew.

Chapter 8

Despite the knowledge she would have an unexcused absence from class on her very first day—Jesse was certain Mrs. Daly would never give her a note this time—she almost enjoyed her AP world history class.

Because of her confrontation with Amanda and her brief conversation with Mr. Irving she walked in just as the late bell sounded. Again the weight of every eye sat full upon her. Twenty-three students and one tall bowling pin shaped teacher stared at her as if she was some sort of nasty specimen under a microscope.

"In the future I would appreciate it if you are in your seat when the bell sounds Miss..."

"Jesse Clarke," she answered and she noted that his eyes held no surprise, no shock. He knew exactly who she was; he only wanted her to have to say her name aloud for the rest of the class to hear...just in case any of them didn't know already.

"Take a seat, Miss Clarke." He wasn't at all pleasant sounding.

There were four empty chairs in the back of the class and one in particular caught her attention...it sat apart from the rest; just like the chair in the next room which the Ghost had taken.

Did he have this class earlier in the day, and was this his chair? Why was it pushed back...away from the others? Intrigued, she immediately went to it and slid in. This caused a stir among the students. Eyes flicked back and whispers ran about the room like a cold draft on a winter day. Even Mr. Johnson's face puckered at her choice of seats, yet he said nothing.

All of this had Jesse wondering what she had done wrong and with a growing sense of unease, she eyed the other students. Some looked back at her with anger or hate and this she was so used to it was neither here nor there to her. However, some of the kids looked back with a touch of nervousness in their bearing. One girl even seemed to shudder slightly after sneaking a peek.

What was going on?

A very unsettling thought made Jesse go stiff in her chair: perhaps the boy she thought of as the Ghost was diseased! Maybe that was why no one wanted to go near him and why his chair sat so far apart. He was probably dying of some sort of communicable sickness: a flesh eating virus, or herpes, or AIDS!

A shiver ran up her back and she pulled her arms close into her sides afraid to touch the very desk she sat in. Surreptitiously, Jesse took a peek at the next closest desk; it appeared clean enough, so she decided to move. Yet with half the class still darting glances back at her it seemed oddly far away and she knew that moving would cause another wave of whispering and likely some cruel giggles as well. No matter, she would just have to chance it; the alternative, staying in a germ-infested chair made her want to rub her exposed arms and wash her hands with bleach.

Thinking she would be slick about it and move once Mr. Johnson turned to the blackboard, she slid her bag off the desk and pivoted in her chair. She was already to abandon the desk when her hand felt something odd. Her head came around and she stared at the wood of her desk.

ALONE

This one word, five inches long and two inches wide, was carved in a rough way, very deeply into the top of the desk. It grabbed her attention and held it; the word seemed as though it was a personal message just for her. She *was* alone, more alone than anyone had a right to be. It had been nine years since she had a proper friend, not since Cynthia White moved to New York during the fourth grade. From that point on the closest thing to a friend that she could boast about were a number of very short-lived acquaintances that died under the power of the herd mentality of small town life.

Abruptly, her self-pitying thoughts were interrupted by a mental image of the Ghost as he drifted through the halls. He had been ignored in the most dreadful fashion as if he were a true and actual spirit instead of a boy. Every eye had slid off him as though he had been visually greased. Every head had turned away at his approach. Indeed, every person looked to have been repelled in some invisible manner, much like the wrong ends of two magnets.

"Wow," the word was as quiet as death. In all her years as *the hated one*, Jesse didn't think it was possible for another human to be as lonely as she was, but now she knew better. That boy didn't even have the luxury of being loathed. He was nothing. If he died in the hall she was sure that the other kids would simply walk around his body as if her were a puddle of something unpleasant.

Her need to change desks left her as her curiosity bloomed and her mind raced over reasons why a person could be so intentionally overlooked. Now that her thinking cap was on it was clear to her that the boy wasn't diseased— there would've been more precautions taken than merely just setting him slightly apart. Yet there was something about him, something distinctly unusual, but what?

She racked her brains for an answer as Mr. Johnson droned on about civil disobedience, a topic that he had declared right off the bat was not going to be on the coming final. When he did this the entire class, including Jesse, promptly tuned him out.

It wouldn't have mattered what he was talking about to Jesse, her mind was on the Ghost. Maybe the boy was a criminal? Someone dangerous.

No, that couldn't be it either. He wouldn't be in school if he was a danger to others, her voice of reason explained.

Right. Then maybe he had some sort of mental phobia of being looked at? Her lips turned down at the thought. People were strange, it was true...but would *everybody* in the school be so helpful as to not look at him? That was so unlikely that she dumped the phobia angle in a flash.

Eventually, after discarding every possible reason for the shabby treatment of the Ghost, including him being a secret agent, or him having such horrid bad breath as to cause immediate vomiting if one strayed too close, Jesse gave up. In her mind there wasn't anything that would justify such cruel behavior.

With the class half over, she took to day dreaming about the boy while running her finger along the rough edge of the carved out word. How someone as cute as the Ghost could be ignored by the girls of the school was just beyond her...

"Crap," she hissed out the word. A splinter had slid up beneath her fingernail and lodged there. The pain for such a small thing was intense and it hurt as much coming out as it did going in. Sucking on her wounded finger, she took a closer look at the carven word. The once tan wood of the desk had been stained a blue-black which suggested the Ghost had used a pen to carve with, and this brought up the question: How long would it take someone to do this? Months?

Had the Ghost started engraving the word *ALONE* on his first day as a senior? And were there more desks like this all over the school? She could picture a much smaller version of the Ghost as a freshman, sitting in the back of a classroom, scraping at the wood, day after day...alone.

She shook her head, saddened by the fact that she had found a person more deserving of pity than herself. It was then she made another discovery. There were more, much smaller, carvings running down the edge of the desk:

S.B.

G.M.J.

J.O.

R. M.- K. M.- N.M.-?

M.C.

Another mystery. They were likely the initials of people the Ghost knew. Actual friends of his perhaps? Maybe people he could talk to outside of school? Possibly they were even the initials of his past...or present girlfriends. This last thought brought out a little *humph* sound from her throat.

No, not girlfriends. Any boy that would carve out the word *ALONE* like that wouldn't have a string of girlfriends at his beck and call. This was something else entirely, but with so little information at her disposal there was no way she could guess at it. Instead she decided to simply ask the source.

Taking a piece of paper from her notebook, she wrote:
Hello,

My name is Jesse Clarke. I'm the girl who tapped you on the shoulder in the lunch-line. I don't mean to be pushy, but I don't really know anyone here at Ashton High and I could use a friend. You seem to be in the same boat. Would you like to sit together at lunch tomorrow? You could tell me all about the wonders of the town of Ashton and for the other 59 minutes, you can tell me something about yourself, ha-ha. Hopefully I will see you then.

Jesse

She grimaced slightly at the ha-ha part, but kept it in anyways. The boy looked like he could use even that pathetic touch of humor. Making sure that no one was looking, she slipped the paper deep into the desk.

Next she took out her pencil and with slow movements, so as not to draw attention to herself, she traced a faint circle around the word *ALONE* and then left a fine line from it leading to the initials. Here she wrote *J.C.-in desk*.

She contemplated adding a heart under her initials, but didn't, since it would just look so desperate on her part. Though in fact she was desperate. Dreadfully so. Embarrassingly so.

The closest Jesse had ever come to a kiss in her entire life came during a fight with a boy named Mike Cuflin two years before. Their faces had inadvertently smashed together and her lips had swelled to twice their normal size. He had also copped a free feel getting up off of her. It was the high point of her dating history.

Still, the Ghost was likely just as desperate...maybe even more so. From books and movies, as well as what she overheard...when nobody had a clue that she was lurking about, Jesse knew that boys had needs. Maybe the idea of her and the Ghost weren't so farfetched after all.

She smiled.

"Miss Clarke, could you please tell me what it is about African-Americans being denied the right to vote, that could possibly make you smile?" Mr. Johnson said in a voice that carried to the back of the room easily.

"Uh..."

"That's what I thought you'd say." Mr. Johnson said in reply to the bewildered little sound that slipped from Jesse's mouth. "If you aren't going to pay attention in class then you will just have to learn at home. See me after the bell so we can discuss the topic of your five page essay that you will hand in tomorrow."

The titters of her classmates drowned out her weak reply of, "Yes sir." The rest of the class was over with quickly and Jesse was sure she knew what was coming. Mr. Johnson would dither about in an attempt to make her late for her final class and this he did, though he wasn't quite so effective at being an ass as he thought he was.

She stood by his desk with a bored expression as he pretended to contemplate what her assignment was going to be. Slowly he flipped through pages of a textbook and said, "Maybe...maybe...maybe."

Jesse only rolled her eyes as the minutes ticked away. She took to staring at the clutter on the History teacher's desk. There was a tiny replica of a cannon from some yester-year war. Facing it was a four-inch tall cavalryman standing up in his stirrups and brandishing a saber. Mostly, however, the desk was simply a place where papers of every sort came to spawn. The top of his desk was layered like leaves on a forest floor, while from the drawers papers poked and peeked and slipped from every crack.

"How...bout...we just go with five pages on..." he spoke slowly, drawing it out. "On Rosa Parks."

"Huh?" Her mind was not on his words, but rather on a picture that she had just noticed amidst the disorder. It showed a smiling thirteen-year-old blonde boy, posing with a tremendous pumpkin in his scrawny arms. Jesse knew the boy was thirteen by doing simple math. At the top of the picture, in gold lettering, were the words:

Gregory Matthew Johnson 1993-2006

Was this his son? Suddenly she found that she was unable to be too angry at the history teacher. "Rosa Parks? Sure I can do five pages. That's no problem." The words came out sounding almost as though she would be doing him a favor by writing the essay. This caused Mr. Johnson to look up at her, but she didn't notice her eyes hadn't strayed from the picture.

He looked at it also and said in a voice that would be the kindest that she heard that day, "You better get going. You don't want to be late."

Chapter 9

Jesse made it to her last class on time, beating the bell for the first time that day, yet she did it only by seconds. Before she knew what was happening her AP Biology teacher began barking out directions to the class concerning their current lab assignment, only he was going so fast that he sound like auctioneer. An auctioneer speaking a foreign language.

Jesse's head spun with how quick everything was suddenly moving in the room. She didn't even know what table she was supposed to be sitting at, and who, if anybody was going to be her lab partner. Kids seemed to be everywhere. Some milled about chatting; others shot about in hurry, criss-crossing the room gathering supplies as if time was against them.

"Mr... uh...," Jesse consulted her schedule quickly. "Mr. Daniels...excuse me?"

The class had only just started, but the man was already in a sweat. He had a wide mouth with large down turned lips; his over-all impression reminded Jesse of a toad.

"Yes, what do you... oh, Clarke, right?" he asked.

She nodded. "Yes that's right. Can you tell me where I should be? All the tables are so...full." Oddly enough, just at that moment the chaos of the room seemed to dissipate and milling teens all looked to have found their seats. Now she could see that there was an empty table right in the front of the class and a table in the back corner at which sat a solitary figure.

A very cute, apple-cheeked solitary figure.

Mr. Daniels considered her question, looking around the room. His eyes passed over the lonesome boy in the back. "I'm sorry, but everyone seems to be paired up already. You had better just take this desk." They were at the front of the room and he gestured to the empty table at her elbow.

"But..." she hesitated for just a second, uncertain. Should she ask about the boy? Mr. Daniels seemed nice enough, maybe he would explain to her why there was so much strange behavior associated with the Ghost? "Why is that..." Too late. She had hesitated a second too long and before she knew it, he was on the other side of the class and she was just standing there with her mouth open.

At least he hadn't been purposely rude about walking away from her, which for Jesse was a first. Rather Mr. Daniels seemed all in a bother. He didn't look capable of *not* fretting. He seemed to act as though everything in the lab was made of eggshells and he repeated the words: *be careful with that* and *hold it gently, don't be so rough*, every minute or so as he scurried around the room.

As Jesse wasn't currently a threat to his lab—since she was just standing there clueless to what was going on in the class—she was ignored by the teacher. And by her classmates in general as well, which was another first for the day. They all seemed preoccupied with glass vials, syringes, and most oddly, disgusting pinky-thick earthworms. They squiggled about themselves in a plastic bucket that sat way too close to her.

Though she wasn't girly-girl squeamish about worms or spiders and things of that nature, Jesse was definitely not a fan. Feeling her throat go tight, she stepped away from the bucket and back toward the table she had been assigned to.

"Mr. Daniels?"

The teacher was shooting by in a hurry and replied, "Just a second," after he had already passed. Great.

"How bout I just sit here looking stupid," she said under her breath. With a long sigh, Jesse took a seat and as she had nothing better to do she took to observing, in the most unobtrusive manner, the other kids around her.

They were an average looking lot. It was as though she had seen them all before in other tired, dying towns. Their clothes were fading or had already faded and were worn through. Some of the kids had on clothes a size too big and were most certainly hand-me-downs, which was expected. These were the children of the parents whose town was disintegrating around them. Jobs were drying up fast in Ashton and money even faster.

For the most part she recognized their faces from her earlier classes. None did so much as smile in her direction. Glares were the order of the day...except of course from her Ghost.

"Here you go," Mr. Daniels said handing her a thick stack of papers.

"Can I ask you a question about..." As she spoke her hand came up to point at the Ghost. "That boy..."

Mr. Daniels interrupted, putting a hand over her pointing finger and gently pushing it down. "No, you may not. This is Biology class. If you have a question about science, I will most certainly answer it. But about boys...no."

"Sure, sorry." Jesse felt the pink slip into her cheeks. "About the class then...what are we doing?"

"Cellular respiration. Have you read over the lab outline yet?" he asked seeming to have forgotten that he had just handed it to her.

"No, you just gave it to me."

"Oh right. Well, you and your partner...I mean, you...look why don't you start by reading over the outline and if you have any questions I'll get back to you."

In the end she did and he didn't.

The outline might as well have been written in Latin and she couldn't make heads or tails of it. Within minutes her hand went up, but Mr. Daniels was so engrossed with a student that he didn't notice. Everyone else did however and their sniggering made her hand feel heavy and she soon dropped it in defeat.

"Let's see...Kreb cycle...$C6 H12 O6 + O2$ TO $6 CO2 + 6 H2O + ENERGY$. Huh?" She mumbled, shaking her head at the spew of random seeming letters and numbers. What was this trying to say? The outline was filled with words that she didn't know or had never seen before: autotropes, glycolysis, respirometer...on and on.

If only she had a biology textbook, or better yet, a partner, then she could figure out what it was all about. The one takeaway that was obvious from the paperwork was that the lab was definitely a two-person job. A quick glance around showed everyone else working with another person...except again the Ghost.

For a long time Jesse watched him and never once did he glance up. He ignored with a precise equality in the fashion that he was ignored. In solitude, he worked as if there was a veil about him, so that he was virtually invisible to everyone but her. Strange...yet intriguing as well.

After a few minutes of staring, Jesse had to admit to herself that she was drawn to the Ghost. Not just physically, though he was a cutie, he was also a mystery that she couldn't rid her mind of. And more than that there was an attraction on a different level. She could feel that in some ways they were kindred spirits: she was cruelly hated, while he was ignored and clearly it was just as cruel, if not more so.

She could see no reason why she should ignore him and without the pressure of the other students, there was a chance that he wouldn't hate her. With a deep breath, Jesse grabbed up her bag and her papers and went to the back of the class. In a flash, all eyes...again except for the Ghost's...were upon her and where the students had been busy as bees only seconds before the room grew still.

It was the longest twelve paces of her life. Each step seemed to dial down the hum and whispering of the students until at last she stood just to the boy's side. Once there the room became so quiet that Jesse could hear her own heart beating in her ears.

Before she spoke, she swallowed. In the quiet of the room it was a surprising loud noise, like she was choking down a strip of tree bark. Yet despite that she greeted him with a pleasant enough, "Hello."

The Ghost didn't stir. He had been reading his lab overview and his eyes went on running over the lines as if he hadn't heard her. Behind Jesse someone snorted in muffled laughter, she forced herself not to look back. Instead she tried again.

"I'm Jesse Clarke...we met in the lunch line?"

Really they hadn't exactly, but his lack of response was killing her confidence. It would be a surprise to some that after the day she'd had that she would have any confidence left at all. In truth it was a fraction of her normal outlook. She was painfully aware of the partially covered stain on the front of her white shirt. Moreover, she knew that her "Barbie" look had suffered a serious degradation as her day had descended into hell.

In spite of all this, she knew that she was still prettier than most. Jesse was also smart and personable and had it not been for her father she could've been popular.

One more attempt, "Excuse me..."

Nothing. The boy went on reading. Now her smile was like a sputtering dying engine. It rose and fell on her lips trying to maintain itself as she stood ignored by the boy. "Excuse me..." she craned her neck around to read the top of his paper "...Excuse me Ky. Do you mind if sit here?"

He turned slightly toward her and her smile, which really did wonders for her face, lit up, though only briefly. He didn't even glance at her, instead he looked down his microscope.

Whispering, interspersed with quiet laughter began behind her, which finally killed her smile for good. Now she was angry. For some reason being snubbed by this boy made her more angry than she had been all day. Here was the one kid in school who was worse off than her yet even this loser wouldn't give her the time of day.

"What's your problem?" she demanded in a carrying voice. The room quieted at once, but Jesse didn't care. What did it matter to her if she was quiet or not? The other students could hear everything regardless if she whispered. They could see her humiliation. Her joke of a life was on display as always.

"Excuse me!" Mr. Daniels called out. He hurried forward from the other side of the room but stopped when he was still ten feet from her. "Excuse me Miss Clar... I mean..." Strangely he seemed reluctant to say her name and he ended just pointing at her and then at the table she had recently vacated. "...Uh... why don't you... come back to this table."

"Fine by me," she replied through gritted teeth. In a fury she went back to her table and flopped into her chair. Now Mr. Daniels came over to her and for once he wasn't overly concerned with his classroom.

He spoke to her, but didn't look down at her, instead he stood facing an equation-filled chalkboard, "I think you need to leave that boy alone and respect his privacy. Can you do that?"

"Yeah. Don't worry about that," she replied and meant every word. She had given him his chance and he wouldn't get another. She had given the entire school a chance and it could burn to the ground with everyone in it for all she cared.

For the remainder of the class she stewed in her anger and whenever Mr. Daniels came by she glanced at her outline. In her emotional state—a combination of hate for everyone around her and apathy for school in general—the words on the paper were simply beyond her. All she cared about was being rid of the school as fast as possible. When the final bell rang she was first out of her chair and first to the door.

"Miss Clarke," Mr. Daniels called from behind.

"Mother-pus-bucket!" she hissed under her breath. What now?

The teacher held out to her the outline on cellular respiration that she had been given. "You left your lab work on the table."

"Thanks," she said and then turned to book it out of there. He wasn't done speaking, however.

"I want you to have this read by tomorrow...I know it looks complicated, but it really isn't." She dipped her head as way of acknowledgement and turned once more...and once more he began to speak. "Oh, your text book!" He spun about and scurried to a deep cabinet.

"Oh goody," Jesse murmured, once more in sotto voce. When he withdrew his head from the enclosure in his hands was a heavy textbook. "Thanks," she said, trying to sound appreciative. Her miserable life wasn't his fault after all.

In keeping with his frantic teaching pace, he barely acknowledged her words with a smile that looked inharmonious on his toad-face. He was then back to bustling about, putting his lab back in its exact order. With a final glance at the Ghost, who was placidly putting away his lab paraphernalia, Jesse left. She had a school bus to catch...or so she thought.

Chapter 10

After being held up by Mr. Daniels, a quick check of her watch showed she still had a good six minutes to catch her bus. It should've been no problem. Except that is for her ankle.

With the temperature outside hovering around freezing, there was no way she was going to try to cross the parking lot, dappled as it was with patches of snow and ice, without her shoes on.

"Crap!" she exclaimed through gritted teeth. Her ankle had swollen even more and now a swath of blue-black ran along the inner aspect of it. Yet she forced her three-inch heels onto her feet and grimaced her way as casually as possible toward the line of busses. According to her schedule, which had everything on it from what bus to take to her locker combination, her bus was the third to last in the line.

It felt like a long way, yet with time to spare she was able to get in line behind the last boy and pull herself up.

"Hi there," she said, giving the bus driver a practiced phony smile...a natural one was simply beyond her at that point. The look that he returned her, a sour overly fake smile had her growing nervous and for good reason. Bus drivers in general nearly always have an evil reputation among students. They could be cranky, as well as Nazi-like in their rule enforcements, yet towards Jesse they ran the thin gamut between surly and vindictive.

This particular one had the needle pegged to a level past vindictive, it was somewhere near malicious. The very evident facts about him also added to her trepidation. The bus driver was relatively young, thirty or there abouts. He smelled of stale cigarettes, was unshaven and though he was not exactly unkempt, his appearance bespoke of one who was on the verge of giving up. Yet he wore a wedding ring and not one that was beaten and worn by age; it looked new.

What sort of newly married man had a job like this? Sadly it was a man without a choice. Probably driving a school bus was all that was left in the job market for him. Jesse had to wonder how much longer he would be able to even keep that job.

Her father, the penny-pinching ass, always cut back on the number of buses and drivers in the local school districts. Close in routes would be axed altogether and the kids would be forced to walk or ride bikes to school. In addition, elementary, middle, and high school starting times would be staggered so that one driver and one bus would be used for each route as opposed to two or three.

It made a certain sense from an outside perspective, but from close up, with the man glaring at Jesse as if it were she who was taking food from his baby's mouth, it was painfully harsh.

He didn't respond to her, *Hi there*, other than to set his teeth firmly in his jaw. Jesse gave a tiny shrug that spoke of sympathy, which she regretted within a minute. The bus was close to being completely full, a first in her high-school experience. There were maybe three or four seats available yet none looked inviting and all had backpacks on them.

"Hi," she said with a cautious smile to a straight-haired acne-ravaged blonde boy. "Could you move your backpack, please?"

"No," he answered in a flat voice that suggested there would be use arguing with him.

Jesse wasn't too surprised; she had seen this kind of crap before. She moved on quickly—three seats down—only to receive the same cold response from some no-neck jock. The friend of Amanda's, whom Jesse thought bore a striking resemblance to a transvestite, was the next person without a seatmate. She wore an expression of happy evil and had a beckoning eyebrow that was raised in expectation. *Welllll? Aren't you going to ask me, too?* The eyebrow seemed to say.

Jesse pivoted neatly on her good foot and marched back up the aisle, laughter chasing after. "Excuse me?" she asked, tapping the driver on the shoulder. He had seen her coming but had turned away to look out the window. At her touch he didn't turn back to her.

"Yeah?"

"Well...um, sir?" She paused, disconcerted to have to talk to the back of his head. In an effort to look him in the face she went around to his side and squatted down near the door. "Could you help me? Some of the other kids won't budge over and I can't find a place to sit."

Still not bothering to look at her, he shrugged. "You can't ride on the bus without being seated."

Jesse reached her limit. "I know! That's why I need your help!" Curse words formed on her lips; barely she was just able to bite them back.

At her tone, the driver finally turned to look at her with eyes that had gone to squints. Steadily, she returned his glare and they locked eyes for a few seconds. He then looked down the length of the bus before replying, "Sorry, school bags can't be in the aisle. I guess you're just out of luck." He pointed to the door.

Feeling as though she were in a bizarre dream she stepped down off the bus but held onto the door. Striving to hold back words that were sure to get her expelled, Jesse instead spluttered, "But...but...what am I supposed to do?"

"You *could* take the late bus," he answered. There was a pause and because of the contemptuous sneer on his lips Jesse knew exactly what was going to come out of his mouth next. "Except there isn't a late bus anymore. Budget cuts are a bitch, right?"

Soundlessly her mouth came open and hung there until the door to the bus closed in her face with an indignant squeal. Then things took on a blurry muffled quality. She could hear laughter and jeering. She could see the faces of the students twisted into obscene hateful shapes. Fingers pointed and balls of paper and other objects came at her from the high angle of the windows.

Busses, that seemed as packed as hers drove by, one after another, filling the air with their nasty exhaust, yet *her* bus just sat there parked, idling. Vaguely, she wondered why. Her chin came up in a distracted unclear curiosity and she could see the driver's face...his lips were moving.

"Get away from the door!" he shouted through the glass, but the words didn't translate into meaning for Jesse. At that moment her thinking was like the taste of sea air, which she could always smell, but never quite taste. It just was too...nebulous? Just too out of reach for her senses.

The door squealing open again brought her back in a snap and she flinched in fear. For some reason she expected the kids on the bus to come off it in a human wave and attack her. Instead the driver yelled again.

"Get away from the door!"

So that was the problem, the bus couldn't leave with her so near at hand. She wanted to stand her ground and not budge, to perhaps force them to let her on the bus by holding it there until someone gave up their seat. However, Jesse was feeling distinctly weak.

Physically, she was exhausted from her stressful day and in pain from her ankle. Yet it was mostly her mental situation that caused her to step back meekly. For some reason, whenever she wore a dress or skirt, which was a very rare occurrence, she felt...small. Like a girl.

Of course she was a girl, but the dresses and the pretty shoes made her want to act like a girl as well. She wanted to smile prettily and have heads turn in appreciation. She wanted to sit with her back straight and her ankles crossed and sip tea and laugh when the boys would cavort and act stupid to impress her.

She had heard that *Clothes make the man*, they made Jesse as well. As long as she wore her bedraggled "Barbie" outfit, dealing with another girl like Amanda, and bluffing her way out of a fight was probably the toughest she could expect to be. Swallowing the shreds of her pride she moved.

In a belch of smoke, the bus drove away with the shouts of the students coming to her, over the sound of the engine: *Have a nice walk home—See you later, bitch!...Good-bye!—Good riddance, you mean.*

And there was more. And there was laughter. And an eraser bounced off her forehead. She watched it leap in jaunty erratic movements over the uneven pavement. With it springing about, it seemed to mock her with its cheeriness, yet despite that, she kept her eyes dead on it. The alternative, to look up and see the other students, while tears formed in hot pools in her eyes would have only added to her torture.

Finally the bus was gone and she was able to look away from the pink eraser. The first thing she saw was Principal Peterson who watched from an open door to the school. He had seen her ill-treatment yet had done nothing to stop it and even as her quickly blurring gaze came to rest on his face, he turned back into the school. The door shut with a heavy sound.

Now Jesse was alone. Strangely, eerily alone. Yet she didn't notice it at first.

"Damn it! Damn it! Damn it!" She screeched out her anger and resentment and her hate. Just then she hated everyone and everything...even herself.

Her ankle throbbed and in her fury she wrenched off her shoe and threw it at the school, where it clicked off the uncaring brick.

"Damn you all," she screamed at the building. Her words echoed back at her unheard by all those that she despised except, that is for her...and the Ghost.

Still placid as ever, the Ghost—though she knew his name was Ky she still thought of him as the Ghost—was just climbing on his bike when he fell under Jesse's hard glare.

"Screw you too, Ghost-boy," she screeched. She meant it simply as a defiant parting shot, only he *reacted* to the words. So perfectly had he ignored the world that day that when he turned his head in the slightest manner, and it was a barely perceptible movement, Jesse was struck speechless for a few seconds.

When she had recovered, he was already starting to pedal away. "Hey! Hey you...hey, Ky!" She called after him. What she wanted from him, she couldn't really say at that moment. She only knew that she wanted him to turn back and look at her. Just for once.

"Hey, don't ignore me damn it! Hey! Ky, you pus-bucket..."

He wasn't hurrying as if he were looking to escape and at first Jesse was able to keep up despite the fact that she gimped along like a raving mad cripple. Yet as soon as he turned the corner of the building and left the empty parking lot, he picked up speed. In response to this she reached down and yanked off her other shoe. This allowed her to pick up her pace.

"I know you can hear me, Ghost-boy," she yelled, huffing and grimacing over her pained ankle. She saw that he was on the verge of outdistancing him and she put her all into her last scream. "Get back here, now!"

Nothing. There was no response from Ky and in a last fit of anger, she hurled her shoe at him. It blinked off his back, probably without him actually feeling it and he kept going.

"Damn it, Ghost-boy," she said quietly to herself, realizing suddenly exactly what she wanted from him. She wanted a friend. She wanted not to be alone.

Turning back to get the first of her thrown shoes, she came to understand just how really alone she was. It stopped her in her tracks. There was absolutely no one in sight.

"What the hell?" she murmured. Jesse had never seen a schoolyard empty like this one had, even the school itself was now dark. Suddenly a shiver went down her back and now she could feel the cold. It was a physical thing that made her desperately want to be inside where it was warm...around people...even people she hated. She ran back to get her first shoe from around the south end of the building and was stunned to see the student parking lot.

Only a few minutes earlier there had been a dozen cars at least still there, idling while their owners had chatted or stared at her as she was left behind by the school bus. But now there was only the cracked and aging asphalt. The lot sat deserted.

Just then, a bone-chilling breeze kicked up and the single shiver that she had felt a moment before started once again, this time thrumming in her chest. It didn't quit itself after a second either as the other one had, but stayed with her and put to rest the last of her anger. What replaced her rage was a ticking apprehension. It ticked up a notch when she pulled out her cell phone to call her mom for a ride, but only got her mom's voice mail.

It ticked up again as she hurried to retrieve her second shoe and saw the Ghost as a tiny figure far down the road that led from the school.

And when she hobbled to the front of the building and saw Principal Peterson start his car and drive off—the last of the cars in the faculty lot—it ticked past apprehension and into fear.

Jesse's fear was a brisk active thing. It spurred her imagination down paths that it was best not to travel and each one of those paths ended in the fearsome image of the Shadow-man.

Though she had barely thought about him at all that day, he was the root of her fear and just then she felt as though she had been left for him...almost like a sacrifice.

With this in her head she was soon scurrying along after the retreating taillights in a gimpy trot. She even waved her hands, hoping to be seen by the principal, yet if he did see her there was no indication and he didn't slow. By the time a minute had passed, the car was no longer visible.

She was now alone. Alone, surrounded by the forest which was perceptibly darker than it had been only minutes before.

The dying afternoon sky was turning a thick gray and was hung with low threatening clouds that lent a particular closeness to the air. It seemed to cling to Jesse in a misty sort of way and it made the dead silence around her greater than it might have been otherwise. She hated to disturb that silence, afraid of what could be in the woods listening, honing in on her position. Yet she disturbed it anyways. To do otherwise meant to slow down; something, that due to her fear, was probably an impossibility for her just then.

Her now hated shoes clacked on the pavement, seeming to grow louder with each step, as did the sound of her own breathing. After a minute her breathing could be considered labored and after another she was panting. Despite her pain she was speed walking down the road, swiveling her head left and right and every few seconds back behind her.

She searched the shadows that seemed to have grown deeper and more tangible in the last few minutes. She searched the darkening forest because *he* was there. The Shadow-man.

He was out there, in the woods, watching her. She knew it. She could feel it. She could hear it.

Despite the agony in her ankle she began running. Across the road, fifty or sixty yards into the woods she could hear the tell-tale cracking of old branches and twigs as something large forced its way through the brush. The Shadow-man had been large...huge really. He would definitely make that much noise.

Jesse pushed herself faster. The road from the school into town was little more than a half-mile long. It was an eight or nine minute walk on a nice day and after a couple of minutes Jesse caught the first sight of the low buildings. It was then that she felt the back of her left leg growing tighter.

"Oh no," she whined low in a panicked whisper. Jesse knew what that feeling meant—her leg was seconds from cramping. With her right ankle burning with pain, she had over compensated in her run and now her left leg was threatening a rebellion. And when it did...

The sound of the Shadow-man grew closer.

"No! Please no!" she cried in breathless hysteria. The cramp had begun. Her hamstring went taunt as though it was run through with a steel cable. The pain was sudden and galvanizing. She grabbed the back of her leg with both hands and squeezed as hard as she could, kneading the muscle, desperately trying to loosen it.

Through sheer will she made it another thirty yards before her right ankle gave out beneath her and spilled her onto the cold pavement. It was a hard fall. She barely got one hand up in time, but still the pavement seemed to jump up at her and smash the side of her face.

Beneath her, the road seemed to tilt and her ears rang, yet still she was able to hear the most dread noise imaginable: from the forest the sound of snapping twigs and the crunch of leaves grew louder...the Shadow-man was coming for her.

Chapter 11

Despite her pain and her ringing ears, Jesse was up in a flash, lurching and reeling down the side of the road. She was crying too, though she didn't know it. Yet it wouldn't have mattered to her if she had. What were a few tears in the face of her coming death? And she was absolutely certain that it was death approaching.

The dead wood of the forest snapped louder under the trampling feet of the Shadow-man, and she could hear plainly the whisper of tree branches against his coat. It sounded so eager, which for some reason made her own terror worse.

She began imagining her coming doom: the Shadow-man would grab her and drag her deep into the forest. There was no doubt that she would fight and try to scream, but he would pin her easily. One of his huge hands would be across her mouth, crushing her lips against her teeth, driving the back of her head into the wet leaves. The other hand...the other hand would be exploring, while his hot breath blew the hair back from the side of her neck. The Shadow-man was excited. She could feel it in the way he trembled and she could feel it hard against her thigh as well. He was excited and eager...

A crash larger and louder than the rest came from little more than twenty feet away just in the brush that ran thick beside the road. Jesse had been winning one tiny battle up to that point... she had yet to look at the Shadow-man. In her mind he was such a horror that she knew if she were to look and see him revealed she would go mad on the spot. Yet the crash had her turning against her will.

Her gaze had been on the road in front of her, down watching her feet. She had been afraid of tripping, of falling a second time, because she knew there would be no getting up again if she did. She was so afraid that she had no clue as to how close to town she had come. As her head came up she saw it was still a few hundred yards down the road...far enough that no one would hear her screaming.

In slow motion, with the world jouncing along to the ungainly lurching of her stride, she turned to see her fate. However, something snagged her eye as her head came around. Movement ahead of her. It was a car.

Relief over-flowed her insides, making her want to laugh... which she didn't, but she did point. Her left hand came up. She found herself pointing at the car, as if to make the Shadow-man aware of it.

You can't kill me now. A car is coming, the point said.

Was that true? Would the presence of a car save her? Since the forest had become silent once again she began to think it just might. She even turned to take a peek into the woods. Other than the dense foliage, there was nothing in sight. This didn't necessarily mean she was safe, since there were dozens of places for the Shadow-man to have hidden, but with the car coming up, she figured that she probably was.

Then she recognized the car and her answer became: probably not. It was the silent black car that had come up behind her only the night before. And just like then it struck a chord of dread in her. She had stopped at the sight of the car, when she had first seen it, but now she resumed her frantic pace.

"Out of the freaking pan and into the freaking fire!" she hissed, as the car drew nearer and began to slow. Which was worse? What was in the car or what was in the forest?

Just before she came abreast of it, the car stopped and idled quietly. It's windows were so darkly tinted that it was impossible for Jesse to see in...until the driver side window slid partly down. Jesse kept walking, keeping her head straightforward as if she didn't see the car, but her eyes were canted to the left. The interior of the car was all in shadows, so it was odd and creepy to see that the driver wore dark sunglasses.

"You ok?" the driver asked.

"Yeah," Jesse replied, still with her head up and forward. Why hadn't she brought her chain and its heavy lock? If she had her chain...she didn't know what she would've done with it, but it would have been comforting at least.

"You want a lift?"

What a stupid question. Was he going to ask if she wanted some candy next? "Thank you, but no. I can't take a ride from a stranger."

He laughed a touch, before putting his car in reverse. It glided backwards keeping pace. "I'm not a stranger. You know that."

He said it so confidently that Jesse turned slightly to see into the car better. The driver was forty-ish with a dark hair and a thick build. She had never seen him before. Jesse tried to walk faster, only her hamstring felt as though there was an arrow imbedded in it and was threatening to seize up altogether.

"You know you're bleeding?" he pointed vaguely in the direction of her face. It was only then that she realized that she'd been blinking something out of her right eye. Her vision had been blurred, but she hadn't known what it was. Great! She was bleeding. Jesse had to wonder at what sort of wreck she looked like now.

"You sure you don't want a lift?"

"No. I don't."

"What's your name?" It was another stupid question and she ignored it. "I asked you a question." Now he sounded distinctly dangerous.

Jesse looked up to the town. Still a hundred and fifty yards to the first shops on this end of town...and there was no one out; the sidewalks were empty. She tried to hobble faster.

"Look, I can make you get into this car." His voice was low. It was the voice of a man that always got what he wanted.

"J-Jesse," she replied quickly.

"And your last name?"

Did she dare lie? This was such a small town that she couldn't take the chance...but to tell the truth seemed insane.

"Well?"

The town was a hundred and twenty yards away and closing with painful slowness. "Clarke," she answered. One-hundred and fifteen yards... one-hundred and ten... She waited for the sudden anger. She waited for the car door to open and she waited to be dragged inside.

That didn't happen.

"James' daughter," the man said. "He's a good man. You're a lucky girl to have him as a father."

Jesse was tempted to repeat her last name again, this time slower, since clearly he hadn't heard properly the first time. Nobody in this town like James, she was sure of it. In fact it would probably be another year before he won even a slight grudging respect. Of course, she could wait a lifetime and still not receive that.

"Yeah...ok," she said, not really knowing what else to say. She was obviously still freaked out and the man stared at her for a while.

"So what happened to you?" he asked.

Should she tell this *stranger* about her Shadow-man? No. The two of them could be working together for all she knew.

"I fell...yesterday and twisted my ankle. And then walking home, I got this bad cramp and before I knew it...I just...tripped. I guess." It sounded very lame. She knew she looked far worse than a simple trip would justify. All the same, she didn't feel that she had to justify herself to him at all.

He smirked at her story. "A fall? You look like you got in a catfight over some boy. You see anyone back that way?" He gestured behind her toward the school.

Was he trying to find out if they were alone? A glance to the town showed her that she was only a block away from its edge. Still too far in the shape she was in.

"There might have been someone in the woods. Over by that low hill on the right."

This seemed to perk him up. "A big guy?" he asked. Truly, Jesse hadn't really seen an actual person, but she nodded anyway. The man grew grim. "Tell your father that you saw *Wild Bill* out here, ok?"

"Is that who the big guy is?" she asked.

Behind his glasses, the man's face went sour. "No. I'm Wild Bill."

Chapter 12

Wild Bill drove off in a hurry toward the school leaving Jesse once again alone. Still in pain, she began trudging along. Thankfully, by the time she came up to where the town proper began, the cramp in the back of her leg had subsided. However, her ankle still killed her and her head was throbbing.

As she passed the one Chinese restaurant in town, she caught a glimpse of herself reflected in the glass.

"Holy crap," she murmured, happy that no one seemed to walk anywhere in Ashton and that she was still alone. The right side of her head was completely covered in blood. The shoulder of her jean jacket was stained with it. She looked like a Halloween exhibit or an extra in a slasher film.

Suddenly, a little gasp escaped her and she flinched back. An Asian man stared at her from the other side of the window. She had been so wrapped up in her own image that she didn't see him at first. He wasn't happy to have her looking in his window and he shooed her away from his establishment with a dismissive flick of his wrist. Jesse was glad to go. Her day was bad enough without being seen like this. She hurried down the street, walking with her head bowed, refusing to look up as cars slowed down and their occupants stared.

Despite her attempts, she was recognized a few minutes later not forty feet from the entrance to the Town hall. Laughter and jeers chased her into the building.

"Yes?" A middle-aged receptionist stared at her over the rim of her glasses. Her tone in that one word made it clear she was seconds from calling the cops on Jesse.

"I'm here to see my father, James Clarke," Jesse replied tersely. The woman's eyes narrowed. It was evident that she disliked her new boss and by extension she didn't like Jesse either. She made no attempt to pick up the phone. Now Jesse's eyes narrowed, matching the woman's. "Did you hear me?"

"I did. However this is not a playground. You can't come waltzing in here as if you own the place, looking the way you do." The lady explained as if she were speaking to a toddler. "This is where the town conducts its business. Perhaps you should come back when you are cleaned up and properly attired."

"I wasn't waltzing. I was limping. Now, I would like to see my father, please."

"No. I can point you to a restroom where you can clean up maybe."

Jesse was in no mood to deal with the secretary of a petty bureaucrat like James Clarke. "You know who I am?" she asked. "You know that I'm James Clarke's daughter and I now reside in Ashton?"

"I don't care if you are the Queen of England. You still can't..."

"I asked a very simple question," Jesse interrupted loudly. "The answer is either yes or no. Do you know that I'm James Clarke's daughter and that I now reside in Ashton?"

"How dare you talk to me this way?" The woman raged. "It doesn't matter who you are. You don't get to come in here and make demands just because your father is the town manager."

"Actually, I get to do exactly that," Jesse replied. "Tell me, what is the stated open-door policy of the current town manager?" The woman's mouth came open and then snapped closed just as quick. "Can't remember it?" Jesse asked. "Well I've heard it a thousand times, so allow me to quote it...ahem...*The town manager will see anyone of the citizens of Ashton, anytime, under any circumstances. My door is always open.*"

At this, the receptionist pursed her lips so tightly that no sound could've escaped her even if she wanted to speak. Nonetheless, Jesse paused for anything the woman might have to say. When nothing was forthcoming, Jesse pulled off her high-heeled shoes, groaned in relief, and walked around the desk in as stately a manner as she could contrive.

The building was small, however Jesse felt as though she was in the final mile of a marathon that she hadn't trained for, and her father's office was an agony to walk to. When she arrived she stumbled onto his couch and groaned again.

"So it's true." James said, breathing out a long sigh of disappointment. "You have been fighting again."

From her sprawled position on the couch, Jesse blinked.

She blinked again and then a third time, slowly, as she struggled to come to terms with the antithetical positions her mind had taken up. On one hand she had the reality of his statement, on the other were her expectations of what she thought he would say when he saw her.

They would not jibe.

"Am I awake?" she asked. The moment was so surreal that she felt that it was a valid question.

"Yes, and you are bleeding on my couch." James replied. "Go to the bathroom and clean yourself up."

"Sorry...I think I'm in the wrong office," she said coldly. "I was looking for my father."

"Jesse..."

She pulled herself up and both eyes were blurry now. "No really, have you seen my father? Do you know what he looks like, because I haven't a damned clue!"

"Don't be like this," he said a touch more soothingly.

"Like what?" she demanded. "I'm just trying to find the man that *claims* to be my father. Perhaps it would help you if I described a father! He's the man who, when he sees his little girl c-covered...in b-blood, doesn't sigh like...he's so put out with having to deal with her. He...he doesn't..." Jesse couldn't go on. Her tears came too heavily and her breath rasped out of her throat in harsh, ungovernable spasms.

"Jesse, I'm sorry. I really am." Her father came around his desk, grabbed a box of tissue, and sat down next to the weeping girl. "You're right about me. I shouldn't have come down on you like I did. It's just your timing was pretty bad. Principal Peterson was just in here two minutes ago."

She thought she could imagine all the bad things the principal had said about her, but she was wrong.

"He said your first day was...well pretty bad. Starting fights, cutting class, being rude to the teachers and disruptive on the bus. In fact, he saw you get kicked off the bus with his own eyes."

Jesse's head spun. "And you believed him?" Deep down, she knew that he would. For some reason he never sided with his own daughter.

"You tell me why I shouldn't," he answered. "We both know you have a long history of cutting class...of starting fights...of lying, especially to me. I don't want to think these things of you, but past behavior is indicative of future action."

Jesse threw-up her hands. "Then I can't win. My past will always keep me as a lower being in your eyes. There's no reason I should even try anymore."

"You should always try," her father said reasonably. "Start right now. Tell me the principal is lying. Did you cut four classes today?"

[89]

"Four!" she exclaimed. "I didn't cut four classes! I missed the first two classes because of placement testing..."

"And the other two?"

Jesse slumped on the couch. "I...uh had a bad day. This cook... he...never mind."

Her father's face was set. "No. I don't think we should never mind. What about fighting? Principal Peterson says you threatened Amanda Jorgenson. There are eyewitness who said you were going to *kick her ass,* out behind the school. And look at you bleeding all over my couch. Are you going to tell me that you weren't fighting?"

"I tripped," she said. There was no use explaining about the Shadow-man. He would never believe it not in a million years. She didn't really believe it.

"You tripped?"

"Yes."

Her father got up and sat back in his chair, leaving her alone on the couch. "What am I going to do with you?"

"Do what you want," Jesse whispered almost to herself. "It won't make a difference. Everyone will hate me no matter what, and you'll side with them against me."

James sighed, his favorite form of communication and then ran his hands through his hair. "Whether you want to hear it or not, this is partly your fault. You never play the game..."

"What game?" she cried out, interrupting. She was close to storming out of his office. She had no idea where she would go, but just then anywhere was better.

"The game of fitting in," he answered. "Yes, I know your situation isn't ideal...but you don't really try. You never give anyone a second chance...ever. Someone smirks at you once and you are done with them forever. You will never have friends that way."

"You mean I will never have crappy friends that way. Remember what you just said about past behavior being an indicator of future actions? I suppose it cuts both ways, doesn't it? There wasn't a single nice person in that school today. And I won't be going too far out on a limb to say there won't be any tomorrow, either." An image of the Ghost...of Ky, came to her. He hadn't been exactly mean to her, rather he was extremely neutral, living in his own world. In fact, the truth was that she had been mean to him, not the other way around.

Her father was full of sighs and another one escaped him before he replied, "If that's your attitude, then you'll be awful lonely and you'll only have yourself to blame."

After her day she could stand a bit of loneliness. It surely had to be better than the hate that had been heaped on her. "I don't blame myself one bit. I blame you," she snarled at her father. "I know you. You're going to fire a bunch of people this week, right before Christmas! How is that really going to help that all important bottom line?"

James rolled his eyes. "I've explained this a dozen times already. First off, there is never a 'good' time to be laid off. It always a painful experience. Second, it *does* help the budget. There is so much unseen cost associated with all these jobs that still accumulates even while they are on winter break. And third, it helps the people themselves."

"How? How can being fired right before Christmas be helpful in anyway?" It was her turn to roll her eyes. "I think your ability to rationalize your behavior, which is bordering on obscene mind you, has gone from rationalizing to fantasizing."

At her little insult he smiled oddly. "You are so smart. I love it when we have these talks and I love you, Jesse. "

This was so unexpected that the fire of her anger was doused...slightly. "I...uh...I'm still so angry at you I could spit." This was at least the truth. Saying, I love you, back to him probably wouldn't have been. She just didn't know.

Not hearing the words back made him smile in a grimacing sort of way. "Maybe you *should* be mad at me, but I'm trying to help..."

"You think that you're helping people by firing them?"

"Yes!" he exclaimed. "You know that I am. I turned around Copper Ridge, Chrisfield, and Denton using these very methods. In the *long run* everyone comes out so much better."

"Everyone but me," Jesse added pointing at her own chest. "In the *long run* your daughter turns into a recluse. In the *long run* she spends half her paycheck on therapy and Prozac...or maybe booze and drugs, who knows? In the *long run* depression takes a hold of her and never leaves and she lives her life hiding in her apartment because all her life she has been hated. In the *long run* you realize that you might have helped the people of all these towns but you have sacrificed your own daughter in the process."

James Clarke leaned back in his chair and stared past his daughter at the wall behind her. "How am I supposed to respond to that? Do I let this town die? There are six-thousand people living in and around Ashton. The un-employment rate is nineteen percent! And the rate of foreclosures!" He stopped for a moment, shaking his head as if thinking about the home foreclosure rate physically pained him. "Jesse, I don't want you to be depressed. I want you to be happy with friends..."

"Then stop being such an ass," Jesse said sharply.

"That's the second time you've cursed in front of me." James Clarke was a striking man, handsome and robust. He had a certain air about him that was greater even than his physical presence. It was probably what made him good at his job; when he spoke, people listened. "I'm being lenient because you've had a rough day, but don't do it again."

Jesse was in a fury, yet so commanding was her father, that she dropped her gaze. "I'm sorry that I cursed at you...but...but I don't know a better word for a man who fires people right before Christmas."

"Try logical," he replied. Jesse's mouth came open to protest this, but when James held up his hand, he silenced her with the gesture. "The average family will spend over fourteen-hundred dollars at Christmas. How many car payments is that? How many months of groceries will that buy? Yes it sucks, I know...but those people who know they are going to be fired will be in a much better place financially. They'll cut back and have a better chance to ride out this downturn."

Jesse hated the fact that his logic seemed sound. It was easier just to loath him without the facts. Then she saw a hole in his thinking: "How is it going to help the economy of Ashton if people aren't spending their money on Christmas. You've told me before that Christmas sales are vitally important to the private sector."

"The simple answer is that people don't shop here in Ashton for Christmas presents. They never have. They go to the mall in Barton."

The explanation of the logic behind the coming firings wasn't much of a salve for Jesse's feelings. Rather it was the opposite. "So, it's all decided then. You get to save the town...again and I get hated...again."

"If you think that all this is easy on me, then you are mistaken," her father responded. "I get my share of hate. I just know that they will come around eventually.

"Yeah, they hate you. I know it. I can see it on their faces...but you have power over them. I'm nothing, so they take their anger at you out on me. And then I come to you...and what do I get? A lecture about fighting!" She was angry. She was in a rage. But she was tired as well. Exhausted she slumped back on the couch, staring out the window.

The clouds were thickening and the day grew darker. She thought about her walk home and uninvited, an image of the Shadow-man came to her.

"Dad, what's with this town?" There was a touch too much silence from her father, which made Jesse take her eyes off the cold sky and glance his way.

"What do you mean?" He knew exactly what she meant. Despite the casual question, he was sitting stiffly in his chair, and where his eyes had held their usual focused intelligence a moment before, they were now guarded.

"What's with the empty streets and the overly crowded library?" she asked, watching him closely. "It's not normal." He started to shrug, which was the closest thing to lie that he ever attempted. "Come on, Dad. I want the truth. I could go ask Wild Bill I suppose..."

"You've met Bill Younger?"

"Yes, twice. Though he didn't introduce himself as Bill Younger. He called himself Wild Bill and he drives a black car with dark-dark windows. You know him?"

"Oh, yeah. I know him," James said, suddenly looking tired as well. "He's with the CID, which is a part of the Michigan State Police. He's a detective heading up a four person task force." He seemed reluctant to go on.

"And?"

"There have been a few murders in Ashton..."

"What?" If she could've jumped up she would have. Instead she had to be content with smacking her hand down on the leather couch. "And you didn't tell me?"

"I didn't want to worry you unnecessarily." Her eyes went big at this and before she could say a word, he continued: "Yes, unnecessarily. You are probably the safest person in the entire town. This man...the killer, doesn't pick his victims at random. They have to have a certain characteristic and you lack it."

He wasn't lying which had the effect of draining most of the fear right out of her. What took its place was a consuming curiosity.

"What's the characteristic? You have to tell me!" she demanded, sounding like an excited girl at a slumber party.

James shook his head. "I don't and I won't. It's a personal thing and though a part of me wishes that you..." He stopped abruptly.

"Me what?"

"Nothing. It's...nothing. Just be glad that you don't have to worry about it."

"How many people has this guy killed?" She felt strangely excited and it must have shown on her face and in her voice. Her father looked at her crossly.

"Listen, keep your voice down," he said with a touch of growing anger. "This is a very sensitive subject in Ashton. I will tell you what I think is appropriate, but you have to promise not to speak about this with anyone."

"Who am I going to talk about this with? I'm friendless, everyone hates me, remember?"

"Oh, I remember," he said and then smiled in an odd cryptic manner. "There have been at least three deaths for sure; one in 2006 another 2007, both boys. And then last year a girl was...strangled."

"Down by the berm? Mom told me not to go down there."

He shook his head. "No, she was found in the cemetery, which is out past the school. But the first boy that I mentioned *was* found next to the berm. As for where is safe and where isn't...who knows. The sites of the deaths have been particularly random."

Jesse was quiet as her mind worked through all of this information and her father sat silently as she did. Finally she spoke, "You said there've been three deaths for sure...did you mean three murders for sure? And were there other deaths?"

James bowed his head to acknowledge her deductive reasoning. "In 2008 three people with that characteristic I was talking about died and in 2001 the alleged killer's son was found drowned in their pool. At first..."

"His son? The police know who the killer is? Why hasn't he been arrested?"

"He was arrested," James replied. "Back in 2006 and put on trial, but he got off, partly due to technicalities and partly due to insufficient evidence." Jesse opened her mouth to ask who the killer was, but her father guessed this was her question. "The man's name is Harold Brownly... he's a neighbor of ours."

"No way!" Just like that, the balloon of her excitement and curiosity burst inside her leaving a nervous sick residue behind.

"Yes," James replied, shaking his head with a pained expression in his eyes. "I'm sorry. When I bought the place I had no clue. Nobody told me. I'm actually thinking of suing the realtor and the previous owner."

"Great. That'll do me a lot of good when I'm dead."

"This is why your mother and I didn't want to tell you so soon. We didn't want you to over react. Look, I've seen all the police reports..." Here he paused and lowered his voice, "...I've even spoken to his therapist. He's assured me that a girl like *you* will be perfectly safe."

Chapter 13

That entire evening she pondered on the concept of having a killer as a neighbor. His house wasn't directly behind hers, but was one house over, yet only a six-foot tall fence separated his yard from theirs.

From her bedroom, if she stood at the right angle, she could see into what looked to be his master bedroom on the second floor. When she climbed up on her bed and peeked through the mostly drawn curtains, she could also see a little into the living room on the main floor.

There wasn't much to see. The house was dark for most of the night except for around ten p.m. when a light came on and stayed on. However, she saw no movement whatsoever, not even the ghost of a shadow, nor the ghost of the Shadow-man. The killer and the Shadow-man were one in the same, she was pretty well sure of that. Her father had described Harold Brownly as the biggest man he had ever seen. She had described the Shadow-man...at least mentally... as "freaking huge" and she too had never seen someone so enormous.

Over all, the killer's house gave her the creeps and except for periodic glimpses, which she would undertake in the most stealthy manner possible, she kept her curtains drawn as tight as they would go.

When she wasn't looking into the killer's house, Jesse sat with her ankle propped up and encased in a bag of ice. She worked steadily on her homework until after eleven when thankfully she finished her stupid essays—complete with bibliographies. They hadn't been asked for, but she knew what sort of teachers she was dealing with.

Too tired to do anything more, Jesse took a last peek at Harold Brownly's silent home and called it a night.

The next morning she woke with a vow on her lips: "There will be no tears today!"

She was living fifty feet from a mass murderer, what could she possibly fear from a bunch of whiny children and a few nasty teachers.

Nothing, her voice of reason said.

Of course in order to maintain her vow she would need a different mindset than the one she had adopted the day before. She had, for the most part, tried to be as sweet and accommodating as she could. Today would be different.

With bleary red-rimmed eyes she went to work resurrecting her old self. She was adept at cutting and styling her own hair and had been doing so since she was twelve-years-old. Jesse had learned the hard way that there was nothing more vindictive than a hairdresser whose husband had just been laid off. Without fear, she hacked off her shoulder length blonde hair, colored it jet-black and then spiked it up.

In a half hour she had gone from Barbie to something else entirely. Though it was hard to tell what exactly...certainly not an Emo-punk or a Goth-vampire wanna-be.

"Someone you don't want to mess with," she said to the cold-eyed girl in the mirror. And that was a true statement. Jesse next applied only the barest accentuating make-up, leaving off attempting to cover the gash above her right eye, entirely. She liked it raw looking.

Next came the clothes that were sure to have her mom steaming. Loose black jeans, a plain black t-shirt and finally, her jungle boots—her favorite pair. They were light and supple, yet would leave a tread mark on someone's cheek if they weren't careful.

After she laced up her boots, she stepped back and looked appreciatively at herself, but then sighed. Since she was about to ask her mom for a favor she would have to at least throw her a bone. From her closet, she pulled out a long sleeve, button up white shirt. Rolling the sleeves halfway up her arms she then tied the shirt about her mid-drift.

"Time for breakfast," she said to herself. Then louder she called out in her sweetest voice, "Mom?"

"Downstairs," came the distant reply.

As Jesse trotted down the stairs she called out again, sweetly, "Mom, can I please, please, please get a ride to *and* from school? I really-really need this." It was either a ride from her Mom, a long and possibly dangerous walk, or worst of all, a bike ride to school.

"No, I can't. Sorry. I have a meeting this morning. Then I'm at the blood bank in Barton all afternoon."

Sarcasm was the first thing that came to Jesse's mind: *What? Something more important than me? How is that possible?*

She stopped on the stairs and rubbed her eyes, feeling the grit of a poor night's sleep in them. Despite just getting up, she was still tired from the day before and this affected her judgment. Jesse yanked off the white shirt and threw it in silent anger at the wall. She was back in black just like her mood.

"Maybe your dad can give you a lift home," Cynthia Clarke called out.

More sarcasm sprang to mind, but she bit it back. It was true her father had given her a ride home the evening before, however that was under special circumstances and she knew him too well to think he would make a habit out of it. There were more important things to him than his daughter.

No tears, remember?

"Right," Jesse whispered. No tears meant she would have to control her emotions. The girl took a moment and sat back on the stairs. With steady breaths she cooled somewhat and her mind was able to think past how her mom was being...and more importantly how she was going to be. Cynthia was going to be a pain, no doubt about it.

"Jesse?" her mom called from the kitchen.

"I'll be right down," she answered back, satisfied that she had kept any petulance out of her voice. It had been close.

She went back to breathing. After thirty seconds she was calm enough to think about her transportation predicament. Her choices were down to the long walk or the embarrassing bike ride. There really wasn't an actual choice involved. She realized this after a brief image of the Shadow-man flashed in her mind; it brought her to a decision quick: she would have to take the bike.

"Damn," she swore, but not in anger. She swore in disappointment. The bike meant that she wouldn't get to wear her favorite coat. It was a gorgeous coat: three-quarter length, coming in tight at the waist and flaring out at the hem...but not too flared. It was black, dark, beautiful. She loved herself in it, but it would be altogether goofy looking on a bike.

Which meant that she would have to wear her leather instead. It was nice also. Black, of course. It came up high, ending just below her ribs. It was very smart looking but there was no getting past it; she would freeze on her bike.

Deciding on oatmeal and a cup of coffee to get her warmed for her ride, she scampered into the kitchen, ready to face her mom.

"Oh, Jesse," her mom moaned, sounding as if she was in pain. "Look at you. Your hair! Why do you do this to yourself?"

The real answer: *to survive* would never be understood by Cynthia Clarke. She did understand about teenage angst, however. So Jesse played that up instead.

"What? You mean, why do I dress in a way that I feel most comfortable expressing who I am?" Jesse asked, glancing around at the still unfamiliar kitchen, trying to remember where the bowls were kept.

Cynthia rolled her eyes. "The girl that came down for breakfast yesterday is who you are. Pretty...sweet...intelligent, that is who you are. Not this." She pointed with disgust at Jesse's hair and clothes.

Her mom was right, the girl from yesterday was truly who Jesse wanted to be. She loved dresses and high-heels, she loved her hair long and flowing, she loved how boys...those who didn't know her...looked at her when she was all made up. The only thing was, that girl, the one with the satin tresses and the big blue eyes, was weak. She was easily hurt and tears fell from eyes at the least provocation.

She couldn't be that girl, not yet.

"Mom, I swear to you that I will wear a long, white dress on my wedding day...and if you ever take me to New York, like you've been promising me for ages now, I'll leave every stitch of black clothing behind."

Jesse found the bowls and then began opening drawers one after the other, searching for spoons. On her third attempt, she found them. Behind her, Cynthia sighed loudly.

"I think I should call your father."

While preparing her oatmeal, which demanded gobs of sugar and a pint of syrup, Jesse remarked: "Dad never notices anything. He saw me yesterday all jazzed up and didn't say boo about it."

"Please go change."

"No, I can't." With her mom staring at her in a huff, the microwave seemed to be taking an age to heat up her breakfast. Jesse could feel her mom's eyes boring into her back. Her emotions started to spin a little inside of her, becoming slick and hard to latch onto.

"If you change your clothes, I'll...I'll drive you both ways to school. There and back, I promise."

Simultaneously this made Jesse want to scream in anger and burst out laughing. This was a promise that would never in a million years be kept. Nothing was more important to Cynthia than her precious volunteering. Where would she be without it? She would be nothing more than the wife of the town's biggest ass and the mother of the town's biggest bitch.

"You'll be there right at three?" Jesse asked. She was pissed. "You know they lock the doors at three?"

[101]

"I could be there around three-thirty," Cynthia responded with a lie. *If* she made it at all, it would be closer to four-thirty. That was how she was. Always an hour late whenever Jesse needed her, but her tardiness was *excused*...there were more unfortunate people than Jesse who needed her.

Jesse shook her head. "An hour up at the school all alone...with a *killer* on the loose..." She let the words hang out there all by themselves as an unspoken accusation.

He mom made another noise that made it seem that she was in pain. "I'm sorry I didn't tell you, but your father asked me not to. He's sure you're not in danger and he thought that you might over-react."

"First off, I don't think you *can* over react to something like this," Jesse shot back. "Second, he could be wrong you know."

"Can you remember the last time he was wrong?" Cynthia paused as if for an answer. "Because I can't."

In truth, Jesse couldn't either. Yes the man was unsympathetic and emotionally stunted, but he was never wrong. "There is always a first time, isn't there?" she asked. "Don't get me wrong; I really, really hope that he's right. I'd just feel better if I knew why he was so sure. He won't tell me."

"And I won't either because you have the irritating habit of doing the exact opposite of what we ask of you. If I told you that this guy only kills boys with blue hair, you wouldn't know what to do first, get a sex change or go to the salon."

"Ha-ha, Mom. I should know..."

"Stop. Just stop talking about this," Cynthia demanded. "I'm completely freaking out about living so close to this guy. I haven't slept at all since we moved...I keep checking and re-checking all the doors and windows. Every time I hear something, I flip out...my stress level is up to hear." Her hand went above her head.

"I bet you're freaking," Jesse said with some sympathy. "I could barely sleep last night myself. If I'm really as safe as you two think, I wish I had never found out we have a murderer as a neighbor. Maybe we should get a gun?"

Her mom started laughing, mockingly. "*You* of all people think we should get a gun? You hate guns. You've always hated guns."

She did hate guns...but at the moment all the scary statistics that had been fed into her at school didn't come close to counter-balancing the fact of the Shadow-man. He was just too present in her mind and she realized that even this little conversation was causing her chest to tighten.

"I know," she replied feeling a little embarrassed. "I guess core convictions aren't what they used to be. It's just that he's so big...and he scares the crap out of me...and he lives so close to us. Of course..." she paused to laugh. "If he came over to borrow some sugar, I'd probably shoot him on the porch."

Her mom nodded. "Yeah, about that, don't let him in the house. If you're here by yourself, lock everything and keep the curtains drawn tight. And always have a phone handy."

"Don't worry about that...I may even barricade the door when you leave." It was supposed to be a joke, but she could easily picture herself doing exactly that.

"Just don't scuff up the hardwood floors," her mom replied, making sure to let Jesse know where she ranked in the hierarchy of things that needed protection. One-step below wood flooring.

Now her chest tightened from another emotion. "Would you also like me to try not to bleed on the carpet?"

Cynthia's face went tight. "I don't need your cheek right now. In fact, I'm late." She got up and threw on her coat. As she walked to the garage, she called out over her shoulder, "I'll see you later...probably around eight."

When the door to the garage shut, Jesse replied quietly, "What happened to picking me up at three-thirty? Was three-thirty just a lie?" She knew it was. If she had taken up her mom's offer she would have been waiting for hours...alone as the day turned darker and eventually slipped away altogether.

Jesse heard her mom's Lexus pull away.

"Cynthia Clarke," she said in a big voice attempting to impersonate a game show announcer. "What's more important: Handing some stranger a cookie and a cup of orange juice, *orrrr* protecting your daughter from a mad killer?"

Jesse then made a face of wild-eyed naiveté. "Oh, that's a toughy, Rick. I *do* think killers are bad, but without a cookie, someone might get woozy. We can't have that. But on the other hand if the killer breaks in here, he might stain one of my knives with Jesse's blood...oh this is such a tough decision!"

The big voice: "You are almost out of time! What's it going to be Cynthia? The cookie or your daughter's worthless life? Tick-tock Cynthia, tick-tock."

"Ooooh...I have to go with the cookie, Rick. I do 'love' my daughter, but cookies bring joy and people really-really like me when I give them one."

"Good choice, Cynthia," Jesse said as herself. She sat staring at her bowl of oatmeal.

Chapter 14

The bike ride was beyond painful. With the temperature at a brisk twenty-nine degrees and a biting crosswind that stung the right side of her face, it was closer to a form of self-induced torture.

At least there wasn't fresh snow on the road. The previous day's clouds had been all show and no snow. Therefore she made good time and was at her locker with a good five minutes to kill. Since she wasn't in the least hurry, she decided to wait there getting warm until the first bell rang.

She fiddled with her lock and monkeyed about in the useless locker—from long experience she knew that her locker would be a magnet for trouble and pranks; as long as it was assigned to Jesse Clarke, it would never be used.

In those five minutes, students meandered by in the lazy way that all teens seemed to walk, and as they passed her they stared unabashedly at her new appearance. By the look in their eyes she could tell that most of them thought that there was *another* new student in school, but then Jesse heard someone whisper her name. Just like that the word 'Jesse' seemed to catch on everyone's lips and she heard it whispering up and down the hall like a cold fire blown on a chill wind.

The bell did nothing to silence the whispers; they followed her into her first period class: English—Creative Writing—Mrs. Jerryman.

Perched on the side of her desk, Mrs. Jerryman, who might have been a beautiful woman at one time, but was now sagging and drooping in all the wrong spots, greeted her students with a smile. One after another they filed in and were presented with this pleasantry. Even Jesse received one. Or at least part of one. The woman's lip rose and her eyes narrowed in equal measure. If it was a smile, it was a disagreeable one.

"Miss Clarke?" she asked. Jesse nodded in answer. "*Interesting* look," the teacher commented.

On the subject of clothing, Jesse had only impolite things to say in return so she kept quiet. Mrs. Jerryman's clothes had been designed for a much younger and smaller woman and the best that could be said about her outfit was that it was keeping her from spilling or sliding out at the edges.

"I saw you yesterday morning in the hall," Mrs. Jerryman continued. "What a complete transformation—you're like Dr. Jekyll and Mr. Hyde. No offense."

No offense? How could that not be considered offensive? The students tittering and elbowing each other all around her sure were enjoying the "inoffensive" remark. Jesse gripped her bag.

No tears, be hard!

"I like the fact that I can change my appearance as it suits my mood," Jesse replied. "It's liberating...you should try it Mrs. Jerryman. You don't want to be stuck as Mr. Hyde all the time do you?"

Silence greeted this little comment, a long silence. At least half a minute, which in a situation like the one Jesse found herself in was very long indeed. As the silence went on she felt a thrum of nervousness at her own temerity.

Mrs. Jerryman only stared at Jesse with hard eyes that clearly indicated that trouble waters lay ahead. Yet, the girl didn't mind the stare so much. She had been stared at in baseless hate, many, many times before.

In fact the stare burning into her face helped. Rather than cowering before it and backing down, Jesse grew angrier with each passing second and she had a right to be angry. She had a right to rip this lady a new one.

When the last of her nervousness left her, Jesse asked with a tone of mock innocence, "Did I say something wrong?"

"Mr. Hyde was the monster that Dr. Jekyll turned into...it wasn't the other way around," Mrs. Jerryman retorted. This was followed by a significant, purposeful pause and then the lady added, "As you well know."

Mrs. Jerryman's lips then formed a hard pink line on her face. Just then they were the only thing on her not sagging and Jesse had to wonder what they would look like if she was really mad.

"You're right. I knew that Mr. Hyde was the hideous monster, but I don't understand why you look so angry," Jesse replied still innocent. Then her eyes came open as if a she now realized her mistake. "Oh, I'm so sorry. I suggested that you looked like a hideous monster and I plum forgot to say *no offence*. My bad."

At this Mrs. Jerryman's face reached zero-lip surface. From the nose down, save for her middle-aged woman's moustache, her face was flat and smooth. Jesse considered it interesting, and it made her want to find out what was the next stage in Mrs. Jerryman's anger transformation would be.

"*No offence* is like magic isn't it," Jesse went on conversationally. "With, *no offence,* you can say whatever you want and not have to worry in the least about consequences. I think that it's wonderful that you taught me something so valuable, Mrs. Jerryman."

Pointing at the door, the teacher seethed, "Get out."

Jesse feigned shock. "Why? What did I do? I meant that as a compliment. *No offence* is great. Really it is. I have to be honest, I didn't think I was going to learn a thing this year; the teachers around here are all so stupid after all..." Jesse paused and held up a finger as if to forestall an avalanche of anger. "...I almost forgot...*No offence*. So when you teach me this right off the bat, when we barely even know each other...it's just great."

"Oh, you *are* rude! Ms Weldon warned me, but I wanted to see it for myself."

"If I'm rude, then I learned from the best," Jesse gave the teacher a half curtsy, holding out an imaginary dress with delicate fingers.

"Get out!" Mrs. Jerryman hollered.

"And where would you like me to go?" Jesse asked in a strikingly calm manner.

She felt great. The normal apprehension that churned her guts when talking to some hateful adult had slipped away, leaving a sense of invincibility behind. She didn't care a whit if she got detention—in fact she rather hoped for a suspension. The idea of a three-day break appealed to her. It would be a nice little run up to the winter break. She could even sleep in. The idea brought a smile to her face.

"I could go down to see Principal Peterson and discuss this wonderful, magical phrase with him." Jesse said, brazenly—putting her own head right on a silver platter, so to speak. The idea only made her smile broader than before.

There was a pause as Mrs. Jerryman looked to be having trouble forming words due to her anger, and Jesse took the moment to glance around. The other students looked on in wonder. They couldn't believe that anyone would ever talk to Mrs. Jerryman in this way. Though most of their eyes held gradients of hate, a few held grudging respect, and one set of eyes held all of her attention.

From the back of the room, the Ghost, Ky, was looking Jesse right smack in her baby-blues. His eyes were wide and intense. The look made her mouth come open; a little sip of air drifted into her lungs and filled her completely. Right at that moment, the Ghost was completely gone and Ky sat in his place. He was just a boy and she was just a girl and there was most definitely a connection between them. She felt it in her chest where that sip of air turned hot.

And then he looked down at the book on his desk and pretended to read. Ky was gone and she only stood staring at the Ghost once again.

Finally, Mrs. Jerryman found her voice. "You would like that wouldn't you?" Jesse blinked at this, trying to play catch up to what the woman was saying. Ky's hazel eyes had pulled her right out of the moment. "I have a better idea," her teacher went on. "Since you are so fond of my teaching methods, I'll give you some extra instruction on the side."

Inside, Jesse glowered, but wasn't much surprised. She could've taken Mrs. Jerryman's insults without saying anything *and* still be forced to do extra work...or she could do exactly what she had: take a stand *and* be forced to do extra work.

She decided to make one more attempt at an early vacation: "Extra instruction? I hope you can teach me how to spit when I talk. I've never met anyone who could do that so well as you. I'm practically drenched."

Mrs. Jerryman's throat began to work up and down; so much so that Jesse worried she was choking on her tongue. At first her eyes bulged and then she squeezed them tight. "In your seats...everyone. It's time to call the roll," she eventually rasped out.

Jesse remained standing until she saw the only chair that was left to her was the one nearest Ky. The sight of it sent a spike through her chest. She began heading that way with dueling emotions: fear and hope. On one hand she dreaded the idea that Mrs. Jerryman would call her away from that one chair and stick her somewhere else. Likely up in the front where she could be insulted at the teacher's whim. On the other hand, she hoped, with more fervor than she had expected, for Ky to look up at her again. All she wanted was one more moment for their eyes to lock once again.

Neither came to fruition.

Ky kept his eyes doggedly down and Mrs. Jerryman seemed perversely pleased with Jesse's seating arrangement. She even gave Jesse a smile accompanied by a little laugh— what this meant was lost on Jesse. Though it did spring to mind a recollection of her brief fear that Ky was diseased...yet he looked so fine.

"As I promised yesterday," Mrs. Jerryman announced. "Since winter break is so close, we will have a little fun this week. I want you to breakup into teams of three. We will be creating limericks....the randier the better...but only to a point. And I will be the judge of that point, so don't go too overboard. I want them ready for tomorrow's class when we will be reciting them out loud."

As she spoke, Jesse cast secret looks at Ky out of the corner of her eye. Again, in the looks department there was definitely nothing wrong with the boy. If he was sick, it was an unseen malady.

"Jesse."

Jesse jumped. Her secret look had turned into a not so secret stare. "Yes...Mrs. Jerryman." For a moment Jesse had been so flustered she forgot her teacher's name.

"Sorry, but you're out of luck in the partner category," Mrs. Jerryman said, not looking sorry in the least. "Everyone is all matched up."

It was a struggle for Jesse not to glance at Ky, who was very much without a partner. Could she dare to hope...

"Instead, I have another assignment for you." Now it was a struggle for Jesse to keep from looking too crestfallen, yet some of the look slipped out anyway. The teacher saw and gave Jesse another one of those unnerving cryptic smiles that seemed to occur so frequently when Jesse was around Ky.

Mrs. Jerryman drummed her fingers on Jesse's desk wearing a considering look. "Let's see... I think that I want you to do a five-thousand word essay instead."

A smirking snide laugh escaped Jesse. "A five thousand word essay?" She glanced at the clock. "In fifty minutes? That's one thousand words every ten minutes. Wouldn't it be easier just to give me a zero instead?"

"It might be, but then what would you learn?"

"I would learn hopelessness." Jesse answered matter-of-factly. "It was something that I was taught in psychology last year. You see when a child is ill treated and given tasks that are beyond her ability to accomplish, she learns to be hopeless...you know without hope. She then stops trying altogether. When we discussed it at school the teacher said that it was...what's the word I'm looking for? Not mean but...?"

Jesse wanted Mrs. Jerryman to say the word, but her lips had pressed together tightly once again and had disappeared. Jesse filled in her own missing blank: "Abusive! That's the word that I wanted. I think he said it could even be criminal...I think. I'll have to check my journal. I keep notes about what happens to me in school in this journal. Names, dates...assignments...everything."

As she had gone on the woman's face grew grim and the flesh of her jowls began to quiver. "Are you done yet?" Mrs. Jerryman asked sourly. Jesse only raised her shoulders slightly and the teacher continued, "I never said the essay has to be done by the end of class. Did I? No, I didn't. You will have until tomorrow. And yes, spelling counts."

Jesse had no plans on doing the ridiculous assignment. She knew it would take every moment of her evening and no matter how good it was she would still fail. "On what topic?" Jesse asked just out of curiosity. She expected the teacher to name some obscure author or some off the wall topic such as: the spirituality of peach-pits, or some such non-sense. Yet she didn't.

Mrs. Jerryman looked thoughtful and then said, "Surprise me, just be sure that there's a bibliography as part of it. I will not tolerate plagiarism. Intellectual theft is still theft."

What an odd thing to say, her voice of reason said.

Yes it was. It almost seemed as if Mrs. Jerryman was looking to trap her into doing some sort of criminal act. Did she actually think anyone would care if she plagiarized? The police wouldn't. Not even the homegrown *Barney Fifes* of Ashton, whom she was certain, like everyone else, would just hate her on sight.

Still, even if they did want to prosecute her, she had a feeling that they would bungle it. After all they've had a killer right in their back yard—right in her back yard actually—for years and couldn't seem to catch the guy even though all he seemed to do is roam the forest looking for his next victim.

Seeing as Jesse wasn't going to do the assignment, she wasn't too worried about being caught by the plagiarism police. "Sure, I love bibliographies; they're my favorite part of any book. Sometimes I will read a research paper and skip right to the end, just to find out where they looked stuff up."

This last bit of nonsense had Mrs. Jerryman rolling her eyes in exasperation and when Jesse took a deep breath to expound on how footnotes got her "randy", a word she had been looking to use ever since Mrs. Jerryman had brought it up earlier, the teacher threw her hands up in frustration and stormed away.

"Good riddance," Jesse said under her breath.

She cast a sidelong look at Ky. He was reading, or so she thought at first. His grey-green eyes were seemingly intent on the book, yet they didn't stroll along the page as they should have. He only stared fixedly on a single spot. Jesse, thinking that she was being cool, reached into bag, grabbed her binder, and then straightened in her seat. When she did, she was a full six inches closer to the boy and practically falling out of her chair.

Opening her binder, she casually turned her head to inspect its far edge as an excuse to get a better look at the boy. She was filled with curiosity over him.

"Psst..."

Jesse turned with narrowed eyes. A plump freckled girl just in front and to the right of Jesse had her head turned slightly back. As if she were a spy, the plump girl made the tiniest eye contact and then gave her head an almost imperceptible shake.

Sadly, this was the friendliest gesture Jesse had yet received in Ashton. Though it might have been "friendly" it was also enigmatic. Was the girl trying to warn Jesse, or was she angry that Jesse was curious about Ky? Jesse raised an eyebrow in question, but just then the girl's face edged over a notch so that she was looking at Ky out of the corner of her eye.

Something seemed to startle her and she faced forward, going pale beneath her freckles. Jesse had to see what had so shocked the girl, it was a desire, a need beyond her ability to control, in fact it would have been physically impossible for her to have stopped her head craning around. What she saw wasn't shocking at all—Ky was simply writing on a piece of paper.

He was writing a note!

It's for me, Jesse thought with a blush of excitement hitting her cheeks. She leaned over the slightest bit more and now her bottom was barely holding onto her chair. Gently, slowly she swayed in toward him and peeked at his note, but Ky's writing hand blocked what he wrote.

She froze in place, waiting with delicious anticipation. Finally he pulled his hand away, slipped the note to the side of his desk, and sat back with the impassive unvarying look of a slab of marble.

Leave me the F*** alone!

Chapter 15

The note was like a slap in the face physically and emotionally and it stunned Jesse for all of a second. Then her anger, that constant companion, rose up fierce inside her. She hadn't been able to contain her curiosity, mostly because she didn't really try, but her anger was another thing altogether.

Sometimes it got away from her, whether she tried to control it or not. Like the time Rick Hobbson had cornered her with two of his friends. Her anger had flared like a sunspot on her mind and it had blotted out all thinking and demanded only action. She had sunk that pencil into his thigh a good three inches. It went in like it was running through warm butter. It went in until her fist ran up hard against his thigh and she felt something grate deep under his skin. The pencil sliding in so easily felt good...at least to Jesse who had grinned wickedly at the stunned look on Rick's face.

She had been lucky not to have been charged with a crime; one of the boys in his shock had blurted out the truth—how they had slapped and punched her...and threatened to do other things of a perverse nature to her. Though in truth they weren't threats, everyone knew that what the boys had planned to do weren't threats.

Sitting next to the Ghost...in her angry state of mind, once more the boy had become something less than human...Jesse stewed, trying to hold it together. It wasn't easy, especially with what she heard coming from the rest of the class.

Whether it was intentional or not, Mrs. Jerryman had her revenge over Jesse's mouthing off. The supposedly randy filled limericks were, judging by the snippets that could be heard plainly by all, not just randy filled, they were also *Jesse* filled.

There once was a girl named Jesse... was the first attempt on every ones lips. There was a problem with this, however. The students had an impossible time trying to find words rhyming with Jesse. They came up with messy but after that they were clueless. This didn't stop them and eventually a consensus winner was discovered. A girl named Hayden came up with:

Poor Jesse had really quite an itch
Too bad that she was such a bitch
Though she looked for a while
She never got a boy who would smile
But found a dog would do in a pinch.

Jesse heard this one at least a dozen times before the end of class and by the last bell of the day, every freshman, most of whom had never laid eyes on Jesse, could recite it. Mrs. Jerryman pretended to be oblivious to what she had set in motion.

With her blood boiling and ghastly images of revenge flashing through her mind, Jesse stormed out of the room within a second of the class letting out. It was a good thing for her that she had calculus next.

Calculus, her favorite subject, helped a great deal to reign in the bitter fury within her. The objectivity of numbers meant that she could compete with the other students on a level playing field. In just this little world, one plus one meant the same thing for everyone. And as another bonus, the class was actually a few weeks behind her old calculus class back at Copper Ridge High. It made her fifty minutes an easy review.

Her teacher, Mr. Shay also helped to calm her. The fact that he loved mathematics was only evident by the gleam in his eye and the speed of his hand as he drew symbols and numbers to form long, wonderfully complicated equations on the chalkboard. The rest of him gave the appearance that he was apathetic, not only towards math, but to life in general. He slouched about in a somewhat slovenly manner, using desks and walls to keep himself propped up. His languid comportment had Jesse wondering if this was how a sloth would look if one was forced to stand upright in a tired suit for any span of time.

Mr. Shay's voice belied his love of teaching as well. He spoke in a monotone that made a metronome sound exciting, and again this was a good thing for Jesse. His droning words coupled with the fluid way he drew out equations had her in a sort of hypnotic state. Jesse watched and listened, her mind absorbed in the math and thus she was able to cool down before her next confrontation.

Ms Weldon sat waiting for Jesse in the art room. She was at her desk, whispering—under her breath, but not too far under—the catchy little limerick that was going around the school. It set Jesse's jaw and instead of repeating her mantra: *no tears*, in her mind, she repeated a new one: *no blood*.

"Do you have your essay, Jesse?" The teacher asked right off the bat. Wordlessly Jesse handed over her work, which was quickly scrutinized. "No bibliography? How am I to know whether or not any of this is plagiarized?"

There was that word again. It sent a warning signal going off in Jesse's mind. "You didn't ask for a bibliography."

Like a lion sensing a weakened gazelle, Ms Weldon moved in for the kill. "You are a senior in high school, Jesse. You have to start taking, not just initiative, but also responsibility for your actions. I'm afraid I'm going to have to give you a zero..."

As she had been talking Jesse slipped out the bibliography and held it out. "Your bibliography," Jesse said after a second, as Ms Weldon only looked at the paper.

Her long face was so tight that when she opened her mouth to speak Jesse was fairly certain that she heard a creaking sound like a rusty car door opening. "Why didn't you give me this with your essay?"

Because I wanted to find out just how much of a witch you were going to be to me, Jesse thought to herself. Aloud she said, "I guess it got separated."

With a smoldering look, Ms Weldon took the paper and then turned dismissively and spoke to the class, "Alright everyone, take your seats. Quiet down, Valerie. I know some of you haven't finished your mock-ups; get them done today. No excuses. Everyone else keep going with your sections. Remember this will make Saturday go smoothly."

When she had finished her instructions, she turned back to Jesse. "Go on. You have a lot to catch up on...wait. Where is your original? Where is your life-sized mock-up? Where is your chalk?"

In confusion, Jesse looked around at what the other students were doing. Her eyes fell on a very large picture of what she took to be Adolf Hitler. "Chalk? I don't have..."

"Then you earned yourself another zero for the day," Ms Weldon said with a silky smooth tongue. She then turned sad and put a long arm around Jesse's shoulder. "I was just talking about initiative. You *wrote* an essay on *I Madonnari* so you must know what the basics entail with street art. Yet for some reason you show up here completely unprepared. Are you looking to fail this class?"

Jesse didn't think she had a snowball's chance in hell of passing the class. Because of her father's stringent methods she had run afoul of many teachers but none had ever been as bad as Ms Weldon and Mrs. Jerryman. Their vitriol was astounding to Jesse.

"No, I'm not trying to fail," she replied, trying to keep herself calm. This was great struggle for her. "Doing the essay kept me busy till after eleven last night. And really I didn't know exactly what the project is."

Still with an arm around Jesse's shoulders, Ms Weldon turned her to face the other students. "Initiative and responsibility, Jesse. These are my watch-words. You couldn't ask any of your fellow students? How tough would that have been?"

It would have been impossible. They were such an angry hateful lot; not a one of whom had done so much as smile in her direction, which in its way wasn't a surprise to Jesse. Her circumstances had forced her to mature faster than her peers and though she still seethed with rage at her treatment, she understood it.

Each one of the students had been affected, not just by her father's tough methods, but also by the down turn in the economy. Impotently, they watched as family members lost their jobs, friends take to food stamps in order to eat, and their childhood homes being foreclosed on. And now, in Jesse, they suddenly had someone upon whom they could focus all their harsh anger.

Jesse saw this and understood. She probably knew these kids better than they knew themselves. Three days ago none of them figured that they would be making up dirty limericks about a lonely girl, but Jesse knew something along those lines would occur. Just as she knew that eventually dog crap would be forced through the vents of her locker, or that her house would be TP-ed with a vengeance, or that her chair in biology or economics would be layered with super-glue.

Although it was only three classes into her second day, Jesse knew all about these kids.

Forced to be in her own little world, she had nothing better to do than to watch them and listen and learn. She saw the jocks and the nerds, the goth-girls and the cheerleaders, the emos, the sluts and all the rest, most of whom couldn't decide what they were or what they wanted to be. She saw them dance the dance of social cohesion, which from her outsider's perspective looked so dreadfully dull. Who cares if Jill cut her hair short again? Who cares if Danny is probably gay?

With hardly knowing any of their names, she knew them all very well. She prided herself on judging character, of grasping the not so subtle aspects of the teen mind.

Except...and there was a decidedly obvious except...there was something pointedly different about the kids at Ashton High. Their rivalries were less acute. Their divisions were aesthetic in nature rather than deep-seated. Their smiles, less. Despite Christmas vacation being only days away, there wasn't hearty, good-natured laughter ringing throughout the halls. Instead there was apprehension and watchfulness.

Jesse had been so involved with her confrontation with Mrs. Jerryman that she had barely noticed the watchfulness. At the beginning of second period calculus, she had been steaming mad, but still something odd was apparent. And then at the start of the art class only a few minutes before, when Ms Weldon had asked the kids to take their seats it clicked. Heads had turned, yes some to glare in her direction, but most turned to see who and more importantly who was not in class. The kids were taking stock, checking to see that their friends were still alive.

That was the difference. The killer attended Ashton High, or rather his presence did. He roamed the halls, riding along on the tops of everyone's minds, affecting everything and everyone. He was there, invisible and never spoken of, but he was there all the same...very much like Ky, the Ghost. In this way the two were alike. They...

"I asked you a question, Jesse," Ms Weldon said, jarring Jesse out of her reverie.

"Sorry. Like I said, I ran out of time," Jesse replied. "May I ask, what..."

She stopped in mid-sentence astounded by what she was seeing. The boy who was drawing the picture of Hitler had just turned it around to work on another part of it, and now that it was facing toward Jesse she saw that the picture wasn't of Hitler at all. It was of her father, James Clarke. The boy had captured his likeness very well, except that he had added the little Hitler moustache and instead of her father's hair being thick and wavy, it was greasy and lay flat across his forehead.

On each of the corners of the picture were swastikas and across the top in bold red and black was: *Arbeit macht frei-- Work sets you free!*

Wide-eyed and incredulous, Jesse asked, "What is this?"

"It's the art portion of the coordinated studies program," Ms Weldon said with all the innocence of a lamb. "We are learning about the importance of peaceable demonstrations as a means of affecting social and political change. Oh, speaking of which, there is a mandatory assembly on Saturday."

Jesse blinked. Saturday? So ingrained into her mind was the concept of the five day school week that the idea of having to go in on Saturday coupled with the bizarre and offensive picture of her father had her head spinning. "Huh?"

Ms Weldon smiled, seeming to enjoy Jesse's bewilderment. "Yes, Saturday. You are actually a lucky girl. Not only do you have the wonderful opportunity to learn about demonstrations, you are going to partake in one as well."

The words coming out of Ms Weldon's mouth were almost a foreign language that needed interpreting to Jesse's mixed up mind. Demonstrations?

"I am? What's it about?"

It couldn't be about war. The war in Iraq was over, and lately no one much heard or cared about what was happening in Afghanistan. Perhaps it was about racism. She hoped not. It had been beaten into her head with such repetition that she was sick of the subject. And what did her father done up to look like Hitler have to do with anything?

Ms Weldon smiled like the cat that had just eaten the canary. It was an unpleasant grin and there might as well have been feathers sticking out of her teeth. "We are protesting the deplorable, Nazi-like behavior of the new town manager. He is destroying people's lives, all in the name of the god that he worships: the all mighty dollar. The town council will be meeting with the town manager on Saturday to rubber stamp his proposals and the entire student body is going to be there to stop them. We're going to surround the building to keep them from entering."

Jesse blinked again. It felt like one long, slow, fluid motion that she could hear as well as feel. "You want me to protest my own father?"

"Why, do you not wish to?" the teacher replied, still smiling, still nasty. "Do you think that it's right to fire so many public servants, right before the holidays? Do you think that this spiteful behavior could, in anyway, possibly help the local economy? Do you think that it's a good idea to deprive children of a first rate education?"

If she had wanted to, Jesse could have answered these questions since she had asked them herself. But that would have meant defending her father. James Clarke was a man she despised three-hundred and sixty-five days a year, he was an insensitive jerk who had always put her needs behind everyone else's, including his own. If anyone had the right to protest James Clarke it was her.

Jesse opened her mouth, not knowing what would come out exactly, but shut it as she realized just how loud Ms Weldon had been and just how quiet the rest of the room had become. Every eye stared hard at her, waiting on her reply. The weight of those stares made her lean back slightly and she felt her mind twirl.

Those stares...were for the first time not all hateful. They looked upon her with a certain anticipation, as if...as if they were giving her a chance to do the "right thing" and side with them against her father. And how she wanted to! This was an opportunity like she had never faced before. It was an opportunity to be liked!

In her mind's eye, she could read the newspaper headline: *Brave Girl Stands Up To Nazi Father!* She could hear the throngs of students chanting her name as she was carried about on the shoulders of the football team. She could see herself dancing her first dance as Prom Queen, and then...her first kiss. Seventeen and never been kissed...that could change!

All she had to do was publicly, in front of most of the town in all likelihood, denounce her father. A simple thing, really. Something she had wanted to do for ages. Only she had wanted to do it for her own reasons and not because she was bullied into it. That thought gave her pause and her mind hesitated long enough for a new vision to slip past the chanting hordes and the long slow kiss occupying her mind.

The image was of her father and her. She could see herself on a podium, standing in front of a sea of people, pointing at him. Her finger was stiff with accusation. Across from her, she could see the look of pain in his eyes at her betrayal. At first this hardened her resolve to side with Ms Weldon... after all what did he know about pain? She knew all there was to know about pain. Jesse Clarke's life *was* pain. Every second of everyday she had to live in pain.

But could she cause pain? Yes, she had been in fights. She had punched and kicked, stabbed and even bitten. Yet all of that was in the moment and always in the moment of self-defense. Certainly, she had been verbally abusive as well. Her tongue could be as caustic as acid, but again, only in response. In all her life, Jesse had never, in the cold light of day and with purposeful intention, meant to harm an innocent person.

"Well?" Ms Weldon asked, and she too seemed suddenly intrigued at what Jesse would say. There was a new look in her eyes. It was as if the teacher hadn't considered the possibility that Jesse would agree to the protest. Jesse could see the cold calculations turning wheels in the teacher's mind. Jesse had wheels as well.

Stabbing her father in the back had other ramifications than just a first kiss and instant popularity. It meant that she might actually pass her senior year. Her last three years had been a struggle, but the first couple of days at Ashton made it clear that she might not pass half her classes. Or if she did, her grade point average might be so low that her only options would be summer school and a community college.

Yet if she stood up against her father...

"Well," Ms Weldon repeated.

"I...

Chapter 16

"I...I'm going to have to think about it," Jesse said finally in a hesitating voice.

"What's there to think about?" a boy asked. She didn't know his name, but she recognized him from both her history and biology classes. "My dad hasn't had a job in two years and when he finally lands something part time your dad comes in here thinking he owns the place and has him fired!"

There was no lie about him in his statement. That he was poor was obvious by the way his clothes hung ill fitting and stained on his gaunt frame. And by the way his hair was limp and dry as straw, Jesse guessed that he hadn't used shampoo or conditioner in months. His hair was clean at least, but had likely been washed with cheap hand-soap. Jesse felt sorry for him and his difficult position, but could think of nothing to say.

As he had finished his little diatribe, the whole class nodded along as though they were the choir and he the preacher. Their support seemed to light a fire under him and he went on growing louder and bolder with each word.

He walked toward her as he spoke, "I've been eating ramen soup every day for months. You ever do that? Eat the same thing over and over again, every single day because your parents can't afford a meal that costs more than fourteen cents?" Jesse shook her head, and fought the urge to look away. She wanted to walk away as well, but kept her feet planted. None of this was her fault. "I didn't think so," the boy sneered.

He was practically baiting her, trying to force her to come to a decision: denounce or defend. "I'm sorry about your father," she replied honestly. "But...but..."

The word *but* seemed to catch in her throat, then her lips seized up and she hesitated. A part of her—the part that she got from her father— wanted to sit the boy down and explain the nuances of budgeting, taxes, and long term planning. Another part of her—from her mom, clearly—wanted to side with the boy unconditionally in the hopes of becoming popular.

The truth was Jesse wanted to do neither. She wanted to be herself. She wanted to be liked or disliked based on who *she* was, not who her parents were. However, that didn't seem to be an option.

As her hesitation drew on, the students grew restless. They began to murmur angrily and started to press forward, seeming to turn from a class to a mob in seconds.

Ms Weldon only watched them placidly waiting for Jesse to make up her mind. The teacher did nothing until the boy whose father had lost his job shoved a desk in anger at which point she stepped forward smoothly.

"Well, Jesse? Do you have an answer? Are you going to join us?" She swept her arm slowly in an arc indicating the other students like a game show hostess showing off a new car.

Jesse's mouth fell open, but she was still too divided to answer. The greatest part of her wanted to belong, yet still something held her back. Ms Weldon saw the indecision.

"How bout we talk about this outside. Everyone else get back to work." The lady then herded Jesse out the door and walked her down the hall. They were silent save for the clacking of Ms Weldon's heels on the polished tile. Jesse drifted along beside her, almost noiseless in her jungle boots.

As they came to the center rectangular building, they entered a set of double doors just off the main office. It was the school's library.

"Hello Carla," the art teacher said, striding past a woman sitting at the tall checkout counter. The woman, a dark haired beauty, gave a nervous smile in return. It seemed to Jesse that the she sat on a rung far down the pecking order in the hierarchy at the school. Yet she was higher up than Jesse and made sure to show it by switching out the smile for a glare.

For her part Jesse only rolled her eyes and hurried along in Ms Weldon's wake.

"Look, Jesse," Ms Weldon said as they went deeper into the library. "This demonstration is very important to the future of Ashton and I'm starting to think that *you* might be very important to the demonstration. You see what a coup this would be? What a strong message it would send to the town council if the town manager's own daughter thought he might be going overboard?"

"I think I understand," Jesse said.

"Good. I know we got off on the wrong foot," Ms Weldon said with a gentle squeeze of Jesse's shoulder. "It's just that there's so much stress on everyone this time of year...because, you know. And on top of that we have all these budget cuts..." Ms Weldon just sort of trailed off.

This left Jesse lost as to what to do or say. Clearly, the teacher had meant for Jesse to take what she had just said as some sort of apology. Only it wasn't an apology. It was just excuses for atrocious behavior, which Jesse felt in no way obligated to reply to. She pressed her lips together.

Ms Weldon saw the look and tried again. "Ashton is a very close knit community. Because of everything that we have gone through we rally around each other and support each other. We can be very good to people who have our same goals in mind. However, people that threaten us may not get treated very well...you understand what I'm trying to say?"

Jesse understood perfectly. She was being threatened...play ball or else. The idea was infuriating and Jesse was so angry she could only nod.

"Good. I knew you were a smart girl," Ms Weldon replied. "Here's what I want you to do for the rest of the period. Take this book." The teacher pulled down a large glossy book. Its cover was a black and white photograph of a man being attacked by a German Shepherd.

Jesse's eyes went wide at the picture. Ms Weldon saw this and explained, "It's a history of the protest movement in America. I want you to see what people have gone through in order to enact social change. It can be very inspiring. I'll be back at the end of class and we'll talk."

"Great," Jesse murmured under her breath at the retreating form of Ms Weldon.

When the teacher was gone, Jesse cracked the book and began skimming. Despite struggling with her own not insignificant issues, she found herself drawn into it. This was mostly due to the vivid and frequently horrific pictures that made up the majority of the book.

The pictures depicted people bravely standing up for what they knew was right. It was astounding to Jesse. She had been taught the basics of the civil rights movement, but the book brought it to life on a whole separate level. Not only was she astounded by what she saw, she was amazed at what she was feeling: inspired.

The self-sacrifices portrayed on every glossy page swayed Jesse's mind in favor of the demonstration. She too wanted to stand honorably with people looking to change the world for the better. She suddenly felt lighter, happier. It was the wonderful fact that not only could she become popular, she could do it by doing the right thing.

Except this demonstration isn't about change, is it? the voice in her head asked.

"Mother-pus-bucket!" she swore silently to herself. There was a part of her that was always contrarian. It could never accept anything at face value. That part of her saw through her self-delusion. The demonstration was not about change, it was about maintaining the status quo. Something her father claimed would destroy Ashton in five to seven years.

"What on earth should I do?" Jesse asked the quiet library books. Just then a person blurred by so quick that Jesse didn't know if it was a girl or a boy. A moment later the person came back and at first didn't see Jesse on the floor. Her eyes were up, scanning the numbers along the spines of books.

It was big haired Amanda Jorgenson. She took a look at a couple of books, grabbed one and was about to leave when she saw Jesse sitting in the narrow aisle. For long seconds the two girls stared at each other, but then Amanda smirked and started sauntering back toward the front of the library.

This was a bit of a surprise. Jesse didn't think that their next confrontation would be so *limited*. But then Jesse heard:

Poor Jesse had really quite an itch
Too bad that she was such a bitch
Though she looked for a while
She never got a boy who would smile
But found a dog would do in a pinch.

Jesse was astounded that the girl would say something so vulgar and so loud in a school library. It took just a moment to get over that amazement and then she was up, spoiling for a fight. There was no bluff in her now. In her black outfit with her ankle taped and feeling better in her supple boot, she was more than ready.

She had a problem however. The school librarian was only a few yards away and Amanda was heading right to her. Amanda was putting on quite a show, swinging her hips jauntily, taunting Jesse in a nyeh-nyeh childish way. The bigger girl even turned back and gave Jesse a smile that said, *Whatcha gonna do?*

Jesse wasn't going to do anything, other than seethe that is.

Carla, at the desk gave Amanda a beaming smile.

"Screw em!" Jesse hissed, turning away. "Screw this whole damn town."

There was no way she was going to help their stupid demonstration. Not now. They could all live off ramen noodles for the rest of their miserable hate-filled lives as far as Jesse was concerned. In fact, if she heard that stupid limerick one more time, she swore that she would figure out how to turn on the hydrants outside of the town hall right in the middle of their god-forsaken street-art demonstration.

Picturing this in her mind actually brought an evil smile to her lips. She could imagine rivers of multi-colored water running down the street...and the cold! If only she had access to a fire-hose. She would show these so-called demonstrators a little history. Would they stand up and do what's right in the face of freezing cold...

But we both know they're not doing what's right, her contrarian voice said.

This one thought brought her rage to a low simmer and destroyed completely her silly and far-fetched imaginings.

It also brought with it confusion and she sat back down to try to figure out what the right thing to do was...or actually since she was in the blackest mood, she tried to figure out how to do the wrong thing in the right way.

"If I help the demonstration to destroy my father's plans then in the end the town will implode economically, and all these jerks will suffer," Jesse reasoned. "But if I refuse to help them...then my father's plans will go through and in a couple of years Ashton will be thriving."

Jesse waited for the contrarian voice to speak up, to find the nuance missing in her thinking that she hadn't caught yet. The voice remained quiet and Jesse made up her mind.

She would help the demonstration. She would be the loudest most boisterous one there. She would become popular. She would show her father that his actions had consequences as well as hers did. She would show him that if he thought he could treat her as an afterthought he had another thing coming. And last but *so* not least: she would help, in the most underhanded way imaginable, a town filled with hateful people to commit economic suicide.

Her own deviousness made her smile.

She pulled the book down from the shelf once again and opened it to the worst picture of the lot: it showed a group of four black men hanging by their necks. Though it turned her stomach to look at it, she kept it open. When Ms Weldon came back, Jesse was going to pretend to have had an epiphany. She was going to jump foursquare into the art project...

In a nearby aisle a cell phone went off, breaking in on Jesse's scheming. The owner of the phone could be heard scrambling about in a bag, cursing in a quiet way. It took her four rings to finally answer and in that time Jesse slipped around a couple of aisles; her curiosity forcing her to get a look at the whispering girl.

"What is it? Is everyone ok?" the girl asked with a strong fearful tone accenting her words. Jesse crept closer until she was just in the next aisle. She was so close that she heard the person on the other end of the line speaking as if she were a tiny, unintelligible mouse.

"Then why are you calling?" The fearful tone of the girl had turned peevish, but then it sunk low. "He didn't get the job? I'm sorry...is he ok?"

Jesse ducked down peering through the books. She saw a girl in a pink sweat suit huddled over a phone.

"Yeah, ok. I know...Mom. I know...I will. Since you called, do you mind if I go over to the bowling alley after school?" There was a pause and then the girl got upset. "Why would you even ask that? I'd never go alone, I'm not stupid. I'm going to be with Jill and Sammy...no not Sam O'Brian; Samantha."

Jesse became bored with the conversation and began to creep away but then she heard the girl respond in a way that froze her in place.

"I know. A part of me just wishes that he'd just kill someone already. This waiting around has got me so frazzled...ok...ok."

Kill? They were talking about her friendly neighborhood killer. The one that could slip over her fence in the dead of night any time he pleased. The thought gave her goose bumps and she rubbed her arms as if winter had come to the library.

"Thanks Mom. I promise I won't spend any money...love you too. When Dad gets back, tell him I love him also, ok? Bye."

In the silence, Jesse slipped back closer to the girl in pink and again strove to look through the books. This time she made out a freckled face that she recognized. It was the girl from her English class, the one that had warned against getting too close to Ky.

Unmoving, Jesse stared at her for a long minutes and the girl never noticed. She knelt in her aisle, holding a small crucifix up to her lips and gazing off into space. She was pensive...no, she was more than that. Her nails were down to the nubs and her lips were frayed and chapped having been bitten and abused by their owner. The girl was afraid.

She was afraid of Jesse's backyard killer. And Jesse was right there with her.

"Hey, you ok?" Jesse asked.

The girl jumped, shocked out of her reverie. "Yeah...yeah, I'm ok. Who is that?"

"Oh...no one," Jesse replied, feeling suddenly like a peeping tom who had just been caught lurking in the bushes. "Uh, just a friend."

Why she should feel weird about talking to another person, especially one who looked like she could use a friend, Jesse didn't know. Yet she did and it was because of this odd feeling that she scurried away, trying not to be seen.

She hid from the freckle-faced girl who looked around for a few minutes before leaving. When she did, Jesse moped back to "her" aisle and sat back down on the carpet. She didn't bother with the book, other than to close it, not wanting to see the poor men with their impossibly long necks.

Her little interaction with the girl had eroded her resolve to help with the town's destruction. Whether the girl knew it or not she shared a bond with Jesse. They both feared the killer. And what's more, the girl had tried to help her. The look she had given Jesse in English class wasn't: *Don't get close to him, bitch!* It was: *I wouldn't get too close to him if I were you.* That was a world of difference communicated in the tiny headshake.

Jesse sighed, suddenly back to being confused about all of her options.

You're not confused.

As always the voice was correct. Jesse had found a person, probably an entire family, that didn't deserve the complete economic ruin of the town. She was sure there were others as well. Did they deserve what she could unleash on them?

The answer had her slumping against the shelves and a feeling of depression got a good strong grip in her soul. There would be no first kiss for her after all. There would only be more hate.

Chapter 17

Now that she made up her mind, Jesse didn't really want to wait around for Ms Weldon. She figured that it would just lead to headache for everyone. Instead, after a quick glance at her watch which told her there was only about five minutes left in third period, she decided that she would just leave a note explaining her choice and then take an extended bathroom break.

Unfortunately, she hadn't come to that decision fast enough. Just as Jesse stood, there came to her ears a steady clack, clack, clack, of heels on tile. The sound of Ms Weldon's approach was unmistakable. Now her options were to hide or face the music. Jesse forced a smile onto her face.

No tears! she demanded silently.

"So, Jesse..." Ms Weldon said the moment she saw the girl in black. "What did you think of the book?"

"Graphic. Very graphic," Jesse replied honestly. She didn't elaborate and for a time there was a silence between them. As it progressed both of their smiles faded.

Ms Weldon broke the silence first. "Yes. We should never shield our children from atrocities or they may not remember important lessons learned from them."

Jesse nodded but kept silent. Her father had taught her a lesson about negotiating. In any negotiations, the side that talks the most usually comes out with the least. And this was a negotiation of sorts. Jesse was trying to negotiate a settlement in which she received minimal damage.

There was no winning for her, unless she chose the "right" side. Ms Weldon had made that clear. The second hand swept around nearly full circle before the silence was broken again.

Again it was the art teacher who spoke first, this time with a note of irritation. "I do have a class to get back to. I need you to tell me right here and right now what your intentions are."

"I can't do it. I can't join the demonstration. But I would like to find a different way in which I can get credit..."

Ms Weldon, her long face tight and her grey eyes like steel, cut across Jesse, "There is only one way. My way. I should tell you that since there are only a few weeks left in the semester that this project will count as practically your entire grade."

"You are not going to count almost four months worth of work that I did at Copper Ridge High towards my grade?"

"I would have to see the work. Do you have it...all?"

Jesse didn't have the artwork. There hadn't seemed to be any reason to hold on to them and plenty of reasons to throw them in the trash. "I don't have them, but I do have my transcripts."

"Of course I will take them into account, but I weigh them against what you do in *my* class. And if you do nothing in *my* class then I have to assume the grades are inflated." Ms Weldon paused to study Jesse. "There is another reason why you should do join us; Ashton is not a good town to be friendless in. You need friends. I would hate to know what would happen to a girl without any friends in this town."

This actually had Jesse's ears perked. She knew about the killer, but not very much about the killer. "Why, what would happen?"

"Oh, this and that," Ms Weldon replied purposefully cryptic. "You know kids can be so cruel."

Was she not talking about the killer then? Or was she hinting about him and would only reveal pertinent...possibly lifesaving information if Jesse agreed to join her demonstration. If she was, then Ms Weldon was nearly as bad as the killer.

"Adults can be cruel as well," Jesse replied. Her blue eyes were ice. "But they are worse than children when they are. They seem to think that they have a right to treat people poorly. When in truth they have the responsibility due to their age and experience to treat everyone with respect."

"Everyone that deserves it," Ms Weldon retorted. "So you won't join the class?"

"No."

"Then you get a zero for today's class participation as well. It's obvious you spent your time down here just messing around instead of reading the book as you were supposed to."

The end of period bell rang, long and shrill. Without another word, Ms Weldon turned on one of her clacking heels and marched away.

When she was gone, Jesse melted against the nearest stack of shelves and clutched her head. "*Then you get a zero for today's class participation,*" she mimicked, sounding like an incredibly stupid Ms Weldon. "*Not a good town not to have any friends...*"

This thought triggered the mental image she had of the killer. His name was Harold Brownly and her father had described him as the biggest person he had ever seen, but when she pictured him, he was the faceless Shadow-man. Jesse was sure that when he killed, he killed as the Shadow-man, not as some big lumbering oaf with a name like Harold.

He would be quick and silent. His victims wouldn't know he was even there until it was too late. It had almost been too late for Jesse. The other night in the forest she had never felt herself closer to death. And no matter what reassurances her father had on the subject, Jesse wasn't going to trust some psychologist with her life.

The late bell rang, startling her out of her reverie. She was supposed to be at lunch, however Jesse liked her black attire sauce free and instead of heading to the cafeteria, she went in search of the periodicals.

If her parents wouldn't tell her about the Shadow-man, then maybe the newspapers would.

Jesse began digging through the old periodicals starting with the not so acclaimed Ashton Gazette. It took her a half hour to go through the past two years of local-yokel blather one page at a time. Surprisingly, there wasn't a single story concerning *any* murder. There were three separate stories about cars being stolen and a plethora of reports about lesser crimes, but no murders.

"Well, I suppose that's a good thing," Jesse murmured quietly as she finished the last of the publications. They sat in a little stack next to her. She stared at them feeling...relief. Perhaps this was all over-blown. Perhaps they hadn't been murders after all; maybe they had been accidents.

Jesse gathered up the stack, patted its sides so it was a neat bundle, and brought it back to the research section. She set it down where she had found it and eyed the top page's headline: *Halloween Festival- A New Tradition!* A picture below the caption showed what looked like a bazillion kids running around a school gym. All the little tykes seemed happily covered in chocolate.

"Lucky ducks," Jesse said good-naturedly.

Unsurprisingly, Halloween was Jesse's all time favorite holiday. As a holiday it crushed Thanksgiving, which was only long, drawn-out enforced "family-time." It easily beat out Jesse's birthday, which was a daylong demonstration of how Jesse's parents really knew next to nothing about her. Halloween even edged out Christmas, which only enjoyed top-runner status because of the long holiday from school that surrounded it.

Halloween was Jesse's time.

Not because she was into "witch-craft" or any of that paranormal non-sense, all of which was complete bunk in her eyes. Halloween was her favorite because she could, for just one night, be someone else. This wasn't simply an appearance thing. Under her make-up Jesse would adopt a new personality, a new way of speaking. She would invent a new background for herself and she would walk amongst the kids who bullied her all year long as a completely different person.

A long sigh escaped her. With a touch of regret she eyed the much larger pile of newspapers that sat next to the Ashton Gazette. It was the Barton Daily. The top paper, unlike the little local one, had headlines that were depressingly real: death in far away countries, oil prices climbing, and dull politicians being dull.

With a grunt she grabbed up as big a stack as she could carry and went back to her corner table. She liked being tucked out of the way. There she skimmed the bold headings for each story until she ran out of actual stories and came to the advertisements for the last minute Christmas Sales. Only one week left!

"Yea! One week left. Yippie," Jesse said in a tired voice. She slapped the paper closed and grabbed the next. At first glance, it seemed identical to the last newspaper: more dreary headlines and then more advertisements for the latest, clothes, toys and computer games. Yet something did jump out at her.

The banner over one sale fairly screamed: *Only nine days left!*

"They must be out of order," Jesse mumbled to herself. She began leafing through the stack, checking dates, looking for the missing paper. Not only did she not find it, she also discovered that there were many other newspapers missing.

Despite that it was still only the seventeenth of December, there were four dates missing. In November there were five and in October only one. Then nothing was missing until she went as far back as March. Three were missing in that month, eight in February and in January, eighteen were missing.

On a hunch, Jesse went back to the Ashton Gazette. All of January was missing as was all of December of 2008. Suddenly the relief that she had felt minutes before went *poof* inside of her. There could have been all sorts of murders during those two months.

Just then Ms Weldon's words floated back into her active mind: *"It's just that there's so much stress on everyone this time of year...because, you know.* At the time, Jesse had thought she meant the holidays, but now Jesse had to wonder if Harold killed only during the holiday season. She hopped up and hurried to the checkout counter.

"Excuse me? Is there some reason that there are so many missing newspapers?" she asked Carla in her friendliest voice. Carla's eyes had narrowed to slits as Jesse had walked up.

The librarian's face went suddenly white. "They might have been lost...or stolen. Or maybe they were never delivered." Jesse was looking for a lie in the quiet responses and found it without effort.

"Or maybe you threw them out," Jesse accused. She hated being lied to, it made her snappish. But worse than the lie, she hated the idea that everyone in Ashton, but her seemed to know about a very dangerous man. This put her a couple of pegs higher up than snappish. "Are you attempting to censor murder? The public has a right to know."

"You don't know what you're talking about," Carla replied, turning away. "Everyone knows."

"I don't," Jesse admitted, hurrying around the librarian to face her again. "That's why I'm trying to research what exactly has been happening around here. The girl that was murdered last year, how did she die..."

Carla cut across her quick. "Shut up this instant! What kind of ghoul are you?" she demanded in a rising voice. "Leave the dead alone and leave the living in peace! I can't believe you. I can't believe how insensitive you're being....get your stuff and get the hell out of my library, this instant!"

For a second, Jesse actually thought that the woman was actually going to try to physically throw her out. It would have been a grave mistake; Carla barely cleared five feet tall.

Jesse had enough. "I'll leave when I'm ready to leave," she replied calmly. "I hate to break it to you, but this is a public school and this is a public library and you are a public *servant*." By sneering through the word "servant" Jesse turned it into a put down.

Carla had been sideways to Jesse, but now she turned. Jesse moved with her, slipping subconsciously into her fighting stance. However, Carla didn't want to fight. She wanted to hurt Jesse.

"You want to know about the girl that was killed last year?" Carla asked in dreadfully quiet voice. "Her name was Mary Castaneda. She was sixteen years old and she was strangled so violently that her windpipe was crushed and her neck was broken. Anything else you want to know? Do you want to hear...do you want to hear...about how the birds picked the flesh right off her face? You want to know what it's like to see your..." Carla choked suddenly and sobbed. There were huge tears in her eyes and they had every right to be there.

When Carla had turned around, Jesse saw for the first time that she wore a little gold nametag. It read: Carla Castaneda School Librarian.

Chapter 18

Jesse walked down the hall in a daze.

She felt empty, as if she no longer owned a soul. She had fled from the library and she had fled from the tears that she had caused to rain down from Mrs. Castaneda's...Carla's face.

"Carla," she whispered to herself. "Not Mrs. Castaneda...it's Carla."

Mrs. Castaneda had a murdered daughter, and perhaps out of all the people who hated Jesse, she was probably the only one with a legitimate right to.

Carla was just a small, pretty lady who ran the school library. A place that Jesse didn't think that she would ever go back to.

The bell rang and Jesse spun in place as four-hundred students flooded the halls. She had to look up at the nearest classroom door just to know where she was. Then she had to dig in her pocket to find her class schedule in order to find out where she was supposed to be.

Just as she was pulling it out, someone smashed square into her and before she knew it, she was on her back, listening to laughter. The blow sent a spike of pain through her shoulder and made her head swim. Whoever had run into her had meant not only to hurt her, but to also break bones if they could. It took a few seconds for her eyes to adjust enough to see who it was that was responsible.

It was the boy from her art class, the poor one whose father had been recently fired. He may have been slim to the point of gaunt, but he was also tall and clearly stronger than Jesse. "You should watch where you're going, bitch," he said to add insult to Jesse's ringing head.

Jesse kept quiet. The boy wasn't alone. With him was another boy that could have been his brother, Amanda Jorgenson, and the blonde girl who once again looked like a boy in a dress. Wincing, Jesse struggled to her feet and as she did she slipped a pencil out of her bag. She had sharpened the pencil herself just that morning. In no way did she *want* to use it, however Jesse wasn't going to get her pretty face bashed in without a fight.

"You got something to say?" the boy demanded.

"I'm just waiting on an apology," Jesse said, not backing down.

The hall went quiet. "Then you'll be waiting a long time, bitch." Snorts of laughter accompanied this, though who could have found it funny Jesse didn't know.

Now Jesse was in a very tough position. She had fought boys before and had lost before, every time. This would be no different; she was too much of a realist to pretend otherwise. Therefore she had to keep from fighting him, but at the same time she couldn't exactly back down either. She had to hit a nice middle ground.

"You're being rude calling names like that," she said, controlling her voice well enough despite the quivering of her chest. "You sound like a child."

"Whatcha gonna do about it, bitch?" he asked advancing.

Jesse forced herself to appear outwardly calm. "Are you thinking about fighting me? A girl, really? You would fight a girl?" she asked, allowing mocking incredulity to enter her voice. "Do you think that would that make you tough? Tell me, do you fight little children also?"

Her tactic of introducing shame worked and the boy paused long enough for Amanda to drag him back.

"She's just a skank, Ronny," Amanda said loudly, walking away with her arm through the boy's. "She's not worth it."

With the fight seeming to be over, a mass milling took place and Jesse was jostled about some more. This time, no one was looking to hurt her and she made her way through the crowd. Her next class was a study hall, which she hoped would be stress free. It was down a long hall and unbelievably she found Amanda and her friends walking in front of her. With a sinking feeling accompanying each step, she watched in horror as they went right into the room marked on her schedule.

"Oh, mother-pus-bucket," she sighed. "Why me?" With another bigger sigh, she straightened her shoulders and strode in.

The period wasn't bad at all. She had feared that the study hall would be more like a rumpus room than a place to review class work or catch up on assignments. Instead, the room remained quiet throughout. The teacher, Mrs. Spiros ran a tight ship and what's more she didn't once harass Jesse.

Jesse was even able to sit alone off to herself. In the back of the room was one of those desks designated as Ky's. She went to it immediately. *ALONE* was again carved into this desk, but in much smaller lettering. This was probably due to Mrs. Spiros, who kept a sharp eye out. For Jesse, study hall was like a mini-vacation from her troubles and she spent the time putting the finishing touches on her essay that was due in history.

She has secretly cheered when Mr. Johnson had given her the assignment on Rosa Parks. Jesse had written a term paper on the civil rights heroine the year before and it was still sitting pretty as you please in a file marked, poetry, on her computer. It was hidden this way because her father thought that every assignment should be fresh and new, for how else could one learn? He also hated poetry to such an extent that it could not be measured with existing technology.

Before history however, Jesse had to deal with economics and with Mr. Irving; it didn't start out well. He greeted her with this: "Miss Clarke, do you have a note from the school nurse for your absence yesterday?"

Jesse would've bet a hundred dollars that he already knew the answer to the question. "No. I was sick...you know...vomiting? I thought it best not to make a mess on the floor, so I stayed in the bathroom."

"You could still go to her and get your absence excused," he suggested with a gleam in his eye.

Right, thought Jesse. The high school was far too small for Mr. Irving not to know her issues with Mrs. Daly. "That's ok, my father is fully aware of my missing class, and..."

Just then Ky came into the room. He literally ghosted between them and Mr. Irving didn't bat an eye at his passing. Jesse, on the other hand was so startled that she lost her train of thought and ended up staring at the boy. This time, she stared not so much out of interest, rather instead out of disappointment. She had seen "his" desk sitting alone and had secretly claimed it as her own, not knowing he shared the same class. Now she would have to find another spot.

"Miss Clarke?"

She turned in embarrassment back to the teacher. "As I was saying, he...my father knows the situation. Were there any assignments due from yesterday?"

Mr. Irving, not the warmest individual to begin with, turned cold. "I don't accept late work. Find a seat."

In her chest, Jesse's heart sunk. If Mr. Irving was against her, then she could add economics to the list of classes she would likely fail that semester.

Jesse glanced around at the classroom. She recognized all of their faces from other classes that they shared and it perked her up a tiny bit to realize that none of the students in the room had yet to be overtly mean to her. It was a victory of sorts. There were three empty seats, two near Ky and one directly upfront.

The one in front was out of the question as far as Jesse was concerned and she started to the rear of the class, it was then that Mr. Irving stopped her.

"Not those seats," he said in a clipped, precise voice.

With the attention of the entire class on her, Jesse went to one in front. It was a bare two feet from the teacher's desk and she felt like butt-kissing schmuck sitting there. But what could she do? In the silence that followed, she busied herself pulling out her binder and pretending to search for a pen. For some reason the class remained quiet around her. It seemed as though Mr. Irving was waiting on her to begin.

"The first thing I want to do is go over current events," Mr. Irving stated. "Luckily we have a local expert on economics here with us today."

Jesse felt her heart stop. He wasn't talking about her, was he? Without turning her head, she shot her eyes to him and saw that he was indeed looking right at her. She looked back at her binder and froze. Even her skin seemed paralyzed, unable to even twitch.

"Miss Clarke, could you please stand up so I can introduce you?" Jesse stood, still with her face pointing down to her binder. "Class, this is Jesse Clarke, her father is the town manager. I hear from reliable sources that she can explain budgeting better than some adults." Other than a few people stirring in their seats, the class was utterly silent.

"Miss Clarke, could you face the class?"

Jesse turned and for the first time that day felt the smallest pain in her ankle. She had turned, but because of the traction of her jungle boots, her foot hadn't. It wasn't bad, just a reminder for Jesse to still take it easy.

"Thank you. Could we ask you some questions?" Mr. Irving asked.

"I'm n-not an ex-expert on anything," Jesse said.

"Really? Ms Weldon said you explained all about baseline budgeting the other night."

"I might have answered some questions." Jesse felt like she was on trial. Strangely, she also felt guilty of whatever it was that she was being accused of. Desperately she wanted to sit back down and bury her head back in her bag.

"Could you answer some questions about your father's proposed budget?" Mr. Irving asked still precise. He was like a lawyer on cross-examination, or a cop giving someone the third degree.

Jesse's face felt suddenly hot. "I don't know what his proposals are exactly, so...no I don't think I can."

Mr. Irving strode to the front of the classroom. "So you're supporting something you know nothing about?"

Jesse was absolutely mortified at her treatment. Her face felt hot. *No Tears!* a distant voice called out from the deep recess of her mind, but to no avail. She felt them coming and she began to blink quickly, forcing them back.

"I-I-It's the same as everyone else," she managed to spit out. "All the other k-kids are all p-protesting and they don't know his p-proposals either."

"Speak for yourself," a boy two seats to her right said. He was loud and his voice was brittle with emotion. Jesse refused to look at him. "I know your father canceled the city's contacts with Waste Management and my dad got canned. What more do I need to know?"

Jesse could have warned the boy that was going to happen. "My f-father always cancels contracts that are longer than two years. It fosters more competition and brings costs down," Jesse replied, straight from memory. "Long term contracts have a tendency to drive competitors out of business. And this makes monopolies out of a few businesses which can then charge what they want, hurting everyone."

When she had finished, Jesse took a long shaky breath. The answer she had given was sound and hearing herself speak had calmed her somewhat. It didn't in any way mollify the boy whose father had been laid off however. He only glared.

"One question, Miss Clarke?" Mr. Irving asked. "Where does your father get the right to cancel contracts that were negotiated, *in good faith,* between two other parties?"

In a small voice, Jesse replied honestly, "I...I don't know." She had no clue how he did it; she only knew that he did.

Mr. Irving sighed tiredly as if this was all a strain on him. "This is part of the reason behind our protest. Not only is your father employing voo-doo economics, he is also doing it in a way that seems more suited to Nazi- Germany than to Ashton, Michigan."

So her father was a Nazi. What did that make her? One of those kid-Nazis...the Hitler youth? She didn't know nor did she really care. Not right then. At the word Nazi, the shaking in her chest and the heat creeping up from her neck changed slightly. It was still there, and was perhaps worse, but now it was fueled by anger.

Jesse gave only a contemptuous shrug and a flip of her hand in response to the teacher, who grew angry at the gesture.

"You don't care?" he asked incredulously.

She wasn't interested in defending James Clarke, nor was she interested in saving Ashton. Earlier she had been, but just then with the glaring eyes of hatred upon her, she couldn't remember why.

"Not when you throw around words like Nazi and...and Voo-doo." Jesse had never heard the term Voo-doo economics before, but it sounded made up and childish in her ears.

"Would you prefer the terms dictatorial and Trickle-down?" the teacher asked.

Without asking, Jesse sat down in her chair. She was done with Mr. Irving's version of The Salem Witch Trials. Just like those witches she was damned either way, so she figured she might as well be comfortable in her torture.

"I'm not my father. I never claimed to be my father. If you have an issue with him, take it up with him."

Mr. Irving was unfazed by Jesse's response. "I hope that you understand my purpose here isn't to anger you. Confronting incorrect ideas is a part of teaching. As an example, there are still people who believe the world is flat, as a teacher it's part of my job to explain how they're wrong."

"And you do that by having me stand up here like I'm on trial. Like I'm some sort of murderer..." Too late Jesse realized 'murderer' was probably a bad choice of words. "Like some sort of criminal?"

"Actually, having you stand is sign of respect," Mr. Irving explained. "When we are both standing, facing each other, then we are equal. You see? When you are sitting, then I'm the teacher and you are the student, which means my statements automatically carry with them more authority than yours. I'm just trying to help you to debate."

To Jesse this wasn't an explanation, it was rationalization. He was still the teacher whether she sat or not. "Thanks, but I don't want to debate."

"Is that because you're taking your father's side, out of love and respect, because he's your father? That's understandable, if you are."

I'm still on trial, Jesse thought. Telling the truth didn't much matter to Jesse just then. She just wanted this little episode to be done. "Yeah, I guess you're right. I am."

"That is very sweet, Jesse. Unfortunately in economics we can't be swayed by emotion like this. Your love, which, I'm sure is..."

Jesse couldn't take it anymore. Her shoulders slumped and she, in a languid motion as if her hand weighed fifty pounds, slapped her desk with the flat of her palm. "I lied," she confessed. "I don't love my father. He's an ass. I just wanted to shut you up, but...I don't see that happening anytime soon."

The class had been for the most part silent, now it went absolutely still as well. They seemed to be expecting some sort of volcanic explosion from Mr. Irving, but instead he turned cold. "Lying is not permitted in this school. When you first arrived you signed the honor code."

"Yeah, sure did. I guess I was lying there too."

"I think maybe you need to leave my classroom," he said in a quiet voice.

"Thank God!" Jesse exclaimed and meant it. She couldn't imagine anything worse that having too put up with Mr. Irving for another minute.

"Take a trip down to see Principal Peterson and explain to him the extent of your disrespect."

Chapter 19

Casually, completely unrushed, Jesse strolled down the empty halls. After all, where was the great hurry? In the past, she had been such a frequent visitor to the principal's office that she knew the routine by heart.

She would drag herself in, pretending to be contrite. She would suffer the annoying looks of Mrs. Daly. And she would sit. And sit, sit, sit. Probably for an hour, but maybe two. She would sit cooling her heels, not because Principal Peterson was so busy, but because that's what principals did. Jesse was sure that at 'principal school' this was the very first thing that was taught to them.

So instead of rushing toward that bit of fun, she slouched around the school. However, this didn't take long, even with as slow as she was going. There just wasn't much to the long two-story, T shaped building. After a trip to the bathroom— she knew she wouldn't be allowed one in her long wait for Principal Peterson—Jesse strolled into the school's office.

"Yes?" Mrs. Daly asked with her eyebrows raised. Her face was expectant as if she had been anticipating this moment for some time.

"Jesse Clarke to see Principal Peterson." The way Jesse said this made it seem as if they'd had a pre-arranged meeting and Mrs. Daly face fell a little.

"Concerning..."

"I have an issue respecting authority figures." Not only had Jesse seen many a principal in her time, she had also seen her share of therapists. In her mind there wasn't much difference between the two. With both it was all sitting around and talking about dealing with the consequences of her actions, controlling her feelings, and working through her negativity.

Mrs. Daly wasn't one for flippancy. "Who sent you down?"

"The Honorable Judge Irving has sentenced me to life without parole in the principal's office." Flippancy was all Jesse had sometimes.

A heavy put-upon sigh escaped Mrs. Daly. "What did you do?"

With the feeling that she had just gone through a mini-version of The Salem Witch trials still upon her, Jesse almost said *witchcraft*. However, a more clever, more exact answer jumped to front of her mind.

"I'm here for the crime of *Heresy*."

Mrs. Daly's eyes narrowed and then glanced down. She was obviously tying to work out what Jesse could possibly mean.

Jesse explained, assuming the air of a parent talking to a child, "Heresy is when you have an opinion that is different...or opposed to that of an authority figure." She didn't really know if the last part was correct, she only knew that charges of heresy only flowed downwards, from those with power to those without.

"I know the term," Mrs. Daly replied coldly. "Have a seat."

And thus Jesse's sentence began.

Her wait to get through Principal Peterson's door extended deep into seventh period and this agitated her. After the bell rang she took to watching the clock.

"Do you know if he will be much longer," she asked the receptionist. "I gotta turn in my paper to Mr. Johnson, he'll be mad if I don't."

This was true enough but also a lie. Jesse didn't care about some stupid essay and neither did Mr. Johnson. She was sure that he wasn't sitting in excitement, desperate to find out her views on Rosa Parks. If anything he was only desperate to flunk her. Whoever heard of a five-page essay as a punishment for daydreaming?

The real reason that she wanted to get to her history class lay in what her mind kept picturing: her desk, the one that she shared with Ky. It fascinated her with its one word message. The carved letters: ALONE was a testament to misery. Couldn't he see that she shared that misery with him? That it would be better to share it together rather than alone?

Even though she had already been rebuffed by him three times, she hoped that it was because she had approached him publicly. That was why she was pinning her slight hopes on the note that she had left him. Urgently she wanted to see if there was a note waiting for her in return.

Jesse didn't find out that day.

Principal Peterson, true to his principal training, kept her waiting until after the eighth period bell rang. Deflated, knowing that checking the desk would have to wait another painfully long day, she went in to see him. She had worried that, in true ogre form, he would scream and threaten, but it turned out that Mr. Peterson really wasn't all that bad. In fact she felt a little sorry for him.

He was clearly stuck in a very difficult position.

James Clarke could in no way legally dictate to either the school or the School Board, any of its policies. He couldn't tell them to fire a single soul, but as the town's main taxing authority he could cut back funding.

And he did.

James was a very smart and ruthless man. His initial funding cuts were such a nightmare that Principal Peterson strongly considered resigning, but then James relented...slightly...with *conditions*. The conditions extended the town manager's purview deep into the workings of the School Board and gave him more control than anyone would have dared thought.

In a way this worked to Principal Peterson's advantage. He was no longer forced to be the bad guy in charge of mass layoffs. The flip side of the coin was that as the head of the school he was pressured to stand up to the town manager. He couldn't seem to win. If he pushed James too hard he would lose his funding. If he was seen not to push hard enough he would lose the respect of his staff and who knows what would happen then. His not-so-secret fear was that they would go on strike, which would be a disaster.

This had all been explained to Jesse in a gleeful manner by her father. The only thing that he loved more than the political infighting was gloating over his victories. Or so it seemed to Jesse.

This one victory put the thinnest silver lining around the maelstrom of Jesse's life. Principal Peterson spent the time with her, not yelling, not screaming, not handing out ridiculous punishments, but, in a not so subtle manner, begging her to get her father to relent and give up more funding.

He didn't know that he was wasting his time and she didn't clue him in. James had *never* taken his daughter's advice when it came to running his towns and he never would. In truth she gave up even trying a long time before.

After a good thirty minutes of veiled pleading, Principal Peterson let her go, with a final word of advice: "Do yourself a favor and try to fit in."

She smiled as best as she was able to after such a stupid remark and assured him that she would do everything she could. As she left his office, she shook her head in disbelief and made her way to her biology class. It might have been smarter to wait out the rest of the final period in the bathroom, but she had to see *him*.

Due to how the world treated her, Jesse could boast of having had only two crushes in her life. The last was in the ninth grade and it was with a boy who would only talk to her when no one was around. It didn't last long. She couldn't like someone who was ashamed to be seen with her and who wouldn't stand up for her.

Now she could record crush number three. Despite the note he had written earlier that morning, she was crushing on him hard. When she entered the biology room she was forced to listen as Mr. Daniels blah, blah, blahed, on and on about the importance of the current lab, about how much of it would go to her grade, about the importance of being on time...and all the while she secretly wished that Ky would look up at her.

He never did.

And that was ok. Maybe even for the best. He probably was so anti-social for a reason and not a good reason either. But he was perfect as a dream. He would always be the handsome boy in her class who was never mean to her.

*What about the note from this morning, telling you to leave you the F*** alone?* her voice of reason asked.

Was it all that mean? Really? He didn't even spell the curse word out completely, which was kind of cute when she thought about it. If that was his greatest attempt at being mean, she would take it. She wished all the kids in school were *that* mean.

These thoughts filtered through her mind as she took her time messing about with the lab paraphernalia. She had no interest in the lab. As far as she could gather, it was a week-long experiment designed for two people. She had till the end of the week to finish it; three class periods. It wasn't going to happen, and she didn't care.

As things were going, she could count on passing only Calculus and study hall...and maybe lunch. English, art, and economics were all definite fails, while history was only a possible fail—she didn't have enough information yet. Biology was in a category of its own. Mr. Daniels didn't seem to have any particular resentment towards her, yet the way the class was structured, with partnered labs, it suggested she would always be behind.

Of course, her father would blame her for her grades. He never cut her a break, ever, and would likely ground her when he found out. This in itself was a bit of a joke. Where would she be going anyway? She had no friends at all. Her normal hangout, the local library, had been turned into a babysitters club by the presence of the town-killer. She couldn't even go for a walk if she wanted to.

Just then the bell rang and she got her wish. Jesse had been going over her pathetic life in a day-dreamy way when the shrill *brrrrinng* made her jump a little. It also made her realize that while her thoughts had been turning in her mind, she had been staring at Ky. She hadn't noticed and neither had he, but the second the bell rang Ky's head came up and he looked her straight in the eyes for the second time.

As before when they looked at each other, her full lips parted and her mouth came open in a small way. It was the best second and a half of her day. He then blinked, gave a little twitch of head, and turned away. Jesse sighed.

She didn't hop up and rush for the door like the rest of the class. What was the point? So people could stare? So they could knock into her? So she could hear her limerick for the hundredth time? All day she had heard snippets of it in the halls as people had passed. No thank you.

It also didn't hurt that she was practically alone with Ky. It was humorous to her as well. The longer she dallied, the longer he lingered. Finally when the halls went from shouts and laughter to an echoey silence, Mr. Daniels seemed to notice them.

"You better get going...it's getting late," he said with a glance at his watch. It was only a few minutes after three. How could anyone consider that late? Before walking out the door, she glanced again at Ky, but he refused to look up or in any way acknowledge her.

She found the hallway, strange. It was so quiet that she felt compelled not to disturb the silence and almost tiptoed along. Ky was quiet as well. Always the Ghost, he made just as much noise as one and she wouldn't have known he was behind her if she hadn't caught his reflection in a bulletin board as they passed. When she got to the rear door that led to the buses and student parking she paused and waited for the last of the cars to pull away before she ventured out into the chill air.

Her breath blew out smokey-white. It didn't bode well for her ride home, but anything was better than walking, especially after her scare from the day before. She planned to ride smack down the middle of the road on the yellow line, and in no way was she going to stop for strangers. That was the plan at least.

If riding her bike had been an option.

As she rounded the corner, she saw her bike as if it was a giant thing. Every surreal detail stood out clear against the backdrop of the red schoolhouse bricks: The rubber tires weren't just slashed, they hung from the bent rims in tatters, the spokes were sprung and twisted wildly as if they had been kicked in, the chain was missing entirely, and even the fork had been pulled back and apart.

Jesse stared. She was dimly aware of a rushing in her ears and then she found herself sitting on the ground; her legs had buckled beneath her and still she just stared. A movement next to her attracted her attention. It was Ky. Unperturbed, as always, he walked past her, climbed on his bike, and began to kick off.

"No, Ky! Wait...wait!" Jesse felt a deep panic that hadn't been there only a moment before. He was about to leave her. Just like the day before she would be very alone. Alone with the man who lurked in the forest.

She was up, sprinting to catch up to Ky. "Please Ky, don't leave me here! Please...please." She begged as she ran, but she begged in a hissing voice, afraid to announce to the world that once again Jesse Clarke would be all alone. She begged and Ky ignored her. He only went on riding in his usual unhurried manner and she might have caught up to him, but she ran out of building.

She went to the corner, but could not force herself to step out of the shadow of the school where she could be seen. "Don't leave me..."

Ky left her. His cruel indifference had her staggering. She was alone again. All alone...

The teachers!

The thought was like a slap to the face and brought her out of the sudden leaden depression that had gripped her.

The quickest way to get to the teacher's lot was to go across the front of the school, something that just wasn't possible for Jesse. There was no cover in the front of the school. It was wide open and she would be seen. A man could sit, tucked up in the hilly forest and see all the front of the school and he wouldn't have to be too far away to read the fear writ plain across her face.

The front was out of the question. Jesse spun and felt a pain in her ankle, a mild warning to take it easy—she ignored this and sprinted with everything she had round the long end of the building.

Hope and fear waged a war within her as she ran, and it was wild stupid hope that had the upper hand. This hope ran straight up against cold reason and rushed around it like water splitting around a stone in a river. Her hope ignored the fact that even the teachers were afraid of the killer. They had rushed out of the school just as fast as the children had the day before. But she still had Mr. Daniels.

Although he rushed about, always in a lather over minor details, he was also easily distracted. She was pinning her hopes that the science teacher had come across an interesting bug or a sparkly rock and that he could still be on the school grounds.

She was close. He was indeed just getting into his car as she rounded the corner of the building, but he was at the far end of the parking lot, a good fifty yards away. Jesse took two steps toward him and then stopped; the battle within her had swung decidedly in favor of fear.

Her growing fear had her calculating the odds of catching Mr. Daniels attention. They weren't good. Jesse was already gasping for breath after her long sprint around the building and she still had another half a football field to go. Not only that, the science teacher's inattentiveness would now work against her. She could see herself running along beside his car, pelting it with rocks, without him even batting an eye.

And if she wasn't able to grab his attention, what then? She would be out there exposed and so wonderfully, deliciously alone.

With that terror filled thought, she retreated back to the side of the building and crouched low near a small juniper bush. Painfully, she watched Mr. Daniel's car toddle off...slowly...very slowly. As it left on its unhurried way, tears filled her eyes, blurring her vision.

She could have caught up to him. But now it was too late.

Chapter 20

As the taillights of Mr. Daniel's car faded and Jesse's eyes filled even more, she shrank back further into the juniper bushes. Normally, she hated the stinging feel of the nasty shrubs but just then, with a panic making her bones ache, she welcomed it and she would have covered herself head to toe if she could have.

If

After a moment she realized there wasn't enough bush for her to properly hide in. Anyone even casually walking by could spot her with ease and it wouldn't take much for someone a little further away...someone slinking through the nearby forest to catch a glimpse.

Jesse knew she couldn't stay where she was, yet she didn't know if she could move either. The bushes were nothing, yet at the same time they were all she had. She squirmed in deeper and laid back, listening to her ragged breathing, feeling the thumping of heart.

A part of her felt silly. The reasoning part. *Why, with the whole town available to him, would the killer choose to hang out at the school after it let out?*

The bike! It was the killer who destroyed it and he knew that she would have to walk home.

Really? the voice asked. *You have no other enemies? And would the killer actually come up to the school in broad daylight and abuse a bike?*

No, the killer wouldn't do such a thing. He was clearly too smart for that or he would've been apprehended long before.

And didn't your father assure you that the killer would never go for you?

Yes, but he could be wrong. There is always a first time for everything.

Then get back to me when he is wrong, the voice replied, confident as always. As usual, it had all the answers to her questions, but what about her feelings? What did it say to the very real feeling that Jesse knew that she was alone and not alone, both at once?

Nothing...the voice was altogether silent on that pertinent fact. This little mental argument took all of ten seconds, but it was many minutes before she eventually got up. It was the cold that finally had her moving. Her tears began to sting her raw cheeks and her jungle boots, though stylish, did little to keep her toes from going numb. She knew, as all kids living in northern Michigan did, the dangers of hyperthermia.

When her shivering started to quake deep into her chest she knew that she had to move, but to where? Her home lay east of the school and slightly north of the ponds, but the killer's home lay in that direction as well. And it was in those woods that she had heard...whatever it was...the day before following along after her.

The main strip of the town lay directly east of her, just down the road, not far at all. Yet it might as well have been on the other side of the planet as far as Jesse was concerned. There was no way she was going to walk down that road again. That left her only heading west, which was the exact opposite that she needed to go, and south.

In her mind she pictured the maps of Ashton that hung on the walls of her father's office. If she could remember correctly, there was a subdivision called Johnson's Farm, to the south of the school. It was probably only a mile or two away through a belt of forest. Would the killer think to watch for her moving in that direction? Was he even around? She didn't know the answer to either question, but without any other options she decided to head that way.

Where she had been a nimble teen dashing around earlier, the cold had turned her into an old crone. Grimacing and hearing her joints pop and crack, she struggled to get up. She even stood hunched over like an old lady, with her arms tuck in close to her chest, trying to stay warm in her light leather half-coat.

Hurrying into the forest helped. It got her blood pumping and her muscles began to relax. Yet what helped her most of all was that nothing seemed to be following after her. The forest behind was silent; the forest in front equally so. This had a tremendous calming force on her mind and once her fears eased, her shivering disappeared altogether. There was no denying that she was still cold, but the affectation her body had assumed stemmed from a purely emotional state.

When she realized this, she smiled and then laughed...very quietly...at how she had reacted. Her reasoning mind had been correct after all: the killer hadn't been out there, or if he had been, he was sitting up in the woods north of Schoolhouse road freezing his gonads off. She laughed again, this time a touch louder at the thought.

Not necessarily. Her annoying reasoning voice was back.

The town of Ashton, with its sub-divisions that crept like tendrils throughout the hills and forests, covered somewhere north of twenty-five square miles. The reality of her situation was that he could be anywhere. *Anywhere.* The word was like an echo in her mind and the truth in it made her stop in her tracks. Just like that, fear crept back into her soul and with it came again the shivering. It started in her hands and quickly ran up her arms, before it then invaded her chest.

Rabbit like, she hunkered down on her heels and tuned all of her senses outward in an attempt to get a greater awareness of her surroundings. The day was cold, but bright and she was able to see fairly well. However, there was nothing to see but the snow-strewn forest. Her ears were perked up and without any wind to speak of the conditions were ideal. However, apart from the hammering of her heart and her barely controlled breathing there was nothing to hear.

After a minute of squatting she had to admit to herself that she was alone. Wonderfully perfectly alone. Oddly or maybe sadly, at that very moment she couldn't think of another person she wished was there in the forest with her. Yes, if the killer was around she would love some company, but since he wasn't...there was nobody. Not even Ky. What had just happened was too painful. It should have been expected, but it was still painful.

Standing, she let out a long slow breath and tried to decide if she had gone south enough. She had been tromping through the forest for a good ten minutes and her idea was to try to get in as deep as possible in this stretch of forest before turning east. What she didn't want to do was get all the way to the sub-division.

Being alone as she was, she would stand out, not only in the eyes of the killer, if he was around, but also to the locals. It would be an understatement to say that she wasn't liked and there was no sense making a target of herself. There was another reason she wanted to stay in the deepest part of the forest and that was despite it seeming to be the ideal place for a murder to occur, she actually didn't figure there was much chance at finding the killer there.

The murderer would be on the edge of the forest looking outward, waiting for a kid to come by all alone. Her horrifying trip into town the day before had been proof enough of that.

Goosebumps flared at the memory and she tried to shake them off. Walking would help she decided and turned south again, thinking to go on a few minutes more before altering her course. Unfortunately, she was off on her judgment of both time and direction. When she finally turned, thinking she was heading east, she didn't get very far when the land changed abruptly. Ahead of her about forty yards the forest seemed to suddenly stop and the land appeared to stretch out, flat and wide open.

"What the hell?" she whispered, craning her neck to try to see properly through the last of the trees. The land wasn't as flat as she first thought, in fact it was decidedly irregular. Jesse started forward, but it was only seconds before she realized what she was looking at. It was the Ashton cemetery. The very place where Mary Castaneda was found strangled to death.

"Oh crap!" Jesse hissed. Without thinking, she went rabbit again, sinking into a squatting position behind a gnarled old tree. Her senses were back on full alert and she stared all about her, straining her ears trying to hear the slightest noise. But there was nothing to see or hear. There was plenty to ponder on, however.

How on earth did Jesse find herself all the way out here? The cemetery was more west of the school than south. In addition, according to the maps, it was a good two miles away, which would mean that she had been walking for at least a half hour. Maybe more.

A quick check of her watch showed the time at 4:12 p.m.

"Oh crap," she hissed again, this time at the watch. Jesse couldn't take her eyes off the face of the watch, still un-believing. How could it be so late? How was she going to get home before dark?

The simple answer was that there was no way she could. This late in the year, sunset was a minute after five, but in the woods it would get dark even before then. And there was no question that she would have to stick to the woods now. The route home by way of the meandering streets was at least seven miles. Seven miles in which she would be totally exposed.

On the other hand the way through the woods was only about four miles, but it was not without its dangers. Jesse would have to cross between the two long ponds by way of the berm. That thought had her stomach aching. For good reason, she feared the choke point at the ponds. The killer could just sit like a spider in a web waiting for someone stupid enough or desperate enough to chance the quick way home.

When she thought on it, neither way sounded safe.

"Please, please, please," she whispered, pulling out her cell phone. "Please give me some bars. Please." It took half a minute for her phone to go through its "wakening" period as Jesse thought it and unfortunately, it was a half minute wasted. *No Service* shown steadily on the little screen.

Jesse didn't have half minutes to waste anymore. Without caring to turn off her useless cell phone she turned straight east and plunged through the forest. It wasn't a reckless plunge however. Jesse's fear was a counter balance unto itself. A part of her—the unthinking panicky part—wanted to run straight home as fast as she could. The other part of her—the over-analyzing part that thought the killer was behind every bush—wanted to creep along at a miserly pace out of fear of making even a single twig snap or just one leaf crunch beneath her jungle boots.

Together, these two pathetic halves kept her moving at a good steady pace. She wanted to head northeast to put her in the deepest part of the woods, however the ground was broken and hilly, and again she turned south by mistake. Cresting a hill, ten minutes later, she saw a slew of tired looking houses out past the edge of the forest. It was Johnson's Farm, the sub-division that she had hoped not to see.

"Crap!"

Jesse turned from the houses, tried to get her bearings and marched off again in the direction that she hoped was northeast. Her main problem lay in the fact that she was new to her surroundings, yet she had an elementary directional problem as well. She had heard, correctly, that the sun moved east to west, but on a southern course. By this she figured that if she stood facing the sun, she would be facing more or less south. She would've been correct if the time had been within two hours of noon. However with the sun almost set, it was dead in the west and so whenever she kept the sun on her right, she wasn't heading east as she thought, she was heading south.

Inadvertently she was not only taking the long way home, she was taking the most dangerous route as well. Instead of being deep in the forest where she thought she would be safe, she constantly found herself coming up on the edge of it.

"Am I lost?" she asked under her breath when she came up on an empty street. It was ten minutes to five...ten minutes to sundown...and it was already worrisomely dark in the woods. The idea of being lost struck her sharply and made her want to abandon the woods, but that empty street...the sight of it chilled her bones. It was so desolate.

She hoped this was the road that ran from the town proper out to the homes at Johnson's Farm and then on to the cemetery. If it was, as long as she kept it on her right, she would make it to the town eventually. With a tightening in her chest, Jesse stared up into the forest. Her idea of sticking to the depths of it was now out the window. Full dark would be upon her any minute and then getting lost was a guarantee...and who would bother to look for her if she did?

Don't answer that, her voice of reason said. Because she was tired and hungry and freezing in her stylish clothes, Jesse ignored her voice of reason. No one would come looking for her. Her parents, if they even noticed that she wasn't home, wouldn't budge except to get a pad of paper so they could list her punishments at being late.

How about her friends? What friends? Ky was the closest thing to a friend and he truly wasn't anywhere near one. He was just a cute boy with mental problems that Jesse had a crush on. The painful fact was that no one would look for her if she were lost.

That's not true.

"Shut up," Jesse said to herself. "Time to get moving."

She began walking again, still in the forest but keeping the road on her right. Sometimes she seemed to stray close to it if a steep hill pushed her in its direction, but mostly it was just a fading grey river barely seen through the trees.

Someone would look for you.

"Stop it," she said out loud and hurried faster.

You wanted to explore this line of reasoning. There is one person who would look for you. And he might be looking for you right now.

Jesse almost clamped her hands over her ears to stop the reasoning voice. Instead she sped quicker, almost jogging along, hoping to see something that would look in anyway familiar. Yet there was nothing...no buildings, no parks, no street signs. The road, for all she knew, went nowhere.

Just then an image of her came to her: she was following the road which ended at an abandoned mine, in its depths a shadow lurked.

She shook her head to clear the image away, but it was replaced by another one. This time of an abandoned hotel, where the doors hung crooked and the windows were shattered and a light in an upstairs room flickered as if from a sputtering candle. In each vision she knew who it was that waited on her arrival.

"Oh crap, oh, crap."

Her fear of the killer and of being lost seemed to be intertwining making each grow greater than they had been. Her panic made her careless and she stepped oddly on a rock and tripped. Her ankle flared and she nearly cried out, yet the possibility of what could be out there, searching for her, had her clamping her lips hard together despite the pain.

She hurried on with a slight limp, and was just wondering how much worse her day could get when, like it was a miracle vision coming to life before her very eyes, she saw lights twinkling in the early dusk. The town was there before her not two hundred yards away. She could see the brightly lit sign for the Ashton Bowling Center standing out like a beacon just down the hill.

"Thank God," she whispered. Powerful relief ran through her; the emotion was so strong that she had to grab a tree branch to keep from sagging to her knees. The feeling was a little astonishing as well. She had never been lost before and the sensation, looking back, was singular and indescribable. Like drowning it had to be experienced in all its horrible reality to be properly understood.

It took her over a minute to calm herself well enough to go on again, and she did heading directly for the lights. However as much as she wanted to Jesse didn't rush the final two-hundred yards. She flitted as stealthily as possible trying to keep to the deepest shadows.

"You're not out of the woods, yet," she whispered to herself. Not even close. If the killer was anywhere, it would be in precisely a spot like this. Just deep enough into the woods not to be seen, but close enough to come out if an opportunity presented herself. She knew she was exactly that sort of possibility, but still it came as a soul tearing surprise when she heard a male voice suddenly speak.

"Who is that creeping out there?"

He was very close only a few feet away and his voice held such a dangerous quality that Jesse froze in place and literally trembled like a rabbit caught out in the open by the wolf.

Chapter 21

"Who is that creeping out there?"

Her fear had paralyzed her to such an extent that Jesse couldn't move if she wanted to. Even the idea of screaming seemed well beyond her at that moment since she was finding it impossible to breathe.

"Come on...show yourself!" the voice challenged. The words held a combination of harshness, violence, and...fear? Was it possible that he was afraid as well? And if so didn't logic suggest that the speaker wasn't the killer; for after all what could make a killer afraid?

The notion unloosened the chains that were wrapped around her chest and just like that Jesse felt she could breathe again. Tentatively, she took a step forward, when suddenly someone else spoke up into the dark.

"It's just me, Mr. Mendel...Kyle's father?"

She recalled the voice with perfect clarity. It was only a few nights before that she had heard it under similar circumstances. Yet she didn't speak up. At his initial utterance, she was so shocked that there was someone else in the woods so close to her that her throat had locked up tight.

"Oh, Mr. Mendel...hey," replied the first voice, quivering a little as if its owner was getting over a scare. It seemed much younger, much more relaxed than it had only a moment before.

"I'm looking for Kyle," Mr. Mendel said, coming forward toward the younger man. "Are you a friend of his?"

"Ky? Well, I uh..." There was an uncomfortable moment of silence after he said this and it took Jesse that much time to figure out why. Ky was Kyle Mendel. It was like a light was thrown on her head and she understood perfectly the awkward moment. Ky didn't have friends, but how do you say that to someone's well-meaning dad?

You didn't. Instead you lied.

"Ky...yeah. We hang out sometimes. I don't know if you remember me. I'm John Osterman. My dad used to work down at the plant with you?"

"Oh right...Bill's kid," Mr. Mendel said in that friendly way of his. Jesse wondered if he spoke that way because of the way his son was so over the top anti-social.

"Look, I'd appreciate it if you didn't tell my dad I was out here smoking," John said. Only then did Jesse see the little ember in his hand. She had thought it to be one of the background lights.

"Sure...as long as I can bum a smoke."

Inside her Jesse felt a strange longing to be near people. She wanted to say something but was a little worried how they would react to her presence since neither seemed to see her in her all black attire so she spoke softly.

"Excuse me, I..." It was all she had time to get out.

"Holy Crap!" John practically shrieked. They both appeared to jump out of their shoes. With her relief at finding other people, she had become giddy and at their reaction she almost laughed.

"Who is that?" Mr. Mendel demanded. His sudden surprise made his voice strident and angry, which stopped Jesse in her tracks. She had been stepping out from the deeper shadows, yet now hesitated.

"It's me, Jesse...I met you the other night, at the berm. Remember?"

"Oh, yes," Mr. Mendel replied. He did not seem altogether happy and Jesse didn't really blame him; she had given him a tremendous fright. John Osterman didn't seem happy either, rather the opposite. He was a silent black shadow that seemed to radiate hate. She didn't recognize his name, but he probably knew hers just fine.

Because of the possible ramifications of that, Jesse silently thanked God for the presence of Mr. Mendel. Who knows what would have happened if she had stumbled across this John Osterman while alone.

"I'm sorry about scaring you like that," Jesse said, stepping out of the shadows and coming up close to Mr. Mendel. Because of the dark, she stood much closer to him than she normally would have and got a good a look at his face. The resemblance between father and son was obvious now she knew they were related. Mr. Mendel was handsome, a shade taller than Ky, and wore his thick hair in much the same fashion as his son. He also carried with him the same sort of intenseness.

At night like that, after her fearful trek through the forest, that intenseness had Jesse stepping back with growing alarm. His eyes were as black as the devil and though he said nothing, she could tell his emotions were running high. He was angry. More so than the situation warranted in Jesse's opinion; she took another step back, closer to John, whom she now silently thanked for his presence. Really what did she know about Jerry Mendel...almost nothing, except for the fact that he had one seriously messed up son. Perhaps Mr. Mendel was abusive and cruel.

"Really...I-I'm sorry about scaring you like that," Jesse stammered out. The silence which had accompanied her first apology had been unnerving and she had felt a dire need to break it. But this second apology was only met with more silence and was worse. "I-I saw Kyle," she said lamely, hoping to spark some sort of response.

It worked.

Mr. Mendel seemed to grow warm at the sound of his son's name. "Really...where?"

"The last I saw him, he was riding his bike down School House road. Just after school." Ky had been maliciously indifferent and had abandoned her. At the moment he had done it there had been hatred in her heart, but now she was clinging to his name.

"Oh, good...I get so worried for him." Mr. Mendel explained. "Are you a friend of his?"

"Uhh..." Jesse gave a glance back at John, foolishly thinking she might get some support. John said nothing. He brought his cigarette up and breathed it in. In the flare of the ember his eyes looked red. Jesse knew his face. He had been standing with Amanda in the hall after Ronny had knocked Jesse down.

Mother-pus-bucket, Jesse thought to herself. She had definitely found out how her day could have gotten worse. Here she was standing in a killer-infested forest with one man who was odd and unnerving and a boy that looked to want to break her face with his fists.

"I'm sorry, Mr. Mendel. I'm new in school, I don't have any...I'm not his friend...yet." She threw that last word in there for two reasons: she felt bad for a man whose son was so bizarre. And she was secretly afraid he'd grow angry again. She'd hate for him to go storming off in a tiff, leaving her alone with John.

Mr. Mendel didn't grow angry. He deflated and looked lost. "That's too bad. Kyle has so few really good friends anymore...but thankfully he has you, right John?"

"Yep...that's right." John was not a good liar, but Mr. Mendel seemed to want to be lied to. "Look, I gotta get back. I don't want anyone getting nervous about me being gone. See you later." This last he said to Jesse. The words made her chest tighten up again as she watched him head down the hill to the bowling alley. Were Ronny, Amanda and that weird blonde girl waiting for him? And would they be waiting on her in a few minutes?

Jesse waited until John was far enough way not hear her and then said to Mr. Mendel, "I have to go also...I have this big paper to write." Technically it wasn't a lie. She did have a paper to write, she just wasn't going to do it.

Mr. Mendel looked to have barely heard. He was staring down the hill at John's retreating back. "Do you think he really is friends with Kyle?"

"I don't know...probably."

The man smiled, perhaps not believing her. "I just hope so. Kyle doesn't have a lot of friends. Not since all of this happened." He waved his hand in the air indicating the woods or maybe the entire town. Jesse understood...not since the killer. "Would you like a ride home? You're not out of my way," Jerry added.

"No...thank you." The reply was instinctive, but sound reasons came to her a second later. Though she had met him twice, he was for all purposes a stranger. Secondly, Kyle was the way he was for a reason; very likely the reason was Mr. Mendel. Third, she just didn't trust him. Of course, she didn't trust anyone in the town just then, with the possible exception of Mr. Daniels, her biology teacher. She didn't trust Mr. Mendel because of the way he had reacted so oddly when she had scared him. Now she knew that might not be exactly fair since a lot of people would've reacted the same way, but trust was trust and it didn't cater to the whims of fair or even of logic.

Logic screamed facts into her mind: She was still a long way from home and the Shadow-man was still out there, stalking. There were moronic teens probably gathering even then for a "Jesse-hunt", and lastly Jesse was just straight up beat down. She was tired, hungry, cold, and in pain, but...

But she didn't trust him.

"Have a good night," she said with a quick wave goodbye. She left him and jogged down in the direction John had taken. Her ankle protested this and when she hit the flat open ground behind the bowling alley, she took to skipping, putting as little weight on her bad leg as possible.

Dangerous as it was she kept to the rear of the buildings, until she saw the Town Hall and then she raced for it. This was another reason she hadn't accepted a ride: her father's office was all of four minutes away from the bowling alley. Chest heaving, she was through the double glass doors in no time.

"Jesse... Jesse Clarke...to see...James Clarke...please," she asked as she expelled great gusts of air.

"Little late to be out jogging. Don't you think?" The receptionist asked. Though her tone and facial expression weren't exactly friendly, they weren't as nasty as they had been the day before. It was something at least. Jesse tried to smile at her little joke, however she was sure it was mostly just a grimace as she continued to gasp for air.

"My father..."

"Is not here."

This was so unexpected that Jesse couldn't quite wrap her mind around it. Twice she looked at the clock on the wall behind the lady and twice it showed a quarter after five. "Where is he?"

The receptionist seemed to consider not telling Jesse, but then she gave a little shrug. "He's at a meeting in Barton. Probably won't be back until late."

What was she going to do now? She had relied on her gut instinct and it had steered right into a corner.

"You can use the phone if you want to," the receptionist suggested. Jesse, who felt as though her brain had been replaced by an old toaster, only looked at the lady not understanding her suggestion. "To call your mother?" the lady added in a voice that was condescending rather than helpful. "You do have another parent, you know."

Jesse lips clamped down hard. What did this woman know about anything? Another parent? Together, Cynthia and James Clarke constituted about half a parent. "I have a cell phone...but thanks."

Turning away from the desk and the grim faced receptionist, Jesse pulled out her cell phone yet didn't dial. She hesitated knowing already the outcome of a call to her mother.

There will only be tears if you dial, her voice of reason spoke up.

Right as always, but what else could she do? The voice was quiet on this front. Yes tears would come and she had every right to them. In fact just looking at the cell phone she could feel them brewing in her eyes. Just then she hated the phone. It represented a world that she wasn't a part of.

In that world a pretty girl like her would have text messages from a hundred boys too chicken to ask her out in a proper way. She'd have a contact list so long that it would take five minutes to scroll all the way through it. Her phone would be as much a part of her life as her heart and that girl wouldn't be able to live without it.

That was a dream girl, living in a dream world. Jesse was not that girl. To her, the little black cell phone was nothing more than an accessory. It was supposed to be for emergencies, but deep down she knew it wasn't. It was her mom's way to feel good about herself as a parent: *I'm always a phone call away if you ever need me*, was a favorite line of hers.

Right. Sure she was.

In the two years that she owned the phone, Jesse had called her mother a dozen times in need of some sort of help. However, nothing ever constituted an emergency in Cynthia's eyes. And Jesse knew this time would be no different. All that would happen if she were to actually dial the phone is that she would be forced, once again, to face her harsh reality: she was alone in this world. There was no one who loved her, no one to protect her, no one to keep her safe and warm. The harsh reality was that she didn't have parents like everyone else did.

To them she was a prop in their upper-middle class theatrical production. Someone her father could beam proudly at and call, "Honey" when others were around and someone her mother could dress up and parade about at her endless functions if a daughter was called for to make Cynthia look better.

And then the prop was supposed to go back into storage and be forgotten until the next time it was needed. This is where Jesse always seemed to drop the ball. A prop wasn't supposed to make waves. *It* wasn't supposed to get in to fights. *It* wasn't supposed to struggle at school and *It* most definitely wasn't supposed to call *Its* mother when she was in a very important meeting—and she was always in an important meeting.

Jesse looked out the window, but with the light behind her all she saw was a strange ghostly image of herself. Her face seemed distinctly featureless, as if she could be anybody...or no one. Without a word, she put her phone away. Jesse wasn't blind to her reality, but all the same she didn't need to be reminded of the sadness of it anymore than she had to.

"Uh...ma'am?" she said to the receptionist. "All I got was voice mail. Do you mind if I wait here for my father?"

The woman's body seemed to droop a little. Clearly she wanted to say no, however she gave Jesse a forced smile. "Sure, but I'm locking up at a half past six and you won't be able to stay after that."

An hour...not much time for her father to get back. Jesse spent her time sweating out the minutes, hoping for the first time since she was just a little girl to see her father walking in the door. She used to like that very much. In fact, they used to be best friends, her father and her. His office had been her playground since she was a toddler and she had sat through more meetings than most adults would ever attend in their lives.

But then he took his first job as town manager. It was in a town rampant with such nepotism that it had been impossible for the previous town manager to fire anyone, since he was related to everyone. The hate had begun then for Jesse. It had started small and then gradually built, and at the same time her father's work began to engulf him.

In the next town they moved to, it was worse.

There the plague had been cronyism, where only those in favor got the good jobs and where only those who greased the right palms got the good contracts. It was a good ole boy network that James crushed under his heel, but in so doing he crushed his own daughter as well. The hatred was dreadful in that town. Jesse turned to her father, but he was too busy. She turned to her mother, but Cynthia turned to helping the poor, something far more self-fulfilling than actual parenting.

Now, in the Ashton Town Hall, Jesse stood staring out the window knowing she could only turn to herself.

"I have to get going now," the receptionist announced at 6:45. "I have to lock up."

"Of course," Jesse replied, smiling and looking the lady in the eye. The girl then took a big breath and held it for a span of three seconds, wondering if was going to be possible to push out the words that were on the tip of her tongue. Jesse needed a ride home. Her mom had told her she would be back after eight, which really meant after nine. Her father wouldn't be home until after ten.

And Jesse was afraid of the walk through the woods. There was a path, so getting lost wasn't an issue this time. The issue was the killer. No matter what her parents said about her not being a likely candidate to be murdered, Jesse felt that the Shadow-man had been near her since she first stepped foot in Ashton.

Jesse needed a ride home and it should have been a simple thing to ask this little favor...only her pride was too great and she couldn't bring herself to do it. After all this was the same woman whom she had made feel stupid only the afternoon before.

"Um..." Jesse said and then her mouth just sat open and her eyes bounced around. The moment became awkward.

"Yes?"

"Uhh...have a good night," Jesse finally said. Inwardly she groaned at her own stupidity. It seemed she would risk her life rather than risk damaging her pride. The receptionist... Jesse swore that if she lived through the night she would ask her father the woman's name...escorted her out the front door and then locked it firmly with a sound that fairly screamed to the dark night—*I'm small and helpless and all alone!* The woman hadn't stepped out with Jesse, she was still safe and warm inside.

"Great," Jesse whispered, swiveling her head back and forth, trying to take in the entire street all at once. At the moment there wasn't anything to see; all the buildings appeared dark and deserted, except the pool hall down the block. That one looked just as packed with people as it had the other night.

The streets were black and wet looking and she hated the idea of walking on them. She felt that she could be seen from a mile away, but without another option she hurried up the block.

Hoping that her all black attire would do something to camouflage her presence, Jesse kept as much as possible to the shadows and there definitely were shadows. The moon, looking like a lop-sided egg, was nearly full and very bright. It was almost bright enough to read by on the north side of the street, but on the other side it gave good gloom and Jesse swept along silent as a cat in her jungle boots.

Her destination was the library. There she would rest, get warm and hopefully summon enough courage to make the trip through the woods to her own little sub-division. She definitely felt that she needed the courage because just then, slipping along like a wraith, she saw shadows move in every dark corner. But then again she wasn't the only one.

"I just saw something move by that red truck," came a girl's loud whisper. Whomever it was seemed keyed up and the whisper carried like a stage whisper.

"Is it that bitch?" John Osterman asked.

Chapter 22

"Mother-pus-bucket," Jesse whined under her breath. She'd been caught by John Osterman and his friends. They were close and getting closer in a hurry. She could hear their shoes slapping the pavement as they ran toward her. It was an oddly hypnotic sound and she found herself near to being frozen into inaction by it. The sound also seemed to drain away the last of her energy and she gave in to the weak feeling in her legs by squatting down next to the car in front of her.

Jesse was seconds from being caught...seconds from being beaten, but strangely she forgot about her chain, with its heavy lock, which sat nestled like hard-coiled serpent in her pocket. Where her hands should have been digging at the weapon, they were instead gripping the rear bumper of a Chevy. The car had once been a bright blue, but was now sun-faded and rusting through.

Blue? She blinked at the car, feeling slow witted. They had mentioned a red truck, but this...

Slipping a touch to her right, Jesse was able to see the red truck that had been mentioned. It was four cars in front of her and as she poked her head out, two people came into view, circling the truck. They were searching for her.

In a flash, Jesse pulled herself back and going to her belly was able to watch from under the Chevy four sets of feet walking about.

"There's nothing here."

"I swear I saw something."

"What do we do?"

There was a pause as the little group took a moment to consider. Jesse didn't wait for an answer. The four of them were standing behind the red truck which meant that if she kept very low and got very lucky, Jesse could slip along the edge of the sidewalk to the next block that was all of twenty feet away.

She was close to making it unseen. The corner of the block was dominated by a long red brick building and just as Jesse darted around the corner, she heard a low shout from behind her.

"Right over there," a girl hissed. "I saw something move."

Rubber soled sneakers pounded up the block after Jesse. Yet she didn't run. After turning the corner she saw how fruitless running would be. The street was literally a canyon of brick. There was nowhere to hide. On both sides of the street the walls were flat save for a slight indention here and there where a darkened entrance lay. Worse, the closest parked car sat halfway up the block.

Jesse would never reach it in time. Her lame ankle was making her gimp along far too slowly. Fight or flight...both seemed impossible, which left only hiding as an option. With pain marring her pretty face, Jesse limped to the nearest doorway and pressed herself into it. It was set back only about a foot or so and anyone but a blind man walking by would see her with ease.

Almost too late did she remember her chain and it might have been better if she hadn't. Because Jesse feared that it would get stuck again, she yanked the chain out of her pocket right as she heard the first of the sneakered feet came around the corner. She froze, trying to will herself to meld with the shadows, unfortunately the lock at the end of its steel tether couldn't freeze.

"I swore I saw..."

Gently, the lock swung as a pendulum. First one way...

"...someone come down here."

...and then the lock swung the other way in a silent arc, until:

Tock—it knocked up against the brick. Jesse's heart leapt into her throat.

"What was that?" one of the girls asked.

"What was..."

Tock—the lock tapped again; much softer this time.
"That. Did you hear that?"

"Yeah, I heard it, Amanda," John Osterman said, sounding peeved. "It's goddamned water dripping!"

Tock—now the lock gave the brick only a light kiss on the cheek and it barely made a sound. The breathing of Jesse's tormentors made far more noise, but still they heard it.

"I guess you're right," Amanda said, perhaps hearing the sound differently in response to peer pressure. It was the only rational explanation to Jesse, who had heard the thunk of metal on brick three times and could mistake it for nothing else. But whatever the reason, Jesse was glad for it. The four teenagers did not venture any further down the apparently empty street.

"What are we going to do now?" asked the second girl; probably the blonde girl that Jesse had seen with Amanda. "I'm getting wicked cold."

"You're cold because you dress like a hooker," John said. "And don't roll your eyes at me. Your mom said the same thing, and so did Amanda."

"I didn't! I swear. All I said..."

"Enough!" John interrupted. "We'll go back to the Town hall. Maybe she's waiting for her dad there."

That seemed to end all discussion. Quickly, and in renewed silence, the pack of human shaped hyenas, as Jesse saw them, strode off in the direction Jesse had just come from.

"That was freaking close," Jesse sighed, letting her body go limp. As she sagged against the wall, the lock thunked against it once more. "And you!" she said to her lock and chain, holding it up at eye level as if it were a wayward cat that she had by the scruff. "You're supposed to be on my side." The mute lock only gleamed dully in the bright moon light.

"Apology accepted. Let's go," Jesse whispered.

After looking up and down the street with all the timidity of a doe in hunting season, Jesse took a right and limped at her quickest possible limp toward the library. Compared to the town, which looked to have died the moment the sun had set, the library was like a beacon of warmth. Every bulb in every socket seemed to be burning away. It lit up the night and drew Jesse in as if she were a moth in summer.

And the warmth wasn't an illusion. When Jesse stepped in to the foyer she was giddy with it. She was giddy for another reason as well; the old biddy who had been supervising the mayhem on Sunday night wasn't in sight. A completely different old biddy was at the front desk, this one looked as wholesome as Mrs. Claus.

Jesse liked the mental picture this conjured up. So much so that she didn't spoil it by introducing herself or hanging around for the whispers to start and the hating to begin. Instead, she made her way down one of the back aisles and noted with even more giddiness how relatively empty the library was. There were probably *only* about two-hundred kids running about the place and Jesse was able to find a table in a secluded spot.

The table wasn't exactly unclaimed. There were backpacks sitting unattended on the backs of the chairs, but since they sported Hello Kitty's annoying face, Jesse simply used her superior status as a senior in high school and moved them to the next table over.

"What a freaking night," Jesse said to the ceiling. The moment she had sat down a wave of exhaustion had her leaning back in her chair drowsing. It was the heat coupled with her body draining stress from her every pore that had her suddenly yawning.

"Gotta stay awake," she mumbled, stripping off her leather jacket. This helped a bit, as did taking off her jungle boot and examining her injured ankle. There was a blue crescent bruise under the swelling. Slowly, painfully she began to work her foot in little circles, trying to loosen up the ligaments.

"This is our table. You're sitting in my chair."

A gaggle of what looked to be sixth graders had walked up and now stood trying to appear tough enough to force an older girl off their table. The girl who had spoken was a pig-nosed, little thing with a brassy voice. Clearly she was used to getting her way.

Jesse stretched and settled in comfortably. "How bout we share? There is a table right there with an extra chair. Drag it on over here."

"I don't want to," pig-nosed replied. "I want to sit right where I was. I'll tell Ms Somersby if you don't move."

"Do I look afraid of Ms Somersby?" Jesse asked, giving the girl a cold hard stare. The girl had nothing to say to this, but one of her friend's did.

"What's that for?" She was pointing at the table. Jesse's lock and chain sat there, looking too much like a weapon.

Jesse put a smile on her face and dragged the heavy chain off the table. "It's a lock for my bike. You guys act like..." Jesse paused as all the girl's raised eyebrows of incredulity. "What?"

The blonde, as leader, spoke for the rest, "You rode your bike here?"

For the first time in hours...for the first time since she watched Ky ride away and leave her to her fate, Jesse thought about her bike. Her dad was simply going to kill her.

"I didn't ride actually. My bike was...it has a flat. I had to leave it at the school; I walked here." The girl's all rolled their eyes at this. "What? You don't believe me? Here, feel my hands." They were only just thawing out. The girls were all properly impressed.

"You really walked here? Are you crazy?" the blonde asked. Before Jesse could answer the quietest girl in the group, and the smallest, spoke up.

"I'm thinking she's new in town and doesn't know any better." Jesse nodded at this and the girl continued, but with narrowed eyes, "That's not a bike lock and that's not a bike chain. And it if it was it would still be on your bike, even if you did have a flat. So why do you have it?"

Jesse like her immediately. "What's your name?"

"Emily Johnson. What's yours?"

"Jesse," she replied simply, as always reluctant to give out her last name. With a warm smile that the girls probably rarely got from a teenager, she added, "Have a seat, girls. I won't bite."

They looked at each other for a moment and then as one, they scrambled for chairs. Emily was shoved out of the way and had to content herself with dragging over the extra chair. Jesse skootched over so that the smallest girl there could be near her.

"I like your boots," Emily said picking up Jesse's jungle boot and giving it a quick inspection.

Not to be out done the blonde spoke up then. "My name is Allison. I like your jacket. I'm going to get one of those for my birthday. I'll probably get those boots too. Are they Italian?"

Jesse had to keep from snorting with laughter. She didn't want to scare away the girls so quick, after all. They made as good a camouflage as she was likely to get in a library. Sitting alone in her black outfit she would have stood out like a sore thumb. But with the girls all around her, she could slink down low in her chair and there was a chance that someone might miss her if they were looking for a solitary girl.

"They're not Italian. They're Jungle Boots made for the Army," Jesse explained, letting the girls pass the boot around. "I gotta tell you. They may be stylish as hell, but my feet are freezing." They were too. Jesse had to get her boot back on before her toes froze right off. However, she had to rewrap her ankle first. Part of the reason it had been hurting so bad was that the ace bandage had uncoiled itself, making a lump in her boot.

"What happened to your eye?" one of the girls asked.

The truth...tripping while running in a panic...was too embarrassing to say. Instead Jesse went with what she hoped was a mysterious shrug.

"What happened to your nose?" Allison asked. This elicited more that a shrug.

"Why what's wrong with my nose?" Jesse replied, running her hand along her pert little nose. There didn't seem to be anything wrong with it.

"It's bent a little...that way." The girl waved vaguely to the right. Jesse glanced at the window and saw her reflection and her bent nose. She touched it, pushing it back where it had once sat. It didn't stay.

"Oh, that's just from a fight." She went back to lacing up her boot.

"Is that why you have the chain?" Emily asked, couching her voice in conspiratorial whisper. "Are you expecting to fight someone?" There was a touch of early onset hero worship in her large brown eyes and she was so cute that Jesse wanted to ruffle her hair.

"You can't be too careful, especially in this town. If that freak Harold Brownly thinks..." Jesse stopped in mid-sentence as all the girl's eyes went wide in real fear. "What?"

The sixth graders all looked at one another and then their blonde leader nudged Emily. "Why me?" the girl asked, but she was only nudged again. Emily crouched low as if this would make her words harder to hear. "Never say his name. He can hear you. No matter where you are. And that..." she moved even closer and spoke even lower. "That chain can't hurt him. Nothing can hurt him."

Jesse nearly scoffed, except she noticed the flare of goose bumps on the girl's skinny arms. "Are telling me that this guy had magic powers?" She tried to ask it without sounding completely skeptical.

All the girls nodded.

"He gets his powers from the dead," Allison said, warming to the subject. "He can walk through walls and turn to shadows. If you ever see his giant shadow, just run!"

Now it was Jesse's turn to get the goose bumps as she recalled the Shadow-man in the forest. She shook off the image, knowing that it couldn't be true. "How can you possibly know any of that? I don't want to sound mean or anything, but has anyone *seen* him walk through walls?"

"The police have...sort of," Allison said. This elicited a round of head bobbing from the other girls. "They had his house surrounded for the last two years and he still got past them to do...*you know what.*"

"Even the police can't watch someone around the clock for two years," Jesse answered back. "It's not possible. They probably got a call somewhere else and..."

All four of the girls were wearing the same—*Sorry but you're wrong*—expression and each was shaking their heads at her. Emily piped up in her little voice, "He only...ya know...does *it* right around the Christmas break. That's why they call him..." She dug in her bag like mad, found a pen and paper, and wrote, *The Christmas Killer*.

Her handwriting was beautiful almost like calligraphy; the words were not.

"And there's more," Allison said, nudging Emily in the ribs. Emily steadfastly refused to write or say whatever it was that the blonde wanted her to. She went even so far as to throw her pen away. None of the girls would write it, either. Allison steamed at this rebellion to her leadership, yet she lacked the guts as well and left Jesse clueless what was so important. The girls then began a secret/silent conversation between themselves as only friends who had grown up together could do. They would raise eyebrows, tilt their heads suggestively, jut their chins, or purse their lips. All of which Jesse followed as if it were Greek.

Eventually, she turned to the window to consider what had been said and what hadn't. Her voice of reason stated with confidence that it was all a myth. The rest of her however, had seen the goose bumps, had watched the girls turn pale, and knew in her heart that something wasn't right about this. She was just mulling over the entire conversation a second time when something on the other side of the window snagged her eye.

Outside the library a familiar face stood under a street light. It was Ky. He was staring out into the forest in the direction of the berm. Jesse could see his breath in wispy clouds. They grew heavier and faster, puffing out of him as though he were hooked to a steam engine and then he began walking with deliberate strides toward the ponds.

"He's due," Allison stated clearly, breaking Jesse from her trance of watching the boy. All the girls nodded in agreement.

At first Jesse thought that they were talking about Ky, but then she realized they were talking about the killer. "He's due? When?"

What came out of Allison's mouth was almost lost on Jesse. She had positioned herself in the back corner and had a great view of this part of the library. Thirty-five feet away John Osterman, flanked by Ronny, Amanda and the blonde girl with the bad make-up came strutting into view.

"Saturday or Sunday at the latest," Allison was saying. Jesse heard, but only on a sub-conscious level. The rest of her mind was taken up with her advancing enemies. "So no matter what you do don't go out alone in the next few days. He has to...*you know*...do it."

Jesse nodded, but as she did, she slipped down even lower in her chair and just then John Osterman's eyes swept right across her. He was looking for a single girl in black, but he wouldn't be fooled for long. With a casual move, Jesse knocked the piece of paper with the words, *The Christmas Killer* off onto the floor. Almost simultaneously she ducked down to get it.

Her hands were shaking. The four of them wouldn't do anything in the library, but she knew if they found her they would definitely do something when the building closed. Jesse grabbed Emily's pants and literally pulled her under the table.

"Listen, I need a huge favor, please," Jesse asked with a voice that quavered in her throat. The little girl nodded with big eyes; she was nervous as well at this sudden odd behavior. "I need you to run to the front desk and yell out as if I was leaving. Say...*Bye* Jesse...really loudly. So we can hear it back here, Ok? Can you do that?" The girl nodded again. "Go, now. Run!"

Jesse helped Emily with a push from under the table. The other sixth graders were all very curious and asking questions. "No matter what don't look under here," Jesse commanded. "Pretend you're doing homework, or there's going to be trouble."

"What kind of trouble?" Allison asked.

Jesse shushed her and then peeked her head around Allison's legs. She could see John Osterman moving slowly toward the back corner of the library. He seemed concerned as if he really expected to have seen Jesse by now. He was even checking corners where smooch-athons were taking place and under desks where nothing was taking place except for at Jesse's table. He was getting close.

"Bye Jesse," Emily's voice floated back. John Immediately perked up. "It was nice meeting you. You'll have to tell me where you got those cool boots. Bye."

Jesse sincerely hoped, for Emily's sake that she would stop right there. As the little girl was going on about the boots, Jesse could see Ronny tearing up the main aisle for the front door and knew that if Emily kept going it might not be pleasant for her. A second later, John abandoned his search as well, and as he did, Jesse scrambled out from beneath the table, grabbed her belongings and raced for the back door.

Chapter 23

A braying alarm cried out immediately when Jesse banged open the back door of the library. At the sound of it a cringe lined her pretty face but she didn't slow down. To slow down meant more trouble than she was ready to handle just then. So she sprinted for all she was worth for the forest trail that led to the berm. There were two hopes in her heart: one- that Harold was on the other side of town and two- Ky was somewhere just ahead of her.

Ky was the first thing that she had looked for when she made her escape from the library. He was nowhere in sight, yet that didn't mean all that much. His lead on her couldn't have been more than thirty seconds and he never really seemed to hurry anywhere. Even as she was sprinting down the faded manicured lawn of the library, she knew that Ky could be on the berm just strolling along.

That was her hope at least.

But to fulfill her hope, she had to get under cover before Amanda and her friends figured out that it was she who had slipped out the back while they had been staring at a whole lot of nothing in the front. Seconds later, Jesse made it to the supposed safety of the dark forest, only it was at the expense of her ankle.

It had her grimacing with each step and every once in a while a sharp groan would escape her. Regardless she carried on down the hill and very soon she could see the two ponds stretching out farther than she could see in the dim light. The berm was visible to her as well and on it a lone figure was making his way across.

It was Ky...or at the very least it was not Harold Brownly, the Shadow-man. The person was far too small to be the killer.

As fast as she could, and it wasn't very fast because the trail was steep here, Jesse climbed down to the berm and began dragging herself across the wide-open space. Halfway across she felt herself flagging. It seemed like she had been under the strain of being chased for hours and there was very little left in her tank; nothing but fumes. Her feet began to weigh her down and her good leg was threatening to cramp up again.

Hope seeped from her as she realized that although she was limping along as fast as she could, and Ky was taking his time as always, she wasn't catching up to him.

This had her nerves frayed to the point of breaking and her breath came ragged in and out, not only because she was exhausted, but also because she just couldn't help it.

Jesse had assumed she would be able to catch up to Ky and now that she wasn't, her fear of being alone in the dark grew. And as she lurched along, she began searching the hills and forests ahead of her, seeking out the massive shadow that would denote Harold Brownly. He was in each one. Each and every one held a killer. Her eyes went wild, darting to each in turn, looking for any movement, and time and again she stumbled, not looking at the trail in front of her

By the time she crossed the berm, Jesse didn't know if she could go on. The forest trail on this side of the ponds was a half-mile long and surrounded by land that was very rugged and thickly wooded. The shadows here were beyond count. Within seconds tears came to her. She tried to stop them by reminding herself of her no tears rule, but that was just a joke. No power on earth could've stopped those tears...except the power that Harold Brownly possessed. Death would stop the tears. In fact, death would stop them cold, they would freeze in perfection right there on her dead face.

Off to her left a sound came to her of something snapping, like a man walking in the woods. If she'd had the strength, she would've run in a blind panic to who knows where, but she didn't. She didn't have any strength left at all and instead of running, her legs folded at the knees and very neatly, she knelt—waiting on her coming doom.

The sound on her left continued. At first, she thought it was coming right at her and she shivered in fright at whom it might be, but then she realized whoever was walking was going to miss her. The man was heading diagonally across her front. Like a slap, the realization of what the noise was had her reeling on her knees. It was Ky. Just then she remembered that the path swung out in a big loop. He was on the far side of the loop and was now heading to cross in front of her.

Jesse couldn't remember how far in front, but her best guess was that it was only a couple hundred yards or so. There was a chance that she could catch up to him...but only if she left the path. Of course this meant that there was also a chance that in the dark Jesse wouldn't be able to find the path again. And that she'd spend the rest of the night stumbling around in the woods until either hypothermia claimed her...or she found the Shadow-man.

"I can't do this," she whispered, to the night. "I'll get lost for certain." That seemed like a true statement. The woods around her were dense and in the dark there were no landmarks for her to orient on; everything looked the same.

You don't need landmarks, you moron, her voice of reason said. *You have a beacon right in front of you. Just follow it.*

Beacon? The moon was behind her and the only thing in front was her shadow, long and dark on the snow. Just then she realized that it stretched out perfectly in the direction that she needed to go. There was her beacon! Wasting no time, Jesse was up and following after her shadow with her head hung low like a bloodhound. She was dreadfully afraid of steering herself off course, so it was that she never looked up until she stumbled across the path a few minutes later.

Then she was happy in a ridiculous way. Her guts had been churning over the idea of missing the path and now that she was on it her relief was so great that she actually cried and laughed at the same time. It was hard to tell which was which. They both sort of mingled on her face and in her chest, making it tight.

However, the laughter dried up, while the tears continued. They slid down her cold cheeks ignored.

She had been waiting on Ky, staring down the path and at first she thought that he had managed to saunter his way past her as she had dogged her own shadow. Then she heard someone coming...only they were coming from the wrong direction! The sound was coming from her right, up the path toward her home, which didn't make any sense.

Had Ky gone up the path a little ways, turned around and come back down? If so why? Certainly not because she was following him. He was too determined to ignore her ever to allow her presence to change his course.

But then who...?

Sudden realization sent her staggering against a squat tree that stood hunched over the trail. What a fool she had been! She had been so afraid of stepping off the trail, so afraid that she would never find it again, when really she should have been afraid to ever set foot on it in the first place. The path that she was standing on not only led to her home, it led to the killer's home as well.

She had known this all along, but for one reason she had ignored it. The reason was Ky. He was a charm against the Shadow-man. Everyone in the town feared the killer, all but Ky. He went about alone where they traveled in packs. He strode the forests, while they kept to their cars. It made no sense. Even Mr. Mendel was afraid for him. He was always out searching for Ky...and where was Ky during those times?

A dread thought dawned on Jesse. Maybe Harold Brownly wasn't a killer after all. Maybe he couldn't walk through walls or overhear conversations from miles away. Maybe he just sat in his home while someone else walked about the town doing the killing. And if anyone could eavesdrop, it was Ky. No one saw him when he was around, no one paid attention, but that didn't mean Ky was oblivious. He heard everything.

Maybe Kyle Mendel was the killer. His disguise: a handsome, apple-cheek, all-American boy, was perfect— while Harold was practically an ogre. It wouldn't be the first time people were judged wrongly by appearances.

"Oh my God," Jesse whispered. She had been following after the killer all along. Just then she felt the first flakes of a fresh new panic settle over the dirty remains of the old. Panic was like the snow in Michigan. It never really went away until the sun had been hot on it for a long time.

If panic had any use in the evolutionary model Jesse didn't know what it was, but her panic just then seemed particularly useless. She froze in place, standing next to the tree. She didn't even have the sense to try to duck around it, yet it would have hardly mattered. He was on top of her before she knew it.

Kyle Mendel came out of the night, looking like the angel of death. His eyes, like his father's, were dark and intense, they swept up the path, and there was something in them. To Jesse's mind it was blood lust. The ruddy planes of his face were no longer handsome. They were hard, twisted into a challenging glare. In his hand he held what looked like a short stick. However as he stopped just feet from Jesse, she heard a very quiet and very unsettling sound: *snick*.

It wasn't a stick he had been carrying, it was a switchblade. The razor edge of it caught the light and it glimmered up at Jesse, hypnotizing her. Though probably only four inches long, the blade was immense in her eyes.

"Is it my turn?" Ky hissed out.

Jesse dragged her eyes from the knife and saw a look of derangement on Ky's face. It was hard to miss, he was right there. Yet he didn't see her. Because of her black clothing and the fact that she had remained perfectly motionless his eyes had taken her for just another shadow.

"Don't ignore me!" he commanded speaking down the path. "Is it my turn, finally?"

His turn? What was he talking about? Very frightening thoughts went through her head in the time it took for Ky to turn and see Jesse standing next to the tree. His turn? Did he and the Shadow-man take turns killing? Was that it? Was that why the Shadow-man had never been caught? He had an accomplice? Or was Ky his apprentice? Learning the art of murder at the knee of his fell master?

"You..." Ky whispered at the sight of her. Mentally, he seemed to be going in two directions at once: the hand that held the switchblade came up and the deadly point was square in Jesse's face, but at the same time his eyes lost their deadly look. His face as well, no longer appeared as cruel as it had. The muscles there were slack, so that his mouth came open a little.

Two seconds clicked by in this fashion with them silently staring at each other and then, without warning, the boy launched himself on Jesse. He was so fast. All she saw was a blur of blue denim and a single silver-white line of the knife as it shot at her. For her part, Jesse had never been slower. Exhausted and stunned, she moved in slow motion, as if she were under water, or in the midst of horrible nightmare.

It felt like a nightmare.

In a blink, Ky had a hold of her shoulders and spun her like a top. Just like that, she was staring up at the moon. It never seemed brighter. Her vision tunneled on it and the world around her disappeared. Yet terribly this didn't last. In her periphery, she saw the knife coming for her throat. It looked deadly sharp. It felt deadly sharp.

Chapter 24

Jesse felt the skin parting on her throat as the knife came to rest just above her carotid artery. Her heart thumped madly and she could feel her pulse tempting the knife. The hand that held the blade was steady like a rock. Even on the verge of murder, Ky was altogether unflappable.

His other hand was in her hair and his grip was like steel. He had her head pulled way back and she panted out her fear up at the night sky.

"If you make any sound...you will die," he whispered in her ear.

This statement was beyond argument. But at the same time there were things that were outside her control. Most were little things: such as the fact that she had wet herself when she first felt the knife. Luckily, she had just gone at her father's office and only a warm trickle came out. And then there was the fact that her legs wouldn't stop shaking. They trembled like a newborn lamb standing in the snow. These were small things. Unimportant things.

What was important to Ky was that her panting was accelerating. She sounded as though she had just sprinted a mile and was getting louder.

"Quiet down!" he whispered harshly. His grip in her hair was now painfully sharp and her neck was being cranked back at a nasty angle. Though desperately she wanted to please him, the pain only added to her fear and her panting became strident.

Just then, up the trail, something—a branch or a dry twig—snapped. It was a small sound, but it could only mean one thing: someone was coming. Ky spun the both of them around and ducked in close to the tree. Another sound—a kicked pebble that hopped among its larger cousins came to the pair. Whoever it was had moved closer. Jesse's panting had practically ceased at the first sound and now she drew in a big breath. This could be her only chance. If she waited and did nothing her death was a guarantee...the killer was overdue after all.

She thought that she would take her chances and scream, however Ky had other plans. Just as she drew in her breath, he released her hair and slammed his hand over her mouth, crushing her lips against her teeth. She could taste the metal of her own blood on her tongue.

"*He* will kill you if he hears you," Ky said. Each word had come from his lips with all the power of a baby's breath. But Jesse only needed to hear the first word: *He*, before she quieted in his grip.

It was the way Ky said it, as if *He* was something powerful, something singular and extremely dangerous, something to be feared above all else. Jesse was properly afraid. *He* had to be the Shadow-man. *He* could mean no other.

And she was right. Harold Brownly came down the trail. For such a giant of a man he moved with surprising stealth. His massive shoulders were at times as wide as the path, yet he barely touched any of the grasping branches that seemed to reach out for him. Behind him, he left tracks that were too big to be believed, yet somehow his tremendous feet always found the sturdy rock or the new powdery snow to come down in. He was nearly as quiet as the shadows that he wrapped himself in.

It was difficult for Jesse to get a true grasp of the man's size. For one she had never seen anyone nearly so big and two, he wrapped himself in a flowing black cloak of some sort. Even his head was hooded against the cold, so that his features were unknowable.

Yet his great bulk was nothing compared to the aura that surrounded him. Being in his presence had opposite affects on Jesse and Ky. Her heart seemed to stop, her breath was caught in her throat, and her trembling ceased. She was for all intents and purposes, a statue— sculpted out of pure fear.

On the other hand, Ky, once unflappable, was now the one trembling. And now it was his breath beginning to sound like a pant. And it was his heart that Jesse could feel thumping into her back. Ky wasn't the terrifying person he had been, not even close. The knife was no longer at Jesse's throat. Uselessly he had it out toward Harold, and somewhere in the last few seconds the blade had changed from fearsome to pathetic. It looked tiny against the immensity of the Shadow-man and what's more Ky was no longer its master. The blade danced about in his grasp as if it was alive and trying to escape his fingers.

Just as Ky did, the Shadow-man came down the trail and paused only feet from where Jesse and Ky stood in the shadow of the gnarly tree. However, unlike Ky, Harold didn't look over and instead went on again after a brief second. Until he was out of sight, the two teens watched him, still in their odd semi-violent embrace.

"Go home," Ky whispered in her ear at the same time that he released her.

Jesse didn't know what to think. The boy had attacked her, threatened to kill her and was now letting her go? Wasn't he afraid that she would go the police?

Her hand went to her throat. It came away wet. "What...what just happened?" she asked in a tiny but incredulous sounding voice.

Ignoring her as was usual, Ky stared down the path. He was still shaking yet his teeth were clenched and she could see him nodding his head in a small way.

Jesse wasn't going to be ignored. She grabbed him by the arm. "Tell me! What's going on?"

"I saved your life. Now go home," he responded, shaking off her hand. He then turned away and began to head off down the path...toward the berm...toward the Shadow-man. Jesse rushed after him and again grabbed him.

"No..." she started to say.

He turned and shoved her to the ground. "Go. Home." He tried to appear tough, but his knife-hand still shook, sending out dancing shards of moon light.

"Are you going to try to kill him?" Jesse asked, amazed. "With that?"

Ky sighed; it was a rattling shaking sound. Her words were clearly undermining whatever courage he had left. "Somebody has to do it." He turned and walked away again.

Unmindful of her sprained ankle, of her exhaustion and even of the Shadow-man, Jesse hopped up and charged at Ky. This time she didn't grab him by the shoulder but went straight for his right hand. Before he knew exactly what was happening she had a hold of it and bit him in the fat part of his palm below the pinky.

With a grunt of pain, Ky's hand sprang open and Jesse had the knife. She would end his little adventure the quickest way she knew how. Turning, she threw the switchblade out into the forest, figuring with the dark and the thickness of the woods he would never find it. That was the plan at least. She threw the blade, but by some foul miracle it knocked off a tree and bounced back to land right at Ky's feet.

He grabbed it up quick. "If you want to die come with me. If not, go home."

"I'll call the police...I have a cell phone." She started to reach into her bag, but he put out a warm hand to stop her.

"The police get thirty calls a day about Harold this time of year. And if you do call, he'll come for you...and there'll be no stopping him. Just please, go home."

This was the end of the conversation for Ky. This time he didn't walk away, he jogged down the path away from her. She knew there would be no catching him, not with her ankle. She watched him until the dark had him all to itself. With an ache in her chest she went home.

It was a long quarter mile. She took pains to move as quietly as possible, not out of fear of Harold Brownly, but because she was desperately anxious to hear Ky's screams. The night was quiet for her all the way home.

Was this a good thing or bad thing?

Her voice of reason was quiet in regards to the question. In fact it had been quiet since she had run into Ky.

After letting herself in through her front door, Jesse limped around the house making sure that every window and every door was locked up tight. She then made sure that every light was on...except her bedroom light. This was purposely kept dark so that she could have the best view of Harold's house as possible.

With a fresh ace bandage on her ankle and her foot propped up, Jesse ate her dinner sitting in the dark of her bedroom. She kept a watch on the killer's house until eight o'clock when something else grabbed her attention. The killer's house was catty-corner to her own. But who owned the house *directly* behind hers, Jesse had no idea...right up until Ky turned on his bedroom light.

"Holy crap!" she spewed.

Her mind was straight up boggled by this. No wonder the boy was all messed up in the head. How do you live next door to a known killer like Harold Brownly your whole life? And Ky's father! She had new respect for him. It must have been a nightmare trying to raise a family under those circumstances. Yes, he might be a bit over-protective, always running about after Ky, but she couldn't blame him one bit. In fact, Jerry Mendel made her own father look *less than*.

For the next couple of hours, Jesse took turns simmering with anger at the way her own parents behaved, worrying about what tomorrow would hold, and secretly watching Ky. There was also time allotted to fantasizing about Ky as well.

The boy was devilishly cute *and* had saved her after all. Perhaps the rescue was not in a manner that would ever find its way into a romance book. But it was something...in Jesse's world it was a very big something.

Near ten, Ky took off his shirt, which was very nice and then turned out his light, which wasn't. A little while later Harold Brownly came home. Jesse slunk back even further in the shadows of her room. There wasn't much to see, that is other than his large shadow which always seemed to be on the move, as if he were a chronic pacer. It was creepy to watch a killer like that.

"I bet he talks to himself," Jesse said.

She couldn't tell from her angle, not even if she borrowed her father's binoculars, something that she was definitely planning on for the next night. A close-up image of Ky shirtless came to mind.

"Jesse?" Her father called out suddenly, making the girl jump. "We're home."

"Ok," Jesse replied, trying to repress the moment of guilt she'd had when her father had broken in on her little fantasy. A moment later, she could hear his heavy tread on the stairs and she steeled herself for what was coming. When he opened her door he didn't look happy. Yet his look was nothing compared to hers—she was worlds beyond unhappy.

"Where were you today?" she demanded as if she were the parent and he the wayward child. "I needed you!"

Her father was silent for a moment. He seemed unsure whether to answer her or yell back. James decided to answer in a quiet conversational voice, "I was in a meeting. I was trying to talk two different manufacturers into moving their operations to Ashton. There's a die casting plant in town that is vacant and it would be perfect for either of the two companies. Does my alibi pass your approval?"

She sighed. "Why do you even care about this town? These aren't good people."

"You don't care about them?" He gave her a very skeptical look and she dropped her eyes. "I chose this town and these people. I made a promise to help. That should be good enough for you. Now it's my turn for questions," James said.

"Let me guess," she shot out quickly. "You got a call from Principal Peterson?" He nodded, made to reply, but she broke in again. "And you are *very* disappointed in me, I know."

James sat down on her bed and leaned back as if he were going to stay a while. "Keep going. You're not done yet."

"Sure...what else did Jesse do today?" She got up to pace but her ankle sent her the message that it was better just to sit for the rest of the night. "Jesse was...flippant, disrespectful...and oh yes, she also lied to a teacher. She told him that the only reason that she was advocating her father's policies was out of love, which clearly isn't the case."

He'd been frowning before, but now he practically glowered. Jesse didn't care. "I can promise you, Dad that it won't happen again tomorrow. I'll be a perfect angel."

"And this is because..."

"I won't be going to school tomorrow."

"Really?" James said.

"Yes, really!" Jesse couldn't help herself and got up to hobble back and forth in her room. "What would be the point? I've been there for two days and I already know that I'm going to fail five of my classes." For emphasis she held up her hand with the fingers splayed. "Oh, and of course everybody hates me. I'm not talking about a few of the students...I'm talking *everyone*."

"I think you're probably exaggerating."

Jesse had to laugh at that. "I'm not. For once, trust me on this. You should see my bike. It's not just a little destroyed, it's completely destroyed. They even took the time to bend the fork. Who does that? And the limerick..." Jesse stopped quickly. The limerick was just too painful. She couldn't tell her father about that.

"There's a limerick?" For the first time during one of their little fights, he seemed sad.

What would he do if he heard the limerick? Jesse got the feeling it wouldn't be good. Her father rarely lost his cool, but when he did it could get apocalyptic.

"Yeah, but it's just stupid kids stuff," Jesse replied, leaving off how Mrs. Jerryman had set the whole thing in motion and then had done nothing to stop it.

"I hope, for your sake, that you can get it together and go to school tomorrow. You know there'll be consequences if you don't." Jesse flopped back down on the far side of her bed and nodded in a small way. Her father continued, "You don't want to be grounded over Christmas break, do you? And then there's the dance on Friday."

He was so out of touch with his own daughter. "Why do you think that I would possibly want to go to a dance with these insects?"

James gave her an odd look. "You don't want to go to the dance? You know it's a masquerade ball don't you?"

Jesse's mouth fell open. "I didn't..." There was *nothing* that she liked more than a masquerade ball. Halloween was fun, but it couldn't compare to the magic of dressing up in fancy gowns and feathered masks. She never went cute. For her it was all about elegance and romance...or at least the possibility of romance.

As an actual Cinderella, she knew there couldn't be a real romance, but there could be a kiss. A first kiss.

She'd been close once. As a sophomore, at her second masquerade ball, she'd found a boy and the night had been perfect. Almost that is. There had been dancing and soft music and talking and laughing. All the while she had refused to answer any question about herself and what's more she hadn't delved into anything personal about the boy. She didn't want to know. Because for that boy and the rest of them the masks were all about hiding who they were, while for Jesse it was all about being herself. The girl in the mask and the angelic white dress was really who she was.

Unfortunately the boy slipped up. He hadn't meant to, but his identity had just come out. Right before they were about to kiss, too. She had never kissed anyone before, but she knew, in her gut...and lower, she knew they were about to. But then he ruined it.

She knew who he was. The year before he had pegged her in the back of the head with an egg as she was walking home from the movies. It had hurt bad. She had a half mile left to get home and she had cried the whole way. Standing there under the glittering ball she'd felt like crying again. That was the thing. Had she been in her black outfit, she might have exacted some sort revenge, but in her white dress there was no hate in her. There was deep sadness, however.

And also hope.

"I want to go to the ball, please." There was a begging quality to her voice and she didn't care.

"Then you have to go to school tomorrow and you have to stay out of trouble."

In a second, Jesse calculated the pain to hope ratio. How much pain would she endure in order to get this one thing? This one thing that she loved more than anything. The answer: quite a bit.

"I will."

Chapter 25

Jesse demanded and received one very important condition to going to school the next day: a guaranteed ride to and from. She didn't explain why to her parents, nor did she mention her harrowing adventures travelling alone the last couple of days. It wouldn't have helped her case in the least; she just stuck to her guns and refused her mom's poor attempts at bargaining.

It was easy since Cynthia Clarke's only form of currency was guilt. Jesse was all guilted out, having reached her saturation limit a long time ago.

"I can drop you off, but I can't pick you up," her mother explained. "You know I volunteered to start up a winter coat drive. We have the first logistics meeting tomorrow at four."

There was no denying that there was a need for coats in Ashton. Winter was long in Michigan and Jesse had seen a number of kids in the halls with tired looking coats sporting homemade patchwork.

"First off, if you pick me up at three you'll have plenty of time to get to your meeting." Jesse explained. "Second, an entire meeting for logistics? For coats? Please, you could do this by phone."

"You certainly are dismissive about what I think is very important matter to the community," Cynthia Clarke shot back. "These people are hurting. They're not like us. They don't have our money."

"I know they're poor. I have eyes, you know. But there were poor people in Denton and Copper Ridge and everywhere else we've been. And there'll be poor people in the next town you move to. You will always have the poor, Mom, but you won't always have me." In a huff, Jesse turned to leave—a bath sounded good before bed. Only her mom wasn't done pontificating.

"I think you need to learn a little about self-sacrifice and helping others. All these poor people you rail against, when have you ever done anything for them? You see everything I do for the poor, but you never once volunteer to lend a hand."

Jesse's teeth came together with a click and she forced them to stay shut tight. To say any of the nasty things that had come springing into her mind would just cause a fight. "I don't rail against the poor. I never have. I rail against stupid people...rich or poor. And I give. You know I give. I just do it my way."

Her way was the quiet unobtrusive way. When hurricane Katrina swamped New Orleans, Jesse had dug into her savings bonds. When an earthquake leveled Haiti, she went back again for more and mailed away the last of her hopes of buying a Camry. She gave, but she gave quietly, the opposite of her mother's method. If there wasn't a chance at an engraved plaque or a page two photo spread Cynthia Clarke wasn't interested.

"Are you going to give me the ride or not?" Jesse asked from the doorway. "No ride...no school." She then went completely still; she said nothing and did nothing. A negotiating trick of her father's. Cynthia had seen it before and knew better that to beat around the bushes anymore, since Jesse wouldn't respond until she got a firm answer.

"Alright."

It wasn't alright with Cynthia or Jesse, since neither was in any way happy, but it would do.

Jesse left her mom stewing over the fact that she had been forced to comply with what she thought was an unreasonable request, and went to take her bath. Lying in the near-to scalding water turned out to be the best part of her day. Dreamily she thought of Ky. She couldn't stop picturing that moment in the woods when he first realized it was she who was standing in the shade of the tree.

His guard was all but down and she could swear that she saw his true feelings in his eyes. Once she got past the fear that is. There was no question the boy had been afraid and for good reason...but there had also been wonder in his eyes. Like he was seeing a miracle instead of a girl. In a sense she had been a miracle for Ky. He would have been dead without her...and she would have been dead without him.

If he hadn't been there, she would've blundered up that path right into the arms of the Shadow-man. The water went chill at the thought and she climbed out. It was getting very late and Jesse decided it was time for bed, but not before she took one more look, one more peek at the extremes dominating her life just then.

Ky and the Shadow-man.

The Mendel's house was dark, not a light visible. This was the opposite of Harold's home. His lights were ablaze and his shadow could be seen pacing...pacing. By the movement, Jesse would have sworn he seemed nervous.

"What did he have to be nervous about?" she asked, her breath fogging up her window, blearing the image. Nothing. A shark only fears a bigger shark and there was no one bigger than Harold.

***

The morning came in what felt like a blink of an eye, literally. Jesse laid her head down and it seemed in the next second her alarm was raging at her.

Her first impulse was to look out the window again. She didn't realize how excited she was to see Ky until she saw that his curtains were drawn tight. It sent a knife of disappointment into her chest.

"Is he going to act like yesterday never happened?" Jesse said to herself.

Yes of course.

A big sigh escaped her at the truth of that. Ky wasn't going to change overnight, not after years living next to a freak like Harold.

What she was sure to be a terrible day was waiting for Jesse and she moved listlessly through her morning routine. The fact that she wasn't going to be walking great distances opened up her wardrobe choices; however, this was counter-balanced by the very real possibility that she would be fighting that day, despite her promise to be good.

The fight had to happen eventually. Jesse wasn't a turn-the-other-cheek kind of girl. Sure she could forgive, and she had readily so, in those very few instances when she'd been truly apologized to. However, from past experience Jesse knew that if *she* turned the other cheek, she'd just be hit again...and again. It would never stop.

Her philosophy revolved around the *Do unto others* rule. If someone wanted to fight, she'd fight. If they'd want to be her friend, then great she'd be their friend. If they wanted to be left alone, she'd leave them alone.

Except for Ky.

"Yes, except Ky. He's different. He needs me to help him out of his shell. And what's more, we are like two peas in a pod."

Yes you are. You're both crazy. He's a loner and you talk to yourself.

"What am I going to wear," Jesse said, looking into her closet. Purposely she didn't think about what her *voice of reason* had just brought up. She was a lonely girl and had slipped into the habit of mumbling to herself under her breath. Whether she could stop it or not, she didn't know; she'd never tried.

With a possible fight in the offing, Jesse chose her loosest pair of black jeans. This wasn't saying much since she liked them tight; she had a good body and she knew it. She then went to pick out a top and at first she almost went with another black tank top, but she decided to throw her mother a bone. Since it was so close to the Christmas break, she went with a deep red, satin top. It looked great on top of the black jeans.

Finally, she put on her long black trench coat. Her very favorite. It hung to mid-calf, was tight at the waist, and flared out just above the knee. When she wore the coat and everyone stared, it made her feel almost like a movie star.

To Jesse, her clothes helped to mold her outlook. If she looked good she felt good. If she looked tough it helped her to feel tough. She had fought a girl once while she was wearing four-inch heels and a mini skirt. The outfit, a onetime attempt at feeling sexy, made her feel weak and...she hated to admit it, girlish. Her black outfit didn't. Though she was only seventeen, it made her feel like a woman: tough when she needed to be, sexy without being slutty, and above all confident.

Flaring her wide lapel, Jesse strutted down the stairs, feeling good. Even her ankle, once again snugged in its ace bandage, barely even sang the blues.

"Ready when you are, Mom," she said, coming into the kitchen. Cynthia Clarke, as per her usual routine, narrowed her eyes at Jesse's choice of attire. Yet the red satin shirt must have mollified her somewhat.

"Oh, the black coat!" Cynthia gushed. "I love that coat. I'm so jealous, I swear to God, I might just steal it one of these days."

"I'm pretty sure that stealing violates one of dad's rules," Jesse replied, happily. For the second time in three days her mom hadn't started in on her clothing...it was some sort of record. "And you know what? You also took God's name in vain, not to mention that you clearly coveted. Any jury in the world would convict you for that. How many sins do you plan on committing before lunch?"

Cynthia looked thoughtful, "Since this isn't Sunday...only nine out of ten, I guess. You know what would look better with that shirt and that coat..."

"Uhg!"

Peter Meredith

"Hush. You're just like your father, you think you know everything," Cynthia said without rancor. "Your black skirt, the one that goes right to your knee. That would look good. We have time for you to change."

Her mom was right; Jesse would look good in the outfit. Unfortunately there was the fight to consider. She hoped it would be Amanda; a good win over a girl bigger than herself would definitely make life a little easier.

"I promise to wear it...when things settle down a bit, ok?"

Her mom rose to her feet, threw back the last of her coffee, and said, "I'll hold you to that. Now, let's get you to school."

The words were barely out of Cynthia's mouth before Jesse felt the first pang of anxiety run through her. It grew as they climbed in the car and when she saw the building nestled in the trees the anxiety turned her stomach sour. But it took another sight to elicit a groan from her.

"You'll never find happiness if you're always groaning and moping around," her mom said, not seeing the hunk of twisted metal that had once been Jesse's bike hanging from a tree near the parking lot of the school. "Your high-school life is supposed to be about fun and laughing and learning. You'll never enjoy it if you have the wrong attitude. Do you think dad has it easy? No, but his attitude is...if life gives you lemons..."

"You make lemonade." Jesse finished the cliché while watching the school. She hated that school and all its lowbred, know-nothing students. "That's not so easy, Mom when all you have is lemons and piss."

"Don't be vulgar," Cynthia said, shaking her head. "You know your dad has these same complaints, but he finds a way. He wants you to find a way too. Adapt and over come, that's his motto. So try it, please. Go in there and find a way to make those teachers, not necessarily like you, but respect you. Once they do, I bet the other kids will come around."

"Unless I catch all the teachers in the middle of a huge orgy in the gym, and secretly tape it, that's not going to happen." The image was repulsive, but the idea of putting the video on the internet brought a smile to Jesse's face. It was sort of an evil smile.

"You're impossible you know that?" her mom asked with a shake of her head. But then she gave Jesse a little wink. "If you do go by the gym, make sure you have your cell phone just in case."

Did Cynthia Clarke just make a joke? Judging by her sly little smile, Jesse would have to conclude that she just had. Weird. She couldn't remember the last time that happened.

"See you at three?" Jesse asked with the car door sitting open. She wasn't going to get out until she got a firm yes.

Cynthia Clarke acted the martyr. "Yes, even though it's going..."

"That's all I needed to hear. Thanks Mom." Jesse gave the door a quick slam and strode away with only a single look back to offer her mom a last wave. Cynthia first gave her glare and then a wave of her own before driving away.

Jesse promptly forgot about her. With so many students going in every direction, she couldn't be distracted with thoughts of her mom. Early morning before the first bell rang could be a dangerous time for her. The teachers were almost all inside, preparing for their classes, while the few parents that were hanging around seemed in a hurry to be off to work.

All of which meant, she was an easy target. Or rather an easier target. Jesse was never easy. She walked with quick steps to the school and despite a few hard stares and a number of whispers, the girl in black made it to the supposed safety of the school. Though her eyes washed over the students in the crowding hall the first thing that she really noticed was one of the posters for the up-coming ball. It was tacked over old notices onto a bulletin board.

The picture accompanying the garish Vegas style headline was that of a girl in white. Her dress was flowing and on her back were arched wings of feathers; she was either a swan princess or an angel. While the poster itself was poorly done, the picture was beautiful. It reached out and set itself deep in Jesse's imagination, where it went to work, building fantasies.

For half a minute she stared at the poster, unaware of the usual chaos of the school hallway around her. In a town other than Ashton, she likely would have paid a price for being so oblivious, yet no harm came to her. The students had other priorities:

"Have you seen Jill?—No—She wasn't on the bus! And I, like texted her thirty times already.—we should call her house...wait, there she is."

"Dude pick up your phone. Come on, man, this isn't funny!...Damn it, he's not answering.—He's probably just in the back smoking. I bet you're freaking for nothing."

"Hey Mrs. Atkins, it's me Felicity. I'm sorry to call this early, but...yeah...yeah. Good! Whew, she had me going there. Tell her to get better, alright?"

The morning routine wasn't even picked up by Jesse's subconscious. She heard none of the frantic tones and saw none of the nervous eyes searching through the river of faces streaming down the hall. For her the picture was all that mattered...until a boy knocked into her.

Her mind might have been far away, however her body was a coiled spring. When the boy jostled into her, she reacted instinctively: turning with the momentum of the blow, she spun, grabbed him and shoved him hard against a row of lockers. Now she would run or fight, depending.

She did neither. The boy was small and weak, a freshman in all probability, and he was afraid. His eyes were wide and when he spoke, he stammered out a very sincere apology. It had been an accident.

Jesse gave him a piercing look and saw there was truth in his eyes. "It's alright, just try to watch where you're going next time."

"That's her..."

"Did you see what she did to that boy..."

"She should be next..."

Sadly, Jesse was back in the moment and heard the whispering. It would only get worse if she stayed in one place for too long. With a quick move, Jesse snatched the poster from the wall and immediately went to find to the nearest girls bathroom. Shutting herself in a stall she again eyed the picture.

The girl in the white dress was so beautiful that Jesse wished she could be her. And she could be, for just one night... but would that one night be worth it? Was it worth having to hear the other kids call her names and make fun of her with their stupid limericks? Was the ball worth having to put up with the teachers and their snide comments and poorly veiled put-downs?

Yes.

Very much yes. These things would happen anyway, no matter what, even if she didn't go. Jesse might as well have her fun. With that decided Jesse now had to figure out how she was going to get through her day without going mad.

"Adapt and overcome," she said, shaking her head in disbelief. Neither seemed possible. She turned again and stared at the picture as if it was going to give her some inspiration. Instead it made her feel a little down. The girl in the picture with her ice-blue eyes and her wonderfully confident smile could do it; she could find a way be good.

Jesse sighed. Promising to be good was one of the easiest things to do; it was backing up that promise that was so difficult. A second later, the bell rang and Jessie sighed again.

She gave herself two minutes before leaving the bathroom in the hopes that the halls would be cleared out some. They were and so it was that Jesse got a full view of Ky Mendel as he strode down the hall with a new attitude.

Chapter 26

It was clear to Jesse that this new attitude of Ky's was just for her. For starters, she was sure that no one else even noticed a difference in the boy. They probably didn't see the tightness in his face, the way his neck was held so stiff, and how the muscles of his jaw were clenched.

Before, he had ignored the world as a matter of habit, a practice made easy by the compliance of the student body of Ashton High. However, Jesse had upset that apple cart and now Ky was clearly setting out, *determined* to ignore everyone around him. The way he kept his eyes directly forward reminded her of one those English Royal Guards, who wore the tall bearskin caps. The ones all the tourists tried to make smile.

She smiled herself as she imagined Ky in one of those goofy hats. His serious, grim face didn't help either and she wondered what it would take to set him giggling.

The idea presented so much of a challenge to Jesse that she almost forgot about her promise to be good. The temptation to break him...to make him laugh, or smile, or even just glance her way was huge in her. She didn't want to be mean. There wasn't an ounce of cruelty in her, she just wanted to connect with him, to let him know she was there for him. The desire to do this was so strong that just as he came abreast of her, and the few kids left in the hall turned away to blot him out of their lives, Jesse had the urge to whisper, so that he alone could hear: *I love you, Ky.*

She didn't and he walked by as if Jesse was only a bug not worthy to be acknowledged. She hadn't said anything because as he drew closer, she couldn't help herself and the corners of her mouth had turned up into a mischievous smile that Ky saw from the corner of his eye. His lips had pursed at this. It was the tiniest movement, but sometimes large things could be read from the smallest actions and Jesse saw the extent of the stress that Ky was carrying about with him.

This was something she could relate to and she wasn't going to add to the burden of it. That his life hadn't been easy was clearly an understatement. Living next door to a known killer, especially a monstrous one such as Harold must have been a punishment all to itself. It was driving her crazy and she only just found out. What would it have been like for a seven-year-old kid? What kind of nightmares would have plagued him? How could he even have slept, wondering when the Shadow-man would come for him next?

It had to have been terrible, so instead of whispering some foolishness, she sighed and watched him head into Mrs. Jerryman's classroom. She would have to go in there next, but there was still thirty-eight seconds left until the bell rang and she wasn't going in any earlier than she had to.

Thirty-seven seconds later Jesse strolled in, trying to comport herself just as Ky had. She didn't envy him. The way he was ignored was bizarre and unhealthy, but at that moment, she could have used a little of it. As she entered every eye was upon her and the class began a low tittering. She did her best to ignore them and went to her seat in the back of the room. This she found had been moved. The day before it had been only a foot or so from Ky's desk, now it was a good five feet away.

It looked lonely sitting back there separated from all the rest of the desks and she tried to come up with an excuse to move it back closer to Ky's. The thing was, he was the one who probably moved it in the first place and it would only upset him more if she were to move it back.

"Miss Clarke, please take your seat," Mrs. Jerryman said, and waited with an air of patience as Jesse sat. The teacher then went on to call the roll. There was another desk empty in the classroom. It drew the attention of all the students.

"David Addison?"

"Here."

"Miss Archer...there you are. Good morning." Now there was a pause. It could only be called a pregnant pause...like the pause just before the Oscar for best actor was announced. "Pam Atkins?" Mrs. Jerryman asked with a clear note of tension in her voice. Eyes flicked around the room and a number of the kids looked to be holding their breath. "Anyone know where Pam is today?"

"She's sick. I called her mom," a girl said.

The reaction by the class to this news was extremely odd. Some relaxed visibly, which was understandable, but some seemed disappointed, which was perplexing. Jesse watched, astonished, and repulsed, as shoulders slumped and sighs—which weren't sighs of relief—crept out of people's mouths. Did they want Pam to be this year's victim of the Christmas Killer? Try as she might, Jesse couldn't remember the girl who had sat in the now empty chair. She certainly hadn't stood out as any more mean than the rest. So why the disappointment? Was she such an unlikeable girl that they were ok with her being murdered? The very notion had Jesse looking at the kids around her in disgust.

He's due. Allison, the sixth-grade girl from the library, had said this the night before with all the solemnity and authority of a high priest. Was this fact? Did Harold Brownly only kill right before the Christmas break? If so, how was this affecting the kids of Ashton? Were they simply desperate for *someone* to be killed so that it could be over for the year?

Jesse didn't know what to think about that and she sat back, not really listening to what Mrs. Jerryman was saying. On the surface the uncaring reaction that a number of kids had displayed was sickening. However, when Jesse thought about her own fear of the killer over the last two days, it made her wonder what kind of stress the kids in the town were under.

All of them, from the dorkiest nerd to the cutest cheerleader, have had to deal with the real possibility of being murdered, on a yearly basis, from a very young age. What did that kind of accumulating fear do to a kid...did it turn them cold inside? Did it eat at their nerves until they were just about ready to throw a party when that year's death finally occurred and they dodged the bullet once again?

Perhaps Jesse had been too quick to judge. What would her own reaction have been if Pam Atkins had been murdered? Would she have cried over the death of this unknown girl?

You'd be relieved. Don't even try to deny it.

Right again. Sure she'd be sad for Pam and her family, but deep down inside of her there would be pure relief it hadn't been her. She'd be able to relax at least a little about the killer, knowing that when her time in Ashton was over, she'd be in her own personal heaven: the hot beaches of Southern California where she hoped to never see snow again.

No she couldn't judge them on that front at least, but she could judge them on how they treated her. At the moment almost all of them were staring back at her.

"Miss Clarke?" Mrs. Jerryman asked. Jesse blinked up at her, knowing the lady had said something, just not what.

"I'm sorry. I was thinking about...something else," Jesse replied. "What were you asking?"

"I asked, if you had a chance to reconsider helping out the town by joining with our protest?" Mrs. Jerryman's tone was surprisingly even, and her expression neutral.

Reconsider?

Why would she reconsider? Very little had changed in the last day that would act as an incentive for her. Jesse made to answer the teacher with a 'no', but just then she saw why she had been asked this at that particular moment. The other students were *all* staring at Jesse and most wore what seemed to be a hungry look to them.

They were the incentive, or rather, they were the threat. Mrs. Jerryman was giving Jesse one last chance to save herself from public humiliation. It was either join the protest or the teacher would unleash her nasty horde and their stupid, poorly rhymed limericks. This gave Jesse pause as she was again put to the test.

Which way to go? She had been dreading her upcoming English class simply due to the limericks and here she was with a chance to skate away without hearing a single one. That definitely appealed to her, yet did stabbing her father in the back constitute adapting and overcoming? Or did that fall into the category of straight up surrendering?

It felt a lot like surrender to Jesse. But the other side of the coin felt a lot like torture. She would be forced to endure the lash of scorn and ridicule, which to a teenage girl could be worse than the real thing. Her mind was all confusion.

If she gave in she knew she could no longer lay claim to principle. But did she have all that much principle to begin with?

Yes

Again true, but what about the flip side—was it in principle that she was playing the martyr for her father? Or was she subconsciously allowing herself to be attacked just so she could win his approval....his love?

Or is it you like the attention?

This thought had her stunned. *I am important,* she thought. *I'm the loose thread that unravels the sweater. I'm the finger in the dyke, without which the town is flooded. I'm the keystone in the center of the arch.*

The teachers at the school sure seemed to think that she was mighty important. That she, Jesse Clarke, was the chink in her father's armor, the key to stopping him. In a way this was an ego boost, knowing that the all-powerful James Clarke needed her more than he knew.

Yet discovering this about herself did not help her just at that moment, rather it had her wanting to scream. It was simply another layer of puzzlement. What should she do and why was she doing it?

Was she avoiding pain, or wanting to be loved? Was she crying out for attention or was she principled? Jesse didn't know. She only knew that right at that moment with twenty-three sets of eyes boring into her she felt backed into a corner and she didn't appreciate the feeling. It got her dander up and made her even more contrarian than she naturally was.

"I had a chance to reconsider," she answered the teacher's question without elaborating.

Mrs. Jerryman eyebrows shot up and remained there for two seconds until she realized Jesse wasn't going to add anything more. "Are you going to help the town or not?"

"I'm not going to help *you*," the girl in black replied.

Instead of getting angry at this, the class almost as a whole, seemed to blow out a collective breath and relax. They wanted this to happen. They wanted to dish out pain. None of them, save Mrs. Jerryman, wanted Jesse on their side.

"Limerick! Limerick! Limerick!" a boy began chanting. In seconds, it seemed that the entire class was chanting along. Yet they weren't all chanting. Ky was Ky and was in his own world, but he wasn't the only one not caught up in the spectacle. There were five or six others, including the plump, freckled-faced girl that had tried to warn Jesse against getting to close to Ky. The girl had her head practically inside her book bag and was rooting around in it with slow and exaggerated motions.

Barely turning her freckled-face, the girl gave Jesse a commiserating look.

It was uncharitable, but the first thing that came to Jesse's mind was: *Coward!* The girl knew this was wrong yet she did nothing. And she wasn't going to either. That one look was all the solace Jesse would receive. It angered her just as the chanting did.

The chanting brought out the blood lust in the students and they were eager to start. Never before had Jesse seen kids so quick to head to the front of a classroom to spill out their verses. Normally it was like pulling teeth for students to share a poem.

No tears! Jesse demanded of herself as the first boy began his limerick. As expected, it was vulgar to the point of an X rating and Jesse was its theme. How could it be otherwise? In this town, where hope was an outdated idea, the students had been raised on resentment and fear. Like their parents, they were angry at how life had treated them, and as much as they would've liked to focus their anger on James Clarke, he was all but untouchable in his high-up office.

They had to settle for Jesse.

She had done nothing wrong to any of the kids around her. Yet she was hated and not just for who her father was. Her clothes were newer and more fashionable. Her look— distinct and rebellious—mocked trendiness, but was in style all the same. Outwardly she appeared fearless, standing up to teachers and students alike. She went about alone, while they huddled together like sheep. She seemed sharp and crisp in their dull world. Yet instead of seeing someone to emulate, they only saw someone to envy and tear down.

They brought out their anger in verse and it was wicked bile in Jesse's heart. The words were designed not just to ridicule but to cause pain. And they were very effective. After the first limerick, Jesse dug out a book from her bag, not seeing or caring what it was.

Calculus! This was her only hope to hold back the tears forming in her eyes. She flipped through the book until she saw a page filled with enough math problems to drown herself in. Or so she thought at first. Only those waters were too shallow and the vile poetry kept slipping in among her equations until at last tears blurred the numbers that she had been trying to hide within.

The rhymes were hurtful, but the over-the-top exaggerated laughter that accompanied each were pure poison in Jesse's soul. She died a little with each outburst, until at last she looked up from her book to beg for them to stop.

The pleading words were on her lips yet they froze there in shock. A girl...Felicity, the one who had called Pam Atkins' mother, had her cell phone out and had it aimed square at Jesse. It took a moment for her to realize what was going on, but then it sank in. She was being recorded. The whole thing was being recorded. Her humiliation...her shame...her pain was being documented.

For what reason?

Don't be stupid. You know the answer to that.

So that the whole world could see. Jesse hid herself back in the book. Tears came harder than before and she had to put her hands to her face. She kept herself in that position for the rest of the class, looking up only once when the freckled-faced girl read her limerick. Hers was about a flower in need of water. It was good...not only did it actually rhyme, unlike many of the others, its message was sweet. And the hidden message, love and the absence of love, was even sweeter.

As the next girl stood to resume the crude word torture, Jesse let her mind dwell on the words of the last message and she was not the only one. Ky was thinking on it as well, or so she hoped. When she looked over at him, his handsome face was tight with emotion, his skin was taunt over a skeleton of steel. He revealed nothing, but he was so doggedly revealing nothing that by doing so he revealed everything.

The message of love had hit Ky hard.

Chapter 27

The limericks continued and only twice did Mrs. Jerryman come close to reprimanding students for going too far in their vulgarity. Both times she allowed the students to finish the limericks and it was only after everyone had settled down with their exaggerated laughing that she would slap a wrist with a velvet glove. On one of the occasions she actually gave helpful hints on how to make the limerick even nastier, just in a more subtle way.

Jesse refused to listen; instead she clung to the sad love poem...

There with waters grow hidden seed
Which all the while lay in its need
A rose, a tulip to be found
Deep in deserts arid ground
And crying, sings of sorrow, to be freed

She whispered the words to herself over and over again, uncaring whether or not she could be heard by the other students or the recording device in the phone.

The cell phone! She could do nothing about the other teens—they thought the worst of her already—yet she could do something about the cell phone.

She could destroy it and she already planned on doing just that. Her initial idea, which came to her the second she saw Felicity pointing the thing at her, was to grab the cell phone and grind it under the heel of her jungle boots. She had yet to come up with a secondary plan, nor did she really need one, since plan A seemed to cover everything she hoped to accomplish.

What about the ball? What about being good?

Right. Plan B then. There was no plan B, and Jesse didn't think she would be able to come up with one either. She had the exact opposite problem as Ky. He was completely ignored, while she was watched with hating eyes everywhere she went. This meant that there would be no stealing the phone on the sly. It would have to be a snatch and grab...which meant plan A...which meant no masquerade ball!

A soft growl escaped her at this.

Just then the bell rang cutting off Mrs. Jerryman's words. The girl in black had no clue what her teacher was saying nor did she care. Jesse was mortified at her treatment. Her rage and humiliation were twin fires in her heart and they made a roar in her ears that muffled all sound.

"Miss Clarke, I'm talking to you."

Ignoring this, just like she was ignoring the looks and laughter that came at her expense, Jesse headed for the door as quick as she could. At the bell, Felicity had been up and had been one of the first ones out of the classroom. Jesse didn't want to lose her in the crush of people that would be in the hall in the next minute.

"Miss Clarke!" A hand grabbed her bag and pulled.

Acting purely on instinct and emotion, Jesse spun. Her face was flush and red, filled with the misery of her shame and her eyes rimmed in wrath were a hard, ice blue. She might have looked like a maniac and her cocked fist certainly didn't help. Mrs. Jerryman actually squeaked in fright and jumped back.

"Oh, sorry," Jesse said and then wondered why she had apologized. In her father's words: 'You mess with the bull, you get the horns'. Mrs. Jerryman was lucky she hadn't been punched in the face. Jesse turned away—whatever the teacher wanted would have to wait—Jesse's need to get the cell phone was an undeniable urge inside of her.

"Damn!" she exclaimed. The exit to the classroom was now backed up five kids deep. With a sigh and a tilt of her head she gave her English teacher an eye. "You wanted something?"

"Yes," Mrs. Jerryman replied in a huff. "Not to be threatened for one."

Since Jesse couldn't guarantee that, not in the mood she was currently in, she only shrugged, hoping it conveyed—*maybe.* "And two?"

The teacher's eyes blazed. "Do you know what the penalty is for threatening a teacher?"

A hundred nasty responses came to mind, but sneaking right up through them came the voice of reason and for once it was unreasonable.

Don't give her any smartass answers...remember the Ball!

Wrong. When Jesse caught up to Felicity, the Ball would be out of the question. Destroying another student's cell phone was likely a sure way to get expelled, and knocking her teeth down her throat was probably frowned upon as well.

If you give her a smartass answer you'll be expelled right now and you'll never catch up to Felicity.

That was right. Jesse swallowed hard, grimacing as she did and said, "I'm sorry that I frightened you. I get a little jumpy when people come up behind me."

Strangely, Mrs. Jerryman seemed mollified by Jesse's apology. "I just wanted to talk to you about the essay that I assigned you."

Jesse narrowed her eyes at the teacher. After what Mrs. Jerryman just put her through with an hour's worth of asinine limericks, she was going to now add this insult onto her as well? "I didn't do it," Jesse said, waving her hand dismissively. "It was such a stupid request that I just assumed you were joking."

"Oh my," Mrs. Jerryman replied, walking to her desk and taking a seat. "Are you looking to fail this class?"

Jesse laughed out loud. "Is there another option?"

Mrs. Jerryman smiled and paused as the last student, Ky, slipped out the door before continuing in a voice kept low, "You know there is another option."

"After what you just put me through?" Jesse gasped, unable to believe the woman. "You think that I would join you now?"

Mrs. Jerryman leaned back in her chair. "I would if I was you. It *can* get worse."

This cooled Jesse's anger, in fact it sent a chill up her spine the way the woman was so confident. "How? How could it get worse?"

"Do I need to spell it out for you?" the teacher asked. Jesse racked her brain yet came up with nothing out of the ordinary: suspension, useless assignments, failing tests, detention. Nothing that would cause this horrid toad of a woman to act this confident.

"So you do need it spelled out?" Mrs. Jerryman said. "Fine...H. A. R. O. l..."

A sharp pain lanced into Jesse's chest as she figured out what the woman was suggesting. "You wouldn't dare!" she cried, interrupting. "You would sic a killer on me? That's accessory to murder...you would stoop to that?"

Mrs. Jerryman couched her voice lower. "I want you to know..." She stopped in mid-sentence as kids began trickling into her classroom for the start of second period. Putting on a fake smile, Mrs. Jerryman resumed, "I would never do it. And I mean that, but if you don't start getting some right thinking into your head...*someone* will. Sooner rather than later. He is due. Now get to class."

The teacher shooed Jesse away with a flick of her hand and the girl was all too ready to leave. She rushed out of there and for the moment Felicity and her cell phone were forgotten.

Would she really do it? thought Jesse. *Would anyone do such a thing?*

The sad answer was yes. Jesse was an outsider and a hated one at that. Yet her father had been confident that Jesse lacked whatever characteristic would make her a target.

What this characteristic was occupied her mind all through calculus. She went over the little she knew about the dead children: there had been three boys and a girl, all were killed in random, or seemingly in random locations. That was all she knew...except that Ky Mendel had asked the question: *Is it my turn?* when he thought that Harold Brownly was nearby. To Jesse, this suggested that Ky possessed the characteristic and the way his dad seemed always to be following around after him, he clearly thought his son was in danger.

What set these kids apart? Yet it wasn't just these kids. All the kids in town seemed downright afraid, not just a few of them. What did that mean? Maybe they were afraid that Harold would break out of his mold and start killing at random.

Jesse didn't believe it. That would mean her father was wrong, and it was easier to believe a town of six thousand souls was collectively less intelligent than her father. So that meant there was definitely a characteristic...and one that her father wished that she possessed. He had mentioned it in passing, but she had been too tired to dwell on it until now.

What physical characteristic was there that her father wished she possessed...a penis? No, there had been a girl killed just last year...unless she was a hermaphrodite...or a cross-dresser. Jesse was grasping at straws now.

If anyone knew the exact characteristic that they all had in common, it would be the boy who had lived next door to the killer for the last ten years. Too bad he would never answer her if she asked. She thought about Ky. She thought about how he looked: his thick dark brown hair, his piercing hazel eyes, his ruddy cheeks, and then she thought about how he looked the night before...with his shirt off.

The end of period bell rang and Jesse jumped a mile out of her seat causing not a few people to laugh at her. Where had the time gone? Another image of Ky jumped into her mind. Right.

With a sigh that was half-longing and half-dread, Jesse gathered up her bag and headed off to art class. It was sure to be another big headache. Her life had turned into a painful yo-yo. Deal with the terrible killer...deal with the nasty people...deal with the terrible killer...

It was enough to make her want to hide in the bathroom all day. The good news, if could be called such, was that Felicity shared this class with her, in fact their tables sat side by side. Getting the phone, unless it was guarded over should be no problem. The problem would come when Jesse threw it down and stomped on it. There would be some frowning at that she was sure and then a trip to the principal's office and then no masquerade ball.

Of course, she could get lucky. There could be fire that consumed half the building, or maybe, for once, no one would notice her and she would be left alone. Neither seemed at all likely. In fact the second far-fetched chance was gone the moment she walked in the door. Everyone of the students glanced her way and more than one snickered.

As the class started and Ms Weldon began issuing orders, Jesse kept her head down but her eyes up, looking for a chance to snatch the phone. It was sitting hooked to Felicity's backpack and would be relatively easy to grab, but also relatively easy to get caught doing so as well. Jesse needed a distraction, unfortunately *Jesse* was the distraction.

Snippets of limericks whispered around the room and the students took way too much of their time trying to catch her eye. Ten minutes into the class, Jesse resigned herself to making as inconspicuous attempt at the phone as possible and letting the chips fall where they may.

Just then Ms Weldon came up to her table shaking her head. "Miss Clarke, either begin working on the assignment or go to the principal's office."

"Yes ma'am." With the teacher right there, Jesse couldn't exactly grab the phone nor did she exactly want to work on the project...but she could fake it long enough for the teacher to wander away. Jesse headed for the supply closet and once there went about gathering anything that might allow her to fake her way through the project long enough to go for the phone.

She even grabbed a can of red paint, but just as she turned away she had a new idea for the paint. Quick as she could, she unscrewed the lid almost all the way and then left the can as precariously balanced as possible on a shelf. There was a good chance that anyone not really paying the closest attention would inadvertently knock it over.

With her arms full, she stole back to her table and started arranging her supplies all the while under the glaring eye of Ms Weldon.

"If you're looking to fail, you're on the right track," the art teacher said quietly. Ms Weldon's attitude was strange that day. She seemed resigned to disliking Jesse, yet at the same time it seemed to pain her to do so. "None of this is correct. You are supposed to be using pastels chalk, not crayon...this isn't the second grade."

There hadn't been much in the closet. "Yes, ma'am. My parents weren't home...and I couldn't really go out...alone," Jesse explained. This was the truth. There was a point the night before when she had remembered her art project and had given all of two seconds of thought about getting the needed materials. "I'm using the crayons to get an idea what sort of colors and image I would like to use."

Ms Weldon's right eyebrow shot up, she couldn't look more skeptical. "The paper is wrong as well. It's supposed to be three feet by five feet."

The largest paper in the closet was two feet wide and one and a half feet tall. "I'm going to draw it to scale," Jesse said, proffering perhaps her lamest excuse of her teenage life, which was saying something.

A sigh escaped Ms Weldon. "Do your best," she said, and walked away to the next table. There her demeanor changed to one of enthusiastic encouragement.

"*Poor Jesse had really quite an itch...Too bad that she was such a bitch,*" a boy recited from behind her as soon as the teacher had stepped away. The limerick from the day before hadn't been topped in popularity...yet. However, if the video of her crying on Felicity's phone made it onto the internet that could change in a hurry, and so would Jesse's life. That video was the sort of thing that could haunt a person forever.

Jesse cast a wary glance back. Her antagonist from the day before Ronny stood a little too close.

"*Though she looked for a while...She never got a boy who would smile,*" Ronny went on. "I have a dog you can use." He pointed to his own crotch.

"Ronny, back to your own table please," Ms Weldon said tersely. As the boy skulked away, Jesse looked to her teacher. There was definitely something about her that was different, a change in attitude that was subtle. The teacher refused to catch her eye. It was almost as if she expected...

"Damn it!" a boy's voice roared from the storage closet. Though she had been hoping for just that very thing, Jesse was as startled as everyone else by the sudden commotion. She recovered quickly however, as the majority of the class, including Felicity, streamed toward the closet.

Jesse went as well, only she detoured to her right and snatched the cell phone from its black case, stuffing it into her rear packet. She kept to the back of the little crowd, remaining obvious, especially to Felicity, but not drawing too close. There were still dangerous...or at least unpredictable elements in the classroom.

"It's just paint people," Ms Weldon said with a raised voice. "Get back to your projects. You are all on a time crunch."

Jesse didn't go back to work, instead she went to the closet and looked at the great red mess; it was surprisingly gory looking for just paint.

"Ms Weldon? Can I go to the bathroom, please?"

The teacher shot her a hard look. "You are supposed to go during passing periods."

"Yes, ma'am. I didn't though and I really have to go now."

In frustration over the mess, the art teacher waved her away. "Fine, take the hall pass and go."

Keeping her face carefully composed, Jesse hurried out and then sped to the nearest bathroom, once again settling herself into a stall. Her first inclination was to crush the cell phone, yet she couldn't bring herself to do it. She didn't know what Felicity's family was like. They could be dirt poor for all she knew and cell phones were expensive. So instead she touched the screen and saw to her delight the menu pop up.

"Not too bright," Jesse chuckled. The girl should've had her phone password protected. Now all Jesse had to do was open up the saved video file and delete the incriminating evidence of one of the worst moments of her life. Just thinking about it made her neck tense.

"There should be a law against teachers acting like..."

A thunderbolt of an idea stopped Jesse in mid-sentence. There *were* laws against this sort of thing and she had the incriminating evidence right there in her hand. She could go to the police with the video...except that she had stolen the phone...and except that the police in Ashton were likely on the side of the teachers. What about the FBI?

Don't be stupid.

Right. The FBI had far better things to do. Going to the media was out of the question, she'd be taking herself down right along with Mrs. Jerryman. And this left, what?

Blackmail.

Her voice of reason was right again. Adapt and overcome. This was what her father wanted after all. With the video in hand, she could pass her English class, and maybe if she played her cards right, all her classes. Looking at the phone her stomach churned. The blackmail would only work if the video showed enough. Gritting her teeth, Jesse pressed the play tab.

In the ten seconds before the bathroom door came open and four girls trooped in, Jesse saw all that she needed to see.

"Who is that?" a girl asked in an inquisitive tone.

In a panic, Jesse hit the stop button and the squeaky voices on the video died away. "J-J-Jane," Jesse spat out. After almost spilling out her own name, Jane was the only thing that came to mind.

"Jane? Jane who?" Amanda Jorgenson asked. The girl's voice, as enemy number one, was imprinted in Jesse's mind and there was no mistaking it.

Her day had gone from bad to worse. Trapped in the bathroom with the odds against her at four to one, the first thing Jesse did was to reach for her lock and chain. It was instinctive mood that resulted in nothing. She'd taken off her coat in the art room to protect it against "accidental" spills and the heavy weapon was still in the pocket she had put it in that morning.

The next thing she did was realize that the tables had turned with regards to incriminating evidence; she had a stolen phone right in her hands. The next few minutes presented itself to her mind in excruciating detail: the girls would want to know who this "Jane" person was. They'd quiz her some more and when Jesse couldn't give satisfactory answers they have peek over the top of the stall. Then would come a minute or so of threats and then they'd rush her and drag Jesse out. If she was very, very lucky they wouldn't notice the cell phone. Jesse wasn't that lucky. The girls would take it from her...maybe before they fought maybe after, but either way they would find out in two seconds the phone had been stolen.

Goodbye masquerade ball, hello jail, and hello Jesse splashed all over the internet as the butt of every limerick joke. Unless that is, she could erase the video in time.

"It's Jane Miller," Jesse said in a small voice as she once again pulled up the tab for recent videos.

"Jane Miller? I know Mike Miller..." Amanda said.

There was a pause and another girl said, "Yeah, Mike has a sister...but it's Danielle. Hey, are we going to smoke these or what? Mr. Johnson friggin times me every time I go to the bathroom."

"Yeah, sure," Amanda replied. Jesse highlighted the limerick video and with a quick sigh hit delete.

"You're not going to go runnin to the principal, are you Jane?" Amanda asked. There was a touch of threat to her voice.

"No...never," Jesse replied still trying to sound meek. She was hoping to come across as a freshman. She glanced back down at the phone and her eyes went wide in puzzlement. The screen read: Please Enter E-mail Address.

What?

"Hey, Jane what grade are you in?" one of the girls asked.

Jesse almost didn't answer. She was too preoccupied trying to figure out what was going on with the phone. "Uh...I'm a freshman."

"Oh yeah? That's cool. Who do you have for homeroom?"

Again Jesse was slow to respond. She had accidentally hit Send as Attachment, instead of delete. Now the phone was asking for an email address. As quick as she could she typed in her own. "I'm in Mrs. Anderson's class." Jesse had no idea if there was a Mrs. Anderson in the school; she had just pulled a name at random.

"Who?" Amanda asked.

Here we go, Jesse thought. Now they would look over the top of the stall and see the one person they hated more than any other. Jesse stood up eyeing the phone—it was taking its sweet time sending the e-mail.

"Holy crap! It's that friggin' bitch!" Amanda Jorgen's ugly blonde friend had her head over the stall and was looking down on Jesse. A second later Amanda joined her.

"You!" she snarled at Jesse.

"Yeah, hold on one second," Jesse answered as if they mattered very little to her. Her eyes were on the phone and the little status bar showing her how much longer the e-mail would take to send. Just about there...

"Let's give her a swirly!" the blonde exclaimed.

There! The e-mail was sent. "You'll regret this day for the rest of your life if you even try," Jesse said in a voice that was far calmer than it had any right to be. The reason for the calmness was that she was still concentrating on the phone. She was now trying to delete the video and her sparring words were coming out of her almost as if she were reading from a script.

"Right," a voice on her right said. "It's four against one. Tina, go stand by the door." Just as Jesse looked up, the blonde girl ducked away.

"Oh, surrounded in the bathroom. It doesn't look good," Amanda said with a grin in her voice. Jesse didn't know if there was a grin on her face to match it. She hadn't looked up again. She was waiting...waiting...there! File deleted. Now Jesse looked up and she wore a grin of her own—a wolf's grin. Chances were she would lose this fight, but there was an even better chance that she would draw blood in the process. Maybe even a lot of blood and after the past few days of hell on earth she had endured she was looking forward to it.

"Too afraid to face me alone Amanda?" Jesse said rolling her head on her shoulders, loosening up.

"Just get out here, or we'll go in after you."

The smart move was to wait and try to fight them in the confines of the stall, where the restricted movement could work to her advantage, but Jesse was actually afraid of the very idea of a swirly. She had been held under water before and the terror that moment had produced was etched on her soul. She would fight them right outside the stall and they would have to drag her kicking and screaming back in.

"Stand back," Jesse warned. There was a girl right outside the stall door...she should have stood back.

Chapter 28

The bathroom stall opened inward and the girl on the other side, a mousy looking brunette, stepped forward with it. Framed as she was, she made an easy target and took Jesse's jungle boot square in the stomach.

Air exploded out of her, while the force of the blow sent her reeling backwards. Jesse followed her out.

"Oh, you bitch," Amanda cursed. She seemed surprised, which struck Jesse as odd. Weren't they just threatening her? Did they expect her not to fight back?

This moment of surprise was all Jesse had time for before Amanda nodded her head at someone to Jesse's right. Just as she turned, Jesse caught sight of movement...a fist was coming in at her. It was expected. Jesse was already in the process of ducking when she felt something jar up against the top of her head. It didn't hurt, nor was it anyway stunning. In fact the blow was feeble.

Like everything else in life, punching took practice. It also took the right mind set. There was a mental balance within each person during a fight. On one hand there was the desire to inflict harm and on the other hand was the universal need to avoid pain. If one's fear of pain outweighed one's desire to cause it, then that person was going to lose.

Jesse had seen it time and again: a girl punching at the same time she was leaning back. There was never any power behind a blow like that, but there was plenty of fear.

This mental aspect was also the reason why girls were foolish ever to fight boys if they could avoid it. Boys were certainly not mentally superior, but they were attitudinally superior. It was in their genes. On a fundamentally sexist level boys *knew* they were stronger than girls and thus their mental balance weighed against fear and towards harm. While girls were generally not born fighters and so they were weighted toward avoiding pain rather than causing it.

Just then in the bathroom at Ashton High, Jesse was glad for this inequity. It allowed her to shrug off the blow and charge her opponent. Jesse smashed into the girl and threw her bodily against the line of sinks. The girl went to the ground. Instead of attacking her, Jesse spun around quick...probably far quicker than Amanda expected. The tall blonde was just in the process of rushing at Jesse, but stopped.

Now there came a pause where the five girls stared at each other in silence. It was wasted seconds for Jesse. Instinctually she knew she should kick the girl closest to her in the face. In a fight where it was four against one that's what you did, but Jesse held back the blow that would have sent the girl to the dentist.

She had never hurt someone in such a defenseless position. The girl had hit the sinks and had fallen to her knees. It would have been nothing for Jesse to send a driving side kick into her face.

"Stay down!" Jesse growled at her. The girl didn't listen. She started to climb to her feet and the room erupted in a one-second spasm of motion. Just like the game red-light green-light everyone moved, but only by a few feet.

The mousy girl Jesse had first kicked took two steps forward; she was still clutching her stomach and grimacing. Tina also took two steps; she left her post guarding the door. Amanda rushed at the girl in black and actually had a hand on Jesse's out stretched left arm, when she stopped. As for Jesse, she couldn't kick a person when they were down, but she could sure kick someone when they were on their feet again. As the girl got up. Jesse shifted her stance, tilting her body slightly left, while bringing her right leg up and in. From that position she was a half a second from uncoiling a side kick into her opponent's ribs.

But like everyone else, she stopped as the bathroom door came open. A skinny twig of a freshman came in and was halfway to the first stall before she saw everyone frozen in place and staring at her. Time and motion seemed strangely out of whack. At the odd sight confronting the skinny girl, she stopped in her tracks and stared right back at them. However, at the same instant that she did this all the older kids started moving once more.

Only they did so in opposite directions from which they had been going. Amanda turned away from Jesse and went to the nearest sink. Tina turned to the door and then turned back again not knowing what to with herself. The mousy girl went into a stall to hide. She wasn't the only one, they all acted like they had something to hide, they were ashamed and rightfully so.

All except for Jesse, who righted herself and walked brazenly to the door. The door represented something strange to her. The margin of her safety lay in the width of one rather thin piece of wood. On one side, were books and learning, and on the other, fists and fighting. The human world could be bizarre at times.

Jesse turned in the doorway. "Face me alone, coward," she challenged Amanda. The blonde stared for a moment and then slid a cigarette from behind her ear. She said nothing to Jesse's dare and pretended to ignore her.

"Lily, if it gets back to my mom that I'm smoking, I'll kick your ass," Amanda warned the skinny girl.

"I don't know, Amanda," Jesse said before shutting the door. "She looks pretty big. Maybe you should get your friends to help." Jesse didn't wait for a response, instead she left.

Breathing hard and beginning to shake, she headed back to Art class, but then stopped, wondering what to do with the cell phone. There weren't many choices left to her, since she felt responsible for its safety. Jesse decided to drop it off in the lost and found bin at the office...she just wished that it was a further walk.

Even with her little tiff with Amanda, Jesse had barely been out of class for two minutes and wasn't looking forward to the next forty-five minutes of it.

The school was sometimes just too small. Within thirty seconds of leaving Amanda and her 'wild bunch', Jesse was at the front office. It was blessedly empty. She didn't know if she could take a dose of Mrs. Daly on top of everything else she'd had to endure that day.

"Probably off, hunting me down," Jesse whispered as she dropped the cell phone into the lost and found bin. "Probably trying to bust me smoking..."

An idea popped into her head. In a wink, Jesse grabbed a piece of paper from Mrs. Daly's desk and wrote: *Jesse Clarke is smoking in the second floor girl's bathroom!*

She then put the piece of paper where it would be easily seen and zipped out of the office. Hurrying until she got to the stairwell Jesse then dallied with a smile on her face. If Mrs. Daly found that note in the next couple of minutes...

Below her, the first floor access door banged open and someone—Jesse's mind filled in the image of plump little Mrs. Daly—came huffing up the stairs. *Holy Crap*, her mind screamed. Who'd thought the woman was so gung-ho on catching her?

You did, her voice of reason said.

Right. The girl in black had no option but to run up the stairs to the roof access ladder and hope that the woman was so single minded that she wouldn't look up the little flight of steps. At the top there was absolutely no cover, or any place to hide. Jesse just froze against the wall, knowing that movement drew the eye.

As Jesse had guessed, it was Mrs. Daly, and she didn't look up. Her eyes were watching the blur of her feet on the stairs. In three seconds she was out the door, while Jesse was flying down the stairs to the first floor. There was no sense hanging around to get trapped a second time.

It took all her will, not to scream out 'revenge!' in the echoey stairwell. Jesse had to settle for a little whisper.

"Revenge."

She took the long way around to the Art class.

"You took long enough," Ms Weldon said the moment Jesse walked in. Jesse blinked a few times, wondering what do you say to something like that?

Do you mention how you were forced to steal a phone to save what dignity you had, and that you then had to fight off four girls, before turning the tables on them? Or did you just mention something about a bad burrito? In the end, Jesse only shrugged and went back to her desk, trying not to smile when her eyes strayed to Felicity. All in all it had been one of the most successful bathroom breaks she'd ever had, except for one minor detail.

She had to pee.

Chapter 29

The rest of her school day practically flew by and other than her challenge to fight Amanda being accepted, it was generally pleasant. Sure she heard the occasional vile limerick but these were easier to ignore when she'd remind herself that without them she wouldn't be passing English this year.

This wasn't a done deal just yet. Jesse figured that she'd try to get Mrs. Jerryman alone sometime in the next day or two and then drop the hammer on her. Just the thought of it brought a warm feeling to her guts.

The rest of Art class breezed by and Ms Weldon even complimented Jesse on her sketch. For the most part Jesse had just scribbled randomly enjoying the mixing of colors.

"I like how you are capturing your anger," the teacher said. "This will work nicely on Saturday." When Jesse's eyebrows came down in consternation, Ms Weldon added, "You do remember that this is a mandatory school assembly?"

Jesse could only smile and nod.

Her lunch period was spent in the warm confines of the front office, more specifically the waiting room in front of the principal's office. This was by design, rather than from an outgrowth of bad behavior. Nowhere else seemed safe and after the previous day's incident with Mrs. Castaneda, Jesse had exiled herself from the library. There was a bonus to sitting in the waiting room of the principal's office: her presence was a complete befuddlement to Mrs. Daly.

The lady had gone to the copier and Jesse had slipped on by and taken a seat. Every few minutes the receptionist would glance at her and wonder what she had done. Jesse had to fight from laughing at this every time.

It was just before the bell that ended fourth period rang that Jesse received her challenge. Amanda Jorgenson came out of the Principal's office looking like she just had her head handed to her.

Principal Peterson looked sharply at Jesse, "What did you do this time?"

Amanda had been evacuating the area in a hurry, but stopped to hear the answer. There was a certain distasteful eagerness in her eyes.

"Oh, nothing. I was just reading this old magazine," Jesse replied with a smile in her voice and on her lips. "It's very interesting." It was too. It was a *Time* magazine from 1990 and it read as if it could have been written a week before. Environment being destroyed, terrible political climate, same things as always. "You know this says the Amazon Rain Forest has been losing a chunk of jungle the size of South Carolina every year and has been since 1978? I did the math. They ran out of jungle four years ago...I bet it's nice down there now."

"Jesse...What...What do you want?" Principal Peterson asked in exasperation.

"Nothing," Jess replied. "I'm just sitting here."

"Oh." The principal didn't elaborate. He only turned and stalked back into his office.

"Did you have fun in there?" Jesse asked the tall blonde.

Amanda's eyes flashed daggers. "You're going to pay."

"I know, but I was going to pay either way. At least I had a little fun first."

"You want to fight me? Just the two of us?" Amanda asked in a quiet voice.

Jesse shook her head. "Really I don't. I want to be left alone."

"It's too late for that," Amanda replied still unnervingly quiet. "I'll fight you tonight; just you and me. Eight o'clock here at the school."

"No. You won't come alone. You're too chicken," Jesse replied. She didn't bother to bring up the fact that she would never travel this far at that time of night, not if she could help it.

"Then down at the berm. You'll be able to see all the way down it. I'll be alone. Eight o'clock...no weapons."

Don't agree to this, Jesse! Have you forgotten the Shadow-man already? You were practically killed just last night.

"Fine...eight o'clock," Jesse heard herself say. It felt like she was possessed, like someone else was running the machinery that made her lips move. Why had she just agreed to that?

Because you are an egotistical idiot, her voice of reason responded. It might have been a reasonable voice, but it certainly wasn't charitable. Yet it was correct as always. Jesse couldn't have backed down from that fight, just like she couldn't have meekly accepted the swirly that had been planned for her in the bathroom. No matter the odds against her.

Just then the bell rang for fifth period and despite the fact that they shared the next class, the two girls went their separate ways. Amanda never made it to study hall and though Jesse did, she didn't study. She alternated between worrying about her coming fight and thinking about Ky. When it came to Ky, she never purposely started to think about him, he always just seemed to slip into her thoughts.

She missed him, which she knew was a very bad sign. Jesse hadn't seen Ky since first period and it was eating at her. It was so bad that she was actually looking forward to Mr. Irving's class.

He won't look at you.

She knew all too well.

When fifth period ended, Jesse waited for Ky and saw that he was still hard at work keeping to himself. It was flattering, since she knew that he didn't have to work this hard for anyone else. As he went by, she slipped into his protective wake and smiled as his shoulders twitched. With him in front, parting the crowded halls, Jesse made it to class unmolested and upbeat. In fact, she was practically perky, the view from where she had walked had been fine, fine, fine.

"Miss Clarke, are you going to be respectful today?" Mr. Irving asked. His eyes told Jesse that he hoped not.

"Yes sir," Jesse said. "I promised my father that I would." Before she knew it her eyes had slid off Mr. Irving's aging face and flicked back to Ky. His head was down, reading a book.

"Your father..." Mr. Irving said this as if it were the most painful subject. "Are you ready to discuss his policies in a calm, rational manner?"

Again? He was going down this road, again? "I...I...uh. Is this necessary?"

Mr. Irving held up one finger to her, while he addressed the class. "Quiet down; take your seats." He then turned back to Jesse and said loudly enough for the entire class to hear, "I'm not trying to pick on you. We're trying to get an understanding of your father's...unorthodox policies..." He was interrupted by snide laughter and under the breath snarky comments. When it quieted, he went on, "He seems to have a poor understanding of economics, and who could better explain his economic policies than his own daughter?"

"I don't know...an economics teacher maybe?" Jesse replied with a shrug.

She had said this pleasant enough for him to smile at her quip. "You would think so...only what he's doing doesn't actually count as economics."

"Then what is it?"

Mr. Irving strolled away from her for a moment so that he had the class's full attention. "I would call it slash and burn economics if anything."

The teacher seemed pleased with the new term he had just coined. He had the approval of a number of students as well, who nodded along in perfect bobble-head fashion.

"This is just like what you were talking about yesterday, when you went on about voo-doo and trickle-down economics," Jesse said, with a first spark of anger. "This is a tactic isn't it? It's called...semetic something."

"I don't know what you're talk..." Mr. Irving began, but Jesse interrupted when a memory flashed into her mind. She had been eating breakfast, while her father was perusing the newspaper and suddenly he was spouting about control of the language and...

"It's called semantic infiltration," Jesse said, the memory of her father lent some authority to her voice. At least in her own mind it did. "It's when you rename terms in order to affect a person's judgment of an idea. Like voo-doo economics. I'm sure that has another name..." she paused, waiting expectantly until the teacher finally spoke.

"Some people call it supply-side."

"Yes! That's semantic infiltration right there." Jesse was suddenly energized. "Who would ever take something called voo-doo or trickle-down seriously. However supply-side sounds respectable enough."

"That which we call a rose by any other name would smell as sweet," Mr. Irving quoted. "It hardly matters what it's called. It's the outcome that's important."

"If it hardly matters then why use a different name?" Jesse paused a fraction of a second and then answered her own question. "Because, when someone can't win an argument on merit, they try to win on deception."

Jesse was coming close to being disrespectful and Mr. Irving's eyes had flashed at the word deception. But then he gave her a little smile. "You suddenly seem well versed in economics. How do you feel supply-side compares to Keynesian economics?"

The question was designed to demonstrate her lack of authority on the subject, something she was willing to admit. She'd heard the word Keynesian before, but barely knew anything about it. "Is that the 'prime the pump' one, or the one from Australia?"

"First it's not Australia...you are thinking of the Austrian school of thought, which is a form of trick...supply-side economics." Mr. Irving explained.

"Then it's the 'prime the pump' one," Jesse said. "Though I'm not really sure what that means."

"Priming the pump is only one of the many ways in which government, when properly run, can control a desired outcome." Mr. Irving went to the chalkboard and began writing the words *John Maynard Keynes* as he spoke. "Keynesian ideas suggest that when an economy is stagnating it can be re-ignited by infusing it with money or low interest rate loans. This is the very opposite of what your father is doing."

"But where does that money come from?" Jesse asked. "Do you just print the money willy-nilly? That's inflation, right? And doesn't that hurt everyone by making the money in their pockets worth less? Or do you take it from the private sector...from companies? If so it means they have less money to spend or hire...hurting the economy even more. "

"Taxes are a necessary evil, Miss Clarke."

"I never thought that taxes were evil," Jesse said considering. "But they can have evil outcomes...which is why I don't think I could be a...Keynesianist? Is that a word?"

Mr. Irving shook his head. "No it's not...but what do you mean by 'evil outcomes'? Is it evil to take from those with plenty of money and redistribute it to those with less?"

"That's not what I was thinking about, but the answer to your question is yes, that is evil. It's called stealing," Jesse replied. "Criminals, who are usually poor, do it all the time and we throw them in jail when they do. Aren't they just redistributing wealth from rich to poor?"

"It's not the same," Mr. Irving said with a touch of ire. "Criminal behavior is not the same as helping out your fellow man by paying your fair share of taxes."

"The rich don't pay their fair share," Jesse replied. This was greeted by heads nodding around the classroom, including that of Mr. Irving. She went on, "They pay *more* than their fair share." This statement stopped the nodding cold.

"Oh, Miss Clarke. It seems your father really has brain washed you," Mr. Irving said sadly. "The simple truth is that the rich can afford to pay a higher tax rate."

"Yes, but we weren't talking about the ability to afford to pay more. We were talking about the idea of fairness," Jesse replied. Again, statistics that were so important to her father that he couldn't help sharing, *repeatedly*, came back to her. "The top one percent of wage earners pays forty percent of all the taxes, while the lower half of the country only pays three percent. That doesn't seem fair to me. To be perfectly fair, everyone—rich or poor—would pay the exact same amount. Not the same rate, the same amount. That would be absolute fairness. Blind fairness. Instead we have this legal form of stealing."

Mr. Irving opened his mouth to reply, but Jesse was on a roll. She'd never really had friends to talk to and her father was usually absent and rarely had time to converse. And now, suddenly, she was given a platform to speak where she wasn't being held up to ridicule at every turn. She discovered that she actually had a lot to say and spoke right over Mr. Irving, who was only going to refute her statement either way.

"It is stealing," she said, in answer to his unspoken refutation. "If you don't pay your taxes, what happens? A man with a gun shows up and forces you into a cage until you pay what he demands. Sure there are courts and all, but the idea is the same. A criminal takes your money because he has the power of his gun...the government does the same exact thing. In no way is that charity. Charity is giving from the heart."

"If you are so against taxes how do you propose paying for infrastructure, defense, schools that sort of thing," Mr. Irving asked. He went to his desk where it looked to Jesse that he was going to start on actual class work. For some reason she felt disappointed at this.

"How would I do it? I would make the United States sort of like a club with membership dues," she replied. "You pay ten percent of your income or get out."

Mr. Irving looked skeptical, "Ten percent? It's not enough for everything that the government does."

"That's because the government tries to do too much...and this is the problem with Keynesian economics," Jesse said, leaning on her chair. "The Keynesians want government to help here and help there, because they are under the delusion that they can control the economy and steer it in a direction they like. But they can't. They never could, otherwise we'd be in a perfect economy by now. All the government does is get in the way of people living their lives and running their businesses. I think that's the main difference between Keynesian and Supply-side. One side looks to the government for answers to all problems, the other looks to the individual."

"And you and your father think Supply side is better? Do you have any clue the harm that comes from this sort of laissez-fare attitude?" Jesse's eyes went a little wide; she didn't know the term laissez-faire. Mr. Irving explained: "It means *Let it be*. It's where there is no government intervention whatsoever and the people are at the mercy of business that can do whatever they want."

"Why do you assume businesses are evil? And why do you believe people are sheep in need of your protection? I don't see people that way." Turning to the class she said, "I bet most of your parents work for one business or another. How many of you think that your parents work for an evil company?"

No hands came up. Jesse didn't know if that was because of their dislike for her or not, she just went with it. "See? I bet there are no evil companies in Ashton. The people wouldn't put up with a company that was stealing or breaking the law. Either way, I don't think Supply-siders want no government, they only want less government. When you boil it all down, Keynesian is about control. Take away all those big words in that book that nobody..." Mr. Irving's eyebrows went up. "...I mean very few people understand and what you are left with is the government trying to control something that can't be controlled."

"What about here in Ashton?" a girl asked. Jesse turned and saw it was the same freckled-face girl from her English class. "My dad says that the town manager is also taking away rights and regulations."

"What rights?" Jesse asked. She had never heard of her father trying something like that.

Even Mr. Irving looked skeptical. The girl started turning a little pink in the cheeks about having said anything at all. "He said the town wasn't going to enforce labor laws anymore."

"Oh that," Jesse said with a feeling of relief. "He does that in every town. He says if a ten year old can be employed watching over an infant or mowing grass, why can't they do other things? If their parents are ok with it why should we keep them from earning a few dollars? And he hates useless regulations. He says they are the quickest way to kill the economy."

Mr. Irving rolled his eyes. "And how do they possibly do that?"

Jesse hopped up and went to the blackboard. "I could explain, but it's easier if I showed you."

Chapter 30

"My father made me do this once when I was eight-years-old." As she spoke, she took a piece of chalk and drew a big T. At the top left she wrote Supply-side and on the right, Keynesian.

"You see, I wanted to have a lemonade sale, so I asked my dad for ten dollars to buy supplies. But he wouldn't give me the money until I wrote out my business plan. You know: how much were the lemons and sugar, how much was I charging per cup, what sort of interest rate he could expect..."

Mr. Irving laughed loud and long. "He charged you interest? His own daughter? How much did he charge?"

"I never got the loan..." She had to stop because half the class was now laughing along with the teacher. Jesse was even able to smile...but that was only because it had been nine years. When they settled down she went on, "He was trying to teach me that there was more to running a business than just slapping a sign on a folding table. Inadvertently, he also showed me how government intervention can kill business."

She paused, feeling strangely confident. Every pair of eyes but one, was upon her and for once they weren't mocking. They were interested. "We'll use the lemonade stand as our proposed business. And we'll keep the ten dollars as our capital to purchase supplies and such."

She turned to the board and wrote on both columns: sugar, lemons, ice, cups, sign, folding table, pitcher.

Although she knew what answer would come to her, Jesse asked the class, "How much are we going to charge per cup of lemonade?" She was suddenly in teacher mode, a mode she did not know she possessed.

"Twenty-five cents," two different students said.

"If we sell fifty cups what will our profit be?" she asked, writing the number twenty-five in each column.

"Twelve-fifty."

Mr. Irving was watching all this intently and was silent up to that point, "She said profit."

"Oh, two-dollars and fifty cents."

Jesse turned back and choked on the words that were about to come out of her mouth. For some reason her eyes had gone straight to the back of the classroom. Ky still wasn't watching her, but he was no longer reading either. His head was turned the slightest bit toward her—he was listening. He was interested. Her heart did a little skip jump in her chest.

"Um...right," Jesse spat out before regaining her composure. "Here both columns are equal...the profit is the same. Can anyone tell me how an interfering government might affect the Keynesian side but not the Supply-side?" Silence greeted this. Even the crickets were quiet.

"I'll start with an easy one," Jesse said, wondering if she would have to fill in all the blanks. "Sugar from Brazil is half as cheap, but the government sticks a tariff on it to protect American sugar farmers. That's great for the few of them, but all the rest of us just got screwed over bad since sugar is the most costly item in your lemonade. There goes seventy cents in profit. What else?"

"A lemon tariff?" someone asked.

"No, but the government is using subsidies to push for all things organic. Organic lemons are being grown more and more and are more expensive. With fewer trees available for normal lemons, what happens to their price? It goes up and you just lost another ten cents."

"What about nutrition labels," the freckle-faced girl added. "The government makes you put them on everything."

"What's your name?" Jesse asked. In her heart there was always hope for a friendship. She searched for signs of it in everyone and this girl had looked Jesse right in the eyes when she had spoken. There had been shyness in them, but no hate.

"Sandra," the girl replied.

Jesse went to the board and began filling in the Keynesian side. Marking off seventy cents for the sugar and ten cents for the lemons. "Sandra is right. Nutrition labels have to be added to each cup—two cents. What else might have to be added to the cups?"

"A warning label?"

"Yes, thank you." Jesse said, nodding to a boy who had earlier that day rhymed runt with an obscene word in his limerick, and received only a very slight reprimand as a result.

"We don't have warning labels on soda and junk food yet, but there has been lots of talk...two cents lost." She turned to the board to add the new figures when Mr. Irving spoke up.

"That is a future *maybe* at the most. It shouldn't go up there."

"Then I have to add a penny for both lobbying and PR to make sure it doesn't happen," Jesse replied. "Every time someone floats these silly ideas, someone else has to fight them and someone has to pay and it's always the business. Anything else..." the room was quiet, but it was a nice sort of quiet. The kids were thinking.

"What about OSHA?" a girl asked, meekly putting her hand half way up before speaking. "When I worked at The Dim Sum I had to watch all these stupid safety movies. There was one that was like a half hour long about washing your hands and another one about not mixing bleach with ammonia and we didn't even use bleach or ammonia. It was such a waste of time."

"Good one. Complying with those sorts of rules cost money, one more cent. Anything else?" Jesse didn't really think any more ideas would come so she only paused a moment. "There's a hundred more that we aren't thinking of. Everything from what sort of markers you use to make your sign, to the height of your table, to what your cups are made of can be regulated and you have to pay for it all..."

"There's also the luxury tax. Don't forget about that." This came from a pale looking boy and it had a sobering effect on the classroom. Everyone looked away from him. Some cast their eyes out the window and others looked to their books.

"Gordon, its lemonade. It's not a luxury item." Mr. Irving said.

"To me it is," Gordon said. "I haven't had lemonade since I don't know when. All I get is water and with the town threatening to turn it off, pretty soon I won't even have that."

Now the room was dead silent. Clearly Gordon's family was on the brink. Jesse didn't know what to do. Did she keep going, and if so, would that appear insensitive? Or did she just wait and let Mr. Irving go back to teaching. If she did wait, Mr. Irving would likely brush over the boy's comment.

"Gordon is right, Mr. Irving." Jesse said. "Anything can be construed as a luxury item. There..."

"In Ashton, used cars are a luxury item," Gordon said quietly. The room remained still. Jesse gave Sandra a look that said *what's going on?*

"Gordon's family," Sandra began, keeping an eye on Gordon to see how he would react. "Owned Triple A Autos. It was a used car lot and it went under a couple of years ago because the town passed a luxury tax."

"It probably wasn't all because of the tax, Sandra," the teacher said.

"It was," said Gordon. "You could get the same car in Barton as you could here but for six hundred dollars cheaper. Who wouldn't want to save six-hundred dollars in this economy? My dad cried when that tax was passed and he cried when the bank took the last of his cars."

What followed that was one of the most painful silences Jesse had ever been a part of. It went on for a half a minute and during it she would have bet money that Gordon was also going to cry. His eyes went red and his face looked hot, but he didn't cry.

"Ok. I think we've heard enough from Miss Clarke," Mr. Irving announced, heading for the blackboard.

"I wasn't done," she replied in a quiet voice. She had a need inside of her to finish and a part of it was because of Gordon. He had a lost look about him, but there was also a desire to *know* in his eyes. Obviously, he had never heard another set of ideas beyond what he had been spoon fed by Mr. Irving.

"You are done when I say you're done."

A little louder she said, "I was just getting to the best part. The *pièce de résistance* if you will. Who wants to hear how this ends?" The kids looked at each other and Jesse was profoundly disappointed when only five hands went up. She thought that she had captured more of their attention than that. Mr. Irving gave her a sour smile and it so angered Jesse that she tried again...from another angle.

"A show of hands...who wants to hear Mr. Irving?" Giggling swept the class, but not a single hand went up. The teacher's mouth came open, but Jesse jumped in first. "The people have spoken. Take a look at our grid...so far, on one side you have a profit of two-dollars and fifty cents and on the other, one-dollar and seventy-five cents. But now, as Gordon has reminded us, we are at tax time and this is where the rubber hits the road. Can anyone tell me what the corporate income tax is?"

No one knew. They were lucky. It meant that they had normal human dads. "The tax rate is thirty five percent, the highest in the world."

A few eyebrows went up and Jesse began to worry that she had over-sold her big finish. "So what is the profit after corporate tax?" she asked.

"About a dollar and fourteen cents," Sandra supplied.

Without looking at the real teacher, Jesse wrote this on the board. "Are we now done?" A few shrugs and Jesse shook her head in a sad way. "I wish. We haven't even paid ourselves. Now instead of a ten-dollar lemonade stand let's say that was a million dollar business. At the end of the day we have either two-hundred and fifty thousand dollars under supply side or one-hundred and fourteen thousand dollars under Keynesian. How much of that do we keep and how much do we put back into the business to help grow it?"

More shrugs came to her.

"On the Keynesian side let's just say we put in twenty thousand to help grow our business...so our take home pay is ninety four thousand dollars...but wait! Now we have to pay our own personal income tax on top of everything else! What would that combined federal and state tax rate be?" she asked Mr. Irving.

He gave her the smallest shrug—*you're on your own, kid*—it said to Jesse. "My guess it would be at least forty-five percent. So that means after working your tail off every single day and risking everything you own...you risked your house, your cars, your children's college tuition...you get to take home about fifty two thousand dollars.

"Some of you may be thinking that's pretty good, but what happens when the sugar tariff goes up? You're out five thousand. What happens when a competitor moves in across the street? You're out fifteen thousand. What happens when the economy starts to slide and the town needs money for their budget?" Jesse left that unanswered, after all Gordon—exhibit A—was right there.

"Now on the Supply side," she said, tapping the board. "You have two-hundred and fifty thousand dollars of profit. Take away the ten percent tax and you are left with two hundred and twenty five thousand dollars." She wrote that number under the Supply-side column and then wrote fifty-two under the Keynesian. "This is the best case scenario. Compare the bottom line of these two; which would you rather have?" This brought out the smiles Jesse was hoping for.

"This is what my father is looking to do—he wants to get the government out of the way of business. Right now the government takes all this money and a lot of it is supposed to help the poor, but look at how many poor you still have, and the numbers of poor people is only growing!" Jesse underlined the larger sum on the chalkboard. "How many more people can the Supply-side hire compared to the Keynesian? With these jobs, how many more people will be lifted out of poverty? Our unemployment rate would practically be zero and there would be almost no need for welfare. In my mind, that's truly helping the poor."

Chapter 31

"Now it's my turn," Mr. Irving announced. "Your column on the left is bare of a few items. You haven't taken into account interest on your loans..."

"I..."

"Don't interrupt. I sat here and listened in silence to your diatribe and now I expect the same politeness from you," Mr. Irving said, sounding as if Jesse had attacked him personally. "You haven't taken into account, rent, utilities, insurance..."

He went on for some time, ticking off the minutia involved in running a business. After a minute he lost the class's attention and Jesse found herself staring at Ky.

"So you see that two-hundred and twenty five is not even close to being accurate," he said as a way of finishing.

"All those little details," Jesse said in response, turning back to the teacher. "I actually factored in under the initial investment of a million dollars. I didn't want to bore the class with lots of little details. But you did bring up even more points that we could discuss. You mentioned energy and fuel costs, those would be much cheaper under Supply-side..."

"I think we have taken up enough time on this discussion," Mr. Irving announced interrupting Jesse. "I don't see it going anywhere. Now if you could present to the class a real world example rather than a fictitious company that you've created simply to showcase the wonders of Supply-side, maybe we would be able to debate that, but since it doesn't exist let's get back to chapter fourteen."

"I do have an example," Jesse said. "A real world one."

The class had been all-aflutter with the sound of books being opened to chapter fourteen, but now they stopped as Mr. Irving looked at Jesse with a mixture of disbelief and loathing. The eyes of the students flicked back and forth between the two...a teacher/student confrontation was always the most fascinating event of the school year and Jesse already had a reputation for putting on a show.

Jesse didn't want a confrontation really, she just didn't want to be dismissed so easily out of hand. Her discussion on economics was like none she'd ever had before. When she had hopped up to discuss her lemonade stand, it was with only a vague notion as to where the debate would lead to. It had been exhilarating. Thoughts had come to her almost as fast as she could speak them and it felt good to be able stand her ground against an adult.

Remember the ball! Don't say anything stupid. Don't blow it.

It was the voice of reason, but also the voice of a chicken. "You asked for a real world example," she reminded her teacher.

"Maybe you should put it the form of an essay," Mr. Irving suggested.

Jesse refused to budge. She neither said yes or no. She only stared evenly into his face. The idea of an essay didn't upset her. What did however, was the fact that if she did write it, he wouldn't bother to read it.

After a few moments he gave her a strained smile, "Fine, I'll indulge you. But be warned my patience is wearing thin."

"I'll be quick," Jesse promised. She opened her book bag and snatched out her thick history textbook. Laying back the cover, she exposed the map of the world which she presented to the class. "Right here...so small you can't even see it is Hong Kong. It's just a tiny little island and it's crammed with buildings and people like you can't believe. I went there two years ago with my parents and it was a real eye-opener."

Her father had been there trying to find companies that would relocate to the states, while her mom had shopped. Jesse had accompanied both during the week and had learned much...from her father.

"Even though it's so thickly populated and has next to nothing when it comes to raw materials...I mean there's no coal, or oil, or even trees...it's one of the richest cities in the world. Why...because it's also one of the freest cities in the world. They have really low tax rates and almost no regulations, other than ones keeping people safe. This is the most perfect example of pure Supply-side economics in action that I can think of. And right next to it is China. It's Keynesian at its purest. They have every resource imaginable, but the government dictates everything and the people are dirt poor. It's a slave economy."

Jesse paused to catch her breath. She had been worried that if she had taken even a moment, Mr. Irving would have stepped in.

"That was wonderful, thanks," Mr. Irving said. "Now, chapter fourteen everyone."

That was it?

Jesse didn't know what to think about this. She had expectations of another argument, yet the teacher just went right into his regularly scheduled pre-planned class. Did that mean she had won the debate? She had refuted, and easily so, the premises of his economic thought, while he hadn't touched hers with anything resembling logic. That sounded like a win to her, so why wasn't he acknowledging it?

She'd been expecting: *Those are interesting points; I should take them into consideration.* Or better yet: *You've really put that into perspective, thanks.*

Jesse stewed on this for the rest of class. Her mind ran over every detail of their debate and came up with even more points to buttress her arguments. Yet she had the feeling that she would be wasting her time if she brought them up. Mr. Irving seemed content in his philosophy despite the fact that she had clearly shown him how wrong it was.

What did that mean? Was Keynesian economics his religion? Was he basing his ideas on faith rather than facts?

Maybe you're the one that's wrong?

That was definitely a possibility. She wasn't omniscient after all. Unobtrusively as possible, she flipped her book open to—Chapter 2 *Keynes and You!*—and read for the remainder of the period. When the bell rang, she wasn't any closer to understanding why he would think it would work as a major philosophy. Her mind twirled and she just had to give up trying to figure out Mr. Irving's rationale.

At least you weren't sent to the principal's office. There was that.

The sight of Ky helped to clear her head. He walked out of the room and she stepped out right behind him. With him clearing the way and people doing their best not to look in his direction, she felt protected being so close to him. It was like he was her own personal bodyguard.

"Room 235 please," she whispered, so that he alone would hear. Involuntarily, his shoulders jumped when she said it. He then went taunt as steel cable and Jesse had to remind herself that Ky had issues. Out of deference to him she kept quiet the rest of the way down the hall.

Jesse didn't immediately turn into her classroom as she came up to it. She was curious. Amanda Jorgenson had been absent from fifth period and with a quick peek into the room next door Jesse discovered that she was gone from seventh as well. It brought a wide smile to her lips. Maybe the girl had been suspended.

Sudden movement to her side startled her. A blur of black leather and blue jeans, came at her. Jesse dodged back, not quite so fast as she needed to be and someone clipped her shoulder hard enough to spin her halfway around.

"Sorry bout that," drawled out John Osterman. He had come out of nowhere and if he had hit her square, he might have sent her face first into the nearest locker. "You should watch where I'm going. If you know what I mean."

"Right," Jesse said and nothing more. Nor did she move. Ronny was on one side of her and John the other. To move meant putting her back to one of them. They advanced wearing goofy grins and she had to wonder if they had been smoking something. But then she smelled the sour odor of cheap beer on their breath. It made her stomach go squirrely, though it was mostly out of nerves. Drunk boys were apt to do anything, even in a crowded hall.

Just then a teacher, an older woman with brassy red hair, that Jesse had only seen on one other occasion poked her head out of her classroom door and barked, "Ronny! John! Get to class." When they didn't immediately leave, she raised her voice louder. "I said leave!"

"Sure thang," John said and spun on the spot. He misjudged his twirl and knocked into his friend which set them both to giggling. Jesse watched them go and didn't move even after the bell rang a second later. They had put a good scare into her and she was afraid that wasn't all they were going to do.

"Excuse me, Miss Clarke?"

Just then Jesse realized the woman was still there. "Y-Yes...Ma'am?" Jesse stuttered still frazzled.

"I need you to do me a favor," she said with a tight smile on her lips. "I need you to cut this 'Bad-Girl' attitude out or don't come back to school...for a few days." The woman nodded her brassy head as she spoke. Her mottled blue eyes fixed on Jesse's. "Do you understand what I'm trying to say?"

"Am I in danger?"

Pain swept the woman's face. "Good, I'm glad we understand each other." She turned and left, shutting her classroom door on Jesse's puzzled look.

A cold chill swept up Jesse's back as she stood in the empty hall. She *was* in danger and not just from the petty bickering of Amanda and her friends. It was the second time that day, she'd been warned by a teacher...what did they know? Had they overheard the other students talking?

"Miss Clarke?" The sudden sharp sound of her name stopped her heart and Jesse jumped a foot in the air. It was Mr. Johnson sticking his head out into the hall. "Should I mark you as absent today? Or are you going to bless us with your presence?"

"Oh...yes. I'm coming," Jesse said and took two steps toward the door, but then stopped. "Can I speak with you? Here?"

"No of course not. I have twenty-two other students waiting on me. If you wish to speak with me do so after class."

"Yes, Sir," Jesse replied, scampering past him and heading for her desk. Immediately her fingers slipped into the word that was carved out on the flat plane of the wood: *ALONE.*

That she definitely was.

The class was full of students and Mr. Johnsons bowling pin shaped body took up a lot of room, but despite that, Jesse felt isolated. It was if she were thirty feet away from everyone else and under a spotlight, with fingers being pointed at her from every direction. Was there a plot to sic the Shadow-man on her? If so, how? There was no way to know. Again her stomach went queasy as her nerves kicked up a fuss.

Settle down. You're not his type.

Right...maybe...who knows? If she only knew what his type was it would be far easier to settle down.

Jesse traced the outline of the carved word almost in a trance and it was sometime before she noticed that someone had erased the light pencil marks she had drawn on the desk. The note!

She had plum forgotten about the note she had left Ky two days before. Too casually, she slipped her hand into the slot of her desk while pretending to listen to Mr. Johnson, yet there was nothing in the desk at all. She even stuck her hand as far back as possible and searched the darkest corners of the cubby. Nothing.

Grasping at straws, she then searched the underside of her chair. Again nothing. She slumped back defeated and dispirited. Ky hadn't written in return and who knows if even read her note in the first place. On its own, her hand went back to the carved word, yet her eyes were drawn to the initials:

S.B.

G.M.J.

J.O.

R. M.- K. M.- N.M.-?

M.C

What were these? Victims of Harold Brownly's?

Probably. The first initials S.B. corresponded with what her father had mentioned about Harold, how he had killed his own son. Scott Brownly? Steve Brownly? Sam, Shawn, Seth...just then, to Jesse it didn't matter the boy's first name.

The last set of initials M.C. had to be Mary Castaneda, the girl who'd been found in the cemetery. The thought of her set a pang of regret through Jesse. It must have been a rough year for her mother, and Jesse had gone and made it just that much worse.

But who were the rest? G.M.J. was likely Gregory Matthew Johnson, the boy whose picture sat on the desk in the front of the room. His year of death matched as well. The rest were just a mystery, especially the three: *R. M.- K. M.- N.M.-?*

Did this mean that it wasn't known if they had been killed by Harold or not? Again unknown. Her eyes wouldn't come off the letters K.M.— Kyle Mendel. Her mind kept filling in his name, which was stupid since although he ghosted around the school, he was still very much alive. But for how much longer? Unknown.

In a zone, she traced the letters, listening to Mr. Johnson teach until later the bell rang.

That was her day in a nutshell. Waiting on bells, waiting on Ky, waiting to see what would happen to her. Waiting, like everyone else in the town, to see who would die next. Why they still lived in Ashton, she didn't know. Or why they didn't gather together and string Harold up by the neck, she didn't know that either. She only knew that the waiting was starting to get to her. It was like an expanding hunk of cold lead in her chest and when she thought about it too much, it made it hard to breathe.

As the other students filed out of the class, Jesse waited for a chance to be alone with Mr. Johnson so she could ask him about the vague warning that she had received. She fiddled about in her bag as if looking for something, but when she glanced up next, he was gone.

"No!" she exclaimed, and then ran to the door. The hall was filled with nothing but students, half of whom stared at her as if she were an insect. Not only had she lost the chance to talk to her teacher, when Jesse looked into the room next door, Ky was gone as well. Now she'd have to brave the corridors without his protection. This wasn't really a problem, she'd done it many times before, she just liked being so close to him.

The girl in black stood out in the fashionably challenged halls as if she had a bulls-eye on her chest, yet she was quick and alert. Two different times people stepped in her way purposely trying to knock into her and both times she dodged with ease. Her biology class was on the first floor and Jesse was only feet away when she saw Ms Weldon come out of the front office.

The art teacher picked her out of the crowd with ease; their eyes locked for a moment and then Ms Weldon looked away. There had been meaning in her look, Jesse was sure of it.

"Ms Weldon?" Jesse called, ducking through the few students between them. "Can I speak with you for a moment?"

"I'm already late," the teacher said turning away.

Jesse touched her on the arm. "I need to know if you think that I'm in some kind of danger."

This stopped the art teacher in place and she turned around with narrowed eyes. "Someone say something to you?" Jesse only gave her a shrug, not knowing if she would be getting the redheaded teacher in trouble by answering fully. Ms Weldon leaned her tall frame back from Jesse and looked down her nose, but not in a nasty way.

"Look," she said, eventually. "You aren't in any more danger than any of the other students..."

"Then why...?"

"Then why the warning?" the art teacher cut in. "Because you are a magnet for trouble. I warned you that this was a bad town to be friendless in and now you are outside the herd, so to speak. Most of these students may not like you, but they won't hurt you. At the same time..." As if she couldn't turn the teacher in her off, she left off expecting Jesse to fill in the blank.

"They won't protect me, either."

"Exactly."

"But the warning seemed more than that...was something over heard?" Jesse asked.

"Not that I know of, but..." Ms Weldon suddenly seemed reluctant to say anything more.

Jesse had just a light touch on her arm before, but now she gripped it, hard. "Please, I need to know."

After giving the hallway a quick scan, Ms Weldon pulled her in close. "There are some in the school who have more reason to be afraid than others. The pressure may be getting to them and they may do *something*. But they may not, I don't know. Now, I've said all that I'm going to say...other than to warn you: don't make enemies if you can avoid it."

"How the heck am I supposed to do that?" Jesse asked in bewilderment.

Chapter 32

The art teacher left a flabbergasted Jesse standing in the hall. Not make enemies? Wasn't Ms Weldon herself an enemy of Jesse's? She certainly wasn't a friend and nor was she neutral. She had actively tried to harm Jesse's academic career and she had practically set her class on Jesse. That sure sounded like an enemy.

Not make enemies! The very idea was too much for Jesse; it would be easier to ask her not to breathe. In a snit, Jesse stormed into the lab room and plunked her bag heavily down on the table. As was usual for her, she was late, but Mr. Daniels didn't seem to notice, because as was usual for him, he was running about answering six questions at once.

Jesse took out her lab work knowing well ahead of time she was going to be killing time instead of doing any work. Even if she hadn't been well behind in the class, her mind was spinning over the idea that there were people actually plotting to hand her over to Harold.

Would Amanda do it? Was this her plan for the evening? It was a possibility. Yet how would she do it? Harold wasn't some demon that you could summon. Would she try to reach him by phone? Not likely with Wild Bill and his useless three-man posse hanging around. Tapping Harold's phone was the first thing they would have done, and Amanda wouldn't want it to get out that she had helped in a murder.

Though he might have saved her two days back, Jesse thought Wild Bill was pathetic. Riding around in a coal black car and keeping to the streets, struck her as stupid; Harold would strike from the forest when he made his move. What was worse than Wild Bill, however, was his team, or rather the small size of it. If they worked twelve-hour shifts, at best there would only be two people to cover twenty-five square miles of town and forests. It made no sense.

But senseless or not it left open the opportunity for someone to set her up, but once again, how? First they would have to give Jesse this secret trait that the Shadow-man was so mad over and then they would have to get her in his path. It seemed impossible, but all the same at least three teachers had expressed concern at the prospect.

"Ugh!" Jesse groaned, with her head in her hands. The whole thing was giving her a headache. It was all useless supposition until she could find out more information, which she vowed to get that evening when her father came home.

Putting it out of her mind, Jesse began making notes in her lab work; she poked at long ugly earthworms, stared down a microscope at squiggly shapes, and generally wasted time. That she'd fail the lab was a foregone conclusion. Even Mr. Daniels thought so. After swinging by to check her progress, he only raised his eyebrows and said, "Ok." Then left again just as quick and never came back. They both knew she was too far behind to catch up and neither really cared.

Doodling her way through the lab made her last class of the day go by rather quick. When the bell rang she slowly put away her equipment, letting the other students go first. She wasn't in a hurry. Though it was tapering off, there was still enough of that stupid limerick business in the halls to make Jesse see red. So she slouched on her desk eyeing Ky and thinking how the day hadn't been half-bad.

Jesse only slouched there for a few minutes. Ky was still extra stiff and getting stiffer. She didn't want to annoy him, so she left while the busses were still pulling out of the parking lot. This earned her a raucous burst of confused rhymes, which she ignored. If it wasn't for the presences of her mother, Jesse would have flipped the kids off with both hands.

But she couldn't do that in front of her mother. Only...her mother wasn't there. Her gleaming white Lexus was nowhere to be seen.

"She's in the front of the building. That's all," Jesse said to herself. "Nothing to freak out over."

However, Jesse was freaked out. Her heart told her that her mom had flaked out on her once again. With that same heart in her throat, Jesse tore back toward the building and saw the back door closing.

"Hold that door!" she cried out to Ky. Ky ignored her and the door shut in her face. "No!" Her first reaction was to rage at Ky, yet her second reaction—panic—followed too close on the heels of the first. The misery of the previous afternoon flashed in her mind: the hunger, the pain, the bone chilling cold, the feeling of being lost, the bullies chasing her, the knife at her throat and behind it all the Shadow-man...always lurking. And there was more: there had been tears, and fear in the pit of her stomach at the knowledge of coming death.

Knowing that death was hunting you was the worst feeling...and she had it again, right at that moment.

This time there was no begging Ky, it would have been useless, nor could there be even a half-second of hesitation on her part. She tore around the building at full speed. She thought that she'd been quick the day before but now she ignored the burning need for air in her lungs and the re-occurring pain in her ankle. Her legs pumped for all they were worth, and Jesse flew along at a tremendous clip with her long black coat trailing out. When she finally made it around the far side of the building she took in the parking lot at a glance: No white Lexus, no mom.

It hurt. Knowing that she had been abandoned caused physical pain somewhere deep inside her. In the spot where there should have been comfort and security, there was only pain. But it was a pain that she had endured many times in the past and would undoubtedly feel again. It was a pain that sadly, she was able to ignore.

Her mom's car might not have been there, but she was happily astonished to see half a dozen cars still sitting idly in the lot. Yet they wouldn't be idle for long. Teachers were streaming toward them and one of them was none other than...

"Mr. Daniels!" Jesse called in a feeble voice. Suddenly the pain in her ankle and the burning need for air was no longer something she could ignore. He was not more than thirty yards away and didn't hear her at first.

"Excuse...me," she tried again, doggedly running forward. As she did she pulled her cell phone out and saw the *light of disappointment* blinking up at her. It meant there was currently an excuse stored in her voice mail. It was always an excuse. Just once Jesse would like to hear a message say: We just bought a puppy, hurry home!

"Excuse me?" she said a second time as her thumb hit the voice mail auto dial. Jesse was much closer now and Mr. Daniels turned at her voice.

"Oh, Miss Clarke...what a...what's the matter?" he asked, sounding concerned at seeing her sudden and startling wide-eyed appearance.

A tiny recorded version of her mom suddenly said, "I'm so sorry I won't..."

Jesse snapped the phone off. There was a volcano of anger in her over being left stranded by her mom, but it was swallowed up whole by her desperate fear. She didn't think she could take another afternoon like yesterday.

"I don't have a ride...and the buses won't let me on...and my bike got des-des..." She had to pause, fat tears ambushed her and they were coming before she knew it. "Sorry...Sorry. I don't mean to make a scene...I just need a ride, please."

Mr. Daniels shrugged and then shook his head, "I can't. I don't have a car here. I'm car pooling." He pointed, indicating the one person in the school who really had a reason to hate Jesse. Carla Castaneda stood on the other side of the low green Volvo.

[273]

Jesse no longer had a heartbeat. It disappeared as she looked into Carla's brown eyes...those same eyes that were sobbing only the day before. Sobbing because Jesse had hurt her in a way no one else would ever dare.

Those eyes told Jesse that she would have a long cold walk home.

Chapter 33

Jesse turned from the green Volvo and looked up to where her fate laid waiting. Her eyes went up into the hilly woods just across the road. If the Shadow-man was hunting, here and now would be perfect. He'd just sit up there invisible to God and everyone and wait for the stray who missed her bus, or for the boy whose mom was running late or perhaps wasn't going to show at all.

He would wait for those unlucky few outside the flock.

Was that how he picked his victims? Was he just penalizing the unlucky ones? Because sometimes Jesse felt like the unluckiest person on God's green earth. Unlike everyone else she had no choice in how she was treated. She could be the sweetest girl in the world and still she'd be spat on. It was her destiny. It was her destiny to absorb the world's hate and anger, its scorn, its bitterness, even its jealousy.

It was a horror to live through, but this time, standing in the parking lot it would be far worse. This time when Carla unloaded her venom on Jesse it would be because Jesse deserved it.

She had not only been rude to Mrs. Castaneda, acting all high and mighty, she had been hurtful as well. She'd caused needless pain. Even if she had done it unknowingly, Jesse had still stomped on the woman's misery.

Her shame kept her from looking at Carla. "I'm sorry about yesterday...I didn't know," she said in a voice of quiet wretchedness.

Jesse decided that she was done running. She would walk down the middle of Schoolhouse road and take her chances. Unable to even say goodbye she started to the road.

"Get in," Carla said from behind her.

Nerve endings flashed throughout Jesse's body at the soft words and she felt her skin come alive in feeling. New and greater tears formed themselves in her eyes and hurriedly she wiped them away before she turned around.

"Hurry up and get in," Carla said with a touch of impatience. "I won't be late picking up my son from day care...no matter what. Not this time." Jesse turned and locked eyes with Carla. The librarian blamed herself for her daughter Mary's death. It was plain to see. What also was plain was that she had forgiven Jesse...despite the pain Carla had forgiven the girl.

The weight of emotions pulled at Jesse's chin and she had trouble keeping her eyes up. She climbed into the back of the car with her head down. "Thank you for the ride, Mrs. Castaneda," she said. "I really appreciate it."

"Don't worry about it," Carla replied. There came a long silence that Jesse didn't know how to break. It ate up the road beneath them until Carla swallowed audibly and asked, "Why don't you have a car? I'm guessing that your parents could afford one."

"I lost my license," Jesse answered, trying to keep the emotion out of her voice.

"Was it speeding?" Mr. Daniels asked. "We have wild speeders around here...in the summer." This last he added almost as if he forgot that the town died, literally as well as figuratively, in the early winter.

"No...it...it." Jesse squirmed in the back seat. "In the last town that we lived in they had too many police officers. They had like thirteen and since the town was small like Ashton, they couldn't afford them all."

"Thirteen?" Mr. Daniels said amazed. "We have six and I swear that's three too many. Except for...around now that is. Is your father planning on firing any of our police force?"

"No...I think he'd normally do that, but under the circumstances..."

Mrs. Castaneda flashed her brown eyes in the mirror. "So how'd you get in so much trouble that you lost your license?"

"Because whenever I took the car out, I had my own police escort," Jesse said, rubbing her head. The memory wasn't pleasant. "I got a ticket every time out. No matter how slow I was going I got a speeding ticket. At stop signs I would have to stop, count to ten and then go, or I'd get a ticket. I had my license for only eleven days."

The car was very silent.

"Well that sucks," Mr. Daniels said.

The way he said it made Jesse laugh. To hear an old biology teacher use the word "sucks" just struck her as the funniest thing she'd heard in a long time and she laughed until she cried.

"Well it does," he added, which had her going again.

She controlled her breathing long enough to give directions. "If you are taking me home first, it's a left at the stop sign."

Mrs. Castaneda had been smiling at Jesse's mirth but her eyes went from brown to black. "I know exactly where you live."

Mr. Daniels stiffened beside her and took to finding the view out the window, a view he had likely seen every day of his life, extremely interesting.

What did she mean by that? Jesse wondered. She asked in a nervous voice, "Do you live around here?"

The lady coughed out a bitter laugh. "No...if I lived around here I'd burn my own house down."

Now Mr. Daniels was practically paralyzed in his discomfort, and Jesse had come down with a case of it as well. Her face went manikin-like in a half-smile. All she could think to say to that was: "Oh yeah?"

Carla's knuckles had gone white on the steering wheel and her slim shoulders were taunt beneath her blouse. "The man who killed my daughter lives right around the corner from you...I guess you knew that right?" Jesse nodded to the face in the mirror. "Every day I used to drive out here and park in front of his house and I would cry and I would scream challenges at him to come for me too. I...I always had a knife from my kitchen with me and-and I would've used it too...but he never came out and I was too afraid to go in."

Next to Carla, Mr. Daniels was a toad-faced stone. Nothing moved on him and perhaps nothing moved in him either. Jesse didn't blame him a bit; the librarian's swelling emotions looked ready to spew out of her either in tears or screaming anger. Jesse felt split down the middle—she couldn't stand to see the pain in Carla's eyes, yet she needed answers, perhaps desperately so.

"Why don't they arrest him," Jesse asked, hoping to tip-toe a fine line.

"Because the police are all so stupid...no offence, Mr. Daniels."

The biology teacher smiled and Jesse could have sworn she heard the stiff muscles of his face grinding together like stones moving against each other. "That's ok. I understand," he said. Then he turned back toward Jesse and explained, "My son is a police officer here in Ashton. They haven't arrested Mr. Brownly for lack of evidence."

"Can I ask...why aren't there more police running around here?" Jesse asked.

Mr. Daniels head creaked on his shoulders as he shook it sadly. "The state has its own budget concerns, and after three years of trying to catch Harold...they are kind of...scaling back." Jesse knew he had been about to say *giving up*, which would have been a mistake with Carla right there. "In the last two years they had sixteen men roaming all up in the hills and up and down the streets and got nothing."

"And now they think it might be someone from another town," Carla added. "Can you believe that? Like we wouldn't notice a stranger wandering around here. How stupid is that?" She cast a quick guilty glance at the man next to her. "Sorry Mr. Daniels, I'm just so frustrated."

He shook his head again. "It's ok. But I've told you before my name is Greg. You haven't been my student in twenty years so stop calling me Mr. Daniels."

"Right...Greg. I can't seem to help myself. I think to me you'll always be Mr. Daniels—my biology teacher from the eleventh grade—the man I threw up on when I stepped on that frog in class," Carla said, once again smiling.

Jesse smirked in the back seat at the image. It was strange to her to see teachers as real people. It was so hard to picture them as being young once: wearing braces, ditching school...accidentally stepping on frogs. Yet they were. Carla was very real. She wasn't just a school librarian; she was a mother and a woman with problems of her own. Carla's smile of a day long gone made her all the prettier and Jesse was loathe to be the one to make it stop, but she had more questions and her house was coming up quick.

"Why do they think it's not Harold?" There was a thousand pounds of hope in that question. Living next door to a killer was a miserable stress. She crept around her own house, peeking through windows, barely breathing, always on edge and always listening. Waiting for that one moment when the wood of the stairs would begin an inexplicable creaking as the Shadow-man came for her.

As Carla pulled up in front of Jesse's house, Mr. Daniels turned back once again to explain, "Most of them do think it's Harold. The only reason some don't is that he's been able to slip through their fingers so easily. On the night of...uh...last year I should say." He paused with a glance at Carla, whose smile was gone—long gone. She nodded for him to continue. "They had four men watching his house and none saw him leave. He just 'floated by like a shadow' as my son put it. None saw him leave, and none saw him return, but they knew he had left. Only they knew it too late. Later when they watched the tapes they could see only his shadow ghost by the camera."

Carla had her face to the window and whether she was crying or not Jesse didn't know, but her voice was thick with emotion. "So instead of admitting that they screwed up somewhere and allowed that great big man to slip right by them. They make up some stupid theory that it couldn't be him. It had to be someone else...a stranger from another town."

"And it couldn't be a stranger?" Jesse asked, fearing that she had gone too far, but urgently feeling a need to know. Now Carla cried audibly and Mr. Daniels became again a toad-like statue next to her.

"My daughter was found in the Ashton cemetery on the grave of Steven Brownly...presented like she was a gift to Harold's dead son. No stranger would do that. Only someone very, very evil would do that."

Chapter 34

After thanking Carla, Jesse got out the car and was inside her house in a matter of seconds. Nothing in their conversation had alleviated her fear of Harold Brownly, instead it exacerbated it. If Harold could slip away from the police and kill right under their noses, how could she expect to feel safe anywhere?

Even in her own home. Jesse checked and rechecked every door and window, knowing all the while what a futile gesture it was. Her doors were not made of cold iron, they were made of wood. A single blow from one of Harold's great shoulders would level them and leave her at his mercy.

It seemed almost safer in the woods. There she could run. Even with her bum ankle she could probably out distance Harold. He was huge and likely didn't have the stamina to keep up with her.

But he's crazy.

Right as always. Crazy people could do crazy things. In her mind's eye she could see Harold stalking her relentlessly—tirelessly, as she grew weaker from exhaustion. He would come on just as he had been for years, and all it would take was one misstep and she'd be down with a broken ankle and then...

With that thought in mind and a cold sweat down her back, Jesse went to the kitchen and picked out a good sturdy knife, one that could disembowel a man. It was a good knife, but against Harold it still didn't seem like much, yet it was all she had. She took it with her to her room and there began a vigil that would last for hours.

She watched and waited. She watched nothing; the two houses were black and blank. And she waited, but for what? For Ky to show up and ignore her, or for Harold to show up and notice her? Neither seemed too appealing.

You're waiting until it's time to fight.

Wrong. Jesse wasn't going to fight. A fight would put her out there...at the mercy of the killer.

I thought you were worried that the killer could get in here?

Jesse growled at her voice of reason. "What good would a fight do either way?" she asked aloud to the empty room. A fight with a girl like Amanda held danger either way, win or lose. If Jesse lost, it would just mean more and more aggravation and would lead to more fights. If she won it could mean that she'd have to deal with Ronny and John, both of whom did not look to be above fighting a girl.

She had not counted on two such losers hanging around Amanda when she had first confronted the blonde on Monday. She had figured that Amanda and her big mouth would be a good lesson learned for the rest of the girls in Ashton high: don't mess with the new girl. Yet now a win over Amanda might very well spark revenge from her two wanna-be boyfriends.

There is option C.

Right...maybe. Option C was what boys sometimes did. When boys fought there was a good chance that they'd be friends afterwards. It didn't make sense and it didn't happen every time, but it *did* happen sometimes. It was as if the fight had to occur for the friendship to occur.

But how did it happen? Maybe they talked afterwards, about sports or girls. Jesse hopped down from her desk where she had been perched and began pacing. As she paced, she began working her neck around, loosening up.

She could do this she decided. She would beat Amanda up...but not too badly...and then sit her down for a chat.

"Maybe I should bring a snack for afterwards," she suggested to the girl in the mirror, while checking the scab over her right eye. It wouldn't do for the wound to open up during the fight. Blood in the eye didn't hurt, but it was distracting. It would hold, she decided.

"A snack is a good idea," Jesse replied to herself, changing out of her shirt. The red satin was just too nice. She slipped on a form fitting black lycra top. It was slick and would be hard to grab a hold of. Next she took off her jungle boots and redid the ace bandage about her ankle.

"Wait! Am I really going to do this?" she asked. "Am I really going out there?" Jesse went back to the window and looked out again. Her voice of reason was silent. She had cause to go out and cause to stay. At this point, all she could do was shrug. When she did, Jesse saw her reflection in the window mirror the movement and this set off a warning bell of alarm.

If she could see herself reflected that meant someone outside could now see in through her window. Quickly she ran to the wall and swatted the light switch down. The room went darker than she had expected and she looked over at the orange glow of her alarm clock: 4:48 pm.

Harold's house was still dark.

Was he in there looking up at me? she wondered. The thought gave her the chills. *Or was he out in the woods searching?* That thought was worse. As long as he was out lurking about in the woods, Jesse decided that she wouldn't leave the house; it was just too dangerous.

Ky came home at half past six and ten minutes later a light came on in Harold's house. Was that coincidence?

Jesse didn't know. She did know a gnawing sense of anxiety that grew as the minutes slipped by. Just after seven o'clock, she saw Harold's large shadow begin to pace, just as it had the night before. This brought on a near fevered pitch of nerves. It meant that she really no longer had an excuse not to go out; it meant that the fight was on.

With a big chest-rattling sigh, Jesse hopped down again and began her own pacing. She would gradually warm up for the next half hour, then grab a couple of handfuls of Double-stuff Oreos put them in a baggy and head down to the berm. It was a good plan. It was a good, nerve-wrecking plan. It was one thing to fight, but it was another to fight at night and it was a whole other ball of wax to fight with an insane killer in the neighborhood.

Was there an alternative? Of course there was, but it wasn't one that Jesse relished. It involved endless hazing, nasty teasing, and being called chicken at every turn. It meant that she'd be looked down upon and with reason.

"A coward dies a thousand deaths while the valiant tastes death but once," she said.

You misquoted that. It's actually...

"Shut up," she said to herself.

Ten minutes before she was to leave, Ky's house went dark. One by one the lights went down and Jesse practically had her nose pressed against the window to see why. There was no way to know from where she was and no likely reason popped into her head. Now her attention was concentrated on Harold's house. If his house went dark too, there was no way that she'd leave, chicken or no chicken. Even if he stopped pacing, she wouldn't go.

A minute later her watched beeped at her. Fight time and Harold still walked back and forth. She hesitated for two full minutes and a large part of her wanted him to stop so she wouldn't have to go... so she would have an excuse to stay and cower.

'Cowards die many times before their deaths; the valiant never taste of death but once.' That is the actual quote.

"Fine!" Jesse snapped at herself, and ran from the room. She stopped in the kitchen, grabbed her Oreos and left, still stuffing them into a baggy.

In seconds, she was practically invisible. In her black attire she blended in with the night and the soft tread of her boots was barely audible even to her own ears. She was a ghost herself as she slipped down the trail. With the knowledge that Harold was at home, Jesse didn't fear what lay before her and hurried down to the berm as quick as she could.

Now that she was moving she calmed considerably. So much so that she was just thinking about inviting Amanda back to her house to freshen up after the fight, when she caught sight of the berm. On it was a lone figure and even from a hundred yards away Amanda's blonde hair stood out against her dark coat. As promised she was all alone.

Now Jesse slowed and took huge breaths trying to focus her mind and control her anxiety. In a minute, she was ready and slipped the heavy chain and lock out of her pocket and laid them next to a tree by the path. No weapons was the rule.

"Show time," she whispered, striding out onto the berm. "Go in fast—keep your weight forward—keep her on her heels." She hissed instructions to herself as she walked. At thirty yards, with her eyes focused on the blonde, Jesse began unbuttoning her long coat.

For her part, Amanda just stood waiting quietly. She barely even moved, as if she wasn't the least bit anxious. The only sign that she was in any way uneasy was in the fact that she was smoking a cigarette. The red-orange ember flared briefly as she brought it to her face and then it went flying to skip across the thin ice of the pond.

Jesse watched its progress and when she looked back to Amanda her breath stopped in her throat.

Far down the berm behind Amanda a shadow came out from the edge of the trees. It seemed a very large shadow, too large to be a normal person. The sight of it smote Jesse's heart, leaving her clutching her chest in fear. The Shadow-man was there!

All thoughts of fighting Amanda left her in that one split second—her mind was only taken up with thoughts of fleeing. Yet she would not abandon the blonde girl, no matter the animosity between them.

"Amanda! Behind you!" she screamed. In what felt like slow motion the girl turned and stared down the berm. Jesse started backing away, but Amanda only stood as if frozen by the sight. Jesse took two more steps away, her feet seemed uncontrollably light. They wanted to fly from there as fast possible and it was everything Jesse could do to hold them down. Yet Amanda wouldn't budge.

"Run!" Jesse ordered. However, the blonde didn't, she only turned and smiled a hard white smile at Jesse. The grin and the pale face around it were like cold death, and were totally incomprehensible. Jesse's mind boggled and contorted on itself. Surely Amanda was afraid of the Shadow-man, everyone was...

Just then the huge shadow coming forward became more distinct and she saw that it wasn't one large man, it was two people dressed in black. Understanding struck Jesse and she spun away from Amanda and her death's head smile. She made to run, only the sight coming from the other end of the berm stopped her and turned her feather light feet to bricks: two more people were heading toward her from that direction as well.

There was nowhere to run. The berm was maybe twelve feet wide; it would be impossible to juke her way past two people on such a narrow strip. Her only other option was to take a chance that her weight on the newly frozen pond wouldn't send her through the ice.

That's not an option! Her voice of reason was also the voice of panic. The waters of the ponds needed at least another week to thicken before they would be skate worthy. To go out too soon would be to face the coldest death imaginable.

Amanda seemed to be reading her thoughts. "I wouldn't go out there if I was you," she said strolling forward. "You'll go right to the bottom. You ever go through the ice before? That pretty coat of yours will suddenly weigh a hundred pounds and it'll suck you down."

Just then her three-quarter length coat felt heavier on her shoulders. She knew if she did go into the water the cotton/wool blend would act as sponge...and it would feel like a straightjacket. The coat would make it seem like she was struggling in black tar rather than water and she would get tired so fast...

Uncertainty raged within her. Every path seemed to lead to pain or to death. Ahead of her were three people, led by Amanda. Behind her only two. Jesse turned and fled down the berm toward her home. She had no real hope she'd get by the two people blocking her way, but at least it was closer to land. That was all that was important to her panic-stricken mind. She had no clue what Amanda planned to do to her, but going into the ice-cold water was her greatest fear...yet seconds later she found herself standing on its flat surface, watching long cracks forming around her.

Chapter 35

In a dead sprint Jesse ran at the two people on the north end of the berm. As she drew closer, the dark revealed John Osterman's thin face and Amanda's ugly friend, Tina. Jesse made her move toward Tina.

It was poorly thought out and obvious. If she had faked toward Tina and then juked back to John she might have escaped. Instead she tried to dance her way between Tina and the water's edge and was mostly successful. However with the margins of safety so thin, 'mostly' didn't cut it.

She got past Tina, however John smashed into her, sending her stumbling out onto the ice. Somehow she managed to stay upright and with horror she watched the ice send out white lines, zigzagging out from beneath her feet. She stood petrified, so afraid to move that she could barely breathe.

In seconds Ronny, Amanda, and the mousy girl that Jesse had kicked in the stomach in their fight in the bathroom, joined John and Tina on the berm above her. They stood blowing out white plumes of breath and grinning at each other.

"What do you want to do with her," Ronny asked in a gleeful vicious manner. He looked like a sick kid who had just trapped the neighbor's cat and was considering whether to shave it or tie a rock to its tail.

"What we came here for," John replied. "But first..."

He left the words out there and Jesse's mind screamed, *But first, what?* "W-w-hat d-do you want?" Jesse's voice shook. Her whole body shook.

"You wanted to fight?" John replied. "We're here to fight." He waved his arm at the little group.

Jesse shook her head. "All of y-you? Th-that's not what w-we agreed to."

"You fight one of us, you fight all of us," John said. "Now come on, you don't want to stand out there all night." As much as she feared the ice, the alternative seemed worse and so she stood her ground.

"I'll get her in," Ronny said. He bent and picked up a large stone the size of a brick and threw it. Jesse cringed down into a squatting position thinking that he was actually throwing the stone at her, but he wasn't. He threw it high in a gentle arc and it landed next to her, embedding itself in the ice, sending out lightning bolts of white lines.

The ice groaned beneath her feet. "No! Please...don't." She begged as Ronny stooped for another stone.

"Then come on in," John said reasonably.

The water was sure death in Jesse's mind, but a beating by the five of them wasn't much of an alternative. "I'll fight...if that what you want. B-but one at a time."

"No way," Tina said, the cold and excitement putting a quiver in her voice. "She's just saying that so she can run."

"It's ok, she won't get past us," John said, holding out at hand to hush Tina. "You want to fight us one at a time? You start with me." John stepped back from the edge of the berm and shooed the others back as well. They fanned out, two on either side of him, making it impossible for her to make a run for it.

"Ok...ok...j-just step back," she said. John was still too close, only about five feet from the water.

"Sure thang," he said, backing up. He was all confidence, while Jesse felt her insides vibrating like mad. She wasn't going to win this, there was no way. He was too big, too long. With his reach, she'd have to get in close. The idea made her want to heave up her dinner just thinking about it.

Yet what choice did she have?

Jesse slid with small fearful movements to the edge of the berm and then stepped onto the rocks. Immediately, she felt a sense of relief. Her pent up breath now came in great gasps which had her enemies laughing at her. She let them laugh without saying a word; she needed all the time that she could get and those few precious moments helped to clear her head somewhat.

"Come on, Bitch. Let's do this," John said, eventually.

Jesse nodded and then rolled her shoulders up and back; she was stiff with stress and that was no way to go into a fight. If she had any chance to win, she needed to be loose, relaxed, and above all quick. He had size and strength; she had speed and experience. Jesse had fought nineteen times in the last five years and that wasn't counting little scuffles like what occurred in the bathroom. In her mind fights weren't fights unless blood was drawn.

Yet for all her experience and speed she knew deep down that she was going to lose. In boxing and wrestling they didn't have speed categories, they had weight categories and for the simple reason: big people beat little people. And John wasn't just a little bigger than her. He might have been thin but he was a head taller than her and outweighed her by at least sixty pounds.

John stood in a relaxed fighting stance; left foot forward, hands low...too low. If he were fighting a worthier opponent, those hands at chest height would have doomed him. They showed he was over-confident, unfortunately that wouldn't last. He would learn. She would teach him.

Jesse came up on the balls of her feet, her supple jungle boots bending beautifully; her hands were positioned at the proper height: just below the level of her eyes. She began to dance in her fighting stance like a boxer, left to right, which brought on gales of laughter from Ronny and John.

The girl in black said nothing to this, she just took the extra seconds to do her best to relax and focus. Her heart beat too fast in her chest; her breathe came out raggedy.

"Get her, John," Tina goaded.

What a nasty smile she wore! Jesse gaped at the blood lust displayed on the girl's vile face. In all her time as the hated one she had never seen anything close and if Jesse had a second to dwell on it, she might have been petrified by the horror of it. However John came on quick and Jesse had to focus, or go down.

He toyed with her—a quick feint that she saw coming. She danced away in an exaggerated movement. This repeated itself a second time, but they both knew that it wouldn't on the third. He knew he would attack for real, expecting her to dance away again and she knew that she wouldn't.

Just as he stepped forward and brought his left arm around to level her, she danced in. Her momentum and his came together at the point where her fist met his chin. The impact charred her all the way up her shoulder; it was expected and she torqued her upper body, following the first punch a fraction of a second later with a hard right. This mashed his lips under her fist.

John's head reeled back and Jesse followed up the one-two with a looping left hook. She was too short. His momentum was now back and the strike, which might have sealed the deal for Jesse, only barely clipped him on the chin. And then his arms were up flailing at her and he stepped back with a shaken look in his eyes.

That was the high point of the fight and the very reason why Jesse thought only a fool of a girl would ever voluntarily fight a boy, especially one bigger than herself. This wasn't Hollywood where a hundred pound girl with twigs for arms could knock out an NFL linebacker with a single blow.

This was fact.

Jesse had used all her strength in both punches, had connected squarely right where she needed to and still John was standing. In a second, his eyes cleared of his shock and then they began to fill with an embarrassed anger. He wasn't going to toy with her anymore.

John came on again: hard, vicious, aggressive. He was much stronger than Jesse, while she was only slightly quicker, yet she evaded his first two blows with relative ease because of the way he was so obvious in his attacks. She would've ducked out of the way the third looping haymaker as well, if she hadn't been suddenly pushed from behind.

Hands shoved her into the path of the blow and it landed awkwardly but heavily on the side of her head. She went spinning to the ground by the force of it, but she wasn't down for more than a second. Fear of fighting on the ground...of being pinned by her much larger opponent...of being raped, had her up as quick as she could. Jesse hated the feeling of being pinned by a boy. All her guile, speed, and skills were useless and always the specter of rape filled her mind. After all, what sort of boy would fight a girl to the point of beating her to the ground and then climb on top her...only one kind.

Jesse used her momentum and was up, dancing left then right as she looked for an opening to strike. Unfortunately, her first two punches had taught John to keep his hands up and he seemed well out of reach.

Angle, angle, angle! her mind screamed at her. Against an opponent so big, there was no way she could go toe-to-toe; she had to attack from the side. She kept up her dance— left, right—right, left—left-attack! Her punch seemed to shock him in its speed, but it did little to hurt him seriously, and worse, as he flung out his long arms, one hand snatched a hold of her fancy black coat.

He reeled her in with it and before she saw what was coming his fist connected with her right eye. Suddenly she lost feeling in her feet and her legs were those of a drunken sailor. Jesse tried to remain up right, she tried to stay in the fight, but without her speed she was just a punching bag for John.

Seemingly out of the black of the night a huge fist appeared and struck her on the left side of her face, turning her around and around until she felt the rough berm on her back. Then like a pack of wild dogs they were on her kicking and stomping.

"Enough! Stop!" Amanda called out and just like that the beating ended and the pain began. The second Jesse had gone to the ground she had balled up to protect herself, and many of the blows had landed on her back and ribs. Every breath was like fire.

"Come on, pick her up!" John ordered. Hands grabbed her and she felt herself lifted from the ground.

She wanted to scream, *Not the pond, please!* Yet it was all she could do to take the tiny puffs of air that slipped between her clenched teeth.

They did not take her to the pond and throw her in. It was not a relief. Instead they carried her to the end of the berm and held her up again a good-sized tree. Tina held one arm, John held the other and Ronny pulled out a grey roll of duct tape.

Amanda stood in front of her and held the strangest thing in her hand. It was a book. John snatched it out of her hands and opened it for Jesse to see what was inscribed on the inside cover:

Happy Birthday!
Your friend,
Kyle.

Blearily Jesse stared at it. The words had no meaning to her. "What?" she asked in a tiny voice.

"It's your birthday," John said. "Isn't that nice. And it must be Harold's birthday too, because we're going leave him a little gift...you."

"No...please," Jesse begged. Tears streaked down her face and in her fear she found a little more breath. "Please, John...don't."

Grimly he shrugged as Ronny began rolling the tape around Jesse's splayed arms. "Then who should die?" John asked. "Me? Hell no! One of my friends? I don't think so. You're the stranger here. You're the outcast. Who would really care if you died? I don't even think your parents would care. Where is your father...Mister high and mighty? Shouldn't he be here to save his only child?"

Jesse's head and chest went limp and she hung by her outstretched arms. She was finding too great a strain to hold herself up and breathe at the same time. "I...don't know...where..." she croaked out an answer. "Please...don't..."

"Sorry," John said. "This is the way it's going to be. But just look on the bright side, when Harold comes and bashes your head in, you'll be saving someone else's life."

Chapter 36

"Amanda, John...my good friends," a soft voice came out of the dark. The words turned Jesse's attackers into living statues. They froze with wide eyes straining to see who had spoken.

Jesse, with a groan, forced her body up so she could see who was coming as well. She was just as afraid as the others, more so in fact. Was Harold come for her already?

No, it was Ky. He strode out of the forest in that slow action of his and stood just feet away. A silence settled on the little clearing. Jesse slumped back down, it was the only way she could speak...or breathe.

"Help...me..." she whispered, "...please."

Ky didn't. He ignored her all together. "Isn't that the book I gave you two years ago? Amanda...my friend."

Amanda began backing away from Ky as if he had the plague and in a second Tina and the brown-haired girl followed suit.

"Get the hell out of here, Ky," whispered John. "This doesn't concern you."

Ky laughed. It was a low chuckle that held the breadth of his misery. "All death in this town concerns me. You...my best friend...know that better than anyone."

"Shut up!" John growled. He was furious, but afraid as well and took a few steps back. Ronny was right there with him. "Stop calling me that. We're not friends and never were. I hate you."

More laughter from Ky. This time genuine. "That won't save you, John Osterman. Because I don't hate you, I lo..."

"Shut up!" John cried. Now he backed away in earnest and within seconds the five teens were halfway across the berm, running from Ky's very odd words. Only then did Ky rush over to Jesse. *Snick.* Out came his switchblade; he began sawing at the duct tape.

"You're going to be ok," he whispered. "Just whatever you do keep your mouth shut."

This was the easiest thing for Jesse to do, she could barely breathe. When the tape was cut away she fell into a ball on the ground desperate for the least breath.

"Come on!" Ky said after a minute. He wasn't looking at her; his eyes were up staring into the forest. He was looking for Shadow-man. His fear focused Jesse enough for her to climb to her knees but that was as far as she got before her head began to swim. The dark forest began to spin and she was afraid she was going throw up.

The feeling vanished however, when she looked up to see Ky slinking away through the trees.

"Ky...please...don't leave me," she blubbered, uncaring about the tears running down her face, or the pain that burned with each breath. All she cared about was her fear of being abandoned. Of being left for the Shadow-man.

Ky raced back holding a finger to her lips. "He's here," the words were so quiet that even so close she could barely hear them. "I thought I heard something on the path, so you have to stop talking."

Jesse nodded and Ky turned away. He was leaving her again! She grabbed at his coat in desperation. "Please...don't..."

Now Ky grew frantic and placed a cold hand over her mouth. "I can either guide you to safety or be here with you when you die. Those are your choices." Jesse let go of his coat; her hands fell back in the snow as if she were already dead. He began again in a low whispering, "Follow me...if I stop, you stop. If you hear me say anything at all just hide as best you can."

When she nodded, he helped her to her feet and she wobbled on rickety legs, clutching his arm with both hands until he pried her fingers away. Ky then became the Ghost, the boy ignored by all the world. As if she wasn't there, he turned from her and headed into the forest but not by the path. He struck out into the thickest part of the woods and watching him go made Jesse want to cry out to him again.

It was hard going for her. The hills seemed dreadful in their steepness and the craggy, root and rock-strewn earth tried time and again to trip her up. To add to that her head swam and her breath came in tiny sips; it was all she could do to keep up with him. He seemed so stealthy, while she lumbered from tree to tree, pausing at each to keep from falling over. As they progressed he completely ignored her; his focus was always up and out, picking his way through the brush in near silence.

Only when she stumbled on a loose rock and set it cascading down the hill they were on did he act like she was even there. Before the stone finished its short journey, he stole back to her. With wide eyes that were full of worry, he grabbed her arm with one hand while the other went over her mouth.

This wasn't needed to keep her quiet; knowing that the Shadow-man was in the forest with them was enough. A series of tiny, stealthy sound slipped out of the night from their right. Closer they came and Jesse felt her life draining out of her. She went weaker and weaker; soon she sagged into Ky's warm body in order to stay upright. He was afraid as well. She could feel him trembling beneath her cheek and his breath was hot and fast on her neck.

But for all his fear, Ky held her with something more than the moment called for. She knew this, it wasn't all in her head, and that's why his cruelty a few minutes later was so devastating.

The Shadow-man circled them. Harold walked unseen; the woods were too thick. In their dark clothing, the two teens were unseen as well and after a short time, Harold turned away and they could hear the light sound of his steps retreating down the hill.

Quickly Ky started moving again and now he didn't lead, but helped Jesse along. This help could not have been more painful. Jesse's left side, where her ribs were undoubtedly broken, screamed in hot agony with each step. She cried softly and moaned in a low voice when she could find the breath to do so, but Ky never slowed. He was bent on saving her life and seemed not to care about anything else.

Jesse should have been more grateful.

They came to the edge of the forest, a hundred yards or so up the street from her house and only then did Ky stop.

"Go and don't look back," he ordered in a growl. "And next time I see you in school don't follow me and stop trying to get me to look at you."

The second they had stopped, Jesse's head began to spin even worse than it had before and she tried to lean on Ky, but he pushed her away.

"Do you hear me?" he asked. "Leave me alone!"

"That doesn't make any sense," Jesse said. "I'm just trying to be your friend."

"Trust me when I say you're the last person I want to be friends with." His face no longer seemed handsome; rather it was harsh and bitter. Uncaring about her obvious pain, he shoved her out into the street where she struggled to keep her balance.

Why? her mind screamed.

Why was he treating her so badly? Why were they all treating her so badly? Was she evil? Was she something so vile that she was worthy of their hatred?

Crying harder than she had before, Jesse fled to her house. The wood and glass was a refuge and she locked herself in. And her heart, she locked that up as well.

Ky had no right to treat her the way he had. How could he want to befriend Amanda and John and the rest of them...they were the evil ones, not her. It made no sense. The whole hating town made no damned sense.

In a mounting fury that turned her soul cold, Jesse went to her room and began slowly peeling away her clothes. New purpling bruises, blotched her skin. They ran up and down her body, and where they weren't in evidence, red welts stood out. It looked like she had been hit by a car. She ached down to her every bone and was quickly growing stiff.

From painful experience, Jesse knew there was nothing she could do about the ribs. A doctor couldn't put a cast on a fracture like that. Unfortunately, time was the only thing that would help and she could look forward to two or three hard months before she could sneeze again without crying out in pain.

The cut above her eye however, could and should be attended to by a doctor. It was now an inch long and Jesse could put the tip of her pinky in it. Her best guess was that it would take a dozen or more stitches to close it.

"Screw that," she said to the mirror. The girl she saw there was nothing like the Barbie-doll that had smiled out at her on Monday morning. The Barbie doll had shoulder length blonde hair, bright blue eyes, and clear unblemished skin. Her only minor defect was an interesting little tilt to her nose.

This girl wasn't the same. Her black hair was cut short, there was a new bruise and swelling on her left cheek, the cut above her right eyebrow was deep and mangled looking, and even the blue eyes were different. There was no longer a hint of optimism to them. Now they held only a profound hatred and a hunger for revenge.

Chapter 37

With her hatred swelling so great within her, Jesse didn't think there was room for any other feelings inside of her, but she was wrong. She had room for shame.

When Cynthia Clarke came home a little while after Jesse, the girl hid herself and her battered face. She made excuses and refused to come downstairs. The same thing occurred when her father arrived. She insisted that she was tired and told him through her door that she was going to bed early.

This wasn't exactly a lie. Jesse was exhausted and after taking as many pain relievers as she thought her liver could handle she dropped into a fitful sleep. Every time she rolled over her ribs spiked in agony and no matter which way she laid her head, her face would start to ache after a while.

Just after six in the morning she gave up trying to sleep and went to her bathroom mirror to see how bad she looked. Not good. Yet not so bad either. If she had wanted to, makeup would have hid the purple-blue bruise on her cheek where John had punched her. It would have also covered up the blue moon under her right eye where blood had crept beneath the skin from her wound. Only she didn't want to cover up her injuries.

"Why should I pretend this didn't happen to me?" she asked aloud. "Why should I be the one embarrassed?" Jesse waited a second for her voice of reason to come up with something. It didn't. It couldn't. There was no reason for her to be the one embarrassed. It was the town and everyone in it that should be embarrassed.

Only they weren't. And that was where Jesse's anger really stemmed. "This town has no shame...they should all be ashamed of themselves!" she stormed at the mirror, and then groaned. It hurt to raise her voice. Jesse opened her bottle of Tylenol and popped six and then went to where her clothes lay in a heap. She'd wear the same outfit as she had the night before, not regardless of the blood and dirt covering it, but because of it.

Then she slipped out of the house on silent feet.

Why? her voice of reason asked. *Why aren't you waiting for a ride?*

"I don't want a ride," she whispered, stepping onto the trail that led to the berm. A ride would not only entail begging her mother, something she was sure she couldn't stomach at the moment; it would also mean endless stupid questions about her injuries.

"Besides, what are the chances that Harold is out?"

The forest seemed empty. It was quiet and still. The night before the air had been charged with fear, now it hung in gentle serenity. Jesse strolled unafraid to the trail and in a few minutes reached the scene of the night's crime. Streamers of dull grey duct tape hung from a tree, and a pool of dried maroon blood lay in the snow at its feet.

Jesse became sick with anger looking at it. They were going to kill her. That was their plan. She was supposed to have been sacrificed to their monstrous god—to appease it, to satiate its craving for blood, and keep it at bay for another year.

You should go to the police.

Jesse ignored the voice totally. Having been a part of small town justice too many times to count, she knew what a waste of time it would've been. Would the police really arrest five of their own? First cousins, nephews, and nieces of theirs? Not hardly.

For Jesse there was only one real justice and only one real way to protect herself. Jesse went in search of her lock and chain...the real purpose for her walk in the woods. She had decided that she wasn't going to go down without a decent fight the next time. The chain, curled like an ice snake, lay in a glitter of new frost right where she left it. She could feel its cold even through her thin gloves as she swung it about.

"Ohh!" she cried, clutching her ribs at the lance of pain. "Ow, ow, ow."

Jesse tried again, going easier, giving her body a few minutes to warm up. The pain limited her movement and she found that the only way she was going to use the chain effectively was in an overhand strike, hammer like. It would do. It would have to do.

You're crazy if you can think you can win a fight, chain or no chain.

"Then what am I supposed to do?" Jesse said to the empty forest. "Run? Hide? Cower in fear? Not me...not me."

In her mind there was no alternative left but to keep fighting. That was just a given—they had tried to kill her after all. As bad as Copper Ridge and Denton had been, at least no one had tried that.

Giving the lock and chain a few more swings, grimacing all the while, she then went to stow it away in her right front pocket, only she couldn't. That pocket was filled with a bag of crushed Oreo cookies.

"You are so stupid," she whispered to herself, staring at the bag. Just like her, the bag had taken quite a beating. Why had she thought that cookies would make any difference? This town only understood pain and fear. There was no love here.

Jesse ate the cookies as she slowly wound her way through the forests. She kept to them, uncaring about the Shadow-man. After all she had her lock and chain; it would make a dent even in his huge head.

You're being stupid. Just because it's a pretty morning doesn't mean Harold isn't lurking about.

Jesse shrugged and dumped the powdered remains of the Oreos into her mouth. Truly right at that moment she wasn't afraid of Harold. She wasn't even nervous about the fight that had to come in the next few minutes. Time was ticking by...or perhaps counting down. It felt like she was walking toward her destiny. She knew what was going to happen...*they* would be waiting for her. *They* would tease and bully her, but they would never stop at that. The Shadow-man was still out there and it still needed a victim...its virgin sacrifice.

And she was even more of a candidate for that dread position now. She could tattle on them, after all. She had the bruises and cuts to show what had happened to her. They would be afraid of what she had already told her parents and what she was going to say to the police—but if Harold was to kill her then all that would just go away.

Then run. You can...

If Jess's voice of reason had anything else to say she didn't hear it. A sudden rush of blood in her ears seemed to drown out any thought other than vengeance she might have had. *They* were waiting for her. John, Ronny, Tina, and Amanda stood by the corner of the school watching the road, expecting Jesse to be dropped off by her mother.

Jesse stepped out of the woods, well away from the student parking lot and it was a few minutes before they noticed her. When they did, she calmly sauntered back under the trees, working her killing arm in large circles.

John would have to die first, she thought. He led the little group across the grassy strip between the forest and the school, while Jesse slunk deeper into the woods. After John went down, Ronny would come at her quick...but he'd be afraid of the chain. He would stay back and because of her injury she couldn't over extend.

"Hmmm," she murmured. A puzzle. How to kill Ronny when he wouldn't commit? The dilemma didn't really bother her; she knew it would work its way out, somehow.

"Look at you, bitch. You got a death wish, don't you?" John asked. He said more than that, but Jesse barely listened. Her mind focused on his range, his bearing, his stance. How the others spread out, flanking him on either side. They looked anxious, especially John. He didn't look good—hungover, and unkempt. Red rimmed his eyes from lack of sleep or worry. Jesse and her chain would fix both of those problems.

The chain was heavy in her pocket and despite it having been snugged up against her, it sat cold on her bare fingers. No gloves for her now. Jesse wanted perfect control of the chain.

John yabbered on for a minute or more, threatening, explaining how she wouldn't be lucky this time, but she said nothing. What was there to say? He had tried to kill her less than twelve hours earlier and he would try again. She saw his feeble-minded plan in his eyes and it was essentially the same as the old one. The only difference was that now Jesse understood the rules they were playing with. This wasn't about teasing, anymore. This was life and death...and a very hard death at that.

So she said nothing and waited, her body a tense spring ready to unleash its vengeance. Finally, her silence goaded him into attacking. He came at her mean and full of menace and she smirked knowing that he would die.

At the last second her weapon came out of her pocket and she let the chain slip between her fingers like a rope of cold hard intestine. The sight of it stopped him in his tracks—just what she wanted. Jesse leapt forward to dash his brains in with that heavy, heavy lock at the chain's end.

Chapter 38

The chain came back and around, wheeling over Jesse's head. She drove it in a sharp arc, straight at the top of John's skull. Foolishly he just stood there with wide, shocked eyes. He didn't even raise his arm in an attempt to block the blow.

"Stop!" a voice bellowed in the cool air. It wasn't a boy's voice. It wasn't Ronny. A man with authority yelled that word.

It was Mr. Daniels. Had it been any other teacher Jesse would have killed John regardless of their presence. However, Mr. Daniels had been, in the slightest way, nice to Jesse and she felt a flash of shame at the thought of him seeing her spill John's brains out onto the snow. She pulled her swing and the chain whistled across the front of John's face.

"What's going on here?" Mr. Daniels demanded, his toad like face pulled tight in his anger. Instead of answering the teens all went silent. John and Jesse only continued to stare at each other. For her part, Jesse would sooner take her eyes off a viper at that distance.

Tina was the first to regain the use of her tongue. "Jesse...she was going to hit John with that." She pointed at the lock and chain.

"What were you thinking, Miss Clarke?" Mr. Daniels asked. "You could have killed him."

Jesse smiled so small that only John really saw it. "Yes," she answered.

"Is that all you have to say?" the teacher asked, flabbergasted by the chill in her one word reply.

"Will it really matter what I say?"

"It might matter to the police!" Mr. Daniels said.

Jesse shrugged. "They were coming to kill me. It was four against one...I have the right to defend myself."

Tina was quick to deny this. "No. Mr. Daniels we weren't going to do no such thing. All we were going to do was...was..."

"Have a smoke!" John finished the lie. He backed away. Despite the cool of the morning, a sheen of sweat lay on his neck.

"Yeah, and she went all psycho," Ronny said, reinforcing the lie. "We were just gonna..."

Mr. Daniels interrupted, "Don't give me that! I saw you. You came up here looking for trouble and I think you most certainly found it."

Ronny wasn't going to give up his lie so easily. "No, it wasn't like that. We didn't want to smoke on school grounds and..."

"Stop. I don't want hear anymore lies." The teacher's hand went up in Ronny's face. "I know what I saw...I just can't believe it," he said eyeing Jesse as though he had never seen her before. Jesse refused to look at him. She knew that if she did the little squiggle of shame that had begun turning in her belly would grow.

Mr. Daniels shook his head. "All of you to the principal's office." The teacher put his hand out for the chain. "Miss Clarke?"

Reluctantly she handed it over.

With the teacher striding along next to her, sighing every few steps, it was an unpleasant walk down to the school. Every student turned their every head and all eyes were on the group. As they passed by the whisperings began.

No one attracted more attention than the girl in the black. With her beaten face, her torn and blood stained clothes, and the hard cast to her eyes, she looked as if she had just come from a war zone. No one wanted to catch her gaze, and if a student did, he was quick to turn away.

An incident such as theirs changed the rules by which principals normally lived. There wasn't the usual agonizingly long wait, at least not for Jesse's attackers. They were seen relatively quick. Through the door, Jesse could hear them taking turns adamantly denying anything beyond looking to have a cigarette, all but Amanda who kept silent. The other three in turn then went on to describe how psychotic Jesse Clarke was. How, out of the blue, she had tried to kill John with her chain.

When they trooped out, John and Tina gave her a look that spoke of future pain, while Ronny and Amanda kept their faces down to the carpet. Jesse thought that she would be next. Instead, she was surprised to see Mrs. Jerryman, Mr. Irving, and Ms Weldon go in.

Their discussion with the principal was much more low-key and nothing could be heard from the other side of the door.

After twenty minutes, Mr. Daniels poked his head out of the principal's office. "Miss Clarke? Come in, please."

The instant she stepped in, Jesse knew she was walking into a kangaroo court. Her guilt had been decided already. There was an empty chair in front of Principal Peterson's desk; she was loath to take it. Just behind it on a couch, three in a row, were her most hated teachers and the idea of them breathing down her neck repulsed her.

She stood just to the side of the desk and raised her eyebrows. "Yes?"

The principal seemed nonplussed by her opening word. "Yes? You act like you don't know why you are here?"

"I'm here so you can know the truth. I just don't know why they're here," she answered jerking her head in the direction of the teachers.

"The *truth*?" Mrs. Jerryman spat out as if the word sickened her. The principal gave her a quick glare.

"First off, I do want to hear your side of the story, Miss Clarke," the principal said. "I asked the teachers to attend because they know you better than I do and I want our little session here to be as open and honest as it can be."

Having teachers in the room was not normal. She could understand the presence of Mr. Daniels, since he was a witness, but the other three spelled trouble. And what did he mean by 'open session'? Jesse had been to enough of these little meetings to know that ordinarily they were private proceedings. None of this made sense to her.

Yes it does, but you haven't put an ounce of thought into it.

Jesse turned to look at the three teachers. They were clearly, visibly, obviously upset. Way too upset. Their outrage was palpable. Strange. Did they care so much about Jesse and her injuries to get this worked up over?

Not hardly. They were sending a message with their feigned ire, and it explained why they were there: they didn't trust Principal Peterson to make the 'right' decision. And the principal's desire for an open proceeding? The principal was afraid of the mob. He wanted a sanctioned outcome, so he wouldn't be at odds with his staff.

Jesse closed her eyes and sighed; the pain in her body matching the pain in her soul. "My side of the story?" she asked. "There is only one side, the truth."

"And what is truth?" Principal Peterson asked, folding his hands beneath his chin.

"Those four attacked me last night, they beat me..." Here she turned and showed off her injuries. "...and left me for Harold Brownly to find. This morning they came at me again and threatened to do the same thing, so I defended myself with that." She gestured at the sixteen inches of heavy chain and the over-sized lock. "My bike lock."

Behind her, Mr. Irving snorted. "That's not a bike lock. Those are inch long links...you could tow a car with that."

"Nevertheless it's what I used to lock up my bike." Jesse *had* used it to lock up her bike, just not very often. The truth was that she needed a weapon that was also not a weapon. She needed 'plausible deniability' for just such a circumstance as this.

"We'll get to the chain in a moment," the principal said. "Do you have any proof that you were attacked?" When Jesse gawped at him in disbelief, he added, pointing at her face, "Besides all of that."

If it had been Jesse looking at a prison sentence for attempted murder, cleaning up the crime scene down by the berm would have been the first thing she would've done that morning. Yet the tape and the blood had still been there at half past six. Was it still there now almost three hours later? Very unlikely and with each passing minute the chances dropped precipitously.

"You shouldn't need any more than this," she answered pointing at her face. "Unless you think I did it to myself."

"Without any evidence, all I have is your word," the principal replied.

"You have more than that," Jesse said. "You have eyes that see. And in your heart you know the truth."

Mrs. Jerryman chimed up from the couch. "I've known John Osterman since he was a baby. We all have, and he may not be an angel, but he's never been accused of doing something like this before. My heart tells me to believe him over some girl who walks around these halls as if she's better than everyone else."

Peterson sat back, looking tired despite the early hour. "Do you think you're better than everyone else?"

"Those are her words, not mine," Jesse replied.

"That hardly answers my question," he said. Taking off his glasses, he began rubbing at his temples. "On one hand I have known trouble makers and on the other a girl who looks, by her bruises alone, to be telling the truth. But without proof...I don't know."

Ms Weldon stood and walked around to stare down her long horse face at Jesse. "Let's say there was a fight last night. I don't know if I blame John." She said to Jesse's amazement. "Mrs. Jerryman is correct. Jesse, you walk around here as if there is no truth but your truth...or your father's I should say. That everything stems from him and that we should be happy with the pittance that he doles out. I warned you. Three times, I warned you to be careful how you spoke and how you acted. But you wouldn't listen. Your ideas are dangerous, Jesse. They are too black and white, and I can see how they would incite anger. If John Osterman did anything at all, he was probably provoked."

Jesse didn't know whether to laugh or cry. She had never asked to defend her father; it had always been pushed on her. In growing fury she kept silent.

"Well?" the principal prompted. "Did you incite him in some way?"

"If I did, it was by telling the truth," Jesse replied, unleashing her anger. "And if he is so easily incensed by the truth that he becomes dangerous, then he should never leave these halls. He definitely won't pose a danger with what passes for truth here."

A gasp and then a glaring silence followed this, but Jesse didn't blanch away from it.

"Let's get to the chain," Principal Peterson said letting out a long breath. "We have rules in place about weapons in school. They are in place for everyone's safety."

"The safety of the criminals perhaps," Jesse said. "Without my chain I wouldn't have been very safe, would I? Either way it's not a weapon, it's a chain and a lock. I know I'm allowed to have a lock for my bike, I just didn't know that there was a restriction on its size. Can you show me in the school handbook where the prescribed gauge of the chain is written?"

The principal looked to the teachers and they looked to each other in silence. Finally Mr. Irving said, "You can play amateur lawyer all you want, Miss Clarke, but the fact is you used it as a weapon. In the handbook it clearly states that anything that can be construed as a weapon is illegal."

"I have a right to defend myself, correct?" she asked the economics teacher. "When I'm attacked by four people, should I defend myself with only those things that *can't* be construed as a weapon? An eraser? A piece of chalk maybe? Or would that be too pointy in your view?" He stood to reply and his smug look was enough to drain away the last of Jesse's energy. Before he could open his mouth she said, "Forget I asked. Pass your sentence and let's be done with this."

But the masquerade ball!

Her voice of reason sounded a lot like a voice on the verge of crying. The ball wasn't going to happen, not for her. She had promised her father that she would be good and she had failed him. His word was law and he wouldn't renig no matter how much she pleaded.

"That's all you have to say in your defense?" Peterson asked. Jesse refused to look up. Her fate been decided long before that moment, and no words on her part would change it. When she didn't budge, the principal rubbed his hands as if they pained him and turned to his teachers, "Well? Should she be given in school suspension? Three days?"

"No that would be a waste with holidays so close," Mr. Irving said. "And besides that seems hardly the punishment for assault with a deadly weapon."

Mrs. Jerryman nodded emphatically. "We should turn her over to the police. This is a criminal matter and not really up to us to decide."

Peterson's eyebrows went up at this, yet he said nothing to it. Instead he addressed another issue. "And John and his little gang? What do we do about them?"

"About last night, it's their word against Jesse's. Unless some sort of proof is given, who do we believe? Maybe she had done these things to herself. It's not unheard of," Ms Weldon answered. "And about this morning...who knows what their intentions were. Yes they might have been going up to those woods to cause trouble, but we can't see into their hearts to know if that was true or not. I say let them go until we go more answers."

Jesse had conflicting feeling about all of this... she wanted to either vomit or faint.

Chapter 39

The police took an hour to arrive and one minute to cuff her. Thankfully the principal's office was so close to the front door that only a hundred or so students got to see the spectacle of her being led away. It could have been worse, but not by much. The officer, big, thick, and blonde, sporting a nametag that read P. Jorgenson, didn't wait for the late bell to ring and the halls to clear.

"Your father is waiting for you down at the station," Officer Jorgenson said, climbing into the front seat of the cruiser. "And he is all sorts of pissed off."

"Uh-huh," Jesse grunted, not really caring. James Clarke had done all this to her and there didn't seem to be much more that he could do. "So how are you related to Amanda?"

The officer glanced down at his nametag seemingly surprised that Jesse could read. "Oh, we're cousins from at least two different directions. Ashton's pretty small."

"It's small, really? I didn't notice," Jesse said, squirming in the back of the car. As they had left the school, they had passed through a crowd of students and someone had hawked a good-sized loogie at Jesse. She was trying to wipe it out of her hair onto the seat next to her. "Oh! Dang it," she moaned.

"Cuffs too tight?" Jorgenson asked. He knew they were. As if she was some sort of dangerous criminal he had cinched them down as tight as they would go. It wasn't the cuffs that had her groaning. Sure they hurt, but it was her ribs, torqued they way they were, that were killing her. "Assault with a deadly weapon...we don't get many of those around here," he said, as though that had been the reason for the tight cuffs and not how his family was involved with her.

"Really?" Jesse replied, rubbing her head on the seat, like a dog. "I hear you get at least one every year like clockwork. You'd think someone as big as Harold wouldn't be so hard to catch."

The officer's blue eyes narrowed. Jesse didn't care. She really didn't care about much of anything. A minute later they pulled onto the street that held both the town hall and the police station. That was when she saw something she did care about.

Harold Brownly. He entered a building right across the street from the police station and with him, looking tiny in comparison, was an officer holding a shotgun. The sight of the Shadow-man sent a tingle running all along Jesse's skin and voluntarily, she slunk down in her seat

"Whoa," Jesse whispered, as her heart took to thumping in her chest. Then louder said, "Did you catch him? What's that building?"

"No, we didn't catch him," Jorgenson said irritably, pulling up to the front of the dinky station. "That's his shrink's office."

"Wait," she said just as he was climbing out of the cruiser. "He's got a therapist? And what's with the cop with him?"

Jorgenson got out of the cruiser, squeezing his heavily muscled body sideways to do so. When he opened her door he answered, "It's court ordered. He got a DUI a little while back and the judge thought some therapy might be all that's needed." Clearly Officer Jorgenson thought the judge to be an idiot.

"And the cop with him?"

"The *police officer* is there because ole Doc Becker is a chicken. Come on. Watch your head."

"Oh! Ow, ow, ow!" He had pulled her out by her elbow and her ribs hurt so bad she came close to crying.

"Gonna play games in front of daddy?" Jorgenson asked in a hushed but nasty voice.

Jesse shook her head and wheezed, "No...broken...ribs." She could barely breathe now. He had her by the arm and was lifting up on it, gently but excruciatingly. Quickly, he lowered her arm.

"Oh, sorry. This doesn't hurt, does it?" he asked, taking a loose grip on her coat. She shook her head, breathing in light gasps. "Your father's in the first interrogation room, he wants to talk to you there."

"No. Just take me to a cell. I don't want to see him."

The officer looked shocked. "My pleasure," he said. "It's where you belong anyways, trying to kill a kid like that."

Jesse said nothing to that and was led through the small building and placed in an empty cell. Before she got there, they were all empty. Her cell held a cot, a sink, and a toilet. It was all she needed. Immediately she went to the cot and lowered herself down as gingerly as she could. She knew it wouldn't be long before her father came, but she was tired and a nap sounded like the best thing. She didn't get a nap just then.

James Clarke was suddenly at the bars to her cell door. "I called your mother," he said as way of introduction.

Unmoving, Jesse replied, "I don't have a mother. I have humanity's paragon of vanity...and narcissism. She demands the world's approval and adoration and she gets it. It takes lots of money and sacrifice, but she gets it every time. And as long as she has your money and me to sacrifice, she'll always get it."

"You don't mean that."

"You love her so blindly that you don't even know her," Jesse replied from the cot. "Her only concern is how my arrest will affect her. How it will make her look in everyone else's eyes."

"I'm sorry you think so poorly of her. And me? What do you think of me?"

"You? You are the worst absentee father possible," she said. "You're not absentee enough! And when you do happen to come around, all you do is mess up my life. You expect me to obey all these rules, yet you never explain them. And you have all these ridiculous expectations of me and impossibly high standards that no one can attain. You seem to forget that I'm only human."

"Do you want me to lower my expectations?"

Now Jesse moved, slowly, grimacing she climbed to her feet. At the sight of her father, she suddenly *felt*. Since she had walked into the police station, she'd been in a dead zone—her outsides were wooden while her insides were hollow. Then she saw her father. Rage bloomed, vibrant and black within her breast.

Jesse jumped at the bars and gripped them as if she could pull them apart. Her week's worth of misery came out in an impassion plea. "Here's what I want. I want you to listen to me!" she demanded. "Listen to me...you destroy this town! Take it apart. Let the banks repossess everything! You said that without you the town was doomed...let it be doomed."

At first when she had sat up, he looked shocked at her appearance but as she made her demand his blue eyes turned sad, while hers were a hot red. She couldn't stop blinking them.

"You're right I can destroy them," he said evenly. "They've built their town on a foundation of sand and smoke. But truly is this what you want?"

"Yes!" she screamed and tried to reach through the bars to grab him, but he was a step away, untouchable for the moment. "The people here aren't worth your effort or my sacrifice. They aren't worth a single tear," she said, though her fevered eyes were filled with them. "Sign whatever law they want...pass all their ordinances and let them build their own little hell right here, where they can rot away in misery."

Her father stood for a time contemplating with his chin down and then said, "How badly you've been treated is appalling and it's because I love you so much that I will do this for you, *but...*"

"No buts just do it!" she shrieked. Her words echoed back to her.

In sorrow James gazed at her cut and bruised face and saw the pain in each of her tears. "*But* you have to tell me, are you willing to lay all your pain on the people of Ashton? Are you willing to destroy all their lives?"

"Yes, they are hating, evil people."

He pierced her with his glance, looking right into her soul. "All of them? Think, Jesse. Have you been treated wretchedly by every single person in this town?"

Immediately she conjured up the image of Ky and for a second her heart thawed. But then she remembered that Ky hated her and had thrown her out into the street and had told her that she was the last person that he'd be friends with. The memory was fresh and full of pain.

She started to nod her head, yes at his question...but then Carla Castaneda's pretty but so sad face came to her. "There is one person that hasn't been mean. A librarian." Could Jesse cause the lady more misery? She felt her head spin.

James brows came down. "Only one? Maybe I should let this town bury itself in..."

"There's also this girl from school...Sandra," Jesse said interrupting. "She's been nice to me. Or as nice as a person can be in this town."

Her father considered. "Two? That's nothing. I would destroy the town for that few. If you could give me ten names, maybe not."

Another face popped into her head. "I forgot to mention this girl...Emily...and there was also Allison and her two friends." There was also Mr. Daniels, he had been good to her, and it wasn't his fault what happened to her today. His son was probably nice too. And Ky...not Ky! But Ky's father appeared to be a good man. And then there was Gordon, the boy whose water was going to be shut off by the town and Mrs. Spiros...

"There might be more." She had a sense of unraveling within her. It was as though her insides had been wrapped in twine and a thread had given way. Her anger unwound along with it. Jesse couldn't hurt these people.

"Perhaps thousands more?" her father asked with a knowing look in his eyes. On this however, he didn't know.

"Not thousands. No way are there thousands of good people in this town," she said wiping her face on her long coat.

"Yes," her father replied. "There are, but many have gone astray. I wish you could look outside yourself and see them as I do."

Jesse felt her ire kick back in. "What do you mean? I see all their hate and bitterness and petty crap. I don't need to look outside myself to see that."

"Perhaps that's true. But you need to look outside yourself to see how they are bound together like no other town," James Clarkes said. "You can't see the love they have for each other...for their homes, for their families, for their neighbors. It's there, but you can't see it. Not yet."

"I can't see it because it doesn't exist."

"You can't see it because you are nothing but a mirror," her father explained. "All the hate that comes your way, you reflect right back outward. All the anger, all the misery that surrounds you is reflected back. That's all anyone ever sees when they look at you."

"You don't know how it is for me," Jesse wailed amidst a fresh wave of burning tears.

"Of course I do because it's the same for me," he said. "In the bad times they hate me and curse my name, but what happens when things go well?"

He paused for her to answer, but she didn't say anything. She abruptly realized that she was missing something. Her father was hated as much as she was, but in the end he was always adored...why?

"I'll answer that," he said in reply to her unspoken question. "Because I never change. I am that I am, regardless of who is around me. But look at you."

Jesse looked down at herself and saw the dried blood, the dirt, the tears stains, the torn clothes, the bruises and lacerations, the cuff marks, and the jail cell. Her father was the exact opposite. He stood tall and neatly attired in a tailored suit and he looked fresh as if he'd had a great night sleep.

"You're an adult..." she started to say.

"No, that's not it at all," he said cutting across her lame answer. "The great difference between us is that I've learned to forgive and you haven't yet."

Jesse was struck dumb—or very nearly so—only small odd sounds escaped her mouth as she struggled to protest this bit of lunacy. "Look at me!" she demanded. "Do you think that forgiving anyone could have prevented this from happening?"

"Yes I do. You've painted yourself into a cell for goodness sakes. Think back to the very first moment that you felt hate here in Ashton."

Jesse's brows creased as she thought back. It was only four days ago but it felt like a month. "Um...I was at the public library and the librarian said something rude about you firing people..."

He cut in, "You know better. I don't fire people; I only cut budgets and make suggestions...go on."

"Well, that was about it. I said something in kind back to her and that was that."

"Thank you for standing up for me...but how did that replying in kind work out for you?"

Jesse was silent. It hadn't worked out at all, the librarian had only become more hostile. James went on, "It didn't work out, because it couldn't. When hate bounces back and forth between two people it only grows and there is no room for anything else."

"Forgiving the librarian is one thing, but what about all this?" she asked pointing at herself. "I was attacked and I don't think forgiveness would have helped...wait!" A sudden ridiculously shocking thought came to her. "You aren't about to tell me to turn the other cheek!"

James smiled and then laughed. "You are so astute! I love that about you."

"No!" Jesse said, dumbfounded. "This is the real world I'm talking about. People attacked me. Do I let them..." The memory of her tied to the tree came to mind and it sent a shiver down her spine. "Do I let my face get kicked in? Do I let Harold Brownly smash my head open with a hammer? And while he's at it am I supposed to sit there waiting patiently in hopes he might see that I'm really not so bad?"

This sobered her father up quick. "No. If you ever come across the killer, you run and you don't look back. Consider that a command. But as for the rest...yes you may defend yourself if attacked. When I suggest that you turn the other cheek, I'm not suggesting that you allow yourself to be beaten. I'm saying that forgiving once may not be enough to turn an enemy into a friend. You may have to endure more."

Jesse pictured the faces of her enemies, John, Amanda, Ronny, Tina. She was tired of enduring more. "I don't know if I can forgive my enemies. It's one thing to say it in the abstract, but when there are real people doing real things...real evil things, I don't know if I can do it."

"It's not easy for any of us, myself included," James said. "I heard you got into a fight with John Osterman. A boy fighting a girl," he broke off shaking his head over the very idea.

Jesse kept her face neutral. The truth about what happened the night before was too embarrassing. All of it, from the Oreos right down to her rescue by Ky and the way he had pushed her away was simply too much.

"We never had boys fighting girls in my day," James said. "So that makes attempting to forgive him doubly hard, but there are things about John you probably don't know. John has been on the killer's list for seven years now."

"The killer has a list?" Jesse asked in shock. "Have you seen it?"

"That was figurative," James said with a smile. "There's no list...there is only that characteristic I had mentioned before, the one the killer fixates on. John has it and has been the ideal victim of the killer's for a long time. I don't know what kind of stress that's like to live under, but it's got to be horrible. Couple that stress with the fact that his dad lost his job two weeks after I show up and voila...you have someone ready to hate."

"I still don't think I can forgive him," Jesse said with a slow shake of her head. "He hasn't even asked for forgiveness. Am I supposed to forgive someone who hasn't even asked?"

"That's up to you," he replied. "You have to make that decision yourself. I only bring up John's situation to show there are things going on in his life that have definitely affected his judgment. We may not even know the real John Osterman at all. He might be a sweet kid if all the rest of this wasn't weighing him down."

Images of John came to her: him swinging his wild haymaker at her face, him in the library hunting her, him in the dark talking to Jerry Mendel...his hands had been shaking as he smoked his cigarette...John had been alone and afraid, just as she had been.

"That's...I...I still don't know," she said.

"I just want you to open yourself up to the idea of forgiveness. That's the first step you need to take. You can't love your enemies without it."

"Oh, God!" Jesse looked around for something to throw at her father. "You are just killing me! Now you want me to love my enemies? I can barely love you and mom."

"That's not how it used to be when you were younger," her father said. "You were full of love. For everything and everyone."

"That was different," Jesse shot back. "I was a kid...everything was so much easier."

"Love, whether easy or hard, is always worth it. After all what is the alternative?" he asked. "More hate? Apathy? Loneliness? Look, I'm saying this to you because I'm worried for you. It's like you've turned your heart off completely and it hurts me to see this."

"I've haven't. I've been trying." Jesse went to her cot and put her head in her hands

"You haven't," he replied. "You say you have, but the truth is you never really tried. You dressed all pretty for one day, passed out smiles to everyone you saw and that was it. You knew it wouldn't work from the get go, because deep down you knew that it would take much more than that. You gave a town of six thousand souls one day to love you and then you turned your back on them. That's not trying."

Her father was speaking to her in a soft voice but still the words stung. He was right. She hadn't tried because she was afraid of being hurt.

But you were hurt anyways.

Yes, she had been, but would she have suffered less if she had opened her heart more? The answer made her hang her head: probably.

"I know what I'm asking of you sounds extremely difficult," James said. "It seems counter-intuitive to love when you're hated, but it does work. Remember Richard Buck from Denton? The city council member who threw his coffee in my face that one time?"

She'd always hated Richard Buck. He had been so mean to her father...yet she knew that they had become close friends. "I remember."

"If you recall he hated me for almost a year, but I never hated back. And now we're practically best friends and if I have a problem, he's right there with a solution."

Jesse mulled over her father's words. He made it seem all so simple, and right there in the jail cell where no one could get at her it seemed simple to her as well. Yet the real world had so many twists and turns.

"I could've had friends," she said after a minute. "If I had been the poster-child against your reforms. There's a protest scheduled for Saturday and they want me to show up and denounce you."

"I know," James said with a long sigh. "And if you do, the town will implode. Things haven't been going as well as I had hoped they would. The town council has been going back and forth about implementing my ideas." He went to the bars of the cell door and leaned his head against the cold metal. "The bureaucracy here is just too dug in, too powerful. You saw Ms Weldon in my office. I've never had a teacher make demands the way she did. She acted like I worked for her not the other way around."

Jesse understood. "She has been leading the fight against you at the school and putting me under a lot of pressure."

He gave a rueful laugh. "I bet she has, but you can't give in. The town council is looking for any excuse to back out of our deal and if they see you protesting me...your own father, it might just tip the scales against me."

"Oh," Jesse said and then smiled. As she did, she felt the last of her tears slip from her eyes. "This town is in real trouble if its fate hinges on me. They all might as well pack up and move right now." Her father smiled at this as well, but there was more sadness in it than gaiety.

"Have you thought about giving in to them a little?" she asked.

"There's no room for giving in. Financially speaking, Ashton is on the edge of a cliff," he said. "This town is too top heavy. There are too few private sector workers to pay the salaries of the government workers. The council thought the answer to their budget shortfalls lay in taxing businesses, but it only drove companies out of town."

How odd it felt to Jesse, sitting in jail and wincing with every movement, to be the one trying to look on the bright side of things. With more cheer than she felt, she asked, "What about those companies you spoke to the other night? I bet you were able to talk at least one of them into moving their operations here." She could tell right away that she had guessed wrong.

"No. Not with the killer running around loose," he said. "They all assured me that once he was apprehended that they would jump at the opportunity. Unfortunately, those assurances don't do us much good in the mean time."

Everything came back to the Shadow-man. He was the center of Ashton and haunted it even without killing. Jesse sat back on the hard cot, ran her hands through her hair, and thought briefly about the special characteristic that Harold was so keen over. It only gave her a headache to do so.

"May I ask about Harold, and that thing which some kids have that draws him to kill?" she asked, hoping that since her and her father were having such a close chat that he would finally spill.

"Are you going to attempt to open your heart?" James replied, looking for a promise. She nodded and he smiled warmly in return and said, "Then definitely not. I know you better than you do. You're the girl who can't help bringing home a stray. Telling you would only open up a can of worms that I can't deal with at the moment, especially with everything else going on."

Jesse dropped her head, but she wasn't going to be defeated. "This is a little embarrassing...I think I need to see a therapist."

Chapter 40

"A therapist?" James asked with more than a hint of suspicion. "You hate therapists."

That was very true, however since no one would tell her what Harold looked for in a victim, she was bound and determined to find out herself. And who knew more about the killer than his therapist?

"Yes," she replied, avoiding her father's eyes. "You and mom are always pushing me to open up. I think it might do me some good."

James shrugged. "I guess I could set something up. Maybe next week..."

"This morning," she said with some urgency. "As soon as possible."

"Are you ok?" he asked this time without the distrust in his eyes. "Is there something else going on that I should know about?"

It was her turn to shrug. "Just teenage girl things...things I don't want to discuss with my dad." That ended his line of inquiry quick.

"We'll go right over," James said, looking more than a bit uncomfortable in his thousand-dollar suit. "Are you ready to leave?" he asked and then opened the cell door.

"That's been open the whole time?" she asked as she slowly climbed to her feet. "That doesn't say much for the police force around here. No wonder they can't catch Harold."

"You aren't being charged with anything," James answered. "I spoke to the DA and I convinced him that it would be in everyone's best interest not to file criminal charges."

Her mouth came open. How did he do these things? Her father held the door open for her, but as she passed, he took her gently but firmly by the arm and held her for a moment.

"I'm sorry. I know that you've been through a lot but I still can't let you go to the ball," he said and paused just long enough for Jesse's heart to sink into the pit of her stomach. "Your mom is right about some things. Appearances do count. It would look bad for you to be arrested one day and be at a ball the next. Do you understand?"

A part of her did. Another part, however, wanted to stomp her feet and tell him how unfair he was being. A final part, a very sly part, began devising schemes...it was a masquerade ball after all.

"I understand."

They met Cynthia Clarke outside in her Lexus. She had refused to step one foot into the police station and instead sat slumped down in her car wearing dark glasses.

"Jesse wants to see a therapist," James said getting into the passenger side.

This announcement went over a little too well with Cynthia, in Jesse's opinion. "Oh, thank goodness," she gushed. "I've been saying for years that she's in need of serious help."

James shot an uncomfortable look at his daughter, who sat in the back seat grinding her teeth. It was decided, by her father, that Cynthia would take Jesse to the appointment and then home. It was decided as well that Jesse would be grounded until further notice.

"Does until further notices mean until Harold kills again?" she asked.

"Or until he's caught," he answered. "Let's give the police some credit. I just don't want you tramping through the forests at night anymore." Jesse was right there with him, she was sick of the forest.

Without an appointment or even an advanced phone call, James led his family into Dr Becker's office and in his usual way of getting what he wanted, he convinced the man to see Jesse immediately. It was such an immediate appointment that the therapist was still working on a file when they arrived. At the top it read: H Brownly.

The answers to all of her questions lay only feet away, tantalizingly close. It was all she could do not to stare at the manila file; nevertheless it drew her eyes until Dr Becker noticed her looking at it and stuck it in his top drawer.

"I've been expecting you, Jesse," he said, once they were alone. This was a shocking opening statement.

Guardedly, she asked, "You have? Why? What have you heard?" What sort of rumors had been zipping around town concerning her? The therapist, pale faced, thinning hair, a body pudging into fat, looked to be the softest person Jesse had ever seen. When they shook hands, his had been so delicate she had been afraid to squeezed too hard.

He gave her a simpering little smile. "It's nothing that I've heard, it's just what I know. You're the only daughter of the town manager...a person with the stress of thousands depending on him. With all that pressure to be perfect, to balance out the needs of so many, someone has to be over-looked. Is that someone you?"

What the man said was so close to the truth that Jesse blinked after an owl-like fashion a few times and then began stammering. "Well, yes...but, I...it's complicated..."

"Take your time," Dr Becker said in a soothing voice. "I want you to feel completely comfortable here. Nothing you say will leave these walls, ok?"

"I'm not here because of my father," Jesse said, after she was able to pull herself together. "I'm here because of the Shadow-man."

Now it was the therapists turn to blink. "The Shadow-man? Could you describe him for me?"

Jesse went on to describe Harold Brownly as she had seen him on her first night in the woods. She dappled her words with enough fear to get his eyes widening and as she spoke, she got the chills and goose bumps jumped up in agreement.

When she finished the therapist steepled his fingers beneath his chin and considered for a time. Finally he asked, "Are you talking about a real person?"

"Yes...Harold Brownly. I have nightmares about him. He comes searching for me in the woods and I run but he's always coming closer and closer. Finally I trip on a rock and I'm lying in the snow and I'm so afraid that I can't move. All I can do is pray he doesn't see me." This was technically a lie, she hadn't dreamt this. However, as she spoke she pictured it so vividly she worried it wouldn't be a lie after that night.

"I see," Dr Becker said after a few seconds to digest her story. "That dream is pretty scary. You feel alone in that dream don't you?" She nodded. "Abandoned?" She nodded again and he went on, "Sometimes dreams can be complicate puzzles to unravel and others, like this one aren't. You feel deserted by your father, who should be there to protect you..."

Exasperated, Jesse held up a hand to stop him. "No that's not it. I'm afraid of Harold! The real Harold, not some dream. That's the issue I want to deal with. He lives so close to me but no one will tell me anything at all about him. Why does he do the things he does? How does he choose his victims...how come he can't be caught?"

"Jesse, all my patients have a right to privacy," he said this with such a sad face that Jesse thought he might just cry. "It's what allows them the chance to open up and the chance to heal. I hope you understand."

Inside Jesse groaned. Was this guy for real? What he said hadn't bothered her, it was how he said it. Dr Becker was like a slightly wimpier version of Mr. Rogers. He even wore a cardigan sweater like the TV personality. How on earth did he go about conducting therapy with a monster like Harold Brownly?

"Dr Becker, I'm not asking for anything private," Jesse said, trying again. "There's information on this man that *everyone* knows. Everyone but me. It could save my life."

The therapist shook his head at her.

The remainder of their hour-long session was a battle of wills...that Jesse lost. The therapist kept up his attempt at trying to tie all of Jesse's problems down to an absentee father. While she kept turning the conversation back to the town's resident killer. She got nowhere. To his credit Dr Becker was an impenetrable vault.

It wasn't an altogether wasted hour. Jesse learned a lot about herself and foremost was that despite everything that had happened to her, she was a strong person. Emotionally and mentally. Yes, she held anger in her heart for the way she was treated, but it felt as though her eyes had been opened by her father. What he had said was true—they hated and she hated. Jesse had to wonder how many of her problems could have been avoided by not feeding into that anger.

Theoretically, her voice of reason said.

Yes, how would it work in practice? How was she going to react the first time someone was a snot to her? Was she going to fly off the handle? Was she going to rip them apart verbally? Only time would tell.

"So how do you think we did today," Dr Becker asked.

"Pretty good, I guess," Jesse replied.

"Isn't that funny?" he asked. "I'm usually the upbeat one. I didn't think it went so well. You've admitted to holding much anger in you, but I don't think you're going to get anywhere dealing with it until you stop denying the true cause of it."

"My father?" she asked, already knowing the answer. This wasn't Dr Beckers fault. Jesse had fed into his suggestions that her father was the root of her problems just enough to keep the session going. Just so she could make her own attempts at getting information on Harold.

The truth was her session had solidified what she had long denied: her father, though a busy man had always been there for her. She seemed always to come to him with anger and hate burning at her insides, yet he was always the same. She would unload her harsh emotions on him, blame him for her problems, try to make him into some narrow minded jerk and still he would be James Clarke. Yes, he wasn't perfect, he worked too hard and carried other people's burdens on his shoulders, but he was a good man.

"Yes, your father," Dr Becker said, his face lingering somewhere between his sad look and his simpering one. She gave him a half-hearted shrug that said nothing, but he took to mean everything. "I think we're going to need some more time together to work this out. What do you think?"

Jesse rubbed her head as if it ached...actually it did ache, but she rubbed it for show. "You're probably right. Can I wait here, while you set up another appointment with my mom? I have a wicked headache."

The soft man nodded, wiggling his soft jowls, and left the room with his day planner in hand. Jesse barely waited for the door to close before she was up.

This is a really dumb idea.

"Since when are my ideas dumb?" she whispered as she slipped around the therapist's desk.

Remember last night?

Right. That had been very stupid. However, this was a matter of life or death. Jesse had the desk drawer open in a flash and there was the file, clearly marked: Confidential. She ignored the word and flipped open the two-inch thick record.

"Oh man!" Jesse exclaimed as she looked at the first page. Every word on it seemed as long as her arm and she had no idea what any of them meant. She began flipping pages and scanning the documents, but knew right away she wasn't going to find what she was looking for. At least not without an in depth search, and thirty seconds was all she had.

Kyle Mendel

The two words leapt out at her from a page. Her eyes darted to the heading: Transcript: *Session H. Brownly 12/18/10*

In a blink, she understood: Dr Becker taped his sessions and then had them typed up. Feeling as though the seconds were flying by, Jesse undid the steel clips and slipped out a small section of the typed notes and crammed them in her pocket. She then re-bent the clips with shaking hands and stuffed the file back in the drawer.

When she looked up, her heart banged once in her chest and then felt to stop. Dr Becker's office door was fully open and he stood squarely in doorway.

Chapter 41

"We could do ten o'clock if that suits you instead," Dr Becker said. He was in the doorway, but just at that moment he had his back turned on Jesse to answer a question from her mom. He would turn around again any second. With wide staring eyes and feet that were as heavy as lead, she took two steps before the therapist turned and stared at her. She stared back. Her brain seemed to have seized up.

"Jesse? You ok, Hun?" her mom asked. Cynthia was gazing at Jesse's forehead and when the girl put her hand there it came back damp. She wiped it on her coat and felt the stolen papers in her pocket; she nearly gasped.

The doctor no longer looked so soft. His eyes were suspicious squints. "What are you doing?" Jesse had no business being right next to his desk and just then she felt to have been struck dumb by the question. Not knowing what else to do she turned trying to buy a second to recover her senses and pointed vaguely behind her. That's when her eye fell upon Dr Becker's diploma.

"I...I was just seeing where you went to school," she said in a stuttering voice. The doctor didn't seem to notice. He brightened at once at the idea someone was interested in his diploma.

"Ah yes, I went to the University of Michigan," he said, jovial once again.

"Go Wolverines," Jesse said on reflex. If she had thought about it she probably would have got the mascot wrong. She could never get them all straight in her head, likely because she didn't care.

"Go Wolverines," Dr Becker replied with a little wave of his soft fist.

"Yes, Wolverines, yeah," Cynthia said with a minimum enthusiasm. "Come on Jesse, I'm starving. I want to get something to eat and then we'll go get your head fixed. You look like you need some stitches. Thank you Dr Becker, we'll see you next week."

Seconds later they were in Cynthia's Lexus with Jesse breathing far harder than the short walk could have possibly demanded. She had been within a quarter-second of being caught stealing confidential papers. What the penalty for that was, she had no idea, but it was probably hefty.

"Chinese or a burger?" Cynthia asked. Jesse made a face and her mom matched it. "I know, not much of a selection...let's do Chinese. I hear the owner is actually Chinese, so that's a plus."

"Yeah, remember that Chinese place in Denton," Jesse said, relaxing as they pulled away. "Everyone who worked there was Mexican and the food tasted like tacos." Her mom smiled at the memory but then turned sad, giving her daughter a thorough inspection.

"Honey, whatever you're doing to yourself, you have to stop," Cynthia said. "You don't look good."

What I'm doing to myself? How could she say such a thing? Jesse's familiar rage flared up, filling her with its protective malice and a dozen snide remarks enter her mind. Her father's first test was upon her. Was she going to lash out over the insensitive comment?

Swallowing the rude words coming up out of her throat, she turned to the window. Jesse watched the little town pass on by and whispered, "She loves me, that's all."

"What was did you say, dear?"

"I said, you love me," Jesse replied.

"I do love you," Cynthia said, giving Jesse a wry smile. "Do I not say I love you, enough so that you have to say it for me?"

Cynthia Clarke *didn't* say it enough, but that was a hurtful truth and Jesse only gave her a shrug. "No one ever says it enough, really," she answered. "You could say I love you to me a thousand times, but if I were to die, would you think that was even enough?"

"You're right about that," Cynthia said with a little laugh. "So I better get started...I love you, I love you..."

Jesse grabbed her mom's arm, "Once is enough...or maybe just one at a time. I'd rather have one really great big one than a thousand meaningless ones."

Just then they pulled into the parking lot of The Dim Sum. "Do you remember the good green tea that I like?" Jesse said getting out of the car.

"Wait," Cynthia ordered, pulling Jesse back. "Do you know who that man is?" Cynthia asked in a whisper, pointing out the passenger side window. "I've seen him hanging around and he gives me the creeps."

Jesse peered out at a car nearby. "That's Jerry Mendel and if you've seen him around it's because he's our neighbor. He lives right behind us. And I thought I was the paranoid one! Hold on..." Jesse stuck a thumb in her mouth and then used it to wipe at her mom's eye. "Sorry, you had some dirt or something there."

Cynthia relaxed in a quick droop of her shoulders. "Yeah, now I know him. I think I'm just on edge, waiting for...you know."

"The next death," Jesse said. "You're right, it's nerve racking waiting for it to happen. But it must be worse for the rest of the town. I've seen the kids at school in the mornings huddled in little groups, watching the busses unload, counting their friends. They all have that same pinched look on their faces."

"I wonder what it's going to be like when it finally does happen," Cynthia said. "Do we bring a casserole? Do we pretend the kid who died never existed? You know...never bring him up in conversation again."

Just then Jesse felt sorry for the people of Ashton. Incongruously, it almost made her laugh. Just an hour before she had been demanding that her father destroy the town, but now she was blinking away tears for them.

I must be tired, she thought. Aloud she tried to change the subject, "I remembered the tea that I like. It's oolong."

Jesse's plan to bite back her nasty remarks to her mother worked. They had the best day together that she could remember, despite their visit to the medical offices of Dr Sarah Becker, sister of the soft therapist. There she had her laceration cleaned out and stitched, a very painful process. She was also checked out, head to toe, an embarrassing process.

During all this Jesse was dying to get home to find out what Kyle Mendel, her ghost, her Ky, had to do with Harold Brownly. His name hadn't been on the transcript just once, it had been all throughout. It was just after three when they were finally released and as small as Ashton was, they were home eight minutes later.

"I'm going to take a nap," Jesse said to her mom. That was part of her plan at least; read the notes, figure out what draws the killer in and then sleep. Jesse's day had been a long one: a near fight in the woods, suspended from school, a trip to the police station, her head shrunk at the therapists and torture at the caring hands of the doctor.

Locking her door, she pulled out the transcript. It started in the middle of a conversation:

Dr. Becker: "And how did that make you feel?"

H Brownly: "I don't recall."

Dr. Becker: "You can't recall how you felt when you first heard your son had been killed?"

H Brownly: "It's been ten years. Upset, I guess?"

Dr. Becker: "Upset? Would that include sadness?"

H Brownly: "Yes."

Dr. Becker: "What about anger?"

H Brownly: "No."

Dr. Becker: "What about guilt?"

H Brownly: "Why would you think that I would feel guilty? He drowned and I wasn't there. That's a proven fact." (Note: client extremely agitated)

Dr. Becker: Please settle down. I'm talking about guilt on a more personal level, not in a legal sense. For instance, did you feel guilt over the fact you left your pool filled so late in the year and over the fact that you left the cover off?"

(Note: client only shrugs at question.)

Dr. Becker: "You barely answered when I asked about you being sad. You deny feeling anger and you shrug at the idea of guilt... Mr. Brownly, I can't say in all honesty that you're cooperating with your therapy. And Judge Te..." (Note: client stands up and begins pacing in a state of extreme agitation.) "I would prefer if you sat or laid back down."

H Brownly: "I know what the judge said. And...and this may not seem like it, but I am cooperating. But what does all this have to do with getting a D.U.I.?"

Dr. Becker: "Are you an alcoholic?"

H Brownly: "No."

Dr. Becker: "An alcoholic doesn't need an excuse to drink to excess, it's in their genes, but an average person is different. There's always a reason for the sort of drunken behavior you were exhibiting. Usually it's obvious, but sometimes it's hidden away deep within them. With you, I'm sure that it's both. The obvious reasons: your son was killed, and then..."

H Brownly: "He drowned. It was an accident."

Dr. Becker: "...And, then there was the second murder and the trial. Your wife leaving you was probably a blow as well."

H Brownly: "I guess I was feeling a little angry back then." (Note: client takes seat on couch.)

Dr. Becker: "Were you angry with Kyle Mendel?"

H Brownly: "What? That...that doesn't...No, I was not angry at Kyle. He has nothing to do with any of this."

Dr. Becker: "Are you fascinated with Kyle Mendel?"

H Brownly: "Why are we talking about Kyle? We were just talking about my drinking."

Dr. Becker: "Because they are related. In your last session, you told me how you held Kyle on the day he was born and that you'd never harm him. Do you ever get feelings of envy or jealousy when you think of Kyle?"

H Brownly: "No."

Dr. Becker: "What about when he's with friends? Does that bother you to see him having fun with them?"

H Brownly: "No. Why should it bother me?"

Dr. Becker: "That's a good question. You've stated that you love Kyle. Can you tell me about those feelings?"

H Brownly: "They're not feelings! Not the way you think. I don't fantasize over him. Son of a bitch! He's lived his whole life next door to me, if I love him it's like an uncle would."

Dr. Becker: "Like an uncle? Do you feel protective over Kyle?"

H Brownly: "Yes." (Note: client's response is quick and strongly affirmative.)

Dr. Becker: How far would you go to protect Kyle? Would you kill to protect him?"

H Brownly: "I don't know...it depends on the situation. Can we go back to talking about my DUI?"

Dr. Becker: "In just a minute. You said you saw Kyle and Mary Castaneda together last year. How did that make you feel?" (Note: client shrugs.) Did you feel she was a bad match, that there could have been someone better for him?"

H Brownly: "How am I supposed to know. I only saw them together once."

Dr. Becker: "Did you see Mary after that?" (Note: client shrugs.) "And do you hear voices? From the TV or the radio?"

H Brownly: "No! These are stupid questions."

Dr. Becker: "When the water runs, is that when you hear the voices?"

H Brownly: "Stop it! I don't hear voices. Why do you keep changing the subject? What kind of therapy is this? You're just trying to get me to admit to something I didn't do."

Dr. Becker: "Can you please sit down? Do I have to ask Officer Daniels to come in here? Good, thank you. I'm trying to get you to open up. To talk to me."

H Brownly: "By getting me angry? I can't even think straight!"

Dr. Becker: "Yes. It's when you're angry that the walls come down. When you're calm you barely say anything besides hello." (Note: client sits.) Now, can you tell me when your fascination with Kyle Mendel began?"

H Brownly: "I'm not fascinated with..."

Dr. Becker: "You are, and to a certain extent we all are. Why is that? Why do you follow him around?"

H Brownly: "Because he is the key."

Dr. Becker: "The key to what?" (Note: client shrugs.) "The key to what, Harold?" (Note: client refuses to answer.) "What do you hope to gain by following him?"

H Brownly: "So I can find out who's really following him."

Dr. Becker: "You're the one really following him. No one else."

H Brownly: "That's not true. The real killer watches him."

Dr. Becker: "When you are following Kyle, have you seen this killer?"

H Brownly: "Yes, a few times, but I can never seem to get close enough to see his face. He always disappears when I get close."

Dr. Becker: "When was the last time you saw this person?"

[339]

H Brownly: "Sunday night, down by the berm. It was him. He ran as soon as I saw him and I lost him in the woods"

Jesse stopped reading for a moment as a chill of understanding swept her. It had been Harold who had been chasing her after all. She'd always known it, but seeing it in writing made her skin crawl. "Holy crap!" she muttered, before going back to the transcript.

Dr. Becker: "What would you have done if you had caught up to him?" (Note: client shrugs.) "Would you have tried to hurt him? (Note: client shrugs.) Or would you have tried talking first?"

H Brownly: "I don't know what I would've done. What would you have done?"

Dr. Becker: "I would've tried talking to him, just like I'm talking to you. I would've tried to help him."

H Brownly: "That's great. You'll help a killer but you won't help me. Why aren't we talking about my drinking problem? That's what I'm here for, damn it."

Dr. Becker: "Your drinking issue is tied up with all of this. You can't pretend otherwise. Now let's get back to Kyle..."

H Brownly: "No! I can't think straight with you asking me all these questions."

Dr. Becker: "You say he is the key? Please settle down, Harold. We have to talk about this, so there's no use getting upset. Everyone thinks that Kyle is the key to these murders; you're not alone in thinking that. I just want to know why you think so." (Note: client shrugs.) "Why do his friends keep dying? (Note: client shrugs.) Harold please, I'm just trying to get your insight on the killer. The only thing we know about these murders is the sad fact that if anyone gets too friendly with Kyle Mendel they're going to end up dead." (Note: client shrugs.)

Jesse read on to the end of the page, but it was mostly questions from the therapist and shrugs from the killer. There really wasn't anything more she needed to know either way. She had found the characteristic that she was looking for and on top of that the reason why everyone so ignored Ky.

"Oh my," Jesse said in tired voice.

After hiding the papers, she laid back on her bed and stared at her ceiling. Her thoughts strayed to Mary Castaneda. Why had they been together? Did she love him? Did she love him so much she was willing to die for him? His love was a death sentence.

"Oh my!" Jesse exclaimed as the words of Ky slipped into her mind: 'You're the last person that I'd want to be friends with.' What did that mean? At the time, she thought that it meant that he hated her, but now...

"No!" Jesse hopped up, barely feeling the sharp protest from her broken ribs.

Yes.

She went to the window and stole a peek at Kyle's bedroom. It was dark and the blinds were drawn, but as she watched, one of them moved. He was there.

You weren't in school and he's been worried for you.

Really? Momentarily forgetting about Harold and the danger he posed, Jesse stared at Kyle's window trying to sort everything out. If she was the last person that Ky wanted to be close to, it really meant that he cared for her more than anyone else.

Ky loves you.

"Oh my," Jesse said, clutching the sill for support.

Chapter 42

"Ky loves me."

Jesse sat on her bed and couldn't stop saying the words. They felt strange on her tongue. She'd never been loved before...not by a boy that is. It made her chest feel like exploding and her feet felt like they could just float away.

"Ky loves me," Jesse said for the tenth time, but then she grew angry. "Why couldn't he be normal! How did I get the one boy in town who *can't* love me to fall in love with me?"

Jesse went back to the transcript hidden in her drawer and re-read it top to bottom. The words hadn't changed and neither had the only possible interpretation of them. Ky loved her, it was simple as that. Yet she didn't know exactly what to do with the information.

Dwell on it until you can't sleep or eat.

Yes. What else could she do? Other than being a guarantee that she would have an early death, Ky would be the perfect boyfriend. He was handsome, strong, courageous, and willing to risk his life for her. Just thinking about him made her soul knot itself and she had to get up and pace.

A wonderful thought stopped her feet. Would he go to the ball? In disguise? There was a chance he would and if so, he would be easy to spot. Quiet and shy, he'd be lurking in the corners.

"Oh, man. I hope so," Jesse said to no one in particular. Just the mere possibility that he would show meant Jesse was definitely going, whether or not she was grounded. She set to scheming and when that was accomplished, she set to napping.

Her father, coming home from work at a little after ten, woke her up. Her body had gone stiff and it was with a groan that she rolled over, "Yes?"

"I just wanted to check to see if you were ok," he said. "Your eye looks much better. Dr Becker has a fine hand."

"Oh, yeah. That was good pain," she said with a smile. Her face hurt to smile so she cut it short. "Take me out to dinner tomorrow night? Please?"

The request caused his face to exhibit pain as well. "I'm sorry. I can't. The protest is scheduled for the next day and we have meetings till way late."

"That's ok, I understand." It was not only understood, but expected as well. But she had to ask just in case. Jesse was simply trying to cover all her bases and James Clarke was by far the biggest. With her father safely entombed in endless meetings, stealing his car would be a snap.

"Could I order a pizza then?" she asked, taking her plan one step at a time. Jesse held out a demure hand.

"Of course," he replied, digging into his wallet. "Mom isn't big on grocery shopping, is she? Here you go." He handed her a twenty-dollar bill. At her look of *more please*, he shrugged. "That's all I have."

"It's Christmas, Daddy," she said, laying it on a bit too thick. "How am I supposed to leave a proper tip?"

"Don't go overboard," he said, handing over what she had been after all along. She pocketed the twenty along with the credit card. He tried to give her a hard look, but it cracked into a smile and he shook his head. "Good night. I love you."

"I was good today," she said suddenly. The words 'I love you' made her remember. "Well, mostly good, but something happened and I didn't react like I have been."

"And?"

"And it worked out pretty good. Thanks for the advice...I love you too." The last words came out of her mouth as if she was speaking them in German. They felt thick and awkward as though they were formed from the wooden letter blocks she had as a toddler. It made her wonder when the last time she had said them was.

Her father's look of happy surprise was enough to tell her it had been a very long time. The look jarred her. It had her questioning what kind of daughter she had been.

[343]

Not a good one if you can't remember the last time you told your father that you loved him.

Right. She couldn't remember. It seemed like years since she had said, 'I love you' to him, while he said it all the time. This made her feel small. He was himself, always, while she had let anger burn away the girl that she had once been. He loved her unconditionally, while she laid blame on him unconditionally. In fact it wouldn't be a stretch to say that she was abusive in the way she found fault in him.

James Clarke came to these towns to help people in need. He put himself out there when no one else would and performed miracles turning around towns that were on their way to destruction. This was something to be admired, yet how did she treat him? She made her problems, his problems. She heaped scorn on him at every turn and called him names under her breath.

All this hit her quite suddenly. She had been a bad daughter...and still was. Jesse had just used pretense to take her father's credit card. Against his wishes she was planning to go to the ball. It wasn't right and she knew it. She opened her mouth to confess, only at that very moment, he bent down and kissed her on the forehead.

"Good night," he murmured and left before Jesse could find the use of her tongue.

"Good night," she replied to the closed door. Right then she resolved to return the credit card in the morning and vowed to be a better daughter.

In the end her vow held, she was a better daughter...just not a perfect one. Her resolve concerning the card didn't make it through the night. Her dreams were filled with soft music and dancing—with beautiful gowns glimmering in the low light. But above all else her dreams were filled with Ky. In every one they were together, laughing and talking as if there was no Shadow-man and no death sentence upon her head.

The dreams were was too wonderful; they were a temptation she could not resist.

In the morning she slept in, knowing both her parents would be gone by the time she got up. She knew if she had seen her father that morning, either he would have discerned her subterfuge with his piercing glance, or she would've broken down and confessed. As it was she had the house to herself.

In keeping with her father's suggestion to open up, Jesse dressed that morning as a girl would. A normal girl, who wasn't trying to keep the world at bay with a hard exterior. She wore blue jeans, a pink top and because for a December day, it was only cool out rather than cold, she added a white down vest.

"Now for the hard part," she said as she slipped to the corner of her window and looked out at the killer's house. Her plan was simplicity itself. She would use the extra set of keys to steal her dad's car from the parking lot at the town hall, drive to Barton, pick up the white costume she had seen on the poster at school, go to the dance, have the time of her life and then throw herself at the mercy of her father. He would find out about the dress and the ball eventually, after all.

But first Jesse would have to brave the forest. The very idea had her hands shaking. From day one the trail had always led to trouble and she was loath to set one foot upon it. However, there was no other way.

With a deep calming breath that did little to calm her, Jesse slipped out of her house and jogged across the street. Once in the forest she slowed but still could see her breath puffing out of her in white plumes. Fear had her breathing hard. Yet the forest was serene.

That is until she reached the berm. She gave it a long look, and then stared up into the wooded hills on its other side. Nothing moved. However the moment she stepped onto the berm a thunking noise came from her left, echoing across the ice. She nearly screamed. Jumping back, she turned ready to bolt, but it was only an old man standing bent over on the frozen pond.

On his feet were snowshoes to spread out his weight and in one hand was an axe and in the other, a fishing pole. Next to him was a little blue milk crate; he was getting ready to ice-fish. Jesse gaped at the man. She was nervous for him; it was too early to be on the ice in her opinion.

It's always too early for you.

Right. Jesse feared the ice, yet the old man didn't seem to. He probably had little to worry about, as small and shriveled as he was.

A few minutes later, she was in the town itself, leaning against an abandoned flower shop, feeling weak as if the short walk had been more of an ordeal than it was. "At last," she said, breathing a sigh of relief. Down her back she felt sweat cooling, while her heart started to regain its normal rhythm. This was another reason she planned on turning herself over to her father after the ball. She would avoid a second trip through the woods. As anxious as she was walking in broad daylight, Jesse didn't think she could handle another harrowing adventure in the night.

Her father's car, a white Ford Mustang, sat in the lot behind the town hall. As if she had every right to, Jesse went to it, climbed in, and drove away. She didn't look back.

Chapter 43

Jesse had been to Barton before, many times, yet never in a stolen car.

"Borrowed car," she reminded herself, checking the rearview mirror for the hundredth time. Borrowed or not, she still felt like a criminal, which made the hour long drive a nerve-wracking one.

Every car coming up behind her became a police cruiser in her mind, so that her hands began to sweat at the sight of a roof rack. She was so nervous that she defied her very nature and forced herself to keep the mustang in check. Despite the near over-whelming temptation to let the car go at a pace it was designed for, Jesse held the needle at fifty-five.

This wasn't easy—the Mustang considered eighty-five a more appropriate cruising speed and when her mind wandered the car's velocity picked up. And her mind wandered a lot. Because of her guilt, her dad's face kept coming to her, and because of her fear—a deep river that constantly ran through her bones—the Shadow-man came as well.

The two men, so large in her life these last few days, were the extremes on the moral spectrum. Her father was good, but in an unbending black and white fashion, while the killer was a pure sadistic evil, untempered by any morality. Together they transfixed Jesse and her world lay balanced between them. It seemed not only right, but smart to keep herself as far from the killer as possible, but she couldn't help thinking that by stealing the car and going to the dance she was edging closer to him.

Then don't go. Turn the car around.

"I don't think I can." It was Ky that kept her on her path. Where did he fit in? He was the forbidden fruit. To taste of it meant death.

Yet, he is also love. Her voice of reason was suddenly, and uncharacteristically, the voice of romance.

"Right," Jesse said, still balanced, but unhappily so. Ky was everything she wanted and everything she feared. The thoughts of him and her father, and the Shadow-man made her mind swirl, until she didn't know what was best.

With one eye on the road and one hand on the wheel, Jesse took from her pocket the flier of the school dance and stared at the glossy picture of the girl in the white dress. She was beautiful—thin in the waist and torso, full in the bosom and just the right amount of flair in the hips. The dress flowed down her body gracefully in a series of over-woven silken feathers. It accented the girl perfectly. Jesse wanted to be her. For just one night she wanted to be beautiful. When she sighed it marked the end of any argument within her of what she would do.

You're doing eighty.

Right. Jesse relaxed her foot off the gas.

Barton wasn't a city exactly; it was nowhere big enough. It was more of a merchandise hub for all the outlying towns in that part of northern Michigan. It was where you went for big-ticket items: a washing machine or a new car. It was also where you went for unique items such as a gown for a masquerade ball.

There was one place in Barton where you went for costumes: *Cassie's Halloween and More!* With her love of Halloween and costumes in general, Jesse was a frequent visitor to Cassie's. As always when she walked in, Jesse's eyes were assaulted by a thousand colors and as always she had to pause in the doorway and take it all in. That day however, she was on a mission and the pause was briefer than most.

"Hi there," Jesse said to a girl behind the counter. It seemed always a different girl. This one was an inch or two taller than Jesse, had big, almost huge, moist brown eyes, and wore a long pink and white scarf. It looped around her neck and the two ends dangled down to her calves. Jesse asked, "Please, tell me that you have this dress?"

The shop-girl took her eyes off Jesse's beaten face long enough to take in the creased poster. "Oh, yes. Everyone wants that dress, but I have to warn you, very few girls actually look good in it. If you're too tall you look like an Albino ostrich and if you're too short you look like a stumpy yeti with wings. You can't be too skinny either, or you get lost in it."

The dress was losing its magic with every word the girl in the pink and white scarf uttered. "Can I at least try it on?" Jesse asked.

"Sure." The half-hearted reply came with a half-hearted shrug.

In the dressing room Jesse slid out of her clothes and then struggled into the costume all the while trying not to grunt with the pain of her broken ribs. The dress was so detailed and inter-woven that she didn't know if she was putting it on upside down or backwards. Even with the help of the sales girl, it took two tries to get it on correctly. When she did the shop-girl grew unexpectedly excited.

"The wings!" she said in rush and dug through the box before attaching two delicate wings to Jesse's back. Only then did Jesse turn around and look at herself.

"Whoa," she whispered.

"I know," said the girl. "Look at you"

Jesse stared and stared. And then started blinking rapidly. When she wasn't bruised and when her hair wasn't shorn and colored, Jesse Clarke was beautiful, a fact that she denied. It was easy for her to do so. The hate that surrounded her colored her vision and skewed her judgment. Yes, she thought she was pretty, but beauty was deeper than that and the hate made her believe that there was something not right about her. Something vile. In her mind, true beauty couldn't mix with something so loathsome as herself.

Yet the girl in the mirror, even with her bruises, was very beautiful; there could be no denying it. "What is the costume exactly...a swan princess or an angel?" she asked.

"It's whatever you want it to be," the girl replied.

The dress had such purity to it that Jesse saw herself as an angel. It was perfect...except for her face. As Jesse stared, all her imperfections grew in her mind; they stood out, becoming more and more repulsive. She put her hand across her eyes to block the view of the mirror. "I-I need a mask. Please, can you get me one? I can't look like this anymore."

The girl saw Jesse's sudden pain. "Honey, don't be like that. You're beautiful. Don't be ashamed of a few scratches."

"But that isn't me!" Jesse cried, pointing at herself. Just then she hated the girl in the mirror as much as everyone else did. That girl wasn't real. That face she wore was an illusion, a mask like any other in the costume shop. Tears were coming now and no amount of blinking would hold them back. "I'm not a monster...I don't deserve to be hated..."

"I'll be right back." Distressed, the shop-girl ran from the dressing room quicker than a fireman to a fire. There was an urgency to her that Jesse felt as well. She had been covering up her true self for so long and now she was desperate to be rid of the mask that she had built for herself.

You are only trading one mask for another.

Yes, but one mask was so much closer to her true self, while the other was a mask of shame, of fear, and of hate. Ashamed she had turned from her natural beauty, thinking there had to be something wrong with her. In fear she hid behind her hard exterior, pretending she was tougher because of it. And the hate that darkened her soul burned out from her eyes and dripped acid from her venomous tongue.

How could anyone like that girl? How could she?

The shop-girl dashed back into the changing room and without asking permission proceeded to slip a mask over Jesse's face. That the mask and the gown had been made for each other was without question. It was white, with small wings coming off the sides. These weren't arched like the ones on her gown, but swept up and back.

The shop-girl made a little noise like a tiny laugh of joy. "You were beautiful before, but now..."

Jesse was perfect. The girl in the picture on the school flier couldn't compare. To see herself from all angles, Jesse turned first left, and then right. Beneath the gown, she felt a wave of goose bumps rush along her skin. The moment, feeling as though she had never been that beautiful in her life and probably wouldn't again, stretched out until the shop-girl spoke again.

"That gown is just fantastic on you," she said not taking her eyes from the mirror. "It's $179 for the dress and..." The girl paused as Jesse snapped her head around.

"One-seventy-nine...is that with the mask?"

The shop-girl looked to be in pain when she answered, "No. The mask is ninety-nine dollars. How much were you looking to spend?"

Jesse's father was going to have a conniption fit already. "A hundred. Sorry for wasting your time." Jesse slipped off the mask, keeping her head down, not wanting to see the mirror now that it was off.

"It's ok, you didn't," the girl replied. "I finally found the girl this dress was made for. That's not a waste of time, not to me. Tell me...?"

"My name's Jesse."

"Tell me, Jesse, can you go any higher? I would love to see you in this dress."

As she slowly and reluctantly began to struggled out of the dress, Jesse said, "I'm using my dad's card...I can spend, maybe as high as one-fifty. After that I'll be outside the bounds of a daughter's prerogative of abusing her dad's credit card."

The shop-girl blinked as if remembering something. "Wow. I just had a moment of déjà vu. What you said sounded so familiar."

Wincing, Jesse pulled the dress over her head. Her shirt came up, exposing the purple/green bruising on her back. Jesse was quick to yank it down. "I'm sure I'm not the first girl to 'borrow' her dad's credit..." The shop-girl had seen the bruising and now her eyes were wide. Jesse felt her cheeks go pink. "It's not what you think, really."

"I know you," the girl said, with wide shocked eyes.

"Oh yeah?" Jesse slid into her jeans with a hard look on her battered features.

"You're Jesse Clarke."

The tension in the little room mounted in a flash. Under her skin Jesse felt her muscles go taut, while her eyes narrowed at the girl with the pink and white scarf.

The girl started nodding. "We went to Denton middle school together. You were in the seventh grade and I was in eighth. We shared a music class."

"Tricia?"

"Yeah."

It was the girl's large brown eyes that Jesse recalled. Just then she also recalled how one time Tricia Freeman had smeared Bengay on the mouthpiece of Jesse's clarinet. Her tongue had blistered and she had cried all the way to the nurse's office.

The memory piled on another: Tricia dumping a glass of milk over Jesse's lunch tray, ruining her meal...and that, piled on another: Tricia stealing her clothes in gym, so that Jesse had to walk home in a January snowstorm wearing only shorts and a t-shirt.

All of this brought out the hate in Jesse. She stepped away from the dress and set herself in her fighting stance, wishing that she had full use of her body. The shop-girl would still lose the fight, that was certain in Jesse's mind, but with her broken ribs, Jesse would feel almost as much pain as she would dish out. That was ok with her.

"I'm sorry," Tricia said, lowering her eyes.

"What?" Jesse asked, completely flummoxed by the words.

"I'm sorry for the way I treated you back then. I-I was really stupid and mean," Tricia said and now her moist eyes were brimming with tears. Jesse stared in growing confusion. Wasn't Tricia going to say something nasty? Was this a trick? Weren't they going to fight?

"You were mean," Jesse said, not knowing where Tricia was going with this.

"I had never been so mean to anyone in my life. I'm sorry. I really am."

"Is this for real?" Jesse asked. It couldn't be. "Do you think that just saying sorry is going to fix anything? Do you remember all the crap you put me through?" Tricia had been a head taller than Jesse back then and fighting her wouldn't have been suicide. There had been no choice for Jesse but to take the abuse that was heaped on her. But not now.

"I remember. I was a real bitch and I understand if you won't accept my apology...I don't think I would either." Tricia walked out of the room with her head bowed.

Accept her apology? "Is that really an option?" Jesse whispered. Tricia had been so vicious and cruel.

Love your enemies.

No! That's impossible. "I hated you, Tricia!" Jesse slammed her fist into the wall, sending a shriek of pain through her ribs. In her seething rage, she didn't care. "I didn't do anything to you!"

"I know...you sh-sh-should have hated m-me." Tricia was crying.

"I still hate you," Jesse screamed. "I do!" Now Jesse came out of the changing room. Her rage was too strong to be denied and in her mind she knew that she was going to hurt Tricia. The girl deserved what was coming to her.

Tricia stood behind the counter, crying. At the sight of Jesse's wrath, she seemed to melt, going down on her knees.

"Get up!" Jesse ordered. "Unlike you, I won't hurt a defenseless person."

"I don't want to fight."

Jesse grabbed Tricia's scarf and hauled the girl to her feet with it. "When did you ever give me that choice?" Jesse yelled. "All I wanted was to be left alone. I didn't want to be hated!"

"I-I didn't hate you."

"Liar!" With a berserker's lust for blood Jesse threw down the skinny girl and knelt atop of her breast. "You hated me...everyone hated me. If you didn't hate me, why did you do those things to me?"

The girl didn't answer at first and so Jesse grabbed her by the shoulders and shook her until she did.

"I-I-I didn't hate you," Tricia said, warbling with the motion. Jesse stopped shaking the girl and she laid back, noodle limp; she wouldn't turn and look at Jesse's hard, red face. "You-you were different, and everyone had this thing about you. It was almost like we weren't allowed to like you...and I went along with it."

"You tortured me because of peer-pressure?" Jesse asked, dumfounded. The idea seemed too far-fetched to even contemplate.

"Yes," the girl said and then began crying to the point of blubbering. "I was angry at what was happening to my family...and you were easy to blame. And it was easy to go along with everyone else, and...and it was easy to take my frustrations out on you. My life seemed to be falling apart, while you seemed to have everything. I know this may sound stupid since you were always picked on, but I was jealous of you."

"How could you possibly be jealous of me?" None of this made sense to Jesse. Her anger faded as her mind dwelt on Tricia's words.

"You were prettier than everyone else and smarter," Tricia said, now looking up at Jesse. "You had money and we didn't. Even your family was better..."

Jesse climbed off the girl and sat next to her, shaking her head. Her mind in a storm of confusion. "You don't know my family if you think it's great in any way. My mom is always running around helping anyone but me, and my dad...no one was hated more than me except for him."

"No. You're wrong there," Tricia said. "People liked him; deep down they respected him and they knew he was right."

"Then why all the anger? Why was he always vilified?"

Tricia finally turned to Jesse. "It's so stupid. People want it easy. They want everything easy. They want the government to do things for them and give them stuff...you know jobs or dog parks, or bike lanes...even silly things like new windows or cell phones. They want everything, but at the same time they want someone else to pay. You see? They even want stuff they don't need or even use, just as long as it sounds nice or important. Remember we had a counselor for every grade in school? No one ever went to them with any problems unless the principal forced them to go...remember Beth Gill? Her mom was one. We all knew what a complete waste it was, but we were like, whatever. We didn't care since someone else paid for it."

Jesse remembered the counselors. In such a small town where gossip ran on the wind and everyone was related in some way to everyone else, counselors were practically useless. Who would take the chance on ever saying anything meaningful to them?

"And my father was hated because he changed everything," Jesse said.

"Well, yeah. He was like the one adult in the town." Tricia sat up and leaned against the underside of the counter next to Jesse. Their arms touched. It was such a casual thing that Tricia didn't seem to notice, but Jesse did. No one had ever sat so close to her. Tricia went on, "Everyone knew deep down we knew he was right, that the way we were going couldn't last. Still we all threw temper tantrums like a bunch of babies. Looking back, I feel like a moron...I think we all were morons. Except for you."

"No. I did some stupid things..."

Gently, Tricia grabbed Jesse's arm. The simple touch from her one time enemy stopped Jesse's words. "No. You didn't," Tricia said. "You were small and quiet and nice. You did nothing to deserve what we...what I did to you. I really am sorry."

Jesse didn't know what to think. The girl had been so hateful, yet now she was nice. Was Jesse supposed to forgive her simply because of this change of heart?

"My father says that I should forgive my..." Jesse paused. She had been about to say enemies, but clearly Tricia wasn't her enemy anymore. "I mean, he wants me to be open to forgiveness...but I don't know if I can. I don't think I even know what the word means. Do I forgive the boy who did this to me?" Jesse pointed at her face.

Tricia glanced up for a brief second and then looked away, guiltily. "That might as well have been me who did that to you," she said in a whisper. Tricia began to slowly shake her head, while staring at her knees with empty eyes. "I-I don't think I could forgive him. He doesn't deserve it. And neither do I."

Chapter 44

"Maybe you don't," Jesse said. "But suddenly I want to forgive you. Maybe time heals all wounds like they say."

"I don't think so," Tricia replied. "Even after six years, the wounds that I caused you are still fresh. Two minutes ago you were going to rip my head off. You scared me half to death."

Jesse laughed guiltily. "I'm sorry, this was all so sudden. Going from the dress, to seeing you and remembering. I didn't mean to scare you so badly."

You did mean it, her voice of reason said.

What? Was that true? Yes, clearly it was.

"Wait. Hold on... I did mean it," Jesse said. Something about this was clicking in her mind. "I really meant to scare you and even hurt you. And now I'm sorry. And I don't want you to be upset with me...I want you to forgive me. Why?" Jesse asked. She wasn't looking for an answer from Tricia; she was following a line or reason. The idea of forgiveness was like a physics theory that she couldn't quite wrap her head around. "Because, I want you to be my friend...but we can't be friends unless I forgive you as well. The question is, can I?"

Tricia smiled; it did nothing to dim the pain in her brown eyes. "I think you're wrong. What you did just now, getting all angry, was understandable. That's easy to forgive, but what about the things you can't understand? Like what I did to you. I have excuses, but they are so weak it's embarrassing. They aren't even excuses at all. How is it even possible to forgive something like that?"

"Maybe you don't forgive the action...maybe you forgive the person," Jesse replied. "Obviously you've changed. You're not the same girl that you were. This new Tricia seems nice and sweet. I could be friends with her, but not until I can forgive her. We could never go forward with that hanging over our heads." Jesse reached out and grabbed the shop-girl's hand. "I forgive you for what you did to me. I want it to be behind us." The words felt silly and right at the same time. Did normal people walk around saying 'I forgive you'? Or did they just say, 'That's ok'?

Jesse liked the word forgive better. What Tricia had done was far from ok.

Tricia sort of laughed and cried at the same time. She dripped tears onto her scarf. "I really am nice. I...I'm not a bad person. I was never so mean to anyone as I was to you. I want you to know that."

"I know. I saw you with your friends and I saw how you treated the younger kids. They all looked up to you."

Tricia wiped her eyes with her one free hand and then asked, "So are we friends now?"

"I hope so," Jesse said, suddenly shy. Her last real friend had been in the fourth grade and just then Jesse felt a little like an imposter. What did friends do? What did they say to each other? A single second of silence passed between the two girls. It was enough to send Jesse into a panic over losing her first friend in nine years through sheer ineptness. She knew she had to say something, only she had no clue what.

Compliment her.

Right! Girlfriends gave each other compliments, while boys did the opposite and put each other down.

"I like your scarf. It's cute. Where did you get it?" Jesse asked in a rush.

"I made it," Tricia beamed. "I picked up crocheting back when our cable got disconnected. It's a wonder all the things you can learn when you don't have a TV. Here, stand up." Jesse stood and Tricia slipped the scarf off her neck and looped it around Jesse's. "The pink and white looks great with what you're wearing."

Jesse took in her reflection. The scarf did go well. Reluctantly, she started to take it off, but Tricia stopped her. "No, leave it on. It looks better on you than it does on me." Jesse opened her mouth to protest, however her new friend shushed her with a look. "You can borrow it and that way you'll have an extra reason to come back to Barton."

"Thanks," Jesse said. "It might be a while. I'm going to be so grounded after tonight."

Tricia's large brown eyes went larger still. "You're going to the Ashton ball without your parent's permission?"

"I'm pure evil, I know," Jesse laughed. "But that's why I shouldn't go over a hundred dollars for the gown. Hey, how did you know I'm going to the Ashton ball?"

It took a second for Tricia to answer. Her mind seemed elsewhere for a moment. "Oh, because for the last two weeks we've had a parade of girls coming through here and it was all they talked about." The girl paused for a moment, again thinking. "Wait here, I know the perfect dress for you in your price range."

Tricia hopped up, leaving Jesse eyeing the masks. When she came back she held a large white box in her hands. Grinning she handed it over. Jesse opened it and became confused. "You said this was one-seventy-nine? I can only do a hundred." In the box, neatly folded sat the angel gown.

"I forgot to mention I can give you a discount."

"You can?" Jesse said, getting excited. "That's so sweet of you. Do you want to help me pick out a mask to go with it?"

"You already have a mask, silly. It's at the top of the box." Tricia pulled back the white tissue paper and the matching mask sat there as delicate as snow.

"I-I...this doesn't add up," Jesse said. "I think this has to be more than a hundred dollars."

Tricia smiled large. "It's a gift."

"A gift?" Jesse felt tears come to her eyes. She had a friend. Really and truly she did, but... "I can't take this. I've nothing to give to you and..."

With a loud happy laugh Tricia hugged Jesse. "You're an idiot. You just gave me a gift! And don't say it's not the same thing. I see it in your eyes that you want to. All these years, I couldn't go a week without thinking of what I put you through. You have no idea what it's like to hurt someone so innocent as you were. To be that terrible of a person. Every time I read in the paper about some poor kid killing herself because of bullying, I would say to myself, 'You did that; you're just as guilty as they are'. It's been eating at me. I've even thought about going out to Crisfield to apologize, but I never did. I was too afraid."

Uncomfortable, Jesse shrugged and gave Tricia a crooked smile. "Afraid? Of little old me?"

"Don't make jokes," Tricia chided. "I feared to see the look in your eyes. I was afraid that you would never forgive me. Even now I don't how or why you have. I just know that I feel suddenly great. I feel lighter than air. I feel...grateful like I've never felt before. It feels like saying thank you can't possibly be enough."

"It's more than enough," Jesse replied. And it was. She didn't need the gift of the dress to feel Tricia's gratitude; it came off her in waves. It made Jesse happy just to be near her.

The two girls chatted and laughed and talked for hours. Tricia was giddy at Jesse's description of Ky and breathless at that of the Shadow-man. They talked about Jesse's troubles in Ashton and reminisced about their enmity in Denton, though in this Tricia was always careful to steer the talk in a complimentary way.

Unknown to Jesse, through foresight and quick wits, she had evaded many more traps that had been laid out for her than she realized. Half the school had been out for her blood, yet she had managed to slip away time and again. Even back then Tricia and her friends had marveled at Jesse's intelligence and perseverance.

Their talk lasted until well after lunch and it was with a heavy heart that Jesse finally said good-bye. She hugged Tricia and promised to come out to Barton as soon as her father would let her.

On the way home, Jesse made one scheduled stop, to get hair dye so that she could go back to her natural golden hair color, and one unscheduled stop. Just out of town the gaudy pink and green neon lights of an army surplus store tempted her. Without her chain and lock, she felt partially naked and completely vulnerable.

The surplus store seemed larger on the outside. Inside it was close and cramped, stocked with every oddity that had ever been associated with the military. There were uniforms by the thousands, a confusion of insignia, ranks, and patches and even a small tank. From the ceiling hung green parachutes and black cannons. Scary looking machine guns, strung with huge bullets the size of her forearm, were mounted about the store.

Jesse had big eyes for the spectacle of it all, but also narrow, sharp eyes for what she came for: a weapon. Wandering around the isles, she inspected everything, but nothing really fit her need.

"What you're looking for is all up here." A man, wearing an impossible to button vest over his round belly and sporting a navy cap that read USS Iowa 51-52, gave Jesse a knowing look. He sat on a tall stool leaning on a glass counter. Below his elbows were a myriad of knives and guns.

"Oh, yeah?" Jesse asked as nonchalantly as possible. She slipped along the narrow path between clothing racks and sidled up to the counter. "You think this is what I need?" It didn't seem like it to Jesse. She couldn't use either a gun or a knife, not if she wanted to stay out of jail.

"It's exactly what you need," the man said. "I know a battered girl when I see one. Here..." The man pulled out a short fat handgun. He clicked open the revolving cylinder, eyed down the six empty chambers and snapped it closed with a flick of his wrist. He then held it out, handle first, for Jesse to take.

"I don't...I can't use that," she said.

"Are you afraid to use it?"

"I'm afraid of what will happen to me if I do," Jesse explained, still keeping her hands to herself.

The man gave her a serpent's smile. "Yes...you should be. Our laws aren't designed to protect the good, are they? It almost seems like our laws were made to help evil flourish." He was right, but Jesse only gave him a shrug. She was nervous and the fact that the man still held the gun only made her feel more so.

"Do you have anything less...violent?" she asked.

The man found this funny and coughed out a phlegmy laughter. "Less violent? Judging by your face, you need to step up the violence. Was it a boyfriend?"

"No, it wasn't a boyfriend...and I don't want to step up the violence. I don't really want to hurt anyone; I just want to keep from getting hurt. Do you have a stun gun or anything like that?"

He gave her a sad look. "Not in Michigan. That sort of thing is illegal in this state. If someone breaks into your home, you can shoot 'em in the head with a gun, but for some reason using a Taser on 'em and just stunning 'em is illegal."

"That's stupid."

"That's Michigan." He tried to say it as a joke, but Jesse didn't crack a smile. Her mind was on the Shadow-man. Turning the other cheek...even forgiving someone like John Osterman was a possibility...a very remote possibility, but it wasn't going to work on Harold Brownly. Forgiveness would be lost on the devil.

"What about pepper spray?"

The man scoffed and rolled his eyes. "I'll sell it to you, but use it only as a last resort. In Michigan we want to protect rapists and child molesters so much that legally we can only sell the watered down version of pepper spray. So zap him and run. Don't look back and don't try to fight him. If you do the pepper spray will get in your eyes as well. Just run, ok?"

"Yeah, just run. That I can do."

"Good," the man said with a nod and a smile. He grabbed a small black cylindrical container and plunked it down on the counter. "That's going to be twenty dollars. I'll need to see some ID and..." The man paused looking at Jesse. She had gone stiff digging through her purse. "You are eighteen, aren't you?" he asked.

Jesse shook her head.

"I don't know what to say." The man gave her a pained look. "Maybe you can have one of your parents come in and purchase it for you."

A grim smile swept her face. "That'll never happen. I'll just...I'll figure something out. Sorry to have wasted your time." She turned to leave, but the man called her back.

When she put her hands on the counter, the old man shot out one of his and took her wrist. "Shoplifting hurts everyone, wouldn't you agree?"

Jesse stared at him not knowing at all what he was talking about. "I...I didn't take anything, honest."

The man ignored her words and picked up a pack of bubble gum. "When people shoplift from me, I have to raise my prices to cover the cost...like this gum." He rang up the gum on his register with his free hand. "Because of shoplifting it's twenty dollars now." He plopped the gum in a bag and slid it over to Jesse. The pepper spray slid over with it.

Understanding hit Jesse and nodding her head she dug in her purse for the twenty her father had given her. Wordlessly she handed it over and just as wordlessly he took it and turned his back on her, allowing her to pick up her gum...and the pepper spray.

Chapter 45

When Jesse arrived at the school four hours later it was in complete lock down. Teachers and parents stood about in knots at all the corners, while others in groups of four patrolled the edges of the parking lot and around the perimeters of the school. Thankfully for them the winter had yet to turn bitter.

Jesse sat in her stolen car and waited for the right cover; she couldn't walk into the school alone. Nor could she arrive too early or too late. So she watched and waited. It wasn't a long wait. Spying a group of costumed students Jesse slipped out of her car and ran up behind them. Close but not too close.

At the entrance of the school, Mrs. Daly stood with some adults that Jesse didn't recognize. "Wow, don't you all just look wonderful?" the receptionist exclaimed. "Who are all these glamorous people?"

"It's me, Ryan," the boy in front said, pulling down his mask. "And that's Jodi and Beth and my little brother, and..." There was only one person left to name. Jesse took that moment to kneel down and fiddle with her shoe beneath her white gown. "And, uh..."

"Hey what's with all the adults?" one of the girls asked. "There's like twice as many as last year."

"It's Harold," Mrs. Daly said, speaking low. "He's disappeared. The police had him under surveillance, but around ten this morning he just up and vanished. They even searched his home. They found nothing."

"No way!" Ryan cried.

"Yes way," Mrs. Daly replied. "So this means we're being extra careful. The principal is even turning a blind eye to smoking. I know that you four don't smoke, but if you know someone who does, they've roped off a little section behind the library. No one will be allowed to leave the building by themselves. You'll be escorted back to your cars at the end of the evening."

The kids in front of her started exclaiming angrily. One demanded that someone should kill Harold on sight, while another posited places where he could be hiding. Jesse slipped around them as they went on and strode away toward the gym dreading the moment when she would be called back and forced to unmask. This was the most dangerous time. Barely breathing, she walked toward the sound of the thumping music and it was only when she made the turn toward the gym that she was able to relax.

She had made it. Jesse was now in the inner sanctum of the school and as long as she kept to herself she would be taken for just another student. However, Jesse didn't want to keep to herself. She wanted to smile and laugh and above all else she wanted to dance. That is why she had crafted a cover for herself. If forced to answer any questions, she would be Tricia Reynolds, junior at Northwestern high in Flint. Currently staying with her aunt Debbie for the holidays.

As the late afternoon hours had dragged by Jesse had invented a hundred particulars about her cover: Tricia Reynolds played the harp, enjoyed skydiving, read a book a day, and had taken ballet until a bull-riding incident sidelined her. Jesse planned on having fun.

Walking into the gym, she paused to stare. If one used their imagination the gym had been transformed into a lush garden, covered over in low-slung misty clouds. If not, then it was just a gym. The basketball nets were still basketball nets only they were strung with stretched white gauze. The folded bleachers were still bleachers only a long forest mural had been taped up onto them.

Jesse had imagination to spare and she loved the room. It helped that the lights were dimmed way down and that strobes flashed with the beat. The music was another plus. Instead of someone's garage-band shredding up chords like a rottweiler chewing on glass, a DJ had been hired. He stood behind a mountain of electronic equipment and kept the throng of kids shimmying and jiggling for all they were worth.

It looked like fun.

After hanging up her coat she went to look for the one boy that she really wanted to share her fun with, Ky. If he were there, he would be lurking along the edges of the crowd; he was too well known to try a cover story like Jesse. So she slipped along unconsciously dancing to the beat as she moved, and in her wake she left a slew of envy.

"That's the dress!"

"Look at her."

"I tried that on, it didn't fit."

"Stop looking at her!"

"I love that gown..."

It all made her smile. She knew that she looked good. After she had colored her hair and applied enough make up to cover her bruises, which was a ridiculous amount, she hadn't been able to stop staring either. But that was the whole idea.

Unfortunately, the one person she most wanted to see her wasn't there. She looked everywhere for him. First, she walked the perimeter of the gym. Then she criss-crossed it. Finally she went from boy to boy giving them each a good stare, yet Ky was definitely not among them. His father was however, and she eagerly waited until he was alone to go up to him.

"Hi Mr. Mendel," she said cheerily. "Are you still looking for Kyle?"

He peered in at her face. "Who are you?"

"Oh. Right, I forgot." Jesse turned from the students and slid up her mask. Even so he shook his head. "It's me Jesse Clarke. Remember, I keep running into you in the woods?"

"Oh right...and no I'm not looking for Kyle. He's at home. This isn't his kind of thing."

Though it was keen inside her, Jesse didn't let her disappointment show. How could he be at home?

She chatted amiably for another minute, gave a perfectly respectable goodbye to Mr. Mendel, and then went to dance, trying not to feel sad. She had to remind herself that Ky was a pipe dream. At the most, they would've had only a few dances together and maybe a kiss or two. After that the clock would've struck twelve and her chariot would've gone back to being a pumpkin.

There would be no happily ever after with Ky. There would be only death in a thousand forms lurking over her shoulder. Just then, a tap on her shoulder made her jump.

"Hi, doyouwantodancewithme?" A sweaty boy stood there in a homemade pirate outfit. His "mask" was a pair of sunglasses that he had pushed atop his bandana-covered head.

The DJ had slipped something slow into the mix and crowds were surging to the dance floor. "Of course," she said. Jesse wasn't picky about her partners. It would have been the height of hypocrisy to have been, seeing as, had she had gone without a mask, nobody would have given her the time of day. The boy danced with her and despite that he kept wiping them on his flayed jeans, his hand on her back sweated through her silk.

"Relax," Jesse told him. "The best part about a masquerade ball is that nobody is supposed to know who you are. Which means you can be anyone. Just pretend that you are James Bond. James Bond never gets nervous around a girl."

"But you're so pretty and I'm just..."

"You're James Bond, remember?"

"But I'm dressed as a pirate!" the boy laughed. "Who are you pretending to be?"

After just giving him the advice to pretend to be someone you weren't, Jesse couldn't tell the boy the truth, that she was finally being herself. "Just an angel," she said.

"Well, you are the most beautiful angel," he said. "Who are you? Are you a freshman too?"

"Didn't I just tell you? I'm an angel...we don't have names." Immediately she remembered that they did, but the boy didn't press the issue and a minute later the song ended. She declined another dance and strolled diagonally across the dance floor...the long way. Before she reached the end a second boy asked her.

He was tall and gangly and when he became a man he would be ruggedly handsome, but just then his feet were too big and his elbows swung out, reminding Jesse of the description of Ichabod Crane. He was sweet and laughed a lot once his nervousness had quelled.

Jesse danced with every boy who asked her, regardless of their costume. She partnered with a cowboy, a karate black belt, even a chef.

After skipping a few songs, her outfit simply wasn't designed for fast dancing, she finally accepted a dance from someone properly dressed. There was a difference between a masquerade ball and Halloween flavored dance. The boy was tall and broad. He was dressed as the Phantom of the Opera and Jesse couldn't help feel her heart beat a trifle harder. He could dance as well and was in no way nervous, but he was persistent. His hands roamed like there was no tomorrow.

"Do you mind?" Jesse asked, grabbing him by the wrist and bringing his hand up to her back.

"No, I don't mind a bit," he replied, grinning mischievously beneath his half mask. "Is that you, Helly?"

Helly? Was that a nickname for Helen? "I'm not telling." Jesse answered. "It would ruin all the fun. I don't know who you are after all."

This struck him as the funniest thing and he leaned his big frame over her in a fit of laughter. It was then that she realized the boy had been drinking. He almost slid off her to the floor, but managed to catch himself just in time. He straightened in a flourish and still laughing proclaimed, "It's me Alan, you dope. That must be Helly underneath there."

Jesse had to grab his hands again, this time to keep him from peeling away her mask. "Stop that! This mask cost a fortune," she admonished him. The kids in Ashton, sober or not, being so poor had respect for money and valuable items. Alan was quick to mumble out an apology and stopped his attempt at taking her mask off.

"One more?" he asked when the song ended. Jesse didn't have a chance to answer.

She was spun about and came face to face with Amanda Jorgenson. Behind the big blonde stood her fellow pack members.

"Let's see who this bitch is who's dancing with all the boys," Amanda growled.

Chapter 46

No, it's too soon! Jesse's soul screamed in anger. She had only been at the dance for an hour and she wanted so much more. Amanda, wearing an outfit that made her look like Maid Marian, advanced on Jesse with her face scrunched into a scowl and her clawed hands out reaching for Jesse's face.

But then Amanda broke into a huge grin. "Helly is that you? When did you have time to go into Barton?"

"I'm not Helly," Jesse said in a gleeful voice. She was anything but gleeful. There were kids all around her and she had no idea who was her enemy and who wasn't. "How could you even think that?"

With a little twirl, Jesse danced away from Amanda's hands, but thumped up against Alan's bulk and bounced forward again toward Amanda.

"Then who..." Amanda began to ask. They were too close, only at arm's reach and with backing away an impossibility Jesse stepped into Amanda, grabbing her arms as if they were waltzing. She pulled her enemy in close to keep her hands from getting to her face and felt her skin crawl as she did it. This was the same girl who had tried to kill her only two days before.

"I won't tell. It's way more fun this way," Jesse said. She gave the girl a spin and Amanda giggled.

"I love this song!" Tina cried suddenly. "Let's go dance." Tina tried to grab both Jesse's and Amanda's hand, but Amanda pulled back.

"Wait. We shouldn't dance with her until we know who she is. After all she could be a freshman!"

"Eek!" one of the girls screamed and then laughed.

"That's not funny, Amanda," another girl said in an irate voice. "Sue and Dakota are right here."

"You know I don't care about that," Amanda laughed. "I was just kidding. But I'm just dying to know who this is. That is just the coolest dress. Who could afford that?"

Jesse's heart went to her throat as heads turned at the question. Clearly, very few kids in Ashton could. A panic started to seize Jesse. "I'll tell, if..." The idea of a dare jumped into her mind. But what? Jesse looked around for some sort of inspiration and saw the gangly boy she had danced with earlier. His elbows still stuck out when he danced and from this view he looked like a...

Jesse turned back to Amanda and said, "I'll take off my mask if you go out on the dance floor and do the 'chicken dance' all by yourself...without your mask on."

The very idea brought on a gale of laughter from everyone around. Much to Jesse's horror, Amanda looked to be considering the challenge and her friends egging her on didn't help.

"Mother-pus-bucket," she whispered. Just then one of the boys that had been standing with Amanda's friends stepped up to Jesse.

"Hey, before the chicken song comes on, do you want to dance?"

The boy had something similar to a Phantom costume on: a loose, black three-piece suit, a Halloween cape, and a simple mask. Jesse gave him a close look before accepting. There was no way she was going to dance with either Ronny or John.

"Sure, I'll dance with you. But how do you know there's going to be a Chicken song?" Jesse said hurrying to the dance floor. "Maybe Amanda won't take the dare."

"I know in the same way that I know that you're from out of town. Wait here."

Jesse wasn't going anywhere. What he had said had stunned her too badly. Was she that obvious? Apparently so. She watched the boy dart through the crowd, passing through the dancers like a breeze. He went to the DJ, dug through his pocket, and ran back. Just as he came up, the song that had been playing ended abruptly and a new one...a slow one came on.

"Do you like Eric Clapton?" he asked taking Jesse in his arms. The boy smelled good and he was warm.

"I don't know," Jesse replied. "Is this him?"

"Yep, it's called *Wonderful Tonight*. It's good to dance to. At least I think so." The boy was strong in his hands and arms; his shoulder was just perfect for Jesse's head to rest upon.

"So are you going to tell me about Amanda?" Jesse asked, swaying to the rhythm. "And how you know she's going to take my dare?"

"She's not...now," the boy answered. "I paid the DJ to 'lose' that song." Jesse looked up at him and caught him staring intently at her. She had to look away. "I also paid him to give me the next five songs."

Wow, her voice of reason said.

Right as always. Jesse wasn't going anywhere for those five songs. She was in his debt. "You were that sure that she would take the dare?"

"Yes. I've known Amanda since I was a kid...heck since I was born." The boy explained. "She was in the crib next to mine at the hospital. I've got a picture of it. And in all that time I've never seen her turn down a dare. So that's how I knew...but then again everyone knows that in Ashton. So..."

"You were right about me. I'm actually from Flint. I'm staying with an aunt of mine for the holidays." Jesse said, feeling more remorse for her lie than she had expected when she had been practicing at home. She was anxious to change the subject. "So, five songs. That's kinda presumptuous. What happens if I don't stay and dance with you? Who will you ask?" She felt his muscles stiffen beneath his suit.

"You're not going to dance with me?"

"Maybe I want to see Amanda do the chicken dance. You ever think of that? I bet that would be the funniest thing ever."

At this, the boy grew uncomfortable in Jesse's arms. He lost the slow beat and stepped back away from her. "It would be funny. I'm sorry. I just thought you were upset at the idea of having your mask being taken off."

Jesse pulled him in close again and picked up the beat. "I was upset, you were right about that...and thank you for helping me out. I will dance with you, it's the least I can do."

He relaxed and smiled. "Don't feel obligated...but yeah it is the least you could do. And I want you to know I won't try to take off your mask. I don't care what you look like under there. Tonight you're beautiful."

The compliment whizzed by, practically unheard. He thought she was ugly! Even though it was the perfect justification to keep her mask on she fought the idea and grew angry in a flash.

"I'm not ugly, if that's what you think," she said. With her hands on her hips she abruptly came to a standstill in the middle of the dance floor. "I just happen to think I look prettier tonight than I have ever before and I didn't want to spoil it. I don't care if that sounds conceited or not. And yes, I am beautiful tonight. It's almost like I've reached my peak, like...like I'll never be this beautiful again."

These weren't the reasons that she wanted to keep her mask on, but they were true nevertheless.

"I keep screwing this up, don't I?" the boy asked staring up at the ceiling. "I'm so sorry. I didn't mean to suggest you were ugly...I just didn't know why you were so afraid to be seen. You...you are beautiful...and now that I know you're pretty under the mask as well, you've become the epitome of beauty in my eyes."

He was so heartfelt in his apology that Jesse relaxed a little. "I think you're laying it on kinda thick."

"I'm not," he answered. "I saw you dancing earlier. More importantly I saw who you were dancing with. I think your choice of partners was why my mind pictured the girl beneath the mask as...less pretty. Really, how many pretty girls would let Charlie McDonald touch them let alone dance with them?"

"Which one was Charlie?"

"The chef."

The chef hadn't been pleasant. She shrugged and replied, "He wasn't easy to dance with, it's true. But I can't turn them down when they come to me."

"And that's why you're the epitome of beauty," he said. "The costume is the illusion of beauty...and your face underneath is what everyone *thinks* of as beauty, but the true nature of beauty lies beneath even that."

Under her mask, Jesse felt her cheeks go red. "Ok stop. I'm not all that great."

"I think you are."

"That's because you don't know me." In a blink of a strobe, she realized what she had just said would take them down a path that she did not want to travel. Deftly she turned their conversation away from herself. They danced and they talked, all the while a chemical thing built up between them. There was an attraction there that they both felt. He sniffed her hair and she pressed her cheek to his chest. Yet for all that, there was also an odd stiffness as well. Jesse knew what was bothering her... This wasn't Ky.

Yes. He's better than Ky.

Perhaps that was true, but only because the boy actually talked to her. How can you have a relationship with a boy who can't talk to you without getting you killed? The simple answer: you don't.

Ky is a pipedream, remember?

He was, yet still Jesse felt obligated toward him. For one, he loved her and for two, he had saved her life, twice. She wasn't going to throw that away, especially on a boy who might spit in her face if she were to take off her mask.

When the five songs had run their course, Jesse prepared herself to turn the boy down. Undoubtedly he would ask for more.

"Thanks for the dance," he said. *Here it comes*, thought Jesse. Oddly, he put out his hand as if she should shake it, and said, "I've had such a fun time, but I have to get going."

What? her voice demanded.

"What? That's it?" Jesse asked, feeling as though the rug had been pulled from beneath her. She recovered quickly. "I mean...yes it's been fun. My ankle was hurting either way."

"Your ankle?"

She started off the dance floor and he walked next to her. "Yes, I tripped in the forest the other night."

He stopped her and looked up at the ceiling. "I've done that before too. Usually when I'm staring up at the stars...I can picture them above us right now." Jesse looked up. It was human nature do so. When she glanced again at the boy he wasn't looking up, he was staring intently at her neck. Self-consciously she touched herself and felt the slight scab where her neck had been cut by Ky's switchblade.

Her mind scrambled for excuses, but couldn't get past: 'I cut myself shaving', which didn't make any sense. "That? It's a uh..."

The boy grabbed her suddenly. "Why did you come here?" he demanded in a harsh whisper. "I didn't think you would be fool enough to show up. What were you thinking? You're in real danger."

There was only one boy in Ashton who spoke like that. "Ky, is that you."

"Shush! What are you crazy? Don't say my name out loud." Ky held her close and his fear was palpable, she could feel the thumping of his heart against her chest. Over the top of her head he scanned the crowds of students to see if anyone had heard.

Seeming to come to some conclusion, he said, "We have to get you out of here." He started to pull her, but she held her ground. This moment was what she had been looking for all night and so she pulled back on his hand. Between clenched teeth, he hissed, "Come on. It's dangerous for you here."

"Only because I'm dancing with you. If you weren't here, what would they do to me that they haven't already?"

His mouth opened and then closed. Even with the mask she could tell that he was exasperated. "Then I'm leaving," he said and turned to go.

Now it was her turn to grab him. "No, you're staying and if you want to protect me don't make a scene. Come on." She led him back out onto the dance floor and pulled him close. The song was a fast one, yet the two slow danced to a rhythm unheard by anyone else.

"This is crazy," he whispered into her ear. "This could get you killed. Why are you being like this?"

Because I love you.

What voice in her head was that? The words jumped to the forefront of her mind and clung there. It was hard to think past them. "Because...because this is all we get. Tonight is it. Tomorrow you'll go back to being ignored and I'll go back to being hated. Our lives will go back to the misery that they were. But I have right now and I'll gladly suffer any pain that they can throw at me just so I can spend it with you."

Suddenly he crushed her slim body into his, wrapping his arms around her in a fierce embrace. She could barely breathe, yet she didn't care and held him just as tight.

Amanda dancing with a boy in a Zorro costume came up close and nudged Jesse. "Get a room," she called out over the heavy music.

Without being disingenuous, Jesse smiled at her. It seemed so strange to do so, but it would have been even more strange not to. Amanda Jorgenson had never seemed more friendly and outgoing. She laughed and danced and hugged enough for two people. There didn't seem to be an ounce of hate in her body.

The same was true for every one there. How many of them had repeated a nasty limerick about Jesse? How many had jeered her as she was left stranded by the busses? And how many had laughed and mocked and spat as she was led away by the police?

All of them? Most of them? At the same time, these weren't the same kids, they just couldn't be. It seemed impossible. How could they hate with such viciousness one day and then show such love and affection the next. She whispered the question to Ky.

"They are good kids, really," Ky said. His eyes were sad. "They've been living under an umbrella of fear for years now and they see death as inevitable. They don't think Harold can ever be stopped." He paused and grimaced. "I think most of them expect you to die and a lot of them secretly hope you do."

Jesse was speechless. Her body swayed, dancing, but her mind seemed to have gone blank. "Then how can you say they are good?"

"If you look at this from their point of view, you might understand. If someone has to die, who would you rather it be? A cherished friend? A loved one, a neighbor, the man who sells you fish at the supermarket...or a stranger...maybe someone who doesn't try too hard to fit in...maybe someone who gets in fights and looks different."

"I would say none of them," Jesse replied, knowing that she was a liar.

"You don't get that choice and neither do they. If someone had to die, here in this gym. Who would you choose?"

John Osterman's face jumped into her head before she had a chance to think twice. No! Wrong. You don't get to pick a person to die in your place! Jesse berated herself, but John's face remained. Finally, she shrugged at the question and then sighed and then hung her head. "It's still not right."

"No, it's not. Sometimes there isn't a right or wrong, sometimes there is simply human nature. And to pretend that it's something that it isn't is a waste of time," Ky said.

"What about you," Jesse asked "Do you picture a face when you think about the next death?"

"Yes...I picture your face."

"What?" Jesse cried in disbelief.

"I picture your face everywhere I go and in everything I do," he explained. "You're always on my mind and every moment I'm not with you I spend thinking of you."

Jesse melted into him, but then pulled back. "You picture me even when you're thinking of the killer? That's just bizarre!"

"No, you goof!" Ky exclaimed. "I was trying to be romantic and change the subject at the same time. Our time is almost up and I don't want to spend it talking about things we can't change."

"Oh, sorry," Jesse said, feeling a blush in her cheeks at her silliness...or was it over what he had said? "Do you really picture my face all the time?"

"Yes."

"I think about you as well..."

The two high school seniors looked into each other's eyes. The music slowed and they began swaying so deeply in each other's arms that the gym fell away and they might as well have been alone.

They were so close that their breath mixed hot with each other. His hands were in her hair and hers were on his back. They drew closer still, until...

Chapter 47

Their lips only brushed when a hand clapped Jesse on the back, stealing her moment.

"It's time!" someone squealed. Before Jesse knew what was happening, hands spun her about, and she came face to face with Amanda.

"What's time?" Jesse asked, breathlessly. She turned her head to find Ky, but like a ghost he had disappeared into the surging crowd. People were pushing forward to the end of the gym that doubled as a small stage and Jesse and Amanda were carried along with them.

"It's time to judge the costumes," Amanda yelled over the din. "Though I don't know why anyone would even bother. You are so totally a shoe-in for first prize."

"It wouldn't be fair, I shouldn't..." Jesse saw a hole in the crowd, she darted through it. The contest was out of the question. If she won, they would demand that she reveal herself. It was the last thing she wanted. Just then a boy in a bear costume knocked into her, making her broken ribs shriek in protest.

"Watch where you're going, Dil!" Amanda said, not noticing that Jesse had been trying to lose her. Shoving the bear out of the way she grabbed Jesse's hand and pulled the gasping girl around the side of the stage. "Don't worry. We rounded up some people in joke costumes just to make it more fun. Go right up there and stand next to Sandra. And listen, if that's you under there, Helly I'm going to pop you right in the nose for being so secretive." She said this with a smile.

Jesse was pushed from behind and found herself mounting the steps up to the stage. She desperately looked for Ky. What she saw instead were over four-hundred faces gazing up at her.

"Crap!" she whispered and turned back to Sandra. The girl's costume stopped Jesse in her place. Sandra was supposed to be a ladybug. She didn't look much like a bug, instead she looked hugely pregnant and splotchy; it was terribly unflattering. Sandra was so uncomfortable up there in front of her school that she seemed ready to puke.

"Is there a way out, behind the stage?" Jesse had to yell over the crowd noise.

Sandra looked at Jesse as if she were seeing a movie star. "Why?" she asked.

"I just need a way out of here! It's me Jesse Clarke! If they catch me..." Jesse couldn't finished her sentence.

The girl's eyes went wide realizing what could happen. She indicated the back of the stage. "Go through there and then head left. It will let you out behind all of them. I...I...will try to buy you some time."

"Thanks," Jesse said, pushing her way through the thick curtain. It was as far as she got in her escape. Sitting on stacks of folding chairs in the back stage area were Tina and the boy dressed as Zorro. Running through Zorro's fingers like a live thing was a long brown whip. It wasn't part of a costume; it was for real.

Turning her back on the whip was a hard thing to do. It made her skin crawl up and down her spine while her stomach turned to knots. She faced to her left, ignoring a question thrown at her by Tina and started hurrying to the exit, only to be brought up short at the sight of Ronny running at her.

"Guys! You'll never guess who I got to go up on..." he stopped short when he saw Jesse in her snow-white angel gown. "Hey, watcha doing?"

The way around Ronny was too narrow for her to get past him. Jesse turned back to the stage and saw Tina sliding off the stacks with an odd look on her face. Quickly Jesse thought up a reason for leaving. "I-I wanted to get my cell phone and call Helly. No one's seen her all night and I was getting nervous."

"I've been with Helly all night," Ronny replied. "Who are you? You don't sound familiar."

"I...I..." Jesse spluttered, edging away from Ronnie.

Just then the curtains parted briefly and Amanda came charging in, her face lit in a gigantic smile. "There you are! You guys are missing it. Sandra is rolling around on stage it's the funniest thing! Come on."

"Wait," Ronny called. "Who the hell is this?"

"It's...it's, I don't know. Does it matter?" Amanda asked. At the moment Amanda seemed the least frightening to Jesse and so she moved toward her. However, she was unable to keep her eyes off Zorro, whom she strongly suspected of being John Osterman.

"It wouldn't matter to me," Tina said. "Except she refuses to tell anyone who she is."

Suddenly a loud crack sounded. Zorro had come off the stacks of chairs and had snapped the whip. The end of it slithered back along the floor toward him.

"Hey, cut that out!" Amanda yelled at him. She then turned and whispered to Jesse. "John's been drinking. It might be best if you take off the mask for a moment. It'll be ok, I promise."

It wasn't going to be ok. Ronny stood a bare three feet to her right, while Amanda had her by the elbow. She was caught. Her words to Ky from earlier came back to her: *I'll gladly suffer any pain that they can throw at me.* This proclamation hadn't included a drunk boy wielding a whip. Jesse was literally petrified with fear and could do nothing as Amanda slowly slid off her mask.

"Who is it," Tina asked.

With her hair back to its natural blonde and all the make-up covering her bruises Amanda could only stare. "I...don't know," she said slowly, but then it hit her. "You...why? Why would you come back here?" Her tone was that of amazement. Jesse clung to it. Anything had to be better than the hate that she had expected.

"Save me," she begged in a soft voice as she felt her eyes fill with tears.

"Who is it?" demanded Tina a second time.

Amanda opened her mouth but no words came out. She only stared into Jesse's eyes in confusion until Jesse was turned about.

Ronny took a moment as well to figure out who she was. "It's that Jesse girl. Holy crap!"

"No way!" Tina cawed. Beyond the curtain a great bout of laughter assaulted them. Tina turned to it for half a second and then saw the mask in Amanda's hands. "I call this," she said and snatched it from the big blonde.

Ronny rounded on her quick. "You can't just call it, we'll flip for it."

"Helly has a mask already. You don't need..." Tina began, but John in his Zorro costume broke in.

"Forget the stupid mask," he ordered. "Get away from her." His whip was drawn partially back.

"No," Jesse screamed as Ronny leapt away and Amanda flinched back. John let the whip fly at Jesse, who at the last second turned. The end of the whip parted the silk and satin of Jesse's white costume as cleanly as if a knife had been taken to it, and then it lashed into her skin with a ferocity that paralyzed Jesse. It turned her into a horrible statue. Her beautiful face twisted by the pain.

A second later someone screamed, "No! Don't!"

By this, Jesse knew the whip was coming a second time and she tried to escape. She could only manage two faltering steps before the whip came again with its fury of pain. Again her body spasmed into a contortion of agony and she twisted in place trying to relieve the pain in some small way. Nothing helped. It seared relentlessly into her back and after a second her legs buckled and she fell to her hands and knees, gasping.

"Stop! Damn it!" Amanda was screaming. "This isn't right..." Jesse felt something pulling at her, but her left hand seemed stuck to the floor. "Run!" Amanda yelled in her ear. On some distant level, Jesse wanted to run, only she couldn't, her hand wouldn't budge.

In a storm of pain, Jesse turned her head and saw the problem. A nail stuck out of the center of her left hand. It was so painless that the hand didn't even seem attached to Jesse's wrist. Pulling her hand straight up off the thin metal freed her and then she was up dragged to her feet by Amanda.

The two girls threw themselves into the heavy stage curtain and fought their way to front of the stage, both falling to their knees the moment they had cleared it. For a span of seconds all sound seemed to stop as four hundred faces stared at the spectacle of the bloody angel.

Jesse could only look up for a few seconds, the pain was still too new, too fresh for her to hold her head up for any longer. Next to her Amanda began spluttering, "Jesse...please. He didn't know what he was doing. He's drunk out of his mind and... and he's been under so much pressure."

"Who is that?" someone screamed. Just like that the auditorium erupted in sound. Over it Jesse still heard Amanda pleading for John, the boy who had just whipped her.

With her face streaming tears and pain racking her body, Jesse yelled at Amanda, "Don't apologize for him! If you want to apologize, then apologize for what you've done."

The words were equivalent to a slap. Amanda's eyes went wide and her mouth worked a moment, soundlessly, before she could speak. Unbelievably she said, "I am sorry...for the other night. I don't know what I was thinking. I...I thought we were just going to fight and then John came and told me what he wanted to do...I shouldn't have listened to him. It was stupid. Really, really stupid and I'm sorry. Ok? I'm sorry."

Jesse stared in astonishment at the girl who had tried to kill her. Was this also the girl that had just saved her from John? And the girl who had been so sweet at the dance? Were they the same girl? How was it possible? And was it possible that Amanda was actually sorry?

If so...

The angel in white astonished herself. Through quivering lips Jesse said, "I forgive you." For the second time that day she forgave someone who seemed beyond forgiving.

Amanda dropped her eyes and just then the lights went out in the school. A dozen hands had been on her, trying to help Jesse up. But suddenly they seemed to disappear. Everything disappeared all save the screams that erupted all about. Someone fell across Jesse and the pain in her back and ribs had her screaming as well until the person scrambled up and away. Then there was nothing, not even vibrations on the wood beneath her cheek.

With a hand that shook, Jesse reached for Amanda, but like everyone else, she seemed to have evaporated with the light. Jesse was all alone on the stage. Alone, until a shadow crept from behind the curtains.

Chapter 48

When the lights had first gone down, Jesse thought the dark complete, yet there was a shadow of deepest black moving toward her. She froze in place, hoping to go unnoticed. It didn't work. The killer came right at her; it was her white gown. It practically glowed like a beacon for him.

"Jesse Clarke?" he asked over the din. With the coming dark, kids had gone berserk with fear. Many had run to and fro shouting and screaming, while the parents charging in from the hallway only added to the chaos.

Jesse didn't want to die. She shook in pain and shock and dread, but she didn't say a word. If he was going to kill her, he would have to do all the work himself. He bent down over her, running his hands over her body, until he felt the wings on her back...and the blood.

"Oh, no!" he cried, unexpectedly. "Jesse? Are you ok? Jesse?"

"Ky?"

"Yes it's me. What happened to you?"

"They...they..." Jesse couldn't spit out the truth. There was a barrier within her that wouldn't allow her to say that she had been whipped. It was too degrading. The way that she had been treated made her feel like a mangy dog and the most that she could say was, "They hurt me."

"Can you stand?"

She searched for his hand in the dark and gripped it fiercely when she found it. "I think so...please get me out of here." He pulled her up. She screamed. Pain ran up the skin of her back, it was so intense that the dark gym floated around her for a moment and she worried that she would faint, but then Ky held her. He was like a rock; steady and strong.

With her back still on fire, she turned down his offer to carry her and only hung on him. She hurt. Everything hurt and she staggered in misery out of a side door. The night was crowded with the hysterical babbling of hundreds of students. They milled about in a belt around the school, afraid to leave the scant protection that it offered.

"Where's your car?" Ky asked, heading toward the parking lot. Jesse pulled back slightly.

"No, we can't go out there. It's exactly what Harold is looking for."

Ky smiled grimly at this. "Harold didn't mess with the fuse box, I did."

"But someone could've gotten hurt."

"Someone did...you got hurt." They were at the parking lot and Ky spotted the white Mustang. "I was afraid what the kids would do. All together like that kids can be scary. They develop a mob mentality, which to me is sort of a funny word seeing as that they don't actually think. It's all about emotion and whoever controls that emotion controls the mob. I didn't know what they would do to you."

"I don't think they would have hurt me any more than I was," Jesse said. "I saw a lot of compassion in their eyes before it got dark."

At the car, Ky stopped and looked at her wounds. His face went hard at the sight and his voice shook. "You don't get it. In a mob, compassion and love are the weak forces. It's hate, fear, and envy that rule. I was so afraid what they'd do to you, but I never thought that they would..." Ky glared back at the school.

He never thought that she would be whipped. She didn't either. "It was just one boy...and he was drunk," Jesse said. He dismissed this with a little shake of his head. She grabbed Ky and turned his face toward her. "Others helped me, ok? You were the one who told me there was good in these kids. You were right; it's just deeper than I thought."

With a long breath Ky said, "Maybe...let me get you home."

It was impossible for her to sit properly and so Ky drove, while she lay on her stomach in the back seat. They used the garage entrance to keep from being seen by Harold, just in case he was about.

Thirty minutes later, Ky asked, "Does that hurt?" He poured peroxide into the hole in Jesse's hand and watched as blood and foam dripped out the other side. He had already cleaned the wounds on her back. These weren't deep, yet burned worse than anything Jesse could remember. She had cried a great deal, but her hand was another story.

"Not really," she said. "Though it's kind of scary." Jesse began working her hand, slowly making a fist and then flattening it out again. In the car, her hand had felt paralyzed. The most she could do was make a bit of a claw out of it. The pain meds had helped. She had taken three times the recommended dose and was now more than just a little groggy and had trouble keeping up right.

When Ky was done bandaging her hand he laid her on her left side and just before she passed out asked her, "Was your night worth it?"

Those moments behind the curtain had been the most horrible time in her hard life. "Yes," she answered truthfully, forcing a little smile onto her lips. Her back would hurt for a while, but her memory of her night with Ky would last until she died. And maybe even longer than that.

Her night went in fits and starts and twice she had to get up for more meds. They made her dull and slow-witted when she woke up and she was too slow to catch a ride into town with her mother. This was a blessing in disguise since Jesse wasn't sure that she could actually sit in a car without crying.

Despite her pain her plan for the day was to go to the protest in *support* of her father and then head to Ashton medical clinic. Of all her injuries, her left hand bothered her the most; she could only make the weakest fist with it, barely able to even grip a pencil. She was afraid there would be permanent damage if she waited too long to have it looked at.

Now her first obstacle of the morning was the forest and the berm after it. She took them both in stride. Jesse carried her pepper spray in the front right pocket of a white coat that she had borrowed from her mom. The little black container gave her piece of mind, even more than her lock and chain would have, since physically she had use of only one of her arms and this she could barely raise above her head without crying out.

The day was brisk and the sky was low hung by thick grey clouds. Jesse wrapped herself twice in the scarf she had on loan from Tricia and set out. It was an uneventful walk; the only person that she saw was the solitary ice fisherman that had been on the ice the day before. He sat on his crate about thirty yards from the shore and as she passed he extended a hand in greeting. She waved and smiled, inside however she said a silent prayer for him. If he went under the ice, all alone as he was, there would be no coming out again.

Jesse's next obstacle was a daunting one. She would have to bypass the four-hundred-person student body of Ashton high ringing the town hall building. Along with the canister of pepper spray, she carried a handful of paper towels. The forecast called for a ninety percent chance of spit.

The crowds of students were there as expected; it was a mandatory school function after all. Yet there was one student that nobody had counted on to actually show up. Ky Mendel stood in the exact center of the walkway. Like the other kids he had drawn on his section of the sidewalk, unlike the other kids he hadn't drawn anything resembling a protest sign. He had drawn an arrow pointing toward the main doors of the town hall and below that was the word: Welcome.

His very presence seemed to guarantee that the protest would fail to keep out the council members. He had a ten-foot bubble surrounding him and Jesse remained spit free because of it.

"Morning," she said under her breath as she passed him by. True to his protective nature, Ky didn't acknowledge her presence other than to clear his throat briefly. This was enough to get her beaming.

"Hi Dad," Jesse said a minute later, poking her head into his office door. "Is this a bad time?"

James Clarke was as dapper as ever and looked in peak condition...except around the eyes. These held a sadness that didn't bode well. "Hi, Honey. Come in."

Jesse heard the anguish in his voice as well. "What's wrong? Did we lose the vote already?"

This actually made him smile. "Did *we* lose the vote? Are you on my side now?"

She nodded her head at his meaning. "I'm always on your side, Dad. When it comes down to it. I'm sorry if it doesn't seem like it."

"That's ok. You have your life to lead. I understand." James turned to the window and looked out. "It's Harold's disappearance that's causing the problem this time. It's making the police look bad and someone has started a rumor that after my first round of budget cuts that I'm going to start laying off some of the police officers."

"With Harold running around loose?" Jesse asked. "Who would believe such a thing of you?"

"You'd be surprised," James answered and then sighed in a way Jesse had never heard. "I actually want to increase police presence but because of my past, not too many believe me. I afraid I'm beaten. I've tried everything, but they won't listen to reason."

"Do you really need the council?" Jesse asked, coming over to stand by her father at the window. "I thought you had...what's the word? Consolidated your power. Can't you just force the laws down their throats? Make them obey?"

"That's not the way I work," James replied. "You know that. Yes I put pressure on them, but they have to want this for themselves."

Silence lay between them as they both watched the same boy. A small group of teachers were talking to Ky, but they might as well have been talking to the breeze. He clearly wasn't listening. Jesse wondered what sort of enticements they were offering him to get him to move.

"I know the secret about Kyle," she said. "How the killer fixates on him."

"Yeah, you were bound to hear about it sooner or later," James sighed again. "It's a messed up story and he's a messed up kid."

"Since I got here he's saved my life twice."

James shot her a glance before returning his gaze to Kyle. "I've always liked that boy," he said. This got them both to chuckling. "You'll have to tell me what happened one of these days. What's he doing down there?"

"He's holding the way open for the council members."

Again James looked at her, this time closely. "He must really...'love our cause' to stand up to the school that way."

A smile that she couldn't have stopped if she tried crept onto her face. "I think he does...I hope he does."

"And you?"

"I love him, too," Jesse said. "I'm glad that you didn't tell me about him. I probably would never have given him a chance."

"Now I'm wishing I had," James said, rubbing his head. "Loving that boy is so dangerous. You have no..." he stopped in mid-sentence.

"I have no idea?" Jesse said with a smile. "I think I do." Her smile then turned down. "But I don't think you have anything to worry about. Ky won't even look at me when anyone's around. He's got such focus..."

James interrupted, "You're wrong. I have everything to worry about. Ky is still just a kid. He may be able to hide his feeling better than most but if his feelings are strong enough they'll show through. Look at his little drawing for instance. Would he have done that if it weren't for you?"

"No."

"That's my point," James said. He then turned and gently hugged his daughter. Her back seared, but she didn't make a sound. "You can't hide love no matter how hard you try. Not even you. Whenever you are stomping around here glowering at me, I know you still love me."

"I do love you." She hugged him back.

"And I love you," James said. "This is nice. We should hug more often."

Jesse agreed. Though her back was burning she kept her father close. "Oh, by the way," she said. "I stole your car and drove to Barton to buy a dress for the dance I wasn't supposed to go to."

"I know. You got blood all over the back seat of the car. The good news is that your mom thinks that she can save the dress. She will have to cut away the back panels and have them replaced."

Jesse stepped back, amazed. "You knew? How?"

James laughed. "I watched you drive away yesterday. You weren't at all slick. Is your back really bad?"

Before she could answer a whistle blew outside. It was nearly nine o'clock. The teachers began to shepherd the students into a double line around the building.

"My back will be okay. Don't worry," Jesse said. "Look, I should get down there. They wanted me to protest so I will...I'm going to protest them."

Just then a cheer went up from the crowd. A man in a dark suit walked up and down the lines of students speaking in a loud voice. Little snippets could be heard through the glass. What he said outraged Jesse. He claimed that James Clarke was as big a danger to Ashton as Harold Brownly. He said that Ashton was turning into a Nazi concentration camp. He made dire predictions of work camps and bread lines. The crowd ate it up.

James watched with a look of sadness on his face. "No," James said. "You can't go down there, it's too dangerous. They are little more than a mob."

Jesse's mind flashed to that one second after she and Amanda had crashed through the curtain. The students had seen her and knew her. They saw the blood, and the pain she had suffered, and not a few of them had shame in their eyes. Jesse's gut told her it would be ok, at least as far as the students were concerned, it was their masters that had her going numb in the hands.

"I'm not afraid of the mob," Jesse said, with a deep breath. "Ky says that it's emotions that rule a mob. It's..."

Her father grabbed her by the shoulders, "Listen to him on this. He right, that's why I don't want you to go out there."

"But you have always told me it's intellect that rules emotions," Jesse shot back. "Those kids down there are only getting one side of the argument. They're getting worked up based on fear alone. I bet if they hear the other side—our side, they'll come around."

James nodded. "Then I should go. I'm not saying you're not smart; it's just that I have all the facts. Budgets aren't easy things to delve into."

This almost made Jesse laugh. "If you talk to them about the budget, you'll just put them to sleep. No offence, Dad, but whenever you go on and on about monetary policies and bonds and debt financing my eyes glaze over."

This actually made James laugh. "What can I say? I find it fun."

"And that's why you can't go," Jesse said. "You can't speak to that crowd, because you're not one of them. You won't connect. I can. I just need to know fully what's going on before I go down there."

"I'm afraid it's nothing you don't already know," James said with a rueful shake of his head. He spoke to her then, and as he did the adults below kept up their inflaming speeches. Her father was right, nothing much had changed from the last town, or the town before that.

Chapter 49

When Jesse had heard enough about the budget issues from her father, she went down to the front of the building and waited there with sweaty palms and what felt like snakes curling and uncurling in her belly. From where she stood, just inside the doorway, she could see that Ky wasn't as effective as she had hoped. The students had formed an arc around him, so that the way into the building was essentially blocked.

Just beyond the arc and looking terribly uncomfortable, stood a group of men and women in business attire. Most of the council was there and with them were gathered many of the business leaders of the town. Jesse recognized a few: Mr. Chu, who owned the Dim Sum and both Dr Becketts.

Teachers formed another group behind the students; they were the most vocal supporters of the man in the suit, who had not tired in his tirade against her father. Scattered among them was the remainder of the council members.

Jesse wondered if she could do this. Public speaking had never really frightened her, however a class of twenty-two students had been the largest number of people she had ever spoken to before. Her greatest fear was that all the facts and numbers her father had given her would simply vanish from her mind the second she opened her mouth.

"You can do this...you can do this...you can do this..." she repeated in a whisper as she waited. Finally the man ended his speech and a chant began. This would be her time. She knew the chant would go on for only a minute or so and when it died from draining enthusiasm, Jesse walked out of the building and into the dark brooding day.

Immediately the crowd went to whispering to each other. To Jesse they sounded like a thousand snakes which did nothing to calm her frayed nerves. As she walked past Ky, she whispered to herself, "Be strong, they won't hurt you." This was likely true, but all the same, Jesse stopped only feet in front of the boy who had saved her time and again. She wanted Ky near.

"Jesse, I'm so glad you came," Ms Weldon said in a loud carrying voice. "Are you going to join our protest against greed and tyranny?"

The students, who had been losing their formation and gathering around the front of the building, quieted, waiting on her reply. Everyone waited for her reply and they seemed to lean in towards her. She shivered beneath her coat.

This was it. Jesse took in a long quaking breath. "I am here to protest," she said in the strongest voice she could manage. "But it is your greed and tyranny that I stand against."

Some of the council members rolled their eyes and scoffed her, while quite a few of the teachers laughed. The man in the dark suit stepped forward. "You don't know what you're talking about, these are public servants! Where is their greed? You don't get rich as a school teacher."

The crowd nodded in agreement and began murmuring. Jesse yelled over them, "Rich and poor are relative! A teacher may not be rich compared to Donald Trump, but they are rich compared to the workers of Ashton." She paused and looked through the crowd. For some reason the few people that she considered friendly seemed to have disappeared and oddly enough only one face jumped out at her. "John Osterman, what kind of car does your father drive?"

The boy seemed shocked that she would call on him, but still answered in a hesitant manner. "He's got a rusted out Buick LeSabre and if it lasts the winter it'll be a miracle." The truth of this was greeted with good-natured laughter.

"And you Mrs. Castaneda?" Jesse asked, holding her hands tight together so that no one would see how badly they shook. "What do you drive?"

The man in the suit spoke before Mrs. Castaneda had a chance to draw a breath. "This is dumbest thing I ever heard! Don't try to make teachers the villains here. It's your father that's the true villain."

The man's bile transformed Jesse's anxiety to anger. "You've had your chance to speak. If these kids are going to protest they should at least hear both sides. This whole protest, when you take away all the rhetoric is strictly about the budget. This is about money, nothing more. All I'm trying to do is give them perspective. Mrs. Castaneda?"

The school librarian stood a little apart from the teachers, holding the hand of a small boy with thick wavy brown hair. She raised her voice, "I have a 2009 Volvo XC90...we paid about forty-two thousand for it."

"There!" Jesse exclaimed. "What is rich and what is poor? If we stretch our imaginations and pretend the Osterman's Buick is worth a thousand dollars, it means Mrs. Castaneda drives a car that is forty-two times more expensive. Would you say that she was rich compared to you, John?"

"Hell yeah!" John exclaimed to the delight of the students around him who laughed and slapped his hand. Jesse's eyes met John's for only a second or two before he turned away. In that brief time she saw shame in them. What did it mean? Was he was sorry for his actions? And if so, did that really matter a hill of beans to her?

In uncertainty, Jesse turned away. "Like I said, there are no Donald Trumps in Ashton..."

"This has gone far enough!" the man in the suit yelled. "You aren't going to lay this on the teachers. They are doing their part despite the anti-teacher rhetoric people like you and your father keep spewing. Public servants aren't the issue here."

"Yes they are," Jesse said. "And it's not just teachers that are causing the problem. It's the whole stinking bloated bureaucracy. People keep using those words, public servants, but these aren't servants. These are your masters!" Jesse cried to the throng of people. "The average school teacher in Ashton makes fifty-four thousand dollars a year! With free health insurance that goes to over sixty thousand a year. That doesn't sound like a servant's pay to me. In fact that's double what the average worker makes. Since when do servants make more than the master?"

"They don't!" someone shouted. The crowd began buzzing over this.

"That's enough," the spokesman for the teachers said, waving his arms to quiet the crowd.

"It's not!" Jesse said, feeling a growing sense of anger. She had no problem with teachers, but she had a problem with people making this much money crying poormouth. "I haven't even gotten to their retirement benefits yet. A retired teacher gets paid to the day she dies. On average Ashton will pay out over a million dollars in retirement pay per teacher. That's a guaranteed retirement fund. How many of your parents have a million dollars in retirement savings?"

"None that I know!" John yelled out. Again their eyes met and again he couldn't hold her gaze.

Evil knows no shame, her voice of reason said. *What John did to you was evil, but the boy isn't evil. He knows shame, he knows regret. You see the apology in his eyes.*

Not now! Jesse couldn't deal with idea of forgiving the boy who had so hurt her...so humiliated her. Not just then with the fate of the town riding on her words, and perhaps not ever.

Ms. Weldon, who had been scowling at Jesse, put on a sad face. "What's with the hate? Why do you insist on hating teachers? It's an important job and unsung, unheralded job."

"I don't hate, Ms Weldon. I just can't stand aside while the truth is so abused. Teaching is an important job, but it's no more important than that of a ditch digger or a waiter." This brought out harsh remarks and boos from the crowd of adults just in front of her.

"Really? You think that low of us? What has your father done to you, to make you so nasty?" Ms Weldon demanded.

"It's not that I think low of teachers, it's that I think highly of *every* job. They are all important," Jesse said and then turned to the crowd. Again, only the face of the boy who had tried to kill her caught her eye. "John, what was your father's job before he was laid off?"

"He was a machinist, over at Carlyle's."

"And was his job important to him? Was it important to you and to your family?"

"Yeah," John said. This time he was very quiet, yet so silent had the crowd gone that the word carried.

"Every job is important, Ms Weldon," Jesse called out, not to the teacher, but to the crowd. "They are important to the individual and to the town. This is why I'm protesting you, Ms Weldon. You represent the status quo that has to change. You know this is true. Everyone here knows. There are too many government workers, making too much money. Why does the receptionist for the town manager make forty-nine thousand a year while the secretary for Mr. Adams over at Carlyle's makes only twenty-eight thousand a year? They do the same job yet one is a government worker and the other is a private worker."

Jesse began walking along the front of the mass of students. "How do we justify paying the fire chief almost one-hundred and fifty thousand a year? He doesn't even fight fires anymore, yet a quarter of the firehouse budget goes to pay him. How do we pay the head librarian ninety thousand and then say we don't have enough money for new books? Why do we pay Principal Peterson over a hundred thousand dollars when tests scores have dropped every year since he arrived? How can Ashton afford all of this?"

Pointing at the protesting adults, Jesse said, "Their initial answer to our budget problem was to tax the rich." This was greeted with cheering from the students. Jesse shook her head. "Why do you cheer? Because you think you got some sort of revenge on them? If you think so you're wrong. They're still rich and you're still poor...in fact this town is more poor than it was. All the rich people moved away, didn't they? And they took their money with them. How did that help you?"

This quieted the crowd. Jesse again pointed at the adults. "Their next brilliant idea was to raise taxes on businesses and we all know how that turned out." The crowd knew and they buzzed angrily in response. Jesse raised her voice over them, "Salaries were cut, hours were scaled back, and people were fired. Who didn't see that coming? And now...here today, what is their new big plan to save Ashton? What is it? Anyone?"

Jesse paused only an instant and then shouted, "They don't have one! That's right. They want to keep things just the way they are. All of you here are protesting to keep Ashton just the way it is. But really, is this how you want to live?"

From the crowd came many shouts of 'no' and 'hell no'. Jesse paused to let the question sink in, this time she paused a second too long. "Liar! Liar! Liar!" the teachers began chanting. It became loud and raucous. She could do nothing but raise her hands in an exaggerated shrug.

Finally, when the chant started to peter out, Jesse went up and down the front of the crowd crying out, "How am I lying? What's your plan?"

Mr. Irving stepped forward. "Our plan is to keep the situation from getting worse. You say jobs are important, but how many people have been fired by your father?"

"None," Jesse shouted. "He has only cut budgets. He has given every department in town the leeway to restructure salaries and operating procedures in order to keep anyone from being fired. Take the library for instance. The library let three part-time employees go, but the head librarian still makes ninety thousand and the other four librarians have an average salary of sixty-two thousand. None were willing to take a pay cut in order to keep the part-time employees on."

"Why should they have to?" someone from the crowd of kids asked.

"Because the town is bankrupt!" Jesse thundered. "You are out of money because of these ridiculous salaries and excessive benefits..."

"Liar! Liar! Liar!" the chant began again. Three minutes passed before they tired. Jesse waited patiently.

"Why are they so afraid of my words?" she called out as soon it was quiet enough. "They call me a liar but they don't refute my words. It's because they can't. The truth is Ashton is bankrupt. We simply can't go on the way we have. And we don't have to; my father has a plan. In order to draw businesses to our town, he's cutting taxes, he reducing fees and cutting red tape. He's putting more money back into your pockets and at the same time he's making it easier for businesses to flourish in Ashton. And when businesses flourish, jobs become plentiful."

Jesse strode back and forth as she spoke and the students watched her and heard. She could see her logic triumphing over the emotion stirred by the man in the suit. It put a grim smile on her face.

"You can either side with them and watch your lives go from bad to worse," Jesse declared. "Or you can side with me and save this town!"

The students looked back and forth from one another, seemingly afraid to commit to the girl who had been so hated only the day before. Then Sandra pushed her way through the crowd and came to stand by Jesse.

"Thank you," Jesse said. Out of the blue she felt tears coming to her eyes and quickly she wiped them away. When she looked up again John Osterman stood in front of her with his head bowed, the sight of him so close caused her to gasp. He said nothing. What could he say? More kids came across to her: Amanda hugged her, Ronny and Tina came with eyes averted. Gordon, as well as a dozen boys whom Jesse had danced with the night before. Most of her economics class came as well and a hundred kids she'd never said a word to.

This seemed to spark a flood to her side when Carla Castaneda stepped up. "Wait!" she yelled. For a little woman her voice was big and it stopped the kids in their tracks. "Jesse, you're right I think we can do more...I think many of us should do more, but I can't join you if your father plans on cutting back the police force. Not with the killer still out there."

"He isn't. I can assure you that he..."

Interrupting Jesse, the man in the dark suit cried out, "I don't think the assurances of a seventeen-year-old kid mean all that much to us. Your father has cut the police budget in every town that he has ever managed and he'll do it here as well! He doesn't care about our safety; all he cares about is the almighty dollar!"

"He does care about our safety," Jesse yelled over the confusion the man's words had wrought. "My father wants to add to the..."

Again Jesse was interrupted. "Words are all you have," he said. "Should we judge what will happen based on her words, or on the past deeds of her father?"

'Past behavior is indicative of future action', her fathered had said to her only the other day. Clearly, since James Clarke wanted to add to the police force there were exceptions to the statement.

What about John Osterman? Will he always be judged by his past actions as well?

Not now! Jesse ran her hands through her blonde hair, feeling a growing exasperation. "My father actually wants to increase the police pres..."

"Liar! Liar! Liar!"

Confusion ran among the students who had sided with Jesse, they stood staring around at each other in uncertainty. Then one walked back the way he had come...and then another. Jesse saw right away that she had lost them and with the chanting keeping her from speaking she wasn't going to get them back again. Their fear of the Shadow-man had overcome her logic.

Once again she felt the pull between the two great forces in the town: Harold on one side and James Clarke on the other. She felt alone and defenseless between them.

You are not defenseless. You have Ky.

That's right. Jesse turned to Ky, what she saw surprised her. The boy's handsome apple cheeked face was set in hard lines and his lips were twisted. He was in a rage over how she was being treated and it showed plain through his mask of indifference.

She wasn't alone after all, she had Ky. The thought made her feel much better and before she knew it she smiled at him to show that everything would be ok.

You can't hide love no matter how hard you try. Isn't that what your father told you?

Was her father right? Was it true? It certainly seemed obvious that Ky had feelings for her. He wasn't concealing it very well...and he was supposedly the master at masking his thoughts. What must she look like? She melted every time she looked at him. Did it show on her face? If it did, and she was certain that it did, then she was doomed.

A stab of fear churned her guts. She had lost the town and now she'd lose her life. There'd be no stopping it. She loved Ky too much to deny the feelings within her. Even then, as she was being castigated as a liar, Jesse wanted to run to him. It took everything she had not to. After all, who else could she turn to, to protect her?

Physically she was too mangled to protect herself. Her father was too busy trying to save a doomed town and the police had proven themselves inept. She didn't know what to do, except to curse Harold's name. He would turn Ashton into a ghost town and her into its lead ghost.

He doesn't have to get both.

That's right; there was a way to stay true to her feelings and save the town at the same time. But could she do it? She laughed feeling suddenly wild, what choice did she have?

Jesse waved her arms to the crowd. "You say you want proof that my father won't abandon you to the killer? Then watch!" she demanded.

With deliberate steps, Jesse went straight up to Kyle Mendel—the harbinger of death—and said with a perfect calm in her soul, "Kiss me."

Chapter 50

Kyle's eyes bugged, but the rest of him went rigid as if Jesse had the gaze of the medusa.

"I've never been in love before," Jesse whispered. "It's crazy how much feeling is inside me. It's like it's going to burst out any second. Whenever I look at you I can't help smiling...people are going to know...I can't hide it. And neither can you...in fact you are even more obvious than me. If I'm going to die..." The crowd whispered and pointed and exclaimed, but when Jesse reached up and grabbed Ky's jacket they went altogether still. Jesse licked her lips. "...I want to at least have a first kiss. Is that too much to ask? Kiss me right now...and make it good."

With shaking hands she pulled his face down to hers. The kiss was worth it. The heat of his breath, the soft warmth of his lips, the thundering of their hearts. She would die, but she'd never trade that moment for anything. A thousand eyes watched the two of them in a silence that was serene and surreal.

The world fell away and nothing mattered; not the protest or the council, not her father and not even the killer. The only thing that mattered was that kiss—it was heaven.

But she had to come back down to earth—if only for a little while.

"Jesse! What have you done?" Ms. Weldon had broke from the crowd and stood staring with an open mouth.

"I've saved Ashton," Jesse said, feeling the moment. Pulling Ky along by the hand...she never wanted to let go of him again...she stepped past the teacher and addressed the stunned crowd. "Who doubts my word now? My father will do everything he can to protect us. Now step aside and let the council through. They have work to do if they are going to help my father turn this town around."

The crowd seemed to part at her words and the gaggle of astonished adults came forward leaving the teachers behind. All but one teacher.

Ms. Weldon stayed close to Jesse. She stared about with frantic eyes; she was searching for the killer. "You need to get inside," she whispered as if Harold was close enough to hear.

"What's done is done," Jesse replied. Snow began to fall; finally winter came upon them.

"Please, Jesse." Ms Weldon grabbed her. "You won, ok? Now get inside. It's too dangerous out here."

"I'll be right in, but there's something I have to do first," Jesse said. "Can you tell my father what happened?" The teacher nodded, squeezed her arm once, and left.

Even with Ky holding her hand, it took a lot for Jesse to stand there, with her insides all in turmoil. It wasn't fear that she was feeling. It was confusion...uncertainty.

The crowd milled. Their talk was loud. Their eyes flicked to Jesse constantly. However, one among them was still and quiet. He kept his eyes to the ground. Jesse stood in the quickening snow waiting for him. He would come to her, but when he did...she didn't know what would happen. What he would ask of her was too impossible to even contemplate. How could she grant forgiveness to the boy who had whipped her, to the boy who had beaten her, to the boy who had tried to kill her?

The real question is, how could he ask you for forgiveness at all?

Right as always! How could he ask? After everything he had done—the nerve of the boy!

Yes. He has nerve. He has courage. Sometimes it's harder to ask for forgiveness than it is to forgive.

That's crap! Jesse's back seared with pain even then. Every time she turned or took a deep breath she felt it as fresh as when it had first happened. Her voice of reason was clearly becoming the voice of ultimate stupidity if it thought that forgiving was easier.

It is. You have all the power. He has nothing. He has to grovel and beg for scraps of your kindness.

Groveling? What about crawling across broken glass? Shouldn't he do that first? What about being whipped? Shouldn't she get to whip him before she granted her forgiveness? Shouldn't she get to kick his ribs in and tie him to a tree?

Then you would be just as bad as he is.

Damn it! It can't be enough that he only asks for forgiveness. There has to be more. Shouldn't he have to prove how sorry he is? Otherwise how would she know if he was truly sorry enough?

You'll know.

Jesse dropped her eyes and saw the snow settling on her sneakers. Right. She would know. Just like love, true remorse couldn't be hidden. If he was truly sorry it would show through. "But he has to really want it," Jesse whispered to herself. Next to her Ky stiffened. Two approached them—one calm, unaffected by the cold and the snow—one jittering and holding himself, moving slowly as though his feet were bricks.

John Osterman had his arms across his chest. He shook. His eyes were red. His Adam's apple worked up and down as if he were choking on something. He was trying to force up words that would tear out his throat as he said them.

A thought struck Jesse then: how much easier would it be for him to go on hating her? Or to make excuses or blame her for what had happened. How much easier would it be for John to act like so many other people and just pretend like it never happened at all?

"I...I..." John faltered. He shook his head from side to side, looking into the falling snow for answers. "I'm sorry...I...screwed up."

"You screwed up?" Jesse asked, with blazing eyes.

"No. I messed up...bad," John said. "I hurt you. I whi...whipped you." A single tear ran from his red eyes and laid a track through the snow clinging to his face. "I was so drunk I could barely see straight...and now... I can't believe I did those things to you. I was terrible, a lot of us were terrible, but still you did this." He made a small gesture toward Ky.

Next to Ky was his father, the other person who had walked up. "You don't really have time for this," Jerry Mendel said, taking her gently by the elbow. "Let's get you inside where it's warm."

Jesse resisted, both Jerry as well as the feeling growing stronger within her. The feeling was a desire to accept John's apology. But a part of her didn't want that. A part of her wanted to be angry. In fact it wanted to be furious. Jesse deserved to be furious. Torn between two conflicting emotions she turned from the three men.

She faced into the bitter wind and was practically blinded by the driving snow. Yet she could see well enough to note how quickly the protest had broken up. Soon they would be alone...except for maybe Harold. This was perfect weather for him. He could be out there somewhere watching in the swirling white madness. Harold wouldn't want Jesse to forgive John. She was sure of that. He'd want her to be as alone as possible.

Jesse didn't want to be alone. She wanted friends, she wanted...

Jerry Mendel interrupted her thoughts. "Really you don't have time for..."

"This may be my only time for this," Jesse said, cutting across him. She turned to John. "I don't know everything there is to know about forgiveness. I don't know how it works; I just know that it does. Your remorse is too obvious for me to ignore and if I don't forgive you it'll eat me up inside. I'm tired of hating and being hated. I'm done with that."

Jesse stepped up closer to the boy. He seemed so emotionally fragile that he looked like he wanted to run away from her. She put a hand out to touch his arm and as she did her shirt stretched along the wounds across her back. It made her grimace.

"I forgive you, John," she said despite the pain. "Just don't ever do that again. Not to me...not to anyone."

"No. No not ever. I promise." He seemed desperate to please and gave her an eager smile. She wanted to smile as well. Just as Tricia had mentioned the day before, Jesse felt lighter, as though a burden had been lifted. It made her wonder what sort of burden she had been carrying. After all she had been the victim. Jesse had done nothing wrong.

Hate is a burden.

Right.

"Are you done yet?" Jerry Mendel asked. His demeanor was less calm, as if he thought that Jesse was just wasting time. "We need to get inside."

After a last look at John, Jesse grabbed Ky's hand and went to see her father. He stood outside his office door wearing a smile so tight that it seemed to hurt the rest of his face.

"There's no stopping you is there," he asked her. "The one person in this town I don't want you showing affection to, you end up kissing him in front of everybody."

"It had to be done."

James pulled his daughter aside. "No, it didn't," he said. "We would have found another way." His tight smile warred against the fear in his eyes that he had for her.

"There was no other way," Jesse replied.

He shook his head in disagreement. "We would have convinced them eventually. We had logic on our side."

"When I was out there, I realized that logic was never going to be enough," Jesse said with a sad smile. "Those people knew that I was right, yet they had no faith in me, no faith in my words. People without faith always need a sacrifice. They are afraid to act, afraid to change, until they see someone go first. Until they see someone willing to risk everything for an idea."

"But...this?"

"You said yourself that Ky and I wouldn't be able to hide our feelings. As always you were right. Until I kissed Ky, it felt like my skin was glass and everyone could see into my heart." Jesse looked back, Ky was closer than she thought. It still sent a thrill through her to have him so near. "I've had life without love. Now I have love...I'm willing to sacrifice my life to have it.

"But I don't think I am!" James cried in anguish. "It's more than I can bear."

"I want you to answer a question: what would you sacrifice for me?" Jesse asked.

He didn't hesitate. "Everything."

"And what would you sacrifice me for?"

Turning those two words around changed the question completely. James took much longer to answer. "Everything." Same word, different answer.

"Exactly," Jesse agreed. "If I'm going to die, it had better be for a worthy cause. To the people of Ashton this town is everything to them. All of it would have withered away to nothing if I hadn't acted the way that I did."

James stared a long while at his daughter before saying: "I'm proud of you, Jesse. You did great out there." These simple words almost had her crying again. She actually felt her eyes well up a bit, but then her dad surprised her by taking her by the arm and pulling her into his office. It was crowded with people.

"Dewey! How many men do you have available?" James asked.

A man shaped as a rounded pyramid shook his jowls in consternation. "Because of this protest they all had to work a double shift. I've only got one patrolman on until tonight, that's it. And the CID guys are all out after Harold. He was last seen in the Tanner sub-division. They're going through it house by house. With all the vacant buildings they'll take all day."

James went grey. "I want one of your men with my daughter at all times...whatever it takes."

Dewey shrugged. "The officer was going to patrol...but with this snow, he wasn't going to see much anyways. I'll have him come by and take her to your house."

James rubbed his temples, looking like he had a headache coming on. "I should be done here around six. Her mom won't be back till later..."

"She can stay with us until you get done," Jerry Mendel offered. Both Jesse and her father jumped at the suggestion but likely for different reasons. Despite the peril of the shadow-man, Jesse couldn't get over the idea of seeing Ky's bedroom. It seemed like the most foolish thing in the world to be thinking about, yet still the thought made her stomach go light.

Chapter 51

At some point the snowfall had graduated to blizzard status, making what would have been an eight-minute ride into a nerve rattling twenty. But at least she got to hold Ky's hand, something that his father seemed to approve of more than Ky. He sat stiff in the back seat next to her, constantly darting his eyes about at the briefest flash of color. And flashes were all he got. Jesse could barely see the forest not twenty feet to the side of the road.

Ky's quiet demeanor didn't change much as they entered the spartan home of Jerry Mendel. Their place was clearly for bachelors only, lacking anything resembling a feminine touch. Ky went to every window, checked the locks, and then briefly stared out. There wasn't much to see.

Jesse stayed in the kitchen with Mr. Mendel feeling like a stranger in a strange land. The house was as chilly as it was barren. It was eerily silent as well. Ky hadn't spoken once to her since their kiss in front of the town hall and Mr. Mendel had been nearly as quiet. Worse than the silence, however, was that when Ky returned from touring the perimeter of the home he and his father did little besides stare at her, making her feel completely uneasy.

It was a blessing when the police officer finally arrived. She had hoped that it would have been Officer Daniels, but it was a man she had never seen before. He seemed ill inclined toward Jesse; eyeing her sourly and with pursed lips. Therefore she used the occasion of his arrival to grab Ky by the hand and pull him from the room.

"You can talk now, you know," Jesse said, easing herself down on what clearly was a rarely used living room couch. "You don't have to sit there all broody."

"Broody?" he asked amazed. "I've never been happier."

Jesse laughed, making sure to keep it a low one so as not to disturb the abnormal serenity of the home. "That's a happy look?"

"Yeah, well, I'm also more scared than I can remember."

"I find that hard to believe," Jesse said. "You've been living next door to Harold for years. I bet there were plenty of times you were more afraid than this."

With a little shrug, Ky said, "I guess, but it's just I've never had this much to lose."

"Oh." That was certainly something. Jesse waited for him to elaborate, which made for a very quiet half a minute. Finally she had to ask, "What's wrong? Really? You're so quiet."

He gave her a crooked little smile, licked his lips, and then shrugged with one shoulder. "There's nothing wrong."

Nothing wrong? His answer, even more than the silence made it clear that something was definitely wrong. Had she made him angry in some way? Was she being too forward holding his hand? Maybe it was the kiss. Maybe it wasn't as great for him as it was for her. "Then why are you so quiet?" she asked in a small voice. "You were much more talkative last night."

Another shrug. "I guess because I got to wear a mask."

"A mask?" She slid away from him. Perhaps he liked her better in her mask as well. He sure seemed to.

Ky shook his head. "I'm making you angry, aren't I? I'm sorry…it's just, I don't…I haven't…"

It dawned on Jesse just then that Kyle was nervous about being this close to her. This immediately perked her up. "It's ok, I'm not mad. I get it now. You've been alone for so long and now…" she ended lamely pointing at herself. He nodded.

Jesse was nervous as well. She felt like she was walking in a minefield; not knowing what was the right thing to say or do. It had been much better the night before when…

A small dose of inspiration struck her and she unwrapped part of her long scarf and wound it around his face, then did the same for hers. "Better?" she asked in a slightly muffled tone.

His eyes, the only part of him she could see, crinkled in reply. "Yeah. I guess I don't know how to be around people so much anymore."

"You'll get used to it again," Jesse said. In her mind she added, *I hope; if there's time to.* The thought gave her the shivers. Hugging herself, she asked, "Why is it so cold in here?"

"My dad keeps getting his hours cut at work. We can't afford too many luxuries."

What do you say to that? "Oh, sorry. Where's your mom?" The question had just come blurting out of her and the second it did she wished she could take it back. First she gets him to admit he's so poor he can't afford to heat his house and now this. "I mean does she live here? In town or uh…"

Ky's eyes shifted away before he answered. "She's, uh…she's in Florida. My parents are divorced." Of course they were. Jesse wanted to slap herself for asking such a painfully stupid question. Ky went on, "She left us three years ago after Jason O'Brian died…got killed. By then everyone guessed what all the deaths had in common. Me. And I guess she couldn't take it."

"Jason was a friend of yours?"

"My best friend," Ky said. "My last best friend. First there was Steven Brownly—we grew up together and there wasn't a day that he wasn't over here playing with me. And then there was Gregory Mathew Johnson. He was murdered in 2006. Then there was Jason. And then…"

Tears came to his eyes all of a sudden and he pulled the scarf up to hide them. "It's ok," Jesse said. "You don't have to talk about this."

He sniffled and then shook his head. "I do. You kissed me...you should know what you've gotten yourself into. I'm a magnet for the killer. He kills anyone I'm close to...it's why I didn't want to fall in love with you." Ky clearly hadn't meant for that to come out. He pulled back from her and the scarf slipped down a little, showing the shocked look on his face. "I mean..."

Jesse had to smile. She was as inexperienced as he was, but his look was priceless. "Don't apologize or worse don't try to take it back. I'm guessing neither of us knows exactly what we are feeling. I've never been in love before so I don't know if this it. But I want to think that it is. Especially now."

"Me too," Ky replied. His apple-cheeks were redder than ever. This might have been the right moment for their second kiss. They moved in closer to each other and were only inches apart when...

"Are you guys doing alright?" Mr. Mendel had stepped noiselessly into the room. His words sent the two jumping apart, but because of the scarf that was still around both their necks they bounced back again.

After a quick gag, Ky answered, "We're fine. Thanks." They both held plastic smiles on their faces until he left again and then had to suppress giggles when he did. When they were able to look at each other without busting out laughing, Jesse realized the moment was gone. And this was ok with her.

Even with the presence of the police officer, and Ky, and Mr. Mendel, Jesse felt an undercurrent of fear that didn't lend itself to romance. Ky must have been feeling something close to it as well, because though he sat back next to her he didn't try anything more than holding her hand.

"Do you want me to finish with what I was telling you about?" he asked. Jess nodded. In truth, she didn't really want to hear it, but since she had voluntarily stuck her head into the noose she figured it would be wise to know as much as possible.

"Two years ago I went and stayed with my mom for Christmas vacation," Ky said, resuming the story of the killer. "I left school early hoping that since I wasn't around Ashton no one would die. It didn't work out the way I hoped. Three people died that year. My dad has family in Mackinaw and Harold went up there and killed the cousins I was closest to. How he knew which three to pick, I'll never know."

"That's terrible," Jesse started to feel a pain behind her breastbone. "And last year? Mary Castaneda?"

Ky suddenly seemed defensive. "If you've heard the rumors that she was my secret lover...it wasn't true. She wasn't. Mary was just in the wrong place at the wrong time. I found her in the woods crying. She'd had a fight with her boyfriend and had stormed off. I made the mistake of thinking I should keep near her...to...protect her." The last words came out as a whisper. He took a few deep breaths before going on.

"I couldn't save her; all I did was draw Harold to her. There was this sound in the woods. I knew right away what it was and I yelled out to Mary to run. She ran...but I think she got lost. Frantically, I searched for her, but I never saw her again...they wouldn't even let me go to her funeral."

There was silence for a long time as each simply stared out at the snow swirling around the window. Finally Jesse asked, "How come he can't be caught?" She didn't want to believe the campfire version of the killer. The one where Harold could hear his name spoken from miles away and that he could walk through walls. "It just seems that a man that big couldn't be missed. There should be eyewitnesses, or fingerprints or boot-prints for goodness sakes. His feet must be gigantic."

"He almost got caught once," Ky replied. "When Gregory Matthew Johnson died there was an anonymous tip that Harold was seen dumping a body down by the north pond. The police rushed over and searched his house. They found Greg's shoes—the shoes that he was wearing when he died—sitting in Harold's garage."

"That's not enough for a conviction?" Jesse asked in puzzlement. "An eyewitness *and* evidence linking him to the murder isn't enough?"

Ky gave her shrug. "The eyewitness was afraid to come forward and the police went into the house without a warrant. It screwed up the entire case."

There's something missing here.

Right. Why dump the body, but take the shoes only to leave them in the garage? Why wouldn't the eyewitness come forward? Finally, how could a man as big as Harold ghost around killing five more people without leaving a shred of evidence either on the victim or himself?

"What I…" Jesse had a question on her tongue, but just then she noticed Mr. Mendel standing in the doorway to the kitchen watching them. Despite the danger to Jesse, Jerry Mendel seemed absurdly pleased that his son had a girlfriend sitting on his couch.

"Go on," he said. "Don't let me bother you." Clearly he was a bother as neither Jesse nor Ky spoke. He got the hint. "Ok…ok. You two can go upstairs if I'm disturbing you that much."

Ky was quick to pull Jesse out of the room. He led her up to his bedroom, which was nothing like she expected. There wasn't a single bikini clad super-model adorning the walls. Nor any posters of fast-backed muscle cars. And the place was neat. No dirty socks or old pairs of underwear.

"My dad doesn't like clutter," Ky explained. "It gets him weird."

Jesse went the window and pulled up the blinds. "Wow. We'll get at least a foot at this rate. What a waste of a snow-day." Just then she noticed Ky's mask that he had worn the night before. It sat propped up on the sill as if it had been looking out at the weather, or at Jesse's room. She went to pick it up, but because her left hand could still barely clutch anything it fell to the floor.

"I thought you were going to get that checked out," Ky said, bending down in a fluid motion to get the mask.

"You can see right into my window," Jesse said, stuffing her hand into the pocket of her white jacket.

"You changed the subject." Ky went to her and pulled out the injured hand. He shook his head at it. The swelling was obvious.

"The hand's not important."

"You think that you're going to die is that it?" Jesse dropped her gaze to the floor. Ky lifted her chin and looked into her eyes. "If I can, I'll keep you safe. I'll give my life for yours." His hazel eyes were beautiful. It wasn't their color or shape. It was the fact that they held so much love for her. Ky moved in closer...

"Sorry to bother you two, again," Jerry Mendel said stepping into the room. Ky groaned at the interruption, but Jerry ignored it. "I'm going to go pick up some take-out from the Dim Sum. Jesse, are you ok with sesame chicken or Mongolian beef?"

She wasn't hungry at all and with her fear sitting like an ice-ball in her stomach she didn't think she would be eating much that day. "You're going out in this?"

"I wasn't expecting company and we don't have anything in the house. You can ask Kyle." Ky's embarrassed look was enough of an answer.

"Please don't worry about me," Jesse said. "I'm really not hungry."

"Actually it's Officer McCew that I'm worried about," Mr. Mendel replied. "I've seen him eat before. He can really put it away. Now you two stay up here and keep out of the way while I'm gone."

Jesse waited to hear his footsteps on the stair before she whispered to Kyle, "He's really not leaving, you know. He's only saying that so that the next time you try to kiss me he'll pop out again."

Though she joked, Jesse didn't like the idea of Ky's father leaving. When dealing with Harold she preferred the layered approach; she wanted as many people between herself and him as possible. Ky didn't seem to like it either. He went to the window and stared out, trying to catch a glimpse of anything that moved. A few minutes later a sound from downstairs caused Jesse to jump.

"Don't worry, that's only the garage door opening," Ky explained. Jesse worried anyways and tense minutes slipped by. She tried not to make it obvious, but Ky saw. "Do you want to go hang out with Officer McCew down stairs?"

"Yeah…kinda I do."

He smiled with a show of bravado, however his hand practically dripped sweat and he moved through the house with more care than was needed. Or so Jesse thought at first. When they got downstairs she realized they hadn't been careful enough.

Officer McCew wasn't in the kitchen.

Chapter 52

Kyle didn't wait for an explanation. *Snick.* His switchblade seemed to leap into existence as if the sinister little noise created it out of thin air.

"Officer McCew?" Ky called out in a low voice. The house was so silent that the officer should've heard. When no one replied, he whispered, "We'll check the bathroom."

Jesse hadn't thought of that. In truth she hadn't thought about much of anything since they first walked into the kitchen. The officer was gone...Mr. Mendel was gone...and soon Ky would be gone. This was such a certainty in her mind that she didn't budge when Ky started walking away. What was the point? She was going to die. This was it. She had talked about sacrifice, but hadn't known exactly what it had meant. The words had sounded noble when she had said them, they even sounded uplifting. However now the words were starting to hit home and she began to regret big time.

"Come on," Ky whispered to her, holding out his free hand. She looked at it dully while inside a foolish part of her considered running away. After all she had never taken off her boots or her coat; she could just run and never look back. She would go somewhere warm and someone else could die in her place.

Ky came back to her. Without asking he began to pull her along. "Stop freaking," he whispered. "If he's not in the bathroom, he's probably out on a call. Remember, he's the only cop on duty."

Not for a second did Jesse need to be reminded of that fact. She knew all too well that if something had happened to officer McCew there would be no one but Ky standing between her and death.

The bathroom was only around the corner. Its door stood open, its interior black. Jesse grabbed Ky's coat and held him close.

"Let go of me," Ky said in a low, urgent voice. "I want my hands free." He had to push her away twice before she stopped clinging. In all her life she had never felt this far gone on the road to panic. She had practically asked to be sacrificed and at the moment for the life of she couldn't remember why.

For love.

Wrong! There was no love in her—there was only an overwhelming petrifying fear. It sapped her strength so that she could barely move her feet. She shuffled along behind Ky like a ninety-year-old woman and it was a struggle for her to keep up.

He went first to the front door, gave the knob a hard twist, and then slipped the chain into place. Next he went to the sliding glass doors. These too proved to be locked. He went to turn away but stopped suddenly and stared. His apple cheeks aged a hundred seasons in a second and his face went grey. Jesse followed his gaze.

Officer McCew lay face down in the snow with his arms flung out and his ankles neatly crossed. The back of his head was caved in. Grey and red mixed there making a gory soup in the bowl of skull, while falling snowflakes ended their short lives in an attempt to cover over the atrocity. They would alight on his still warm flesh, pause as if time would always be on their side, and then disappear, becoming nothing.

Jesse saw this occur a thousand times before Ky grabbed her and started moving. She allowed herself to be moved. She was a snowflake. All her life the winds of fate had blown her in every direction and in Ky she had finally found her pedestal. The one place where she could unfold the gossamer wings of her soul and rest. Yet how brief that rest. A single kiss…and now she would become nothing. She would disappear like all the rest and soon she'd be forgotten.

Ky dragged her into the kitchen. He picked up the useless phone and held it to his ear. She could have told him it wouldn't be working. Her destiny was to die at the hands of the Shadow-man—he would not forget the phone.

A noise, heavy tread upon stairs announced the presence of Harold. He came from out of the basement and stood in the doorway wearing a long black coat over his massive frame. Huge black boots were upon his feet.

"Did I kill yet?" he asked.

For an answer Ky flew at him and drove his knife into the man's chest. Harold didn't seem to notice, not even to flinch. He only reached out to Ky and pulled him in close.

"Did I kill yet?" he asked again, searching Ky's face. Ky had regained his color. His cheeks were flared a bright red and his eyes were now the brilliant green of a summer forest. He balled a white-knuckled fist and punched Harold square in the face…once and then twice before the giant retaliated with a single blow. Ky's legs buckled and he fell in a sprawling heap.

Surprisingly Harold seemed far more upset about this than Jesse did.

"Kyle!" he yelled, giving the limp form such a hard shake that the boy's head flopped around grotesquely. Still Jesse wasn't upset; her mind was too far-gone down the road of terror. Her only action upon seeing Harold come out of the basement was to press herself up against a cabinet. This was the extent of her running as well as her hiding. She could not hide from destiny.

Again the giant yelled, "Kyle!" Then he looked around and saw Jesse for perhaps the first time. "Did I kill yet?" he asked grabbing her shoulders. The answer was both yes and no. He had killed, but he hadn't killed the right person...the person he was meant to kill.

"Am I supposed to kill you?" Harold asked her.

Somehow Jesse managed to let out a whisper, "No."

"Then who? Who do I kill?" he demanded.

For some reason Harold wasn't at all what she was expecting. Confusion and insanity lay behind his eyes, but surprisingly she didn't see even a touch of evil. Jesse thought for sure she would see sick depravity, blistering hate, and a fire of rage in his eyes but instead she saw fear and puzzlement.

The way he asked *who do I kill?* Made it seem that he was really unsure. Was he so far gone mentally that all she had to do was name a proper substitute and he would leave her alone? Faces flashed through Jesse's mind; a long list of everyone she had met in Ashton. Who would she name to die in her place?

"Who?" he asked, growing angry, and Jesse was shaken into a daze. Faces came to her, but her tongue refused to pronounce names. Jesse looked down at the linoleum and waited for her doom.

"It has to happen," Harold told her, after he had waited as long as he would. "Everyone says so. They all say so." He brought his thick fingers to her throat. They were surprisingly warm and strangely clumsy. He gripped her about the throat but at such an odd angle that when he began to squeeze she feared that he would break her neck rather than strangle her.

Jesse's face went redder than Ky's ever had and then instincts took over and she fought back. She could breathe, but only in tiny gasps and her first action was to pull down as hard as she could with her right hand on Harold's left thumb. It gave her enough room to make one great gasp of air. When she exhaled, the words "I…forgive…you." Came hissing out.

In truth, she didn't forgive him. She hadn't had time to even contemplate forgiving this monstrous creature. She only knew that forgiving Tricia, Amanda and John had practically worked miracles and Jesse had never been in more need of a miracle than at that precise moment.

Unfortunately, her words backfired this time.

Chapter 53

Harold wasn't looking for forgiveness.

His eyes went wild and in a flash he threw Jesse across the room. She hit a cabinet *above* the stove, dropped like a stone, clipped off its sharp-edged surface, and then crashed to the floor.

Every part of her burned with fresh pain, but it wasn't enough for Harold. He lifted her to her feet and then smashed her head into a cabinet. The wound above her eye opened up, sending a splash of blood running down the fake wood panel. She could barely breathe from the pain in her back and ribs, while her left hand was useless from the elbow down. She would have collapsed if Harold hadn't kept pressure on her head against the cabinet.

"I don't need you to forgive me!" Harold raged. "I didn't do anything. I never killed anybody!"

The way her face was pressed against the wood she had a blurry vision of Ky on the ground. He lay unmoving; she would not be saved. "Look what you did to Kyle. Ask his forgiveness," Jesse demanded through her bruised lips.

Harold did look and as he did his hand relaxed against her face. "I didn't mean it. I never meant any of it." He let her go completely and she was barely able to hold herself up especially with one useless hand and the other digging in her pocket for her pepper-spray.

Smooth and easy as a gunslinger the little can slid out of her pocket and the lid flipped off before her arm was all the way around. And then she paused with her hand extended as if she were the snowflake and had all the time in the world rather than a girl seconds from death. She waited until Harold turned back to her and when he did she shot a line of the foul liquid into his face.

In a second his face went red and his eyes watered as he grunted. With one arm he scraped at his eyes and with the other he reached for Jesse. She didn't move. She could barely move. Instead, she allowed him to grab her and as he pulled her in close she dropped the pepper-spray and plucked Ky's knife out of Harold's chest. Ky had stabbed far too high to cause any real damage.

Jesse didn't make the same mistake. Before Harold knew what danger he was in, she stabbed the blade straight up under his sternum, galvanizing the man. As if attached to a live wire Harold went stiff, going straight up on his toes to try to pull himself off the blade, but Jesse pushed the knife up with him. For seconds he grabbed at her wrist with his way too large hands, but they lacked strength and purpose. All at once the giant collapsed in a thunder onto the linoleum, shaking the kitchen. He laid next to Ky, making a little hee—hee sound high up in his throat.

The knife was still stuck in him. With his chin up, Harold looked at it as if unsure exactly what it was. Eventually he got the nerve up to pull it out and when he did, his breathing relaxed a little. He held the knife up to get a better look at it and then slid it over to Jesse.

"Fin—ish—the—job," he said in between wheezes.

Jesse pushed in the switchblade, so that it looked again like nothing more than a little brown stick and then she lowered herself to the floor. Her foot was only inches from his. If he wasn't everything that she had expected, his feet sure were. The tread on the bottom were as wide as a snow tire. She looked at the little grooves and notches. They were dry and dirt free so that they looked new.

"I can't do that to you," she told him.

He turned his red face to the side and looked at her down the length of his body. "Please—every—one—hates—me."

The words struck a chord in her soul, amazingly she felt sorry for him. "Everyone hated me too…but…I…" Harold wasn't going to find acceptance the way she had. His road was going to be much harder. "You're just going to have to try. You're going to have to ask for forgiveness…"

"I—did—not…"

Just then the garage door opened, she could hear it rattling up. Was that Mr. Mendel? What time was it? How long had he been gone? Jesse tried to blink away the cobwebs of her mind and she wasn't quite done when he came in as silent as a cat.

"Harold!" he exclaimed. Jerry walked up and stared down at the bleeding giant. He glanced once at his son and then turned to gaze in amazement at Jesse. "What the hell happened?"

Jesse could barely lift her eyes from the floor and could only shake her head.

"Jesse, I'm talking to you," he demanded.

"Why are you back so soon?" she asked. His boots had left a damp track from the garage.

He came to stand over her. "What does that matter? I forgot my wallet. I…"

For all of three seconds the girl fixated on the damp tracks from the garage, and then Jesse let the switchblade sing free and in a quick motion mingled Harold's blood with Jerry Mendel. The blade entered his thigh midway up and when the man jerked back in surprise the thin metal snapped off.

"What the hell?" he screamed before falling to his knees.

"That's for Mary Castaneda and for Officer McCew and for Gregory Matthe…"

"Don't say his name," Jerry growled through clenched teeth. His eyes had become nightmare dark.

Jesse eased back away from Mr. Mendel. "I'll say his name if I want to... Gregory Matthew Johnson." Everything that she had expected to see in Harold she now saw in Jerry Mendel. "You're the evil one here. You're the deceiver. You've been killing all this time and pinning it on Harold. You've driven him mad."

Jerry laughed, pushing himself to his elbows. "Yes. How did you know?"

The fact that Harold had clearly been set up after Gregory Matthew Johnson died was the first thing that had Jesse wondering...though at the time her fear had limited her thinking. Then there was the fact Jerry was always so 'worried' over where Ky was when in truth Ky was the safest kid in town. It was the perfect excuse to hunt victims: *Are you a friend of Kyle's?* How many times had that been asked? Then there was the fact that Harold supposedly escaped to kill so easily time and again.

All that added up to strong circumstantial evidence, but the real kicker was: "His shoes were dry and his hands were warm," Jesse said, getting her strong right arm under her. "He didn't kill Officer McCew and drag his body out into the snow. Harold looked dazed coming out of the basement; I bet he's been down there since yesterday waiting for Ky to…"

"To lead him to whom he's supposed to kill?" Jerry sat up. "It looks like he almost beat me to it." Jerry grimaced and laughed. "I can't believe it. You stab someone over a pair of wet shoes. You're even worse than my ex-wife."

"I didn't stab you for that," Jesse explained. "It was how you looked at Ky. It was so evil. Every time you kill I bet you picture his face."

His eyes went to slits. "The one boy I want to kill the most," he snarled, "is the one boy I can't. But he has his uses; he leads me to the perfect victims, every time."

"Except he led you to me." Jesse hopped up just as Jerry lunged at her. He came away with nothing but an end of her scarf and this she ripped out of his hands.

This made Jerry smile. "Good one. Almost got you. I'm glad he led me to you. You'll be the best of them all. The town manager's daughter…the girl who stood up to the crowd. You don't know how badly I wanted to kill you right there in front of everyone. But I resisted and I'm so glad I did."

"Dad?" Ky stared up at his father. His handsome face was marred by confusion. "What...what's going on?"

Jerry had turned to his son at his first word, but then he looked back at Jesse. She could see him eyeing the distance. He would make a jump for her any second. What was the best course of action? Did she run and leave Ky in the hands of his psychotic father? Or did she try to stay and fight.

Run. Ky is safe as long as you're alive.

Jesse didn't hesitate.

Chapter 54

Straight away she turned and ran, fleeing into the garage. She then slammed through the door that led to the back yard. Immediately the wind and snow blinded her, so that she staggered forward with her bad left arm in front to her face. Behind her, she heard the door slam a second time. Jerry was coming.

The thought spurred her on and she was at the fence separating her home from the Mendel's a second later. Despite the pain raging across her body, she climbed the fence clearing it just as Jerry jumped up at her. Ahead, made blurry by the shifting snow, was her own home.

Is the back door locked?

Yes. You were too afraid of the killer to leave anything unlocked. And don't try the front either.

Right. Her keys were in her left coat pocket. It would be a gamble getting them out with her bad hand. Besides, her house was not a refuge. Jerry would get in sooner or later. With the only officer on duty dead, she couldn't call the police. Nor would calling her father help. He was a blizzard away. She'd be dead before he got close.

With a heavy heart Jesse ran around the side of her house. Going through the gate she dashed across the street and into the forest. She had no plan brewing in her fear stricken mind, other than escape. If she was lucky she would outdistance Jerry. After all he had a knife in his leg, while all she had was a spinning head from being slammed into a wall… a claw for a left hand…searing pain in her back and ribs…the lung capacity of a newborn…and an ankle that screamed out warnings with each step.

It was her ankle that scared her the most. One misstep and he would be all over her. She tried to go light on it, but the snow and uneven ground made everything a roll of the dice. Her luck held for over two hundred yards of up and down trail and then out of the blue she was pulled backwards by the neck.

"No!" she screamed. "No...No!" Struggling against what felt like hands on her neck she kicked herself over only to see that she wasn't being choked by Jerry Mendel. Her long scarf had come loose and the end had snagged on a branch. Her first impulse was to take the scarf off her neck, but the wide lops of the crocheting had caught on a button so that she was as good as leashed.

"No, no, no," she whined, feeling tears mixing with the snow on her face. Jerry was just a dark figure in the swirling chaos of white. He was at least fifty yards back, hobbling toward her but gaining every second. Frantic she ripped at the scarf until it finally gave up its hold on the branch.

She then turned and fled. The whiteout conditions were so bad that after a minute Jesse lost the path. One moment, it was there underfoot and the next she was surrounded by nothing but trees. She spun around to look for Jerry, but with the thick forest she couldn't see him.

Yet she knew he was out there, coming for her. Her panic took over the remains of her mind and forced her to run at break-neck speeds and it wasn't long before she stepped oddly on a rock hidden by the snow. There was a snapping sound; a stab of pain, and then snow blinding her as she rolled down a short hill.

Pitching up against a downed log, Jesse immediately stuffed a hand into her mouth to keep from screaming. The agony was so intense that she lost focus on the Shadow-man...the real Shadow-man, not caring where he was. She could only sit there rocking back and forth whimpering and crying into her hand.

Get up! Get up! He's coming, her voice of reason screamed.

"Yes…right," she said through her tears. At first her right leg could hardly stand even a little weight but after a minute it didn't get better, yet she was able to go faster. Jerry Mendel came lunging out of the white only ten yards behind. Covered in snow, head to toe, it was clear he'd had his share of falls as well, yet he was driven by maniacal forces that Jesse couldn't understand. His eyes were wild and imbued with a pure desire to kill for pleasure's sake.

This horror of a man filled Jesse with such fear that the pain in her ankle became a distant scream and she was able to drive herself on despite it. Long hard minutes took their toll, but somehow Jesse was able to lengthen her lead. She never knew by how much since she refused to look away from the ground in front of her feet, but gradually his hoarse ragged breathing dropped further back.

And then she came to the pond. It stopped her in her tracks.

She hadn't come to the berm, which was somewhere off to her right. Instead she came straight up on the ice.

"Oh, no," she said shaking her head in disbelief. She had no choice but to cross. If she went left or right along the edge Jerry would have too much of an angle on her and would be able to cut her off. However, crossing the ice in a blizzard seemed like certain death. She hesitated.

Go!

"Right," she said in a tremulous voice. Stepping out onto the ice she knew that she had made a mistake. For one, her ankle couldn't get any purchase and it was forced to bear more of her weight than she could stand. She cried out with every step. But worse than that was the driving wind. After seconds on the ice, she had no idea which way up was let alone where the other side of the pond lay.

Still she had no choice but to go on…and on. The agony she was in made her wonder if it would've been easier to have been killed by Harold in the warmth of the kitchen.

Next to her something blue skipped by and she flinched back so sharply she almost fell. What was that? It reminded her of something, but what wouldn't come to her until it was almost too late. Just when the gaping four foot hole in the ice seemed to erupt at her feet, she pictured the little ice fisherman sitting on an old, blue milk-crate.

There was no stopping her forward momentum and so she threw herself forward hoping to find the other side of the hole able to hold her weight. It did, but she hadn't been close to clearing the hole.

Her lower body went into the frigid water and where she had been panicked before over Jerry Mendel, she went absolutely mad with fear now. She scratched at the ice with her gloved hands while she kicked and scrambled with her legs for everything she was worth. How long it took she had no clue, but eventually she made it out of the water and slithered to her feet again.

Only to be brought up short by the neck again. There was no branch behind her this time.

"I always thought ice-fishing was for idiots, but holy cow I caught a big one," Jerry Mendel called out into the freezing wind. "Turn around!"

Jesse was sure that if she turned around that she would not see a man but a demon. She couldn't force herself to look…not until Jerry gave another yank on the scarf and she felt herself tip precariously toward the hole. With little penguin-like steps Jesse turned, as she did she put a hand to the scarf feeling where it was caught on the button. She dug at it furiously.

It wouldn't come loose; the loops of the crocheted material had entangled themselves too deeply. It wasn't coming off, not right there, not right then, perhaps not ever.

The scarf, long to begin with, now stretched across the hole. At the other end of it stood the Shadow-man in the fullest of his vile terror. His eyes were inhuman, wild and black, so black they seemed to shine in the white madness around them. No smile was ever so full of dread and woe, Jesse felt stricken by it. She feared that he would eat her with those white teeth...that he would take her into some hole in the world and chew on her until the cold turned the remains of her flesh to wood.

"Holy crap!" he exclaimed as she finally made it all the way around. "This fish isn't just big, it's huge. It's the great Jesse Clarke! The girl who thinks the world revolves around her." He capered in delight on the slick ice, seemingly unaffected by the cold. "Look how scared you are. All your talk of faith, yet you shiver with fear. Why so afraid? Don't you have angels who will catch you if you fall?"

For an answer, Jesse only shivered the greater. She had no clue what he was talking about.

"I didn't think that it would be you," he shouted, winding his end of the scarf around his arm, pulling gently on Jesse's neck as he did. She tried to grab the scarf to pull back on it, but her gloves, wet from when she fell, were now turning stiff with ice. She looped her arm around the scarf just as Jerry had. This little move almost toppled her.

Jerry smiled with glee over this. "I thought it would be someone else, but you kept showing up...only to be saved time and again. Where are your guardian angels now?" He waved his arm gesturing to the white wilderness. Foolishly she looked. There could be no one out there. It was impossible. And even if someone was out there, would they dare come on the ice?

"I'll be your angel, Jesse," Mr. Mendel said, giving the scarf another little tug. "I'll save you...just tell me who I should kill instead of you. Name someone and we'll go together. I'll teach things you won't learn up at that high school."

"No," Jesse croaked out. The sound of her voice was a bit of surprise and only then did she realize just how tight the scarf was about her throat.

"Don't you want to live? Aren't you craving life? I could just walk this leash around the hole and we would be back inside in a few minutes...just give me a name."

She had been tempted by Harold in the same manner yet despite her pain and her fear, denying Jerry was far easier. His words were less substantial than the wind. "You're nothing but a liar!"

"No, I'm a god!" Jerry roared, giving the scarf another tug. "Worship me!" Again he yanked, but this one was far sharper and Jesse fell to her knees at the lip of the hole. Her death lay in front of her, deep and dark.

You wanted to be sacrificed, her voice of reason said.
Not like this!

Pain is pain. Death is death. Every way would be equally as bad. Your love could not be hidden and sometimes...unfortunately...this is the price of love.

"No, please," she begged the voice of reason.

The killer answered instead: "What's wrong? Did you think this was going to be easy? Let me tell you, I was never going to make it easy for you. Not when I saw how you strutted around this morning preaching to the people acting as though you were better than them. And then I had to stand there and watch how you made John Osterman whine and debase himself before you; begging for forgiveness as if you were a queen. But worst of all was when you spoke about sacrifice!

"How brave you were up there in your Father's chamber where it was safe and warm. Look at you now, cringing and begging. You are no better than the rest of them, in fact you're worse. You're like a snake-oil salesman trying to peddle paradise to the people of Ashton. You don't know the first thing about this town. If you did, then you'd know that I hold this town in the palm of my hand.

"Ashton goes to bed and I haunt their dreams. They wake up wondering where I've been, whom I've visited while they slept. All day they worry about me... all day they fear me. And for good reason, I have the power of life and death over them."

He ended this by giving Jesse another yank and she felt something come loose at her neck. She ran a hand over the scarf and discovered that the scarf hadn't come off the button, but the button had come of the jacket. Now the scarf was only looped once tight around her neck and then wrapped around her arm.

She could escape, popping the scarf over her head, if only he would look away for a second.

"You....you d-don't have the p-power over life," she stammered through numbing lips. "I do. You only have power over death. You're a murderer, remember? But I have power over life." The conviction of her words had him pausing and she went on, "If I die here it will mean someone else will live." This made him laugh, but it was a cold sound that matched the wind. He didn't look away.

"You still think your death is some sort of sacrifice?" Jerry asked in amazement. "You've been dragged to edge of your life against your will. You didn't step forward voluntarily. You ran, remember? Some sacrifice you are...and now you are going to claim some sort of nobility in your actions?" He paused shaking his head at Jesse. "Your death isn't going to be noble. You'll die with ice water pouring down your throat and no one will find your rotted corpse for months. The only thing your death will do is make my legend even greater."

"But Harold...and Ky? People will know who did this," Jesse said, watching him, preparing to move, thinking incorrectly that she was about to escape.

Jerry sighed, a sound matched by the wind. "Harold will have to die of course. His death will make me a hero. And I'm afraid Kyle will have to die too. It had to happen sooner or later, I always knew that it would. I will find someone else to act as a beacon, don't worry."

The breath went out of her. Ky dead? That couldn't be. That couldn't happen. Right then, with her body core temperature dropping to dangerous levels and her pains fading into numbness, Jesse realized that she was beyond caring about herself. She knelt one inch from a death that up until that very moment, she had feared more than anything. Now she feared something else more: the death of her love.

The very thought made her soul ache. Jesse knew there was only one way to keep Ky safe and it wasn't by escaping. It was by taking the very hardest path.

You know what you have to do.

"I have to truly sacrifice myself," Jesse said.

You talked about sacrifice. Now you must live sacrifice. You can't run from it.

"If I do, Ky dies," Jesse said, nodding, understanding. If she ran and lost Jerry, he would go back and kill Ky. She would do anything to keep that from happening.

Jerry Mendel asked, "What?"

She ignored the question, feeling the same eerie calm, the same moment of peace she felt right before she kissed Ky. It brought a smile to her lips and then Jesse yanked hard on her end of the scarf. She was small, terribly undersized compared to Mr. Mendel, and with only a fraction of his strength. Yet she almost pulled him into the water with her surprise move. He slipped, pin-wheeled, and then pulled back on the scarf to hold himself up.

In response, Jesse let the wound up scarf come off her arm. Two things happened: the scarf immediately went tight around her throat, like a hangman's noose, and she lurched forward, barely keeping herself out of the water. The second thing to occur was that the unexpected slack sent Mr. Mendel's upper body back and because of the ice, his lower body shot forward.

With a cry, he fell over onto his back. Now the scarf went ever tighter around Jesse's neck and the extra pull sent her face first into the water. She knew this was going to happen. She planned for this to happen. She wanted it to happen. It was the only way for her death to have the power to save a life. As she was thrown forward she flung out her good right arm and caught a hold of one of Jerry's boots.

Boots are worn tight in Michigan. Everyone knows that. You wouldn't want to lose one in a snowdrift. Jerry's were tied tighter than normal and so when Jesse got her fingers entwined in the laces and began to pull as hard as she could there was no chance for the boot to slip off.

The water was dreadfully cold, yet she hardly noticed, in fact she thought that it would be colder. Jesse was focused on one thing: saving Ky's life. And that meant ending Jerry's. From beneath the water, she got her legs up under the ice and heaved back, pushing herself deep into the dark water. With nothing but the frozen surface for purchase, Jerry slid in with a strangled cry.

He immediately began to thrash, kicking out in wild animalistic fear, but his right leg had a hundred pound anchor hooked to it and in seconds Jerry too slipped beneath the surface. Jesse didn't want to die. Desperately she wanted to live, but she knew there was no chance of that now. Therefore, instead of fighting Jerry to get back to the surface, she pushed them both away from the hole with strong sweeping scissor kicks.

She hadn't moved them far before Jerry's left foot kicked her right hand, breaking her hold on his boot. She tried to grab it again. However Jerry was still in a complete panic and one of his thrashing legs kicked her square in the sternum. A great gout of bubbles shot out of her and a second later what felt like steel ice flowed into her lungs.

It didn't hurt and was more confusing than fearful. Her body didn't know what to do. Her lungs hitched in her chest, filled with water, and then relaxed almost completely. She could feel her diaphragm pushing the water in and then out again in slow motion. It was strange and oddly a little comforting—there would be no more pain. Her misery was finally over and so were her fears. For herself, as well as for Ky. He would live.

Jerry Mendel had kicked her away and got to the frozen ceiling of the pond, but the hole in the ice was off to his right. Ten feet down, Jesse had a perfect view of it and watched with a growing serenity as Jerry punched and scraped frantically at the ice, but in vain, there would be no getting through it. And in his frenzy he moved slowly but steadily away from the hole.

She turned away from him, not wanting her last view in the world to be of that monster.

Instead she pictured Ky. She remembered him in the woods at night with his knife to her throat…pretending to ignore her in class…walking behind him in the halls…slow dancing with him in the gym…holding her hand in his room. She died feeling his one kiss on her lips.

The End

*

Author's note:

This work and its sister novel, *A Perfect America,* have as their underpinnings the works of both Ayn Rand and CS Lewis. Although Objectivists generally clash with Christian apologetics, it does not have to be and when one informs the other, the result can be intriguing. If you enjoyed The Sacrificial Daughter I would suggest:

A Perfect America

Phil Tarsus is a dreadful instrument of State justice. He's an Inquisitor, a man who makes a living rooting out and executing those people who have been charged with treason. Guilt or innocence mean little to him--he has quotas to fill after all. Yet when he unwittingly stumbles upon a secret involving someone high up in the new American government, he becomes a target himself. Unfortunately for Phil, there's nowhere to run that the government can't find him.

In the year 2122, in the perfect state of America, the government owns everything...from the shoes you wear, to the apple you eat, to your next door neighbor. The government owns everything and is everything. Under these conditions Phil can trust no one but the man he's slated to murder next.

What the readers say about A Perfect America:

"A Perfect America is the rarest thing: a perfect dystopia."

"Prepare to be scared for your future..."

"...a very scary place. In this world, humanity has been replaced by conformity."

P.S. on a self-serving note, the review is the most practical and inexpensive form of advertisement an independent author has available in order to get his work known. If you could put a kind review on Amazon and your Facebook page, I would greatly appreciate it.

[440]

Fictional works by Peter Meredith:

A Perfect America

The Sacrificial Daughter

The Horror of the Shade Trilogy of the Void 1

An Illusion of Hell Trilogy of the Void 2

Hell Blade Trilogy of the Void 3

The Punished

Sprite

The Feylands: A Hidden Lands Novel

The Sun King: A Hidden Lands Novel

The Sun Queen: A Hidden Lands Novel

The Apocalypse: The Undead World Novel 1

The Apocalypse Survivors: The Undead World Novel 2

The Apocalypse Outcasts: The Undead World Novel 3

The Apocalypse Fugitives: The Undead World Novel 4

Pen(Novella)

A Sliver of Perfection (Novella)

The Haunting At Red Feathers(Short Story)

The Haunting On Colonel's Row(Short Story)

The Drawer(Short Story)

The Eyes in the Storm(Short Story)

Made in the USA
Columbia, SC
12 September 2017